Jan '12

A SMALL DEATH
IN THE GREAT GLEN

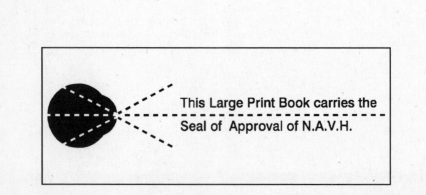

This Large Print Book carries the
Seal of Approval of N.A.V.H.

A SMALL DEATH
IN THE GREAT GLEN

A. D. SCOTT

THORNDIKE PRESS
A part of Gale, Cengage Learning

Detroit • New York • San Francisco • New Haven, Conn • Waterville, Maine • London

GALE
CENGAGE Learning™

LIBRARY OF CONGRESS CATALOGING-IN-PUBLICATION DATA

Scott, A. D.
  A small death in the Great Glen / by A. D. Scott.
    p. cm. — (Thorndike Press large print crime scene)
  ISBN-13: 978-1-4104-3072-4
  ISBN-10: 1-4104-3072-3
  1. Boys—Crimes against—Fiction. 2. Journalists—Scotland—Fiction.
3. City and town life—Scotland—Fiction. 4. Highlands (Scotland)—
Fiction. 5. Large type books. I. Title.
PR9619.4.S35F38 2010b
823'.92—dc22   2010028962

Published in 2010 by arrangement with Atria Books, a division of Simon & Schuster, Inc.

Printed in the United States of America
1 2 3 4 5 6 7 14 13 12 11 10

To my mother and my sister
in memoriam

PROLOGUE

He dressed the boy's body whilst it was still warm. Getting the clothes back on was easy. Such a skinny wee thing, the body weighed next to nothing. No, no weight at all.

Dark came around five o'clock this time of the year and an hour or so later most people would be home in front of the fire. No moon either, luckily. Time to move, in the deep dark before anyone came looking; now was the time to get rid of him.

He hefted the boy in a fireman's lift over his left shoulder. Feet against his back, head and arms dangling down in front. His nose rubbed against the wool of the child's jacket. The body had lost its smell; that sweet savory tang of boy had gone.

The old greatcoat had once been home. He had slept in it, sheltered in it, flames and flying embers had singed it but not penetrated the thick felted wool. Just the job.

Carefully he draped the coat over the body, fussed with the folds, arranging the collar to cover the head, making sure no stray hand or foot poked out. He gave a slow birl, checking the effect in the hall mirror. Fine. Looked natural enough.

The streetlights, dim and far apart, were on one side of the road only. Large sycamores overhung the footpath, a sighing tunnel of black. He walked confidently, out for an evening stroll, his burden lightly carried. Not far to go. He met no one. But anyone noticing him and his bundle would never look twice.

The last part was tricky. An exposed track, a hundred yards or so, ran up to the canal. Gorse, whin and elder bushes would give no cover. Luck was still with him. He reached the lock, peered through the dark, nothing, no one, not a sound.

Holding it by the arms, he lowered the bundle. Feet, body, head then arms, it slipped down into the vortex. No splash, just a sigh as the water closed over the wee soul sending out ripples that set the stars dancing in the still water.

The man, clasping his hands, muttered a prayer, smiled a half smile, put the greatcoat on. All done, thank goodness.

ONE

McAllister rolled yet another tiny piece of copy paper into the huge old Underwood typewriter. Needs the arms and the strength of an orangutan to type on this monster, he had often thought. Deflated ghosts of discarded prose lay crumpled in a top hat on the floor behind his chair. The typing was smudgy, faint; changing the ribbon was not an editor-in-chief's job.

"The obituaries are the only opportunity to be creative on this rag of a newspaper and I can't find anything remotely interesting to say about this man's life. Nor his death."

Elbows on the high reporters' table, he cupped his chin in both hands, emphasizing his resemblance to a black-clad praying mantis. Deadline loomed.

Rob and Joanne paid no attention to their new editor-in-chief's comments. Five months and they were almost used to him.

They worked on, busy with all the "wee fiddly bits," as their subeditor called them. Livestock prices, community notices, school concerts, sporting fixtures, traffic infringements — if being drunk and in charge of a horse could be termed a traffic offense; all the usual fodder for a local newspaper in 1956.

But news? That was for the Aberdeen daily and *The Scotsman* to provide. As Don McLeod, subeditor and all-round fusspot know-it-all told him when he started on the *Highland Gazette,* "We're a local weekly, here to publish local information — not some scandal-mongering rag from down south."

McAllister hit the return on the typewriter as though he was whacking the gremlins of spelling mistakes from the bowels of the huge machine.

"I mean, how can I be expected to write a decent obit?" He waved his notes at them. "All he ever did was attend meetings, chairman of this, treasurer of that, he was even on the committee for the Highland Games. May as well publish minutes."

Rob looked up. "Well, he's been summoned to the final committee meeting of them all. I don't know which angel keeps the minutes, but your man undoubtedly has

10

an in with Saint Peter."

"That'll be right," Joanne contributed. "He went to Island Bank Church for forty years or thereabouts. An elder of the Free Kirk, no less. Bound to have a free pass straight to heaven."

"And I bet in school all he ever got were B's." McAllister had lost them.

Rob grinned, relishing his role as straight man. He loved hearing the editor-in-chief expound on life, liberty and the state of Scottish football.

"How's that then?"

"To get A's in exams shows you as clever, different, a smidgen better than your peers. And God help those that stand out. Conformity, thy name is Scottish."

"But I got A's at the academy."

"Point proven."

The newspaper would be finished by late afternoon, well in time for the final touches from the subeditor and typesetters, then the printers. McAllister despaired of a paper where meeting a deadline was easy. He glanced at his two reporters. Neither had had any real training, and Joanne worked only part-time. Her husband resented even that. Her mother-in-law backed him. Women didn't work — it showed up their husbands, made them seem incapable of

11

providing for their family.

Don McLeod, chief and only subeditor, racing aficionado, keeper of dark secrets, walked in, ignoring Rob, as usual, but nodding to Joanne. She embarrassed him; too young, too bonnie, too smart, too married. Besides, like the boss she was an outsider. "Boss, a word?" He gestured toward the office.

McAllister gave a theatrical sign. "Tell us *all.*"

Don glanced at Joanne before continuing. "I just heard — they've fished a body out of the canal. A wee boy, he went missing last night, the lockkeeper found him first light."

"Oh no, the police were at the door last night looking for him," she cried. "The poor parents."

"And you never thought to say anything before now?" McAllister glared at her. "This is a newspaper!"

Don grimaced. He was right. A newspaper was no place for a woman.

The steep hill that ran from the *Highland Gazette* office to the castle was cobbled; hard to walk on in the best of weathers, lethal in the rain. In the open expanse in front of the castle Flora Macdonald stood on her plinth, a stone Highland terrier at

12

her feet. His raised paws and expressive face seemed to be begging Scotland's most famous heroine to forget Bonnie Prince Charlie and the failed rebellion.

"You're right, boy." Joanne patted the dog's cold head, laughing at herself. "Flora, take heed. No man's worth the wait." But Flora's sightless eyes kept staring out to her homeland in the Western Isles.

Joanne Ross was affected by weather. A premonition, an almost visceral feeling, heralded a change. A distant storm she felt in her bones, well before the clouds formed. She moved in time to the weather; her tall lithe body stepped lightly in summer and strode into winter. Her eyes changed from blue to green with the light, her hair changed from brown to red in the sun, her freckles ebbed and flowed with the seasons.

She found a bench out of the wind, keeping a close eye on the black-backed gulls suspended over her impromptu picnic, their sandwich-detecting radar on full sweep. One especially large bird hung effortlessly in a thermal current.

Joanne went into a dwam, floating with the gull. Floating over the castle braes, over the river, across to the cathedral without a single wing movement, he (for it always seemed a him to her) drifted on toward the infirmary, back over to the war memorial, disappearing into the tangle of the Islands.

She could feel herself nestling into the shoulders of the gull, oily satin-smooth feathers smelling of fish. Up into the thermals they floated, taking in the river, the town, the hills, the mountains, the Great Glen, the faultline that fractured the Highlands. Peaks and scree-strewn ridgelines were mirrored in the ribbon of deep dark lochs. Glens clad in a faded tartan of heather and bracken with splashes of green outlining abandoned crofts emptied by the Clearances were cut deep by drunken burns and rivers. A fierce and stunning landscape; it made Joanne want to sing.

The cathedral bells were the first to strike two o'clock. Four more sets of chimes followed, overlapping, discordant.

"A whole hour of sun." Joanne smiled at the novelty, stood, shook the crumbs from her skirt, ready for the rest of the day. Then, remembering the boy, she shivered, fearful for her own children.

"I'll meet the girls after school today."

"Now I don't want you two going anywhere near the canal."

The children looked at each other. First their mother collecting them from school,

14

next a lecture. This was summer talk. No one went up to the canal in the cold. Although the secret den near the canal banks occasionally tempted them even in chill autumn, they had not been there for weeks. A dark sandy bowl in the roots beneath the elder and whin bushes, it was a perfect hiding place. In the long summer holidays, that is. Autumn, and rotting elderberries, wet slippery leaves and damp earth, made the den dank and scary.

"Another thing, do you still have that den in the bushes near the canal?"

Annie jumped. She knew it. Mum could read minds. How did she know about the canal? She held her breath, waiting for her sister to give the game away. Wee Jean squinted up through her thick fringe, saw Annie's glare and decided she was more afraid of her than of their mother.

"No, it's too cold and too dark." Annie was emphatic.

Joanne believed her eldest child. This time anyway. Then came the next puzzle.

"Do you know a wee boy called Jamie?"

"No" came Annie's automatic reply. Then, "Well, there's a boy called Jamie but he's not in my class. Not in Wee Jean's class neither."

"But you know him," Joanne persisted.

"We sometimes see him on the road home. He's in Miss Rose's class."

As Joanne well knew, ages and sexes didn't mix when you were eight and a half and six. Her mother's questions alerted Annie, but she knew asking would get her nowhere. They reached their gate. Joanne wheeled her bicycle through, then turned back to her girls, her voice unusually stern.

"If I ever catch you or hear from anyone that you have been up the canal banks, your father will hear about it."

That meant the belt. Whilst not a frequent occurrence, just the threat of a leather belt on a little girl's bare bottom, always "for her own good," was terrifying for Wee Jean. To Annie, the humiliation was worse than any pain. They ran up the stairs to change out of their uniforms. Behind the closed bedroom door Annie grabbed Wee Jean's arm. She leaned over her wee sister and whispered fiercely, "If you say one word about Jamie, a giant worm'll go up your bum when you sit on the lavvy pan."

"I won't tell, I won't. I'll never tell."

And she didn't, but constipation and a dose of syrup of figs were the inevitable consequence.

Later, in bed, lights out, curtains closed against the night, Mum and Dad fighting downstairs, Wee Jean cowering under the blankets, Annie thought it through. Why did Mum ask about Jamie? And where was Jamie anyway? Sick again? Fearty, scaredy-cat Jamie, they often didn't see him for days — asthma he said.

Annie pulled the eiderdown over her ears, vainly hoping to muffle the sobs from her parents' bedroom. Almost asleep, she felt a small warm body climb in beside her. Jean hated it when Mum and Dad fought. She let her sister coorie in, tried to drift off, but the remembrance of walking home, playing their game, of that last glimpse of Jamie, before they ran off, abandoning him, terrified they might not reach their house before their father came home, kept her from sleep for a good two minutes.

"Truth, dare or got to," the girls chanted, "truth, dare or got to!"

They kept it up till Jamie, wee, skinny, timid Jamie, finally gave in.

"Truth!" he shouted, scared of the girls but pleased to be one of the gang at last.

"Truth," said Annie. "We-e-ll. Is it true, you eat poo?" The other girls shrieked with laughter at the very mention of the rudest word they knew.

"Big poo number two, big poo number

two." The girls circled him, chanting, laughing, no malice in their game. He joined in, relieved. They didn't push him or try to pull down his pants, nor accuse him of being a wee lassie.

On they skipped like skittish lambs, Annie, her sister, the two girls from their street, the boy Jamie, on they meandered through the darkening autumn, down the long long street, lamps coming on, past the respectable semidetached Edwardian houses, past the prewar bungalows with their neat gardens, past the big old mansions with their big old trees and their dark noisy birds settling for the night, on their way home from school.

One particular mansion with graveyard dark trees the children avoided, crossing to the other side of the road, pushing and shoving, telling stories, and making ghostly noises to scare themselves. The curving gravel driveway disappeared into a tunnel of sprawling rhododendrons, but the double doors, set with vivid stained-glass scenes of some forgotten Victorian martyrdom, were clearly visible through a gap in the shrubbery. Annie stopped. The other girls ran on ahead.

"Come on, Jamie, it's your turn."

"Don't want to," he said, frightened,

knowing what was coming, "don't have to." He was near to tears.

"Cowardy cowardy custard, stick yer nose in mustard."

"No a'm no. I'm no frightened." But he was.

"Well then?" taunted Annie.

Jamie knew. They'd played this game many a time. As yet, no one but Annie had dared. Simple enough: run through the legs of the menacing crablike rhododendrons, run across the oval of gravel in front of the house, run up the steps to the big dark door, reach up to the big brass bell, pull hard, run for the road as though the devil was at your heels, run, run, run to the safety of the dim scattered streetlight, grab the lamp-post, bending double from the stitch in your side, panting, grinning, triumphant . . . did it!

A distant ringing but this time, the first and only time, the door opened. Annie and Jean peered through the rhododendrons, eyes popped wide open, giggling with fascinated fear. The other girls were long gone. Annie's games were too scary for them. A pool of light, like a pulsating evil halo in a horror film, backlit the misshapen figure that seemed to fill the double door frame. Annie grabbed her sister's hand, and they

fairly flew up the street, terrified the bogey-
man was on their heels.

They raced round the corner and ran till
they could run no more.

"I've a stitch in ma side." Wee Jean stag-
gered, her wee legs trembling, peching like
a collie dog, winded after rounding up an
unruly flock of sheep.

"What was thon?" her voice squeaked.
"What was that, in the door?"

Annie had been as terrified as her sister
but would never show it. "It was nothing."
Now she was scared her sister would tell on
her. "It was nothing."

"Yes it was, I saw it, a great big black
thing."

"Aye, a hoodie crow. That's what it was.
And it'll come back and peck your eyes out
if you tell Mum." She poked a finger toward
her sister's eye.

"I'll no tell, promise, I'll no tell," Wee Jean
wailed.

So the hoodie crow was destined to become another of their secrets, their thrills,
their nightmares.

Flushed from running, from fright, they
walked quickly home, clutching hands,
holding on tight against hoodie crows,
bogeymen, the dark starless night and their
dad's temper. And Jamie, poor, always-left-

behind Jamie, was abandoned yet again. But Jamie was a boy. He would be fine. Bad things only happened to girls, everyone knew that.

"Where is everybody?"

Rob, late as usual for the Friday morning postmortem, grinned at Joanne and grabbed her copy of the paper.

"Hey, get your own."

"I daren't go downstairs. The office is unhappy with me over my phone calls to Aberdeen. I didn't put in for an approval chit for long-distance."

The *Highland Gazette* came out on a Thursday. Serving the town and county as well as the far-flung outposts of the western Highlands, it was a newspaper with a long history — and not much had changed since its inception in 1862. Advertising on the front page, a monotonous diet of county council, town council and church notices interspersed with the goings-on of various community groups; the highlight of the paper for some was the prices fetched at the livestock market. For others, Births, Deaths and Marriages was the first page they turned to, the obituaries the best-read section of all. Rob skimmed all eight pages of broadsheet, pausing only to read his own contributions, then gave the paper back to Joanne.

"It's not folded right. You've made a right bourach of it."

The phone rang.

"*Gazette.* Right. Uh-huh. When? Right. See ya."

Rob stood, pulled Joanne up by the hand, the mess of newsprint floating to the floor.

"A reprieve. We've one hour — back here at ten. McAllister's out with Don, so are we. I'll shout you a coffee."

"Seeing you're paying, how can I refuse? And how come the boss is away with Don McLeod? They're usually bickering like some old man and his wifey."

Rob, reluctant to admit he didn't know, just shrugged. Then dashed down the stairs.

"Race you."

Off he sprinted, his overlong barley-colored hair billowing out in the wind, giving him a close resemblance to a dandelion. For many a local girl, Rob was the epitome of a dashing hero of some ilk; a Spitfire pilot perhaps, a film star maybe, a romantic character in *The People's Friend* possibly. He had a look that charmed. Even before he turned on his best blue-eyed, American-teeth smile. Whatever it was, all agreed he was a heartthrob.

The two friends linked arms, strode through the stone arch out onto the bridge, a biting sea wind channeling down the firth, blowing the river into delicate white horses, stinging their ears and eyes. Below, the drowned paving stones of an ancient ford were clearly visible through the whisky-colored current, which at high tide deepened to a darker shade of full malt.

The café on the corner served toasted sandwiches, pastries and its own ice cream and, wonder of wonders, had a real cappuccino machine. Huge, gleaming, its strangled gurgle and hissing blasts of steam could rival the *Flying Scotsman.* Next door was the chip shop, which also served as a social center after dark.

Gino Corelli shouted above the noise as Joanne pushed through the doors.

"*Bella,* how are ya? Shame, you just missed Chiara. An' Roberto, ma boy, I seen your father a wee whiley back. Sit down. Sit down. I bring the coffee."

Gino, dwarfed by his chrome monster, beamed across the café at his daughter's best friend, his cheerful chatter drowned out by the milk-frothing thingwayjig. He had been proud of his English until the day when Joanne told him he spoke Scottish English. The ensuing explanation as to what was English and what was Scottish became complicated.

"Ah, I get it." He beamed like a torch on a wet Highland night. "Like you have Italian and you have Sicilian. Like in my village." He now cherished many Scottish words and phrases, although their usage was haphazard and often hilarious.

Joanne leaned back into the fake leather of their booth dreamily taking in the creamy, frothy bliss of a cappuccino and the highly imaginative gelato-colored murals of famous Italian landmarks.

"I wish I could go there." She nodded up at the hot-pink lava pouring out of Vesuvius down to a turquoise sea.

"Me too." Rob sipped his coffee. "Mind you, it's probably changed a bit."

"Bill was in Italy during the war. His regiment had a hard time of it. Sicily, Naples, Monte Cassino. The Lovat Scouts, all the Highland regiments, had a hard time. I doubt Messina looks like that anymore."

Her husband, her handsome brave soldier boy, had survived the battles but not the war. Towns and villages everywhere had their share of ghosts and the walking shells of lost men, boys most of them. Gone to fight in distant wars, fighting the battles of others, again and again the Scottish regiments had been in the thick of it. Mothers, sisters, wives, children, they too were the victims of wars, the unacknowledged victims. Down the centuries, in hopeless situations, in harsh conditions, when all looked lost, "Send in the Scots" was the cry of the generals — the Black Watch, the Lovat Scouts, the Cameron Highlanders, the Seaforth Highlanders, the Gordon Highlanders, the Highland Light Infantry, along with the thousands upon thousands of wild colonial boys. They're tough, they're fierce, the generals said. They're expendable, they thought.

Rob peered through his hair, watching Joanne spoon up the last of the coffee froth. He had been at the *Highland Gazette* a year, Joanne six months, hired because she could type and because McAllister had taken a liking to her. Long-legs, nut-brown shoulder-length hair, bright blue-green eyes, big smile, light freckles; a "bonnie, bonnie lass" incarnate. She loved swinging on the children's swings, her bicycle, knitting, reading, singing and listening to music. And she was a battered wife.

"Come in, number seven," Rob teased.

"Sorry. Away with the faeries."

"Life is but a dream, ssh boom, ssh boom, life is but a dream, sweetheart."

25

Rob mimed the song, a rolled-up copy of the *Gazette* for a microphone.

"Aye. You have that right." A laugh, a shake of the head; Joanne rejoined 1956. "And you've been hanging about with thon Yanks again."

"You should come, Joanne. You'd love it. They've got this great dance band and all the latest records from the U S of A."

"Me? Me dancing in the canteen at RAF Lossiemouth with American airmen? I can just hear my mother-in-law. To say nothing of my husband."

She had loved going to the dancing with her chums in the ATS during the war; dancing to Glen Miller tunes was her favorite. She had met her husband on the dance floor. The very idea of going to the airbase or the Two Red Shoes in Elgin thrilled her. But reality drowned out the daydreams.

"So what's the drama with McAllister? We never miss a Friday postmortem."

"Maybe something about the wee boy in the canal."

"It doesn't bear thinking about." She shuddered. "McAllister is furious with me for not mentioning it, but I'm only the typist. A policeman knocked on every door down our street, the girls were asleep and I didn't like to waken them. Besides, I didn't know if they knew him and I didn't want to upset them, they're too young."

"Aye, accidents happen." Rob rose, went to pay, but Gino, flapping and waving his hands, was having none of it.

"Away with you, away." He grinned at Rob's protestations. "An' I have something else for you. A wee birdie told me a sailor jumped off a Baltic timber ship down at the harbor. Lookin' for a lassie to cuddle I'm thinking, but now gone, lost, he is. Might be a story, *sì?*"

Sounds of fierce arguing came spiraling down the stone stairway. Rob loved a good fight. He bounced up the stairs two at a time, Joanne fast behind. The square reporters' room, with high ceiling, high square reporters' desk, huge bulky typewriters standing along its edges like unexploded bombs, was not a good place for an argument. No room for gesturing, too close to your opponent in the narrow space between desk and walls, too far across the table for "in yer face" poking and pointing. But they managed it. The shouting paused only for a thundering "Shut the door!" from McAllister. He continued his diatribe, punctuating his sentences with slaps on the tabletop. Joanne sidled past Don, wishing she could turn down the volume knob.

"This paper has been going since 1862," Don interrupted. "We never run stories like this. That's gutter-press-from-Glasgow style." He waved the dummy layout at the editor.

"This rag will never see 1962 if we don't start doing something different." McAllister gesticulated back. "This is a human interest story. A child has been found, in the canal, dead, with no explanation, for goodness' sake!"

"Aye, but no need to make such a meal o' it! Accidents are all too common wi' bairns — farms, rivers, the sea, falling off or into something or other. It does no good to put the wind up folk. Scaremongering — that's what this is." He waved the layout pages. "And sentimental. Gossip and scandal'll be next. The father of the chapel will never stand for it neither," Don warned McAllister.

"Well, he'll be without legs if we don't. And another thing, I don't see how you can possibly defend all these outdated trade union practices we have here. I run this newspaper, not the father of the chapel."

"Round one to McAllister on points." Rob started to clap.

They turned, and to Joanne's amazement,

they both stopped. And both men lit up, Don with his Capstan Full Strength, Mc-Allister with his Passing Cloud. Joanne opened the windows, shifting the jam jar of hawthorn sprigs onto the reporters' table. Fallen berries lay on the white windowsill like drops of blood in the snow.

The argument was not new. It had been a sniping war for the first three months after McAllister was appointed editor-in-chief over Don's head. A shaky truce had been observed over the last three months, Mc-Allister agreeing to "see how things go" but adamant the front page must be changed. He won that battle and a temporary truce was called. That truce was now over.

"Sit," McAllister commanded them all. "The postmortem on last week's paper." He stood, picked up a copy of the *Gazette,* held it high with one hand as though it had been used to clean up puppy poo, then carefully tore it in two. Then into four. He dropped it into the top hat, turned, and demanded, "Anyone else, any further comments on last week's rag? No? Right, let's see if we can't do better than that shite."

Silence.

Don smoked furiously, sending out fumes that would shame a Clyde tugboat. Admitting to being fifty for the last few years, he had been with the *Highland Gazette* forty years. A short man, balding, beer belly, scruffy, wearing the same tie his mother had given him on reaching his twenty-five years as a newspaperman, a subeditor right to his bones. He sided with the compositors, the printers, the father of the chapel. The *Gazette* had been going well nigh a hundred years; why change?

"I'll follow up on the child in the canal. We may be a weekly but this is important to a safe wee community like ours." McAllister wanted the meeting over with.

"My girls are at school with him," Joanne volunteered.

"Anything else you haven't told us, Mrs. Ross?"

Joanne blushed, furious with herself.

McAllister gave a theatrical sigh. "Rob, what have you got?"

"Eh, well . . ." He thought frantically. "I've heard a seaman jumped ship. He was crew on a freighter out of one of the Baltic ports. I'm just away to ask at the police station."

"What for?"

"What? Well, they're the ones who're looking for him — an illegal alien, I think they call him."

McAllister shook his head, reminding himself that there was not a real newspaper person amongst them except Don, who, McAllister privately thought, had been around since the printing press had been invented.

"Where, who, when, how and why," he counted out on his elegant long fingers. "The polis may help you with the first three, but the rest? That's for real newspapers. Get off down to the harbor, laddie, and don't come back till you have a real story. Right?" He turned to Joanne. She sank lower in her chair. In this mood, the dark hair and dark eyes and equally dark expression on McAllister's gaunt face made her feel as though she was about to front the Spanish Inquisition.

"I'm on the usual."

He stared.

She mumbled.

"Women's Institute, Girl Guide and Scouts news, school stuff . . . oh, and there's advance notices on Halloween parties I need to sort. You know," she finished lamely, not knowing what was wanted of her.

"Right. But maybe in amongst all that, you could find a story."

Her blank look annoyed him.

"I know, I know, you're only the typist as you keep telling me, but *try*. Something with a beginning, a middle and an end — preferably with the middle bit being of interest to our readers." He saw that he had lost them. "Right, here beginneth the lesson."

The chuckles from Rob and Joanne were somewhat forced. Don kept ignoring the proceedings, but the atmosphere did lighten slightly.

"Let's all try something new. Let's try to imagine that we are in the middle of the twentieth century, not the nineteenth, and that life as we know it is changing. Or is about to change. And if it's not, at least we can nudge it in the direction of change." He stared out of the window, watching the racing rain clouds as they scudded west to catch the mountains. "God knows we haven't made a great fist of the first half." He caught himself, shook his head and continued. "All I want is stories with some meat on the bones. Let's try anyhow. Now away with you both. Bring me some excitement."

"What on earth did you do that for?" Don glared at him when they were alone again. "You know we can never print anything that's different."

McAllister gave his skull-like smile and lit another cigarette. "We'll see."

TWO

McAllister stood on the gleaming red door-step of the terraced fisherman's cottage. The curtains were drawn, as were those of its neighbors. He took a deep breath, then knocked. The door opened reluctantly. Peering out from behind it was a woman with a blotchy red face and haunted eyes.

"I'm sorry to intrude. John McAllister, *Highland Gazette*."

"You'd better come in." She turned, and he followed her into the dim front parlor. The mirror above the unlit fire was shrouded with a shawl; a crowded china cabinet squeezed into one corner; a sideboard covered with pictures of their son stood by the window. Jamie's father sat hunched at a heavy dining table that filled the remaining space. The room smelled of beeswax polish and damp. McAllister shook hands and murmured condolences to a man lost in grief and guilt.

33

"One of us should have been home."

McAllister could not answer that.

"Mr. Fraser, could you tell me something about Jamie? I'd like to do a piece in the paper about him."

"The police think it was our fault."

"Surely not."

"No one is here when Jamie comes home from school. We both work. He was up at the canal because no one was here to look after him."

"Where do you work?"

"On the buses. I'm a driver, my wife's a clippie."

"I used to be in the office but I went on the buses eleven months ago," Mrs. Fraser explained. "We wanted nice things for Jamie. The shift work pays more." She glanced toward a complete set of encyclopedias, as if to lessen the guilt. "He's excused from swimming. I wrote to the school. He'd never go near the canal. Not even with his da. He's a timid wee soul." She had yet to change her tenses. "An' I wasn't here to make his tea."

Her husband didn't move. "He near drowned as a bairn. I was fishing and he fell in the loch. Only three he was. Terrified of water ever since. He never goes near the canal on his own. Never. He won't even

34

cross the river by the footbridge, has to be the big bridge so's he canny see the water. He was delicate, our Jamie."

Their whole lives were devoted to Jamie, McAllister could see that. They told him about his school, his obsession with trains, his stamp collection, small episodes in a barely lived life. They told him of their faraway Hebridean home and their family and them speaking Gaelic amongst themselves. McAllister was gentle, allowing the silences of grief to float between sentences. He listened until they had talked themselves out.

"May I have a picture of Jamie? Would you mind?"

"I've two of these." She handed him a picture of a small boy, all bony arms and legs, clutching his mother's hand beneath a towering tractor. "This summer at the Black Isle Show." She pointed to a merry-go-round on one side. "He loved that." Her eyes glazed over at the memory. "Will you find out what happened to my laddie, Mr. McAllister? He'd never ever go up there on his own."

McAllister had seen grief; as a cub reporter sent on similar interviews, as a war correspondent in Spain, as a crime reporter in Glasgow. And grief had consumed his own mother.

"His friends, tell me about his friends."

They looked at each other in bewilderment.

"I don't know about that. . . ." The woman looked away. "He liked his own company." She couldn't look at McAllister. "He didn't mind being by himself." She gestured to a train set beneath the table. "We had to work so much. Buses run on Sundays too so he had to stop going to Sunday school. . . ." The shadow of guilt hung over her like a cloud darkening an already gloomy sky, becoming tears that dripped onto her cardigan, making no marks in the Fair Isle pattern. "We just wanted the best."

McAllister realized he had stepped into a well-worn argument. Breaking the Sabbath observance must have been a huge step for them, adding to their guilt immeasurably. Her husband stood. He had had enough.

"Many bairns his age were already working when I was a boy." He glared at his wife. "Well able to look out for themselves." Then, looking down at the carpet, he added in desperate justification, as though the sin had already been flung in their faces, "It doesn't matter what the kirk says about Sundays, you have to look after your family first."

It was time to go, McAllister knew. Stages of grief, like stations of the cross, were a ritual. There was no need for him to hear of their innermost fears, their self-recrimination and rehashed arguments and all the other stages of grief that loss of their only son would surely bring. All this he knew only too well.

Walking gingerly on the wet cobbles, down the narrow street, back to the office, a thin mist shrouding him, he hunched his shoulders and pulled down his hat against rain and melancholy and the knowledge that Jamie's parents had now entered the realm of the half people — parents who bury a child.

Rob decided that a motorbike was essential to life as a star reporter. His mother's respectable gray Wolseley was a woman's car; he couldn't keep borrowing it.

"I'll be twenty-one next year" — as though that made him an adult — "I'll buy the bike myself," he told his parents, and gave a solemn promise to never drive with a drink in him and never to use the bike if there was even a hint of black ice. They capitulated.

Saturday was a half day at the *Highland Gazette,* but not for part-timer Joanne. She had Fridays and Saturdays off and was usually scrubbing floors, catching up on the washing, weeding the vegetables or plucking a chicken for the Sunday dinner at this time of the week. This morning, however, she was at the office early to meet Rob, who was off to chase the story of the missing sailor — at least that's what he told Don. But first, they were hoping to buy a motorbike. And it was Don, Rob reasoned, who had taught him to never let the facts get in the way of a good story.

Joanne knew about motorbikes. She'd been a dispatch rider in the uncertain days of 1944. She knew a surprising amount about the internal combustion engine.

"The most important thing is —"

"Carry a spare spark plug! I know," said Rob.

They drove to the outskirts of the town. 'Round the back of the bungalow belonging to an usher at the magistrates' court gleamed a red Triumph 650. Rob walked around it a few times admiring the color. Trying to look knowledgeable, he sat on it, barely hiding his longing.

"Hop on the back, I'll take ye for a drive," the owner offered.

"Could Joanne take it out? She's the friend I was telling you about. The one from the army."

"You niver said anything about your soldier friend being a lassie."

Joanne quickly launched into a technical spiel, asking all the right questions about cylinders, carburetor, power-to-weight ratio, then got down on her haunches to inspect the engine. Rob fooled around with the usher's three children in the back garden, staying well clear of the discussions. Then they mounted the bike, Joanne driving, heading out toward Culloden to see how it handled the hills and bends.

After she had some fun putting a few scares into him, Joanne shouted over her shoulder, "This is a great bike, immaculate condition, as we in the classifieds would say."

Rob left her to strike the deal. His role was to hand over the cash.

"You owe me one. I'll add it to the ever-growing list," Joanne reminded him.

"You can always borrow my bike."

"I'll hold you to that, but meanwhile babysitting would be a good payback."

"Don't you need someone for tonight? You're off to the Highland Ball, aren't you?"

"Thanks, but I'm fixed. The girls are going to my sister's. They love being with their cousins, so it's fine."

They waved their cheerios. Rob roared off on his new Triumph. Joanne drove the McLeans' car back, looking forward to a chat and a cup of tea with Rob's mother.

The tip had come from Don McLeod. As ever.

"Right, laddie, I've set it up, just mention my name."

"Great, I'm looking forward to a run on the new bike."

"Why you want to go chasing after some Polish seaman is beyond me; he'll be just another manny wanting to get out of his country — not that I blame him."

"McAllister wants some human interest stories."

"This is a weekly newspaper, not some women's sob-sheet," Don shouted. But too late — Rob's motorbike boots could be heard at the bottom of the stairs.

The trip down to the harbor to meet Don's informant was Rob's chance to try out his new image. He fancied himself as Scotland's answer to Marlon Brando. I'm off down the waterfront, he joked to himself. He drove out of town, past the old fort and the Black Watch barracks, crossed the rail tracks, opening up the throttle along the shore road through the salt marsh fields with tinkers' ponies dotted around like clumps of dirty melting snow. Quarreling gulls and feeding migratory birds took no notice as he sped past the town dump toward the harbor. Right in front of the window of the Harborside Café, he propped the Triumph, hoping everyone would notice the gleaming machine.

A blast of steamy warmth hit Rob as he opened the door. His cheeks and ears tingled with the sudden change in temperature.

"Were ye born in a barn, Rob McLean?" Mrs. McLeary, the café's owner, cook, waitress and cashier, shouted. He shut the door quickly. She was a scary woman. A man in work overalls sat alone at the corner table. He grinned up at Rob.

"So you're Rob. How're you doing?" They shook hands. "Maybe it's nothing, but Mr. McLeod is always interested in tips."

"I bet he is."

"Aye, that's right. But usually of the horse variety." The man laughed. "Let's order. It's been a long night."

"Sorry I'm late. I just bought a bike."

"It looks grand. So, breakfast?"

"Aye, on the *Gazette*."

Rob nodded toward the wharf as they

tucked in. "Another world out there."

Three ships, six fishing boats and a filthy dredger stood along the busy wharf where the river flowed into the firth. Timber from Scandinavia, coal from Newcastle, cement and building supplies were the main cargoes in, grain for the distilleries the main cargo out. Its ancient beginnings, its connections with the Baltic Hanseatic League, the departure of emigrant ships during the Clearances, the everyday trade of centuries, had made the deep harbor the most important in the north. For a small town, the port brought the exotic: foreigners who spoke no English, who looked different; romantic names and ports of registration painted above the Plimsoll line, strange flags flapping. An Eskimo from a Greenland fishing boat, resplendent in traditional sealskins, had once come into the café. Mrs. McLeary had served him the usual fare of a big fry-up and stewed tea. He paid in coin of the realm like anyone else, she said.

Over extra-strength tea and light fluffy rolls bursting with bacon, Rob took notes, trying to keep the grease stains off his notebook. Born nosy, he was good at this part of the job, the chatting, the questioning; he was intrigued by the minutiae of other people's lives — excellent traits for a journalist.

"So what made you go and look?"

"The boat's registered in Danzig, their last port was Tallinn, but they were shouting in Russian. I could hear them clear. Sound carries across water at night."

"Are you sure it was Russian?"

"I was on the Murmansk convoys. I can tell Polish from Russian. And German." His tone was sharp, not used to being doubted by a boy.

"As I was saying, there was fierce arguing. Then it went quiet. I did ma rounds so it would have been maybe half an hour afore I heard a big splash from round the other side o' the ship. Across the river there was a boat, a salmon cobble it looked like, waiting for the turn in the tide to take them upriver, so I thought. Then a short whiley later I saw two folk pulling summat aboard."

"What was it?"

"Couldn't tell, the moon was keeking in and out from behind the clouds. I still had to check the Bond House and by the time I got back there was nothing and nobody."

Rob paid for the nightwatchman's breakfast and, intrigued by the romance of the port, the ships, the foreign sailors, he made for the wharf.

I really need a leather motorbike cap and

jacket, he thought.

Slipping past the guard's hut, making his way down the line of huge iron bollards squatting like sumo wrestlers along the water's edge, he noticed one ship lying separate from the others.

"It's yerself," Constable Grant shouted from the top of the gangplank. Not much older than Rob, Willie Grant was front-row-forward big.

"So where's this runaway Russian, Willie?"

"He's Polish."

"Thanks." Rob grinned.

Realizing he'd let on to something he wasn't supposed to, Willie Grant sulked. Rob changed tack with "Did you see thon new goalie Thistle has? Jammy hands. They'll put one over on Caley next week, you'll see."

Five minutes of minute detail followed as to why Caledonian Football Club would always beat Thistle. Rob judged his moment as Willie blethered on.

"So where is he now, Willie, this Polish fellow?"

"No one knows nothing 'cept that the sailor is no here. The captain doesnae speak English an' Peter the Pole, yon engineer manny, he came down to help us 'cos he speaks a bit o' Russian an' all. But the

44

ship'll be sailing bye 'n' bye, no reason not to. The Polish fella just wants a better life, most like."

"Ta, Willie, you're a pal."

"You never heard nothing from me, mind."

Frozen from the biting wind, Rob returned to the café to jot down some notes. He sat staring out of the steamed-up window, nursing another mug of tea. The vista of harbor, river and firth seemed to be melting, cranes alongside the wharf looming like giant storks; distant fishermen rowing out their nets were tiny figures dissolving in and out of the watery scene of sea mist and steam. He tried to picture that night. Someone, something, thrown overboard at the right time of the tide would drift with the flow of the river straight to any waiting boat. The swift currents where the river met the narrow waters of the firth were notorious. Maybe they were smuggling, Rob hoped. Vodka in unlabeled bottles was readily obtainable. Usually in this very café.

Rob was a romantic. He looked and thought like a nineteenth-century romantic; very out of place in a small Scottish town. He had once been told by a teacher at the academy that his curiosity and wild imagination would one day land him in a lot of trouble. Instead it had landed him a job. This will make a good story, he decided.

"Do you know where I can find Peter the Pole?"

"Mr. Kowalski to you," Mrs. McLeary informed him. "He's away up Strathpeffer fishing, is what I heard."

"I heard it's Glen Affric he goes," someone else joined in.

"Up the glens anyhow." She never missed out on a conversation, overheard everything and was known locally as "radar lugs." Her cruel metal curlers, half covered by a head-scarf with a Stags at Bay Scottish landscape, were rumored to be antennae.

"Anyone heard anything about the sailor that jumped ship?" Rob asked around.

They had all heard of it, the police had been round asking questions, but Mrs. McLeary had to reluctantly admit to know-ing nothing new.

"Thon big tinker camp down by the shore," one customer suggested. "The river could have washed up a body or such like along there."

"Nah," said another. "A body would float down the firth on the ebb tide and be well upriver on the flood tide."

"The tinkers miss nothing. Tell ye nothing neither." The local gave Rob a mock finger wag. "An' if you go nosying around, mind the dogs don't get ye, and don't bother takin' thon shiny bike o' yours. It'll be stripped for spare parts afore you can blink."

Talking to the tinkers was a great idea, Rob thought. He'd do it. But first he had to work out an approach. You didn't just walk into a tinkers' camp. All the old tales from childhood surfaced. Not that his parents had ever said anything. But the myths of tinkers kidnapping bairns, stealing everything not nailed down, and the all-round general mischief that ensued whenever their horse-drawn caravans appeared — the stories were still vivid. He had once asked his mother, after a tinker woman had come to the door selling lucky white heather, were the tinkers Gypsies? Scotland's Gypsies maybe, she had said, but no, she went on to explain, not the same people as Romanies. An old, old race of Gaelic-speaking people was all she knew.

So, yes, he'd go to the camp and ask questions. Impress McAllister. Make this a real story. His confidence in his ability to charm had yet to be dented.

Along the burns and rivers that tumbled through the glens, autumn reigned in bright scarlet and dull gold. Birch, oak, beech and rowan formed small thickets dotted among the rusting bracken. Higher on the hillsides, bands of gloomy conifers followed the contours of the land. A purple watercolor wash of heather softened the boulder-strewn hills of the upper glen, with snow lying lightly on the tops and deep in the shadowed corries.

Peter Kowalski knew this wild empty landscape well from his time on the construction of the hydro dam. Gangs of displaced men, locals and foreigners alike, lived and worked in the remote glen, dealing with the cold, the backbreaking work, the scars of war, desperate to earn a stake for the future. Poland was lost to him, and he had worked hard for his new life. He shared the pain and he shared his skills with those who had neither country nor family to return to. He taught simple engineering, filled in forms in English, helped men apply to the Red Cross for news of lost family. And he listened.

Pleasure came from the small things; tickling for trout, watching the birds, the eagle hunting, stalking the deer. Cloudscapes of great beauty highlighted the four-seasons-in-one-day phenomenon that was called weather in Scotland, but often it was dreich for days, sometimes weeks, on end.

"Dreich, I like that word," Peter had said when it was explained to him. The rolled "r" and the harsh "ch" conveyed the texture and color and feeling of the days of gray. He thought Scotland much like Baltic Poland in weather, if not landscape — drawn-out rains, mists and damp, cold, dreich days with an absence of light.

The directions from the tinkers were good and clear; trees, rocks, turns in the river were the markers. He had reached his destination.

A note had come to Peter's office. He had read the Polish words, surprised by the letter, but had agreed without thinking to help a fellow countryman. He knew that deportment to labor camps, imprisonment on false charges, starvation, any number of horrific things were still happening to those in occupied Poland. Escaping was no easy matter either. Peter Kowalski had no hesitation in making his decision.

The tinker boy who had brought the message told him the man was sheltering with them, that the man was well but frightened of being found by the police. The necessities listed in the letter were boots, cigarettes and vodka. Whisky would have to do.

He had picked up the man on the north side of the canal, agreed with the plan to move him away from the town into another county and had taken him to the deserted croft in his work van. The tinkers were unhappy having him at their encampment; the town and the police had a bad enough opinion of them without giving another excuse to raid their caravans and campsite.

"A good hiding place." Peter looked up to the high fold in the hills for the clump of birch and rowan that obscured the entrance to the hanging glen.

Now midafternoon and turning very chill, it had been two days since he had taken his fellow countryman to the ragged cottage and outbuildings. Even in the seventy years or so since the last of the Clearances, a small area around the fading settlement was clear of vegetation. As with the graves on the battlefield of Culloden, the heather had not grown back. Locals were reluctant to go there. Memories of exile were fresh in these parts. And this glen was the realm of the faeries, another good reason to keep away.

Peter whistled a well-loved tune from his childhood. Silence, then a figure material-ized under the lintel of the long-gone doorway. Meeting his compatriot for the second time reminded Peter of approaching an unbroken horse. Food, whisky and cigarettes were offered. The gifts were accepted, but no thanks were given.

"The police are questioning everyone at the harbor, especially your captain and shipmates."

"The police!" The man flashed a look of pure hatred. He had used the Polish slang word for the militia, the hated occupiers of their homeland. He was edgy, defensive; he paced through two cigarettes, glowering resentment at his rescuer.

"It's not like that here, they're decent local lads. And you did jump ship. No papers, no nothing."

"What about that thieving murderous bastard of a captain? He tried to kill me. Why is he not locked up?"

"Because he has papers. According to the law he's done nothing wrong. He reported you missing a whole day after the event. Late, but not illegal."

"He only reported me to keep the ship's manifest in order — and to spite me. He stole everything. My papers, all the money I had left, and he took . . ." He stopped, lit another cigarette. "He meant to kill me."

"He pushed you overboard. Maybe it was an accident."

"He beat me. Hit me on the head. Put me into the water semiconscious, in the dark."

"The ship sails this afternoon."

51

"Now you will abandon me." This was a statement. No blame was implied.

"We are Polish. You need help. I will do all I can to get you legal here."

Of course Peter would help, had already helped, but the stranger's surly manner did not aid his own cause. And Peter suspected he could not talk about it. Whatever the reason, the man was a walking suppurating wound. He had briefly told Peter of his escape from the Polish coast to Tallinn, through the Baltic marshes, through the minefields that studded the coastal waters. He mentioned the Nazis, years in a Russian labor camp and a large bribe. Why he had to leave and not endure as his fellow Poles were still enduring was another mystery.

"I must return to town. I'll get you out of here as soon as possible, but I still think you should turn yourself in. They are good people here."

"No."

The man turned and faded back into the black of the ruins without farewell.

Gino Corelli could feel the heat of the tears hovering on his daughter's long thick lashes. She was his life and his soul, he would often declare, but this time he could not reassure her. He had promised.

"Where is he?" Chiara asked again. "You're treating me like a child. Why all the mystery?"

"Maybe your future husband couldn't cope with any more discussions about bridesmaids' dresses." Joanne walked into the middle of the argument and hugged her dearest friend.

"I didn't hear you come in."

"Too busy harassing your poor dad."

"Peter is supposed to be here. Now I hear he's off up the glen fishing. Honestly, I thought he wasn't like some other men" — she glared at her father — "disappearing whenever I want to talk about our wedding arrangements. It's only six weeks away."

"Well, I hope you've not forgotten your promise to help me get ready for the ball," Joanne reminded her. "That's tonight."

"I'll leave you two beautiful girls to talk." Gino kissed them both, glad of the reprieve from his daughter's questions. The sooner Peter got back the better. He hated secrets. For him, the marriage of his only child was sad and joyous all at the same time. Peter Kowalski was a wonderful man, Gino knew this. But Chiara was his only child, all he had left. His wife, his parents, two brothers and a sister had disappeared along with most of their village during the liberation of

Italy. Gino had been lucky. Captured in North Africa, he had ended up in a prisoner-of-war camp in Scotland. Along with British Italians interned for the duration, he had worked on local farms, made friends in the camp and stayed on as there was nothing left, nothing to go back to. He sent for his daughter and his only surviving sister after the war had ended.

"The band, Papa," she called after him. "Don't forget, that is your job. I want Italian dancing. Scottish as well."

"Your cousins from down South bring their accordions. We'll have Italian-Scottish dance music."

Chiara grumbled to Joanne about her elusive fiancé but was soon distracted by the problem of the bridesmaids' dresses.

"Two of my cousins are so short and round that most dresses make them look like the dancing baby elephants in *Fantasia*. Anyway, enough. I'll punish Peter by asking him to decide on the designs. Let's get you ready for tonight."

Laughing, teasing, gossiping, Chiara finished the hem on Joanne's dress, laid it on the bed, then started on her hair.

"This is the first real dance I'll have been to since we were married, nearly ten years."

"Finished." Chiara looked critically at her

54

work, then enveloped them both in a choking mist of hair spray. "You'll be the belle of the Highland Ball." Joanne picked up the dress, held it against her, caressing the deep forest-green silk taffeta.

"I love this. Thank you, Chiara. I'd never have chosen the design myself. Far too daring." A moment of panic seized her. "I hope Bill approves. This evening means a lot to him."

"You look gorgeous. Like Ava Gardner but far prettier — and not nearly so much showing." They laughed. "Your pearls, they're perfect with the dress."

"My grandmother left them to me." The memory of her cherished grandparent, the only one to keep in touch with Joanne after her disgrace, saddened her.

The doorbell rang. Bill had arrived to collect her for the ball. He waited in the doorway looking equally splendid in his regimental Fraser tartan dress kilt. Joanne felt a lurch of animal attraction when she saw her handsome charmer of a husband, grinning at the two women like a fox at the henhouse door. Chiara gave a wolf whistle.

"You're almost a married woman. What would your fiancé say?" Bill teased Chiara and smiled at Gino but wouldn't come in.

"I'm not his possession, I think what I

like." Chiara was quick.

Joanne walked toward him, a mohair stole draped over her shoulders, and did a quick birl for his benefit. Bill was delighted.

"You look beautiful."

"Don't sound so surprised."

"It's a bit revealing."

"She looks like a film star." Chiara turned to her father. "*Si*, Papa?"

"More beautiful than any fil'im star." He kissed Joanne's hand and escorted her to the car. There was not much Bill could say after that, but when they reached the entrance of the Caledonian Ballroom he reached for the stole, pulling it over her cleavage.

Just like his mother, she thought, and sighed to herself.

The drinking, the heat, the volume of talk increased steadily. The men had regrouped around the bar; their wives stayed at the tables to embark on the character assassinations that passed for conversation among the "ladies." Joanne sat watching the band, half listening to the conversations around her, and did not catch the opening salvo.

"Sorry, I was miles away."

"We were just saying, dear, how unusual your dress is." The woman across the table smirked at her. As the wife of the town clerk she assumed the right to be first with the velvet dagger.

"It's the latest fashion from Paris." Joanne smiled. "Well, at least the pattern is. The fabric is Italian. A present from my friend Chiara Corelli."

Another of the tightly permed and tightly corseted brigade around the table got in the next barb — "Ah yes, the chip shop people" — and duly received appreciative sniggers.

The next harpy took her turn. "You must be a very busy person, dear. A successful husband, two young children, a job on the *Gazette,* I hear, *and* you make your own clothes too! Still, I'm sure it saves money."

"The silk wasn't cheap," Joanne started. "It was a *Vogue* pattern, and . . . I enjoy sewing." She was floundering.

"Mrs. Ross, may I have this dance?" McAllister appeared behind Joanne's chair. He nodded around the table. "Ladies."

The chorus returned his greeting, disappointed at having their prey snatched from them. But Joanne clearly heard the final judgment as they headed for the dance floor. "Just who does she think she is?" Enshrined in the well-worn phrase were all the petty jealousies and small-minded prejudices of a small town.

"Knitting before the guillotine, I presume?" McAllister held the tall slim figure lightly as they swung around the floor, Joanne's fury vibrating through his hands.

"Something like that."

"Jealousy, my dear, plain and simple."

"In my homemade dress and my granny's pearls, I hardly think so."

"In your elegant creation and heirloom pearls, with your chic hairstyle and natural beauty, not forgetting your obvious intelligence, they have everything to be jealous of, Mrs. Ross."

"Why, thank you, kind sir. Now you're making me blush. But thanks for rescuing me. I never saw you as a knight in shining armor."

"I will endeavor to keep up the illusion."

They stood at the edge of the crowd waiting out the next dance.

"You know, no matter what I do, I never seem to get it right."

"They're like hens at a pecking party. Anyone different, anyone who stands out, gets the full treatment. Just be yourself and never mind what anyone thinks."

Joanne caught sight of her husband across the room.

"It's not my feelings that matter."

Standing at the bar with his cronies, he

was watching her. Another whisky was shoved into his hand and Bill Ross turned back to his new friends. Joanne shivered; an autumnal gust of fear ran through her. She tightened the stole in an attempt to ward off the goose bumps.

The next day being the Sabbath, the band had to pack up at eleven. Tables were cleared, the bar shuttered, and the last of the drinkers went dribbling down the stairs. Joanne was waiting for Bill by the revolving doors. McAllister waved good-bye across the foyer, then disappeared from the pool of light out into the dark street, a cold wind with the promise of rain his companion on the short walk home. He was nearing the corner when a sharp cry cut through the quiet. He turned. Under a streetlight a woman was sprawled backward across a car bonnet.

"Joanne." McAllister was startled by the intimacy of the scene. He went to intervene, saw she was with her husband, Bill Ross. It was none of his business. He ducked quickly around the corner. He stopped. Coward, he told himself. Went back. By now they were in the car, drawing away from the pavement. He hurried home, cheeks burning in the raw cold night. Aye, he thought, she was right;

I'm certainly no knight in shining armor.

The attack had started on the walk to the car when Joanne had instinctively made for the driver's side.

"I'm driving." Jingling the keys in her face, Bill then shoved her, sending her flying backward onto the car bonnet.

She stifled any protests. Arguing only made it worse. He drove fast, took corners fast, fairly flying across the bridge. Few cars, no cyclists and no police were out this late. They made it home — a miracle. She slunk through the back door, shrinking herself into as small a target as possible. He tackled her from behind. One arm around her throat, the other hand pulled her round by the hair. Hairpins scattered to the floor. A gargoyle face, a few inches away, spat at her.

"You're no better than a hoor. Showing me up like that." An overpowering blast of whisky and malice made her try to turn away.

"We had a nice time." She hated herself for pleading. "It was a lovely dance. You enjoyed it too."

"You have to show me up, don't you? You just have to be different. Everyone was staring at you. And telling them you made your frock yourself. That la-di-da latest-from-

Paris shite."

The punch caught her square in the middle. She doubled over, gagging, bitter bile filling her mouth. The kick caught her full on the hip, flinging her across the room. She landed awkwardly, one leg buckling under her. Bill had never touched her face nor anywhere that bruises might show. Curled up, she kept muttering, "Sorry, sorry." He always stopped when she capitulated.

"Here. Have it. Have the lot." He threw a flurry of banknotes, followed by a painful shower of coins. "Go on. Get a fur coat, the best you can find. I'll no have a wife o' mine show me up."

She didn't move until she heard the car leave. Every breath was painful. She gathered the banknotes, put them in the tea caddy, glad that there was enough to buy the girls new winter boots. She clutched the banisters, hauling herself up the stairs, her hip stiff with pain where the kick had landed.

In Annie's bedroom, the chest of drawers dragged across the door, spoiled dress abandoned like a discarded dishrag on the floor, in the too small bed, she lay there, silent, sore, all crying done, smelling the comforting fragrance of child, drifting down

into sleep, her last thought: Thank goodness
my pearls didn't break.

THREE

All that Rob knew about war came from watching Pathé newsreels in the cinema. In front of him, the desolate scene of the tinkers' camp emerging from the haar reminded him of images of displaced peoples in makeshift encampments strewn all over Europe. Caravans, lorries, vans formed a semicircle. Picked-over carcasses of skeletal vehicles hovered around the outside, ghosts at the feast. Traditional dwellings, "benders," made from birch saplings and tarpaulins sealed with tar, huddled near the mounds of scrap metal, rubbish, smoldering fires and washing lines. Children, chickens and mangy dogs roamed, hungry scavengers picking through the bones of the camp. The northern boundary, the municipal dump, was alive with a coronet of circling seagulls. The railway line marked the southern boundary. Westward, multiplying industrial warehouses were creeping over the remaining fertile land. Eastward, coastal mudflats and salt marshes seethed with wintering birds, greylag geese competing for the lush grass with forty or so horses. This was the winter quarters of the travelers, the Summer Walkers, as they called themselves; the tinkers, tinks as the townsfolk called them when they wanted to perpetuate the myth of a child-stealing, curse-laying, thieving, outcast, scourge-of-Scotland race of outsiders. Fear, that's what his father had told Rob. In the past the Traveling people were respected for their skills, their music; they were, are, a vital part of agricultural life in the Highlands, he told his son.

Rob stood beside his bike in the gusting breeze, coming all the way from the Atlantic and the Isles, blowing down the faultline of the Great Glen to meet the North Sea.

"Hiya, is your dad here?" A girl, seven or eight, appeared, stared at the stranger, mouth open, a clot of yellow snot hovering above her top lip. A boy, twelve or thirteen, materialized and stood staring, mesmerized by the shiny red motorbike.

"Can I have a shot on yer bike?"

"Hop on. Then I'd like to speak to your father."

Once around the fields, with a spurt of speed on the last hundred yards, they skidded to a stop. The boy jumped off and ran.

"Hey, we had a deal," Rob shouted.

"On your own heid be it then." The lad disappeared into one of the larger caravans. A man emerged from the doorway.

"Away with ye! Get the hell out o' here."

Dogs circled, barking, snapping at Rob's boots, peeing their territory on a wheel as he sat astride the bike. Children joined in with whooping war cries. A stone flew past; another landed close by. Rob's new friend watched, laughing. A shout from the man in what Rob took to be Gaelic and the boy took off across the fields toward the ponies. Looking back, he gave Rob a cheery wave, his red hair a beacon in all the surrounding shades of gray.

On the Monday, Joanne took the bus to work, too sore to cycle. Her hip ached and she prayed she wouldn't cough; the bruising around her ribs and solar plexus made even breathing painful enough.

"Good night on Saturday?" McAllister smiled across at her as she joined the others for the news meeting.

"Great, thanks. Yourself?"

"Bored out of my mind." He sensed her deflation. "Apart from the dance with you, of course." The attempt at gallantry failed.

Sitting hunched in the chair, she seemed somehow diminished. He tried putting it down to Monday morning, but the echo of that cry, the flicker of stills from the night street scene had flooded his long Sunday.

Mrs. Smart, the *Gazette* secretary, sat poised, ready to take notes; Rob fiddled with his notebook; Don waved a fistful of copy paper to start the meeting, summarizing the next issue's content: road widening for the main A9 south, ferry changes for the crossing to Skye, prices fetched for this year's potato harvest, petty theft from a council house building site, golden wedding celebrations, plans to convert the Victorian poorhouse to an old folks' home, all the usual.

"The fatal accident inquiry on the child's death —"

"Aye, *accident*," Don muttered.

"— will report back after the usual inquiries, but a postmortem has been ordered, just to be certain." McAllister glared at Don. "Anything else, anyone?" Silence. He asked again. "Is there nothing new for this week or shall we just change the date and run last year's pages?"

"I doubt anyone would notice the difference," Rob said cheerfully.

"You're employed here to make a difference, laddie."

The editor's ferocious tone made Rob jump. He quickly explained his search for the "Slippery Pole," as he had dubbed the missing sailor.

"Why didn't you ask me?" Don grumbled. "I'd have got you an in wi' the tinkers."

"Thanks, I might take you up on that. A foreign tribe down there. I know they know something. But no one gets past those bairns — nor the dogs."

"If you ask me, it's a job for the police to find him, not for some boy who fancies himself as a Scottish version of Scoop to chase after." Don glared at McAllister as he lit a new cigarette from the previous one.

"Joanne, how about a wee piece on the Highland Ball?"

"You were there" — Joanne didn't even look at McAllister as she spoke — "you do it. I'm only the typist, I've not got an *in* with anyone."

Everyone stared. This was not the Joanne they knew.

"The committee secretary will send notes as usual." Don made a peace offering.

"That's what I'm trying to get away from." McAllister, still digesting the sharp reply, reminded them of the new policy. "We'll get who made a speech, who made a toast, who sucked up to whom, a list of the prominent guests. Riveting stuff. Something fresh and lively, a bit of gossip, that's what we need. It's right up your street, Joanne."

"Depends on who the gossip is about," she muttered.

"Like that, eh?" Don gallantly intervened. "I can just imagine it. You turn up looking smashing, the belle o' the ball, you get dumped at a table of council wives wrapped up in their superiority and their fox furs wi' claws still attached; you've been given orders to suck up to them whilst your man goes off drinking wi' the big boys to also suck up to them, then, when you step out onto the dance floor —"

"With me as her Prince Charming," McAllister contributed.

"— you show them a thing or two. I bet every man there was wishing you were his wife instead of the battle-axe he came with. Grace Kelly of the Highlands, you are."

"But you weren't there."

"Aye, but I know what it's like."

"I'm in agreement with Don, for once — belle of the Highland Ball." They applauded. Joanne turned crimson. The atmosphere went back to normal.

"Why don't you give it a try." McAllister spoke through a shroud of cigarette smoke.

"Don't forget revenge is one of the perks of a journalist's job. Get a dig in, but keep it legal. Don'll sub it and if it's too close to the bone I'll take the blame — as usual."

Somewhat flustered, decidedly more cheerful, she nodded. "I'll give it a try."

Peter Kowalski had asked Mr. Silverstein to have the tray of wedding rings ready. He enjoyed talking to the old man from one of the few Jewish families in the Highlands.

"Don't worry. Only the best quality, like we agreed."

"The matching ring for me?"

"My workmen will think you're a big girl, having a ring made." He laughed, knowing this would make one more story around the town about the weird ways of foreigners. The jeweler's shop was in the Victorian covered market where many small family businesses congregated in long arcades. A large covered produce section had fruit and vegetable stalls, fishmongers and butchers, and at the northern side was the furniture auction room.

Chiara was meeting Peter at the jeweler's. Pleased, relieved, at last she had her explanation for all the whispering and secrecy between her fiancé and her father.

The bell on the door pinged, and in bounced a flushed and happy Chiara, her aunt Lita trotting behind. They exchanged greetings in a mixture of languages before settling down to the serious business of choosing the rings.

"Choose for me too," Peter said. "Mr. Silverstein will make them up for us."

Chiara took a long time, trying on this style and that, most of which looked identical to Peter, then after a debate in Italian with her aunt, who was more impressed by weight than design, she said, "This one. Matching rings, please."

"A good choice." Peter squeezed Chiara's hand.

A handshake for Peter, a kiss on the hand for Chiara, a bow to her aunt, a promise to find suitable gifts for the bridesmaids, and Mr. Silverstein saw them to the door.

Chiara and Aunt Lita lingered in front of the gleaming window display, discussing gifts for the bridesmaids. Peter peered over their shoulders. Then his world fell apart.

In the soft full lights, nestled in blood-red velvet, amongst antique rings and brooches, was his mother's diamond and ruby crucifix.

That it was his mother's he had no doubt. His grandmother had worn it before her, and her mother before that. It was a family tradition that the cross was passed down to the first daughter of each generation. His mother had never been without it. In spite of its value, she had worn it every day concealed under her clothing.

Peter felt faint. "A moment, my love." He went back inside and hurriedly asked Mr. Silverstein to put the cross aside for him.

"You all right, my boy?"

"Maybe a touch of fever or something."

The old man accepted the lie.

Peter walked the short distance from the jeweler's to the Station Hotel in a complete daze. Chiara, holding his arm, chattered away like an excited sparrow. Business acquaintances and friends smiled as the couple made their way through to the dining room.

"Almost a ritual, this, eh? We seem to see you every week."

"It is," Peter replied. His engineering company relied on contacts and, more important, council contracts. The man speaking to him, Mr. Grieg from the town council, was just such a person to cultivate. Peter had to swallow his dislike of Grieg's self-important, hail-fellow-well-met hand-shake.

"Did you receive the wedding invitation, Mr. Grieg?" Chiara too knew the game.

"Wouldn't miss it for the world."

They were shown to a table. Peter dropped into the chair, trying to maintain his composure. He glanced at the menu, knew he couldn't eat, the very thought of food . . . He put it down to delayed shock.

"I think my stomach has had too much haggis."

"You never eat haggis," Chiara replied. She saw that he was even paler than his usual white-blond-hair, pale-blue-eyes paleness.

"Oh, right. Are you catching something? Do you want to go home?"

Gino was in the kitchen when they returned. "What's wrong?"

"His stomach, Papa."

"Italians, we never get upset stomachs." Gino smiled. Then, looking again at his future son-in-law, seeing his carefully disguised distress, he fetched some water.

"Thank you. And perhaps a walk?" Peter asked the older man. "Fresh air is good for me."

On their way to the jeweler's, Peter explained.

"Are you sure?"

"Absolutely certain. I revered that necklace as a child. I know every stone in it. I remember the stories — the diamond that is not as good as the others because when it fell out and was lost, my father couldn't afford another of the same quality."

He told Gino that when his father could afford to replace it with a better diamond his mother had refused, saying that it would remind them of harder times, now long gone. "My mother told me the history of the heirloom, showed me the pictures of her mother and also her grandmother wearing it. It came in turn to the eldest daughter of each generation, from mother to daughter."

Saturday being a half day, the shop was shuttered, and as they waited for an answer to the bell, Gino was still struggling to make sense of the story. How on earth could this Polish family necklace have ended up here, out of all the places in a still shattered Europe, here in this small Highland town where Peter had made his home? Mr. Silverstein had the same problem.

"This crucifix is my mother's." Peter was adamant.

"I believe you. Please, your word is enough for me." Mr. Silverstein had to sit down. "You know, when he came into my shop, I was suspicious. He said it was his mother's, but now he had no family. He said he needed the money to start his new life and couldn't get a good price in Tallinn. I believed him." Mr. Silverstein was deeply embarrassed. "So now we must find this sailor, find out how he got your mother's jewelry. I will help all I can."

Peter felt betrayed. He had done everything he could to help the missing sailor, even putting himself at risk with the police. His compatriot must have known, must somehow have taken the necklace from his mother, must have known of his mother's fate. And he had not uttered a word to Peter.

Mr. Silverstein turned to Gino.

"I never trusted a Russian before, now look where it gets me. Receiving stolen goods; I could lose my reputation, my business."

"Russian?" Peter was puzzled. "The missing sailor is Polish."

"Never. I am Russian, I know."

"Describe him."

"A bear of a man. Big beard. Dark. Dangerous. He wore a captain's uniform and spoke Russian with a northern accent. Murmansk, I am thinking."

"That's not the missing sailor. He's Polish

and fair but darker fair, not like me."

The three men were at a loss to explain the what or the how or the why of the mystery. As Gino and Mr. Silverstein discussed one theory after another, Peter sat staring at the necklace, lost in thought, memories jostling for position like restless horses at the start of a race.

"The day I left to rejoin my squadron I didn't know I would never return," he started his monologue. "Our estate bordering the Baltic marshland is isolated. War was coming, we had no doubt of that, but we never guessed how bad things would become." He lit a cigarette for support. "I said good-bye to my parents. I never dreamed it was a final farewell. Then I went back to my old unit in the Polish air force."

The two older men nodded. So many stories had been shared; all different, all the same — heartbreaking.

"We'd been to early mass, my mother wearing her crucifix as always, this time on display, worn as a soldier would, proudly. I left straight after the service. My father understood. We were officers. It is our duty to defend our homeland. I never saw them again. I have never heard from them." Winter sky-blue eyes clouded, he paused.

"I will always feel we were traitors for fleeing Poland. But what could we do? We escaped. They didn't. Now, once again, Poland is a prisoner."

Mr. Silverstein and Gino Corelli listened silently, their shoulders bowed by the weight of their own memories.

"When we landed in Scotland, me and many of my countrymen joined the British forces," Peter continued. "But I, I had it easy, stuck here in safety."

"You served your country. An engineer does just as much as a pilot. You saved lives." Gino was adamant. "Now it is in the past."

"My homeland is occupied. Different enemy, same result."

"We sold my wife's wedding ring." Gino's voice was harsh. "My sister Lita sold everything to join me here."

"We all did what we had to do."

Mr. Silverstein put the cross into its red leather box. "This is yours."

Gino and Peter both reached for their wallets.

"No, no. It is my present for Chiara, for you both. I insist. Take it, take it." He shooed them away with flapping hands.

"I even remember the box." Peter picked it up, shivered. A picture of it lying on his mother's dressing table came sharply into focus.

His future father-in-law looked at Peter. "Home now, ma boy."

"I will find out what happened, Mr. Silverstein, and keep you in the picture."

"Thank you. But be quick. The Russian captain said the ship is sailing away very soon."

"But he will want his Polish seaman back — or at least some papers from the police to explain what happened. Big trouble for him with the authorities in Tallinn if he returns without a crew member," Peter explained.

They left with profuse thanks, bows, handshakes and a promise to keep in touch.

As the two men walked down Bridge Street, making for home, Peter realized his stomach was empty and his mood bitter.

"He lied to me, Gino. This Karel Cieszynski, calls himself Karl, I help him and he lies. He is the only connection I have to my family. The Red Cross hasn't been able to get news. I must know. I must go back up the glen. Get the truth from him. My God! Why didn't he say something? My parents, how he knows my family, why he is here, he told me nothing." By now he was babbling.

"Tomorrow." Gino held his arm. "First thing in the morning. It's too late now. Nearly dark."

And pausing in the middle of the bridge, the river red-gold from the rays of the dying winter sun, Peter offered up a brief prayer to a God he no longer believed in. The tall somber figure and his short round companion standing alongside him were each wrapped in their own memories, their individual realms of loss.

Don drove them to the bleak council housing estate on the edge of the firth near the ferry crossing to the Black Isle. Joanne had invited herself. She had always wanted to meet the famous Jenny McPhee.

"Mine's a gill of the Glenfarclas, the 105 proof. Thanks for asking." Always one for a decent drop, Ma McPhee wasn't going to let this chance go by.

Joanne sneaked glances at the clan matriarch. She had expected someone older, decrepit. Mrs. Jenny McPhee at fifty was a handsome woman, although her life had been spent wandering from season to season. She had raised seven sons in caravans and benders and byres. She was one of a small group of Travelers who still traveled the roads in a caravan in the summer months and who kept up the traditions and secret tongue of her people.

"Aye, that'll be right," Don said cheerfully. "McKinlay's it is and be thankful."

This bar was for desperation drinkers only. The green-tiled interior, marginally more welcoming than a public toilet, had a malt-brown bar with trough and brass foot rail stretching the length of the room.

"We'll away to the back bar since there's ladies present."

"As long as you're buying, Mr. McLeod."

Jenny gathered her bags, leading the way, and the three of them settled down in the small room, a coal fire and comfy chairs making it seem more like someone's front parlor, the impression spoiled only by the smell of a room seldom used and of spilled drinks from the sticky carpet.

"Ma man." Jenny indicated a photograph of a stocky figure leading a pony with three rosettes prominently pinned on its halter. "Black Isle show, 1936."

More rosettes, their ribbons faded and dusty, sat atop pictures of ponies, proud men holding them on halters. Quite why Joanne identified them as the Travelers of the North she wouldn't have been able to say, but they were clearly of that tribe. Quite why these photos were up on the wall of this saloon bar was another mystery. But Don knew; Mrs. McPhee, née Williamson, matriarch of the clan, singer of renown, keeper of the old ways, kept hushed her talents as a shrewd businesswoman.

"All right then," said Don, "what's this about?"

"Money, what else?"

"I thought it was about grazing and camping rights."

"That land down by the council dump and all along the shore has been used by farmers and drovers and Traveling folk for forever. It's historic those fields, it's the end of the drove roads from the West, where they rested and fed their cattle whilst waiting to sell at auction. That land belongs to the town, not the town clerk. He's got what you call an *interest* in all this. In other words he's making a nice wee commission on the side."

"Aye, I always heard that it's common land." Joanne knew a little about the dispute from her husband. He had his workshop in the burgeoning industrial estate that was taking over the grazing land.

"It should be left for everyone to use, not sold off," Jenny insisted.

Too much money to be made. You need ᵉ than common-law grazing rights to fight the council," Don pointed out. He knew that most of the communities in Scotland had an instinctive dislike of the tinkers but the agricultural cycle of much of the northeast would have been hard-pressed without these seasonal laborers, especially after the losses of the war. Stones needed to be lifted after the spring plowing, ditches cleared, walls mended, the raspberries picked, the tatties harvested. And the womenfolk selling lucky heather, the menders of pots and pans, the river pearl fishers, all had their part in Highland life. Yet they were outcasts.

"You're looking right peely-wally, lass."

Joanne looked up at shrewd currant eyes examining her.

"I fell off my bike."

"How's that man o' yours? I mind him as a laddie wi' holes in his breeks." Not much escaped Jenny.

Joanne couldn't help laughing. Her mother-in-law would have been mortified to hear Jenny speak this way of her precious son. They all knew each other; the families came from the Cromarty part of Ross and Cromarty. They had worked side by side on the farm where Granny Ross had been brought up.

"Bill's out west a lot of the time, Loch

Carron way, building houses for the council."

"Aye. I heard that. And I heard your man has some fine new friends." It sounded like a warning but before Joanne could ask, two red-haired men walked in, one a younger version of the other, both unmistakably Jenny's kin.

"Ma," they said.

"Don." The older one grinned, showing the missing front tooth that gave him the look of the fighter he was.

"Jimmy." Don nodded a greeting back. "Yer mother has been giving me the low-down on the land at the Longman. Maybe I can stir things up a bit. My new boss likes a bit of what he calls 'color' in his stories." He wanted to add, but didn't: And they don't come more colorful than you lot.

"So, maybe you could do a wee something for me."

"Oh, aye?" Jimmy McPhee was averse to doing anything without good reason.

Jenny laughed. "What's the use? The *Gazette*'ll never get the council to budge for some tinkers. Now, if it's thon sailor you're wanting to find . . ." She held up her empty glass.

ne and Don had barely stepped into

the office when Rob jumped up.

"There you are. I've been looking for you. The school called and —"

Rob didn't have a chance to finish the sentence.

"What's happened? Is it about my girls? Are they all right? When did they call?" Fear for their children's safety, a hitherto almost unknown emotion, was now never far from the minds of parents of the town.

"They're both fine."

"For goodness' sake, sit down, lass," Don commanded. "Right, young Robert, what's this?"

"The school rang to say that all the children are being asked if they know or saw anything connecting to the wee boy who drowned in the canal. The children who knew him are being questioned and parents can be there, if they want to that is. Routine, they said. About three o'clock they told me."

"But I already asked my girls," Joanne explained. "Annie assured me they hadn't seen him." Then an awful thought came to her; Annie would swear black was white if she was in trouble.

"I'll give you a lift over there," Don offered. "As for you, young Robert, a wee bird whispered something in my ear about a faerie glen and a hidden Pole. And I expect

83

a suitable reward when you get your big story."

"In my will," Rob promised solemnly.

"In the Market Bar or no more tips for you."

Detective Inspector Tompson terrified children. Dogs hated him too. His immaculate uniform, his dour expression and his dead-cod-cold-on-the-fishmonger's-slab eyes elicited silence, not answers. Woman Police Constable Ann McPherson longed to take over the questioning. Inspector Tompson was having none of it. She was but a woman. He was in charge. But the previous three girls had told them nothing of any use and had left the room in tears. Joanne sat to one side watching the interview in despair. The policeman was intimidating the child.

"Tell me again about that afternoon, Annie. You were walking home from school. You were with your friends, your sister and Jamie."

"I don't remember."

"For heaven's sake! The other girls said you were all together!"

"I forgot. Sometimes Jamie's no at school. He's sick a lot." The policeman's impatience ⸃ught out Annie's stubborn streak. "And ⸃oesn't always walk home with us."

"You were playing a game."

The child focused on the floor. "No."

"You were ringing doorbells and running away."

"No."

"You saw a stranger."

"I never saw nothing."

"You must have seen something. You were with him."

"We went home."

"You're testing my patience." He tried again. "Tell the truth. You've done this before — ringing doorbells and running away."

"No."

"Not what I heard." The inspector's harsh voice was loud in the headmaster's small office.

Joanne was looking down at her hands, clenched in her lap. Frustrated, trying not to intervene, she knew the policeman would get nowhere with her daughter. Heaven knows, I've tried often enough myself and never succeeded, she thought.

"You know what happens to liars, don't you? Your mother and father will punish you. No doubt the headmaster will deal with you too. Six of the best with the belt, that's what you need."

He nodded toward the headmaster, who

85

was sitting in a corner, Inspector Tompson having commandeered his desk, and he too was trying hard not to intervene.

Again silence. Joanne knew that nothing now would make her daughter talk.

"Annie." WPC McPherson spoke softly.

The child would not look up.

"Did you see where Jamie went? See any strangers? Anything unusual?"

Silence.

"Your wee sister said she saw a bogey-man."

"She's only six. She makes things up."

Joanne looked sharply at her eldest daughter. If anyone made things up it was this one.

The inspector suddenly stood. "I've had enough of this nonsense." He marched out in a fury, WPC McPherson shrugging an apology as she followed, leaving behind a vacuum of silence.

"This is a very distressing situation for everyone," Mr. Clark, the headmaster, said with a sigh as he closed the door. "Tell you what, school finishes in fifteen minutes, why don't you collect Jean, leave early, and you could all have a talk on the way home. And if I can be of any help, Mrs. Ross . . ."

Joanne, walking home, holding hands with

a subdued Annie and Jean each side of her, realized that they were retracing Jamie's final journey.

"That's where Uncle Rob lives." Joanne, trying to change the atmosphere, pointed to a bright 1930s bungalow standing in what had once been part of the estate of the big house.

"Uncle Rob lives there?" Jean was surprised. "Is he no frightened of the hoodie crow?"

Joanne stared at her then and cautiously, conversationally, tried to make sense of the child's blethers. "The hoodie crow?"

"Aye, the hoodie crow that stole Jamie."

Joanne stopped. Turned to both children and told them, "You can't make up things like that. This is serious."

Neither child would look at her.

"If you know anything, tell me. I promise, cross my heart, you won't get into trouble if you tell the truth."

"No one ever believes us 'cos we're children."

Annie was scuffing her school shoes on the pavement. Joanne had to stop herself from shouting at her, shaking her. She took a deep breath.

"I'll believe you if you tell me what you know. And we'll not say anything about ringing doorbells. This time."

Annie was about to deny it, admit nothing, but something in her mother's voice stopped her. Hiding the truth was giving her nightmares. Maybe her mother would believe them.

"We just want to know why he didn't go home. It's not your fault, what happened to him. Do you understand?"

They nodded.

Both were in complete agreement, they were adamant, they told their mother, over and over; a hoodie crow had taken Jamie and that was the last they saw of him.

The next morning's meeting was "housekeeping," in McAllister parlance. They worked through the many small tasks, discussed what to run, what to discard, they brought each other up-to-date on their articles and reports and worked steadily through the morning to the heavy rhythm of typewriter keys and the ping of the return bell.

"I know, it's a big place out there in the glens," said the editor, chatting with Rob as they both leaned back, stretching tired arms, between articles, "and I don't need to tell you again, but if you find the Pole, talk to him before he's locked up, there'll be a wee story in it. Whichever way it unfolds it'll be interesting. And Don, that council story — I like it. I have a feeling about it. All these new housing and industrial developments are too much of a temptation for the unscrupulous. So fill it out, a bit more background. And check for legal problems. I don't trust Mr. High and Mighty Grieg or any other councilor not to sue us on this one."

He left them to it. The clatter of typewriters, the regular ringing of the phone, Don up and down the stairs taking copy to the comps, Rob in and out to who knows where. Eleven thirty struck from the church clock. Joanne made tea but there was only Don and herself at the reporters' table.

"Thanks, lass." He wrapped both hands around the mug and nodded to the half-sorted pile of copy paper. "I can see the renowned Scottish education system has failed miserably with the boy. Punctuation is where he pauses for breath."

"That's Rob for you. He knows you'll fix it."

Joanne was having problems of her own. One arm was still tender from the beating, making typing hard; sitting was also uncomfortable, but the main problem was that she had no idea how to even begin the report on the Highland Ball.

"Don, can you help me?"

The clocks across town struck a quarter to twelve.

"You've got one minute, no more."

"I don't know how to put this. I know the *Gazette* usually publishes a list of who attended the ball and not much more." She waved the clippings at him, caught the eyebrows raised in exasperation. "What?"

"It's easy. Who was sitting where. Who didn't attend. And throw in a wee description of the getup the posh damochs were wearing."

Joanne looked puzzled.

"Who was sitting at the provost's table?"

"You know . . . the lord lieutenant, legal folk, a laird or two."

"All as it should be," Don informed her. "How about the town clerk's table?"

"Businesspeople and councilors and the wives. A man from some big concrete company in Aberdeen, a builder, an architect . . ."

"How do you know?"

"Bill and I were at that table."

"Specify the host. List his guests by name and business."

"Why?"

"Those in the know will quickly figure out

who's in favor. Or who's begging for favors. Then there's your revenge. Give back thon fishwives as good as they gave. 'Mrs. Uppity from Lower Auchnamuchty, also known as Mrs. Town Clerk Grieg, was resplendent in pink with a Princess Margaret décolletage and matching tiara.' Everyone knows she's fifty-seven if she's a day and shows off her wrinkly bosom any chance she gets. 'Her husband was seen in close proximity to —' then name some young lassie . . . I'm joking, leave that bit out, even though everyone knows he's gey fond o' a sweet young thing. Then add that the Honorable Mary Mc-Callum was unfortunately unable to attend. That'll get them all going 'cos she, the Honorable, is always a revered guest but she's had a huge bust-up with Mrs. Lady Provost. So, rather than endure a seat at a second-tier table, the Honorable Mary comes down with a mysterious malady."

"Don, you're a genius. I'm going to enjoy this."

The sound of a cyclone rushing up the stairs brought Rob, still in his motorbike gear, flying into the room.

"They've arrested Peter Kowalski."

"Peter? Arrested?" Joanne sat down. "What for, for heaven's sake?"

"You're sure?" Don was equally skeptical.

"Look at this."

Rob waved a smudged paper, obviously the last of at least half a dozen carbon copies.

"Mr. Peter Kowalski has been detained, charged with aiding and abetting an illegal alien. Anyone with information on the matter of a missing Polish seaman, Karel Cie — szy — nski, no idea how to pronounce that, is asked to contact the police on Central 257."

"Poor Chiara, I'll phone her right now."

"No, wait." Don marshaled his team. "Joanne, go over and talk to your friends the Corellis, see what's what. I'll let McAllister know — he's friends with Peter the Pole. Rob, you have a chat with your special friend. WPC Ann, is it? And don't look so glachit. Nothing passes by me."

"Aye-aye, sir."

"Forget the facetious bit, laddie. If Mr. Kowalski is any friend o' yours, you might want to put him in touch with your father. He'll be needing a good solicitor. The town prison is gey cold and grim. Better still, Joanne, you get hold of Chiara Corelli, tell her to call Mr. McLean. I'll tackle the inspector." Don reached for his hat. "Arresting Peter the Pole — the usual overkill from Tompson."

Rob was halfway out the door. "Oh, I nearly forgot. . . . Joanne, my mother wants to talk to you. Something about a bell, or bells. Hell's bells, maybe."

FOUR

Chiara was shivering-white-cold furious, every word she enunciated in rapier-sharp, rapid sentences. "Anything else you forgot to tell me?" Her black eyes bored into him. "To protect me?"

Her father stood silent, head bowed, like a wee boy about to get the strap. The comfortable, well-proportioned sitting room of the Corelli family home, curtains drawn against the chill autumn night and fire ablaze in the large hearth, was often the setting for heated family discussions. Family fights were unknown. Arms windmilling, voices raised, heated discussions about important things such as pasta, the color to paint the chip shop or gelato versus ice cream were the most this family ever argued about.

"*Cara.* Please, we try to do what is for the best." Her tiny aunt stood in the doorway, hands wrestling with invisible knitting, trying to support her brother.

"Oh really? Well, it didn't work. And, Aunty Lita, I can't believe that you too hid this from me." She stared at her. "Peter was hiding a DP, a displaced person, who is on the run from the police. But none of you told me. You thought I should be protected like a little princess. That is such an insult. What next? Oh yes, you forget to tell me my future husband is in prison. Yes, yes" — she held up her hands to ward off the excuses — "I know he's out on bail now. And I have to hear from Joanne that he was arrested. Do you know how that made me feel?" Especially, she thought, since I always lecture *her* about trust in a marriage.

Her father called out when he heard the front door opening.

"*Cara,* where are you going?"

"Out." And the door slammed.

"What's wrong?" Chiara stood shivering on the doorstep like a bedraggled little bird, lost in a storm.

Joanne tried to steer Chiara into the kitchen, but the girls were pulling her by the hand in the opposite direction.

"I've had a big fight with my father about Peter and —"

Joanne shook her head imperceptibly and gestured with her eyes toward Annie, who had immediately latched on to their conversation.

"Later," she mouthed.

"Play with us, Aunty Chiara," Jean pleaded.

"We're about to have mince and tatties, Scottish haute cuisine. Join us."

Chiara smiled at Joanne's feeble joke.

"And Bill's out late so we can have a good blether."

She knew Chiara didn't like Bill. But then he too had made it clear he had no time for "turncoat" Italians. And she had no idea where Bill was tonight. When he was home he was monosyllabic. Joanne put it down to guilt. And more and more, especially when he'd been drinking, he'd spend the night in his workshop. So he said. The business had problems; that much she had been able to twist out of him. But her husband didn't believe in a woman knowing a man's business.

"It's no him. It's the drink." Granny Ross always had an excuse for her son.

"That's the Scottish national anthem," was Joanne's retort.

The girls had had their story and were now in bed. A wind was up, rattling the last of the leaves from the rowans. The two friends sat each side of the fire talking quietly, on their third cup of tea.

"What really gets me is that I thought they — Peter, Papa, Aunty Lita — were all doing secret wedding stuff. They were keeping a secret, all right — a secret missing Polish seaman. My own family, my fiancé, didn't trust me. They did it to protect me, didn't want to worry me, they said."

"That was wrong." Joanne knew the feeling of being shut out.

"Aiding an illegal, something like that, that's what he's charged with. Peter was seen crossing the canal bridge, heading north, with the sailor in his car. The idiot! This could affect Peter's business badly, our business too. I know some in the town still think of Italians as cowards, turncoats, traitors — that's a mild way of putting it. I've heard much worse. We're not responsible for what happened in the war, I was a child! Papa suffered! My mother was killed." Chiara was becoming more agitated. "And so many Italians who were born here, been here for ages, were interned in camps — just for being Italian, for being on the wrong side."

Joanne didn't know what to say. She knew the sentiments of people in wartime. Prejudice had nothing to do with being rational.

"I'm going to tell Peter I can't marry him."

"Chiara! You can't. You love him."

"I love him to bits but if we don't trust each other, there can be no marriage."

There was nothing Joanne could say. It was too raw a subject for her.

The fire had burned down to a deep devil red. From the wireless in the corner, the round plummy voice of the BBC announcer introduced Mahler's second symphony. The opening chords began, the music a salve for raw emotion. Slowly, surely, as the adagio led into the opening movements, Joanne opened up.

"I've never known real trust," she began quietly. "It's not the way Bill sees a marriage. He tells me what he thinks I need to know, no more. He doesn't share, doesn't talk, he provides for his family, that is what men do, but talk? Discuss things? Share his thoughts? I think that only happens in films and books, and even then, you have to be a foreigner. No Scottish man would talk ever about his dreams, tell you he loves you . . ."

"Except Rabbie Burns."

"Aye, Rabbie. Goodness, would you not want to marry him?" They both laughed.

"Even though we had to get married in a registry office," Joanne continued, "the 'love, honor and obey,' especially the 'obey,' is how Bill thinks it should be. As for love, well, he does love me in his own way. Honor, I don't think he's ever wondered what that means."

Chiara sat silent, slightly uncomfortable at the intimacy of the conversation, but knowing Joanne needed to talk to someone.

"You probably guessed, but yes, we 'had to' get married. We barely knew each other. End of the war, a handsome soldier laddie swept me off my feet. I brought complete disgrace to my family. My father literally barred me from his door, very dramatic it was, biblical, well, he *is* a minister, and he has never spoken to me since . . . nor my mother." She shook her head and forced a smile. "I wonder how many war brides have the same story. After all that death, we were avid for life, for a new start. We were intoxicated by our survival when so many . . ." Her throat started to close up. "Another cup of tea, that's what we need." She rose abruptly.

It was the last thing Chiara needed, but she was used to the Scottish custom of endless cups of tea in every situation.

Settled back in her chair, Joanne determined to be more cheerful.

"I saw Margaret McLean today, she told me that Annie has a game of ringing doorbells and running away."

"That's my girl." Chiara smiled.

"I'd be too scared. I was a right goody-goody, a true daughter of the manse."

"Me too. All Italian girls are supposed to be princesses."

"When I was little I thought God was my grandfather. My father called him 'our Father' when he preached his sermons. But my mother used God to threaten me. You know; He was watching, He knew when I hadn't tidied my room, knew what a naughty girl I was, all that kind o' thing. I suppose I was lonely, my sisters being much older than me, but I had books, books were my escape. When I first read *Jane Eyre,* I used to fantasize that my mother was like Mrs. Rochester and that my real mother would one day appear."

"And you wonder where Annie got her imagination from."

"This time it's Wee Jean with the fantasies, some nonsense about the wee soul Jamie, the boy that drowned, being taken away by a hoodie crow."

Chiara stared at her.

"It's a horrible big black bird that eats carrion and waits around at lambing time for the carcasses of dead and sometimes not so dead lambs."

"Euch!" Chiara shuddered. "Children have great imaginations; they need to explain the things that scare them. A crow, that's a new one. But this wee boy drowning, so terrible for the parents, the family."

"Aye. It doesn't bear thinking about."

Angus and Margaret McLean were sitting quietly together over their ritual evening G&T. Rob had wine, a taste he had acquired when on exchange holidays with French family friends. He was desperate to ask questions, knew that his father rarely expressed an opinion and wouldn't speculate nor ever break a client's confidence. Rob and his mother knew none of those restraints.

"My, my," said Margaret. "A fine mess."

"Peter did give assistance to the man, a person the police wanted to interview, the procurator fiscal can't ignore that," her husband gently pointed out.

"Maybe Peter didn't know the police wanted him when he helped the man," Rob offered.

"Ignorance is no excuse in law. And please remember, you're a reporter. You investigate. You report. And you inform the police if need be. It's not your job to play detective."

"Don McLean is always telling me the

same thing. I'd like to find this sailor, though. A great story."

"We all would. For Peter Kowalski's sake." Angus McLean looked thoughtful. "The police will have checked the trains and roads and of course boats. This man can't have vanished. If you believe he is up the glens, why don't you go to Beauly? Ask Dr. Matheson if he has anyone on his list who would notice unusual goings-on in the glens. You know country people; no one can walk across a field without someone seeing them. You never know." An afterthought struck him. "Dr. Matheson knows Mr. Stuart, the head gamekeeper up Cannich way. There's not much escapes his eye. What with his precious pheasants and stags and the salmon, he's always on the lookout for poachers. He would spot a stranger, if that's where this Polish man is."

"Thanks, Dad, I might just do that. It's worth a try anyhow."

"I also seem to remember," Angus went on, "the old ghillie, this one's father, he knew Peter from when they were building the dam. They played together."

"Football?"

"No," laughed his father, "the fiddle. Though in Peter's case it would be the violin. A good player, I'm told. Classically trained. I recall them playing at one or two dances at the Spa Pavilion in Strathpeffer. Peter was far too good of course, but they rattled off a fine jig."

Margaret agreed. "Yes, that was fun, wasn't it, Angus?"

Rob could never imagine his father having fun. Enjoying himself, yes. But fun? Still, it was a good lead and the prospect of being out and about on his bike appealed to him.

"Thanks, Dad, I'll give Dr. Matheson a call right now."

"Give him our regards," Margaret called after him as Rob left to use the phone in the hall. She turned to her husband. "You do know something."

"Only one thing for certain. Peter Kowalski is a good man. Inspector Tompson needs someone to charge, makes him look competent. The police here have the added problem of searching in Ross-shire, in a different jurisdiction. Peter's a foreigner. For some, that means he must have done something. So, this arrest is opportune."

"No one would believe anything bad about him." Margaret was certain.

"Maybe," said Angus, "but I'm afraid I don't have your faith in human nature, and people believe that the police are always right. 'No smoke without fire' sort of thing.

Peter Kowalski could lose a lot more than his reputation if he ends up with a police record."

Rob arranged to meet the young ghillie. Young Archie had inherited his father's job and his love of the glens. Even though retired, old Archie Stuart was "fit as a fiddle," as he told everyone who asked. In late Victorian times the estate was at its peak. As a young boy, he always knew he would follow his father in the service of the clan chief, lord of the vast estate. Vast in square miles. Vast in glens and hillsides. Nearly empty of people. The people, rounded up like cattle, had been driven to the four corners of the earth. Rob had heard there were more Highlanders in Canada than in the Highlands.

Rob drove up the steep winding track to the gamekeeper's cottage at the top of the glen. The scars of the clearances were visible still. Ruined croft houses, remains of dry stone dykes marking lost fields, now reclaimed by ferns and gorse and whin and heather, a brighter shade of green on the hillsides showing where crofters had fertilized and cultivated the land, now they were empty, except for the sheep. Only ghosts and the faeries remained.

In this particular glen, what land had not been claimed by the sheep was now under-water, flooded to bring electricity to the towns and villages of the rich farmland below, to a booming population born to replace the souls lost in two world wars.

Rob reached the only habitation at the very head of the glen, and with the engine switched off, the silence of nature — with the birds, distant water, a low drone of insects and the wind rustling the birch and rowan and setting the pines to sighing — he took it all in in a second and was enchanted.

"Come in, come in." The old man wel-comed Rob heartily, shaking his hand. The grip was excruciating. Rob tried not to wince.

"Pleased to meet you, Mr. Stuart."

"Archie, lad, call me Archie. Mind, now they call me Auld Archie. How's your father? And your mother? I remember her fine from the dancing in the Strath. A fine bonnie lass your mother. Didn't think young Angus had it in him to land such a catch."

"Young Angus?" Rob was bemused. His father young was a strange concept. "It's good of you both to see me." He nodded to the younger replica standing behind the table.

"Aye well. It's been on my mind to talk to

someone. I just never got round to it."

"There's not much to tell anyhow," joined in young Archie. "It's not as if them old crofts have been lived in for near a century. Didn't his lordship sell that one off?"

"Not sell, no. An understanding I heard. And only to Peter," Auld Archie explained.

"Peter? Peter the Pole?" Rob was excited. His trip up here had not been wasted.

"I thought that was why you came, lad."

"Oh aye. To help Peter. But we can't help Peter till we find this other man, the other Pole. Peter's been charged with hiding him, Mr. Stuart."

Father and son looked at each other, shocked.

"Charged, you say? Well, well. That changes things, surely it does."

"My father's his solicitor, and he got Peter out on bail," Rob explained. "But the best way to help Peter is to find this missing sailor and persuade him to turn himself in to the police."

"Da, you might as well tell him." A look went between father and son.

"He's no sailor, lad, that I *can* tell you. He wouldn't know a half hitch from a granny knot."

His son nodded in agreement.

"No, we thought he was Peter's friend.

Peter asked us to keep an eye out for him and take up some supplies. Not that your man was grateful. Oh no, always girning on about summat."

"You say he's gone?"

"Aye, he's gone aright."

Rob was stunned. "So where is he? Do you know?"

"Aye, we do that, young Rob. A cup o' tea?"

"No thanks." Rob recovered quickly. He knew Highland etiquette. You waited. Talked about this and that. The son would follow the father, saying nothing except to agree or back him up. "Well, only if you're having one. That would be fine."

The old man in his widower's kitchen made a fine cup of tea, but no homemade cake appeared, only shop biscuits, and Rob was starving. He tried to sit still as he waited the excruciatingly long time it took the kettle to boil on the wood-burning stove. He tried to stop his fingers tapping invisible typewriter keys, writing up his scoop in his mind. He could see the headline: "Local reporter finds missing Pole." No, ". . . missing sailor." No . . .

"Sugar, lad?"

Early afternoon saw Jenny McPhee, with

Joanne at her side, lead a curious procession down the street and stop in the mud-patch garden of a gray-harled council house that looked as though it had been designed to encourage a quick turnover of tenants via the mental asylum or suicide. If there was grass, it was in single blades. Trees were sticks with a side limb or two poking up through the moonscape. Broken prams, rusting bikes, skeletons of cars and vans and broken dreams, made a playground for the tribes of bairns and dogs that roamed the council house scheme.

Joanne had taken the phone call.

"Don, it's for you."

She couldn't help but hear the conversation.

"No, Jenny, I canny come over. Jenny, I've a newspaper to put out. Aye, uh-huh, no, I haven't the time. No. Really? Hold on a wee minute. . . ." He turned to Joanne, raising his eyebrows in a question.

"Yes, I'll go." She had no idea why or where she would be going, but anything involving Jenny McPhee intrigued her.

"Jenny? Joanne Ross will be over. And remember, you'll owe me."

He scribbled down an address and hung up. When he explained, Joanne was at a loss as to why she should be there.

"A witness, that's what Jenny wants. No one, especially Inspector Tompson, will ever believe a tinker. They want you there as a witness to whatever the blazes is going on."

They stopped outside one of the houses. Jenny quietly gave the orders. "One of you, round the back. Jimmy, Geordie, wi' me."

Firmly clutching her disreputable bag under one arm, she banged on the door. No answer.

"Keith, Keith." Adding quite unnecessarily, "It's your ma."

"Keith?"

"Ma eldest." Joanne was astonished. How many more McPhees were there?

"Not a drop o' common sense that one — for all his fancy education. And living in sin, he is. What's the world coming to? We're Travelers and proud of it. No sin in our family." She smirked. "Weel, a few close calls maybe."

She continued banging on the door.

"I'm comin'. Hold yer horses." A voice echoed down the hallway.

The door was opened by Keith McPhee. That he was a McPhee there could be no doubt. He had the ginger hair and as many freckles as stars in the sky.

"Ma, Jimmy, I've told you. It's no good.

I'm not going to change my mind."

"Where's your manners, boy? Are you no going to ask us in?"

Keith stared at Joanne, glanced at the woman hovering at the end of the hall. "It'll have to be the kitchen. We have a friend staying. He's . . . he's sleeping."

Joanne and Jimmy followed Jenny, and the three of them sat round a small table in a small kitchen with Keith standing by the sink, Geordie waiting in the hall. The unknown woman stood by the door, ignored. Joanne was curious; no doubt this was the scarlet woman. Older, late thirties maybe, well dressed, a country air about her, she would not have been out of place presiding over a Women's Institute meeting. And the kitchen was tidy and nicely decorated with lace tablecloth and lace curtains and a busy lizzie in a pot on the windowsill growing up and over, framing the view toward the firth. Joanne wondered all over again what on earth was going on.

No introductions were made, so Joanne smiled at the stranger. "Joanne Ross, pleased to meet you."

"Shona Stuart. Pleased to meet you too." The woman blushed.

"It's no you we've come about, lass. It's your visitor." Jenny started. Half a second later there was a commotion in the hall. Jimmy McPhee ran out, sending the chair flying. He returned dragging a tall stranger, held on one side by Jimmy and on the other by Jimmy's clone, Geordie.

"You've picked the wrong McPhee to run into, Mr. Missing Polish Seaman," chortled Jenny. "Ma Jimmy may be half a foot shorter than you but he wis the army bantamweight boxing champion." As most Scottish fighters were bantamweights, it was quite a claim to fame.

Everyone was still for a moment. In the crowded kitchen, with no one sure of the next move, Joanne took charge.

"Shona. Why don't you and me make a cup of tea and then we can all sit down and sort this out."

"Aye, lass, a nice cup o' tea would be welcome." Jenny McPhee reached into the voluminous bag, then handed Shona her contribution, a half bottle of whisky.

"Add a wee drop to mine, would you?"

Shona Stuart was so astonished at Jenny's even speaking to her that she forgot the invasion of her house. And everything else besides.

"She's not such a bad soul, ye know," said Jenny in a loud whisper to Joanne. "It's that boy of mine that's led her astray." This of a man nearing forty.

Another knock at the door.

"That'll be Allie, ma second-youngest," Jenny explained. "He was out the back in case thon one" — she nodded toward the stranger still held in Jimmie McPhee's embrace — "made a run for it."

Keith went to open the door to his brother. Rob was there too. So was a wind-blown and bowlegged Auld Archie Stuart. Rob had given him a lift on the back of the Triumph all the way from Glen Affric.

"Dad!" cried Shona in astonishment.

"Lass," he replied.

"Archie," said Jenny.

"Jenny," came the reply.

"Will somebody please tell me what's going on?" pleaded a completely confused Joanne.

"So?" Don demanded when they were back in the office.

"Well, I went up the glen to meet Archie Stuart and brought him back on my bike," Rob began. "It was terrifying. He's a hopeless passenger, leaning the wrong way into bends and everything —"

"And I went to the council house, like you told me," Joanne chimed in, "with Jenny and Jimmy and Keith and two, or was it three more McPhees, and this Polish sailor was there, oh, and Shona Stuart, and Rob turned up with —"

"Haud on, haud on." Don held up his wee stubby pencil for silence, then hauled his short stubby body onto a stool by the big table, rearranged the piles of paper in front of him, reached for his spiral shorthand notebook. "Right. Ladies first."

"Righty-oh." Joanne took a deep breath, organizing her thoughts. "We" — Don waved his pencil in the air — "sorry, Jenny and I, sorry . . . Jenny McPhee, myself, I think three McPhee men, including Jimmy, went to the house down the ferry, where we met Keith McPhee, who is living there with Shona Stuart —"

"Archie Stuart the ghillie's daughter?" Don looked up from his squiggles.

"And Archie Stuart the ghillie's sister," Rob added.

"Wheesht, wait your turn," Don warned him.

Joanne stopped, confused. Rob jumped in.

"This Polish man, Karel Cieszynski, had a fight with the captain, who is Russian, of the Baltic timber ship, and who had the Pole onboard illegally, for money, and the Polish man — Karl, as he wants to be called —

jumped or was pushed overboard into the river, if you believe his story, that is. It was an ebbing tide and he was picked up by some tinkers who were fishing" — Don snorted — "or poaching for salmon," Rob acknowledged with a grin. "And they, the tinkers, took him to their camp down by the council dump and let Peter Kowalski know about him because he was Polish and" — Rob picked up the look on Don's face — "and because there might be a reward in it for them. And because this Polish person knew Peter Kowalski's name."

"Curious, that," Don commented.

"So Peter took the man up to his fishing camp, an old but and ben up Glen Affric, because the man didn't want to go to the police until he had a chance to return to the ship to collect his belongings. So he said. Then the man Karl got young Archie to take him back to town so he could confront the captain and get his belongings and young Archie took him to the only person he knows in town, his sister — who is the fiancée of said Keith McPhee, son of —"

"Aye, I know all that." Don stopped him and continued squiggling furiously.

"So where does Jenny McPhee come into all this?" Joanne queried.

"There has to be something in it for her." Don looked up. "No, I take that back. It's most likely because Peter Kowalski got charged. That put the wind up them. See, Jenny McPhee, all tinkers, know that if Inspector Tompson and his ilk had their way, tinkers would be charged with any and every crime ever committed. So it's in their best interests that this man hands himself in and the less said about their role the better."

"But they rescued him and, at the time, had no idea he was wanted by the police," Joanne protested.

"What's that to do with the price of fish?" Don shut his book, slithered down from the high stool, stuck his pencil back behind his ear and reached for his hat. "Right, Rob, you finish up this story. We'll see how much we can print. Joanne, it's getting late, off home to those bairns of yours." He caught her grateful look. "They'll be fine, you know; children have to learn one day that they too can die. It's all part of life." He patted his pocket to check that he had his cigarettes. "If anyone wants me, I've gone to see a man about a horse."

"In the Market Bar," Joanne and Rob chorused.

■ ■ ■ ■

The afternoon had been a long one for Angus McLean. Not only had he had to deal with a recalcitrant police inspector who was ignorant of the law as far as illegal aliens were concerned and was determined to charge Karl with something, anything, but Angus also had to sort out the legal status of both the Polish men, an area of the law he was not familiar with. Contested wills and property disputes had been the highlights of his career for the last ten years.

Inspector Tompson had gained his position in the police force as a direct result of his time as a military policeman, not from merit. A man with no imagination, no empathy, he had no understanding of the decisions some men make when death and despair are all around. He saw them simply as foreigners.

Angus McLean, solicitor, husband, father and well-liked citizen of the community, was a kind man. His mildness belied a tenacity that had often surprised clients and judges, but never his wife. While a student in Edinburgh, he had glimpsed the underbelly of Scotland's so-called egalitarian society; in the tenements off the High Street, the Cowgate, off the Royal Mile, in the drinking and gambling dens, on street corners where women huddled in doorways and on church steps, waiting for customers, Angus had witnessed another world.

"All things bright and beautiful, all creatures great and small . . . The rich man in his castle, the poor man at his gate." That was the Edinburgh of his youth.

A subdued group gathered around his desk — Gino, standing bail for his prospective son-in-law, Peter Kowalski, and Karel Cieszynski.

"Well now." Angus started the proceedings. "The procurator fiscal's office says the charge against Karl — may I call you Karl?" He took the nod as a sign to continue. "It is all quite simple — illegal entry. There's a good chance an application for asylum will be looked at favorably; we will gather some sponsor and prepare the case. I'm hoping the charge against Mr. Kowalski — Peter — will be dropped. Now, I understand you are staying with Keith McPhee."

"He has offered me a room." The voice came out tobacco stained and weary, the accent thick but understandable.

"Yes, well, we may have to review that situation," Angus McLean hurried on, "and I think perhaps, now that we are all together,

117

you should explain to us exactly how you come to be here."

Karl hesitated. "My English is not so good."

"Good enough." Gino wanted an explanation now.

"Karl," Angus interrupted, "you will have to tell me — us — what happened if we are to support your application for residency in Scotland."

"I am ashamed I have made trouble for Mr. Kowalski."

Peter said nothing. He was so angry he felt he would explode and a seething silence was his way of keeping his temper in check.

Karl took a deep breath, sat up, backbone straight, a vagabond transformed into the long-lost Polish gentleman. He accepted a cigarette. Gino was smoking, Peter had a Balkan Sobranie alight and Angus was coping, just, with the fug-filled room.

"It happened so fast," Karl started. "Poland betrayed, invaded. We were rounded up like ducks and told we had new owners. That is our history. I was an engineer in my father's mine so they needed me, but the Nazis turned the mines into death camps. To them we were human refuse, from Poland, then Czechoslovakia, the Netherlands,

Norway, everywhere. I survived, but not my father."

What he couldn't tell them about were the deaths by the day, the hour, of men and women, boys who had never left their mothers, dying as they slaved at the coal face, bodies pushed into unused shafts, someone else stepping up to take their place.

"But how did you get here?" Gino was impatient. Everyone had their stories.

"Sorry if I do not tell it right. I must explain from the beginning. So." He continued. "The Russians liberated the mines, ha! I and a few other survivors now were sent to the Urals, to the coal mines there. Punishment for working for the Nazis."

"My God." Angus could not comprehend the horrors Karl had endured.

"I was lucky, you could say." Karl gave a short barking laugh. "I was given a supervisor's job. They needed mine engineers. I had privileges. Later I married a fellow prisoner, a Ukrainian. She also survived a labor camp only to be rounded up by the Russians. But her health was not good. We had some small freedom in that camp, a small life, but a life. We found love. Now she is dead."

He stopped. He couldn't tell them of the swing he had made her, the swing that had brought back her smile, the smile she had lost when she was dragged from her home by the Russians, the smile she found again as she swung herself up to touch the red apples with her toes.

Angus rose. "A drink, Karl? Anyone?"

"I want to finish. I can never say this again."

"A dram first." Angus kept a Tomatin Distillery malt. "I certainly could do with one." The gentle Highland voice sent out an air of calm.

Karl took a swift slug of the water of life, then plowed on.

"I buried her in the orchard under an apple tree. I left her where she was happy."

Gino envied Karl that. *He* had not been able to bury his wife; he had been a prisoner in North Africa before being sent to the camp in Scotland.

"One Russian helped me after my wife died," the story continued. "The war was over, we were free — ha! Free! It took three years of my pitiful salary to bribe my way back to a mine job in Poland.

"I didn't want any of the Russians to know my background. I am from the bourgeoisie. I am just a miner, I told them. When I arrived back in Silesia, it is very hard, but in the country people eat better. In winter they hunt wild birds, that is if you know your way through the minefields. In summer the forests are full of people searching for fruit, nuts, mushrooms. It is like the Middle Ages.

"Then I get permission to visit my family village. I find that my mother is dead also. Then I meet my mother's friend Madame Kowalski, Peter's mother."

Peter leapt from his chair, his long strong arms grabbing Karl by the lapels, shaking him, shouting, swearing at him in Polish, yelling, "She's alive? What do you know? Why didn't you tell me?" followed by un-repeatable curses and finally tears.

Angus's secretary came bursting in to see what the commotion was. Gino reached up, patting his future son-in-law on the back, trying to soothe him as one would soothe a heartbroken child; Karl slunk lower in his chair, doing nothing to ward off the attack.

Angus waved his secretary out with "It's fine, it's fine" and when the commotion had subsided, he topped up the glasses with a healthy dram of whisky.

"I must tell you," Karl said simply. "I must go on." He took a gulp of the spirits and took up the story again. "My mother's family is Jarosz, they have been trusted servants on the Kowalski estates for centuries."

Slowly, recognition dawned on Peter. He

nodded.

"Madame Kowalski knows Peter went to Scotland. She had news from a priest who works with the Red Cross. She learned of the town where you are. She wants me to escape, to find her son, and she says to me to have a new life. She gave me gold. This is how I am here."

Tiring visibly, he looked down at the floor.

"First, I had to find a ship. Gdansk, anywhere in Poland, is too dangerous, many guards, traitors reporting anyone looking for escape. So I take many months, through the marshes and forests, to make it to Tallinn, then weeks to find a captain who would take me. I give him all the money I have left.

"When we arrive here I want to go to the police. But the son of a Russian bear, he said no. He knows there will be big trouble for losing a crewman when he gets back home. He asks for more money, but I have none. He asks me what I hide in my coat, I don't tell him. He hits me, I hit him, but he is big, big man and he throws me into the river. I nearly die. But the fishermen catch me and take me to their Gypsy camp. That is my story."

The rough kindness of strangers who had helped him out on many, many parts of his journey was a story for another, later time. And the final cruelty, the irony that broke his carefully constructed carapace of courage, what he was unable to tell his listeners just yet, was that he had failed in his mission. On the cusp of freedom, the precious, carefully guarded package, carried on the long march across the occupied Baltic states, across the North Sea, the package entrusted to him by Peter's mother, carefully hidden deep in the pockets of his greatcoat, was lost, stolen by the scoundrel of a sea captain.

It was Gino who broke the long silence.

"We have the necklace."

"The necklace?" Karl stared in shock. "Madame Kowalski's necklace?"

Angus McLean looked completely lost.

"Why did you not tell Peter about his mother and the necklace?" Gino continued, "I do not believe you tell us *all* your story."

The reply was a short sharp bark of a laugh, perhaps a cough.

"How to explain my idiocy, my cowardice, my failure . . ." He stopped, momentarily lost in thought, then stood, drew himself up and, in a quaintly old-fashioned gesture, bowed from the waist.

"Mr. Corelli, I promise you, as a Polish compatriot and a gentleman, I did not steal

Madame Kowalski's necklace. Please believe me it is my deep regret I lost it. I came back to the town to get it from that lying Russian thief. But then I am told that the ship has sailed."

Gino did believe him. He knew the times threw up strange tales. He knew you could never judge a man for what he did in the darkness of war. His innate kindness overtook his doubt. "Hold up, my friend. We will explain all later. First we must feed you." Gino smiled up at Karl. "My sister and daughter are waiting."

FIVE

The next day there was a distinct late-autumn briskness to the air. The hurry-hurry-it-will-soon-be-winter wind, intent on clearing the last of the leaves, sent them scurrying along the riverbank. They tumbled this way and that, tiny disembodied hands attempting to escape the cruel blast. The wide shallow river, sprinting the short journey from loch to sea, had an icy hue, reflecting the pale blue of the high sky. The snow line on the distant mountains crept lower with each passing day.

Rob, Joanne, Don and McAllister came into the office over the space of two minutes. Discarding coats, scarves, hats, mittens and, in Rob's case, extravagant motorbike gear, they gathered round the table.

"Right, a quick review of what we've got for tomorrow's paper. Firstly, Rob" — McAllister poked the pages of the article before him — "I like this, necessarily brief for the moment, but nicely put. I know all the shenanigans with the Polish man and the tinkers can't be written up, and I can't say as I blame them for wanting to keep out of it, but still, this is good. So, fill me in on the status quo of the lost-but-now-found Polish gentleman."

"Peter Kowalski is out; the other man, Karl, or Karel I-can't-pronounce-it, was in, all hokey-cokey like, one Pole in, one Pole out, but now he's out on bail too," Rob informed McAllister. "But my dad, sorry, Mr. McLean the solicitor, believes it will all be fine. He's now working on sorting out the legalities of the Polish not-sailor's status."

"I still don't get why the tinkers will say nothing," Joanne started.

"Don't want trouble," Rob told her.

"But they're the ones who rescued him from the river and can back up his story of his being beaten up."

"They helped a wanted man. End of story as far as Inspector Tompson is concerned."

McAllister felt sorry for Rob. "When it's all sorted you can write this, make it a big story, human interest stuff."

"Aye . . . when!"

"Patience, laddie, you're only a cub reporter. You'll get there one day. Joanne next.

I love the bit you did on the Highland Ball."

"Don helped a lot." She was pink with pleasure.

"Right, next. Anyone got anything more on the wee boy in the canal?" The editor raised the one subject they had all unconsciously been avoiding.

"I've got my spies," Don said, "but nothing so far."

"I've nothing either," said Rob. "My contact, she said not much is happening. The fatal-accident inquiry convenes again tomorrow. Of course it would be a day after deadline."

"We'll make a newspaperman out of you yet. Right, anything else?"

"I like your piece about the boy." Don looked uncomfortable even slightly admitting he may have got it wrong. "You're right, boss, telling a wee bit about him coming from the Islands to start a new life, his school and his train set, well, it made it all the more real, his death. And leaving out the parents, that was smart." He noticed Joanne's puzzled look. "In case they did him in or something."

"Don!"

"Wouldn't be the first time, lass."

"Thanks, Don." McAllister perused the layout spread across the table. "It's not big changes I want, or at least not yet, just a wee bit of the color of life. And yes, death." He ticked off the pages and passed them over to Don. "Right." He stood. "Let's get to it, we've a paper to put to bed."

The sound and smell of a newspaper were quite different on press day. The clatter of the presses, although in a sub-sub-basement, made its way up the three flights of spiral stone staircase. The newsroom smelt of ink on paper, acid on metal, and the many cigarettes needed to produce a newspaper. The office staff had left and the printers were engaged, deep in the dungeons of the building, in their dark secret art of picking up the type, setting it with meticulous precision and very small tweezers, with, courtesy of union rules, only Don McLean allowed to stand in the hallowed area of the stone to check the proof pages as they were printed up. Toward midnight the presses would roll and another *Highland Gazette,* the most recent in ninety-odd years of the *Highland Gazette* would be printed.

But at eight o'clock on this Wednesday night, it was well dark, October black starlight dark. The lights from the eyrie in the heart of the town were a lone beacon; everything except the pubs and the chip shop had closed long since.

Don was working steadily checking pages. The old newspaperman's trick of reading the typeset pages upside down and back to front never ceased to amaze Joanne. Thinking to stir up mischief, Don had thrown out a tidbit of gossip on an outgoing ring of smoke, as he and McAllister finished up their night's work, leaving the printers to get on with their job. "By the way, a friend of yours said to say he was asking for you."

"A friend?"

"Mr. Grieg."

"The town clerk? He's no friend — barely an acquaintance."

"Not what he says," Don informed him. "Bosom pals you are. So he tells everyone and —"

Before Don could continue, McAllister stopped him.

"Hold on." Eight o'clock had just finished striking on the church clock. "My stomach thinks ma throat's been cut. What do you say to a fish supper and a dram back at my place?"

"Make that fish, black pudding, a double portion of chips, two pickled onions and a pickled egg." He counted the order off on his fingers. "All them pickles go well with ma pickled liver."

On the climb up the brae to McAllister's house, like big boys without their mother to stop them, they tore open the newspaper and tore into the finger-burning fish and chips. The biting North Sea wind made them glad of the hot package keeping at least the hands warm. Once home and with a beer each, they settled down, feet on the fender by the kitchen fire, content.

"He's a fly one, thon Grieg, no doubt about it," Don started. McAllister waited expectantly. "Look, John, there's a story there. I can smell it. But pinning it down? The man seems to be everywhere when it comes to getting hold of land. At the right price naturally. The land where the tinkers camp every winter — which is now to be industrial land — that place has always been traditional common land where the drovers from the west left their beasts before the auctions. Now the town council is taking it over. Fair enough, times change, there's few drovers left and it is some of the only flat land left in town. But a wee bird, well, two young blokes from the planning office, told me they were uneasy at some of the deals being done. They'll talk. Off the record, naturally."

"Naturally." McAllister thought about it. "You have a good nose. If you say there's a story there, well and good. Goodness knows there are enough people in local government everywhere with their fingers in the pie. There's a lot of money in this postwar building boom and it's not only the cities that have avaricious local governments." He gazed into the fire, giving it some thought.

"From what I know, I think this is only one man with ideas above his station. Fancies himself as a laird, I hear. He's started by building a great big house, an abomination of a baronial-style mansion, on rezoned land west of town."

"The *Gazette* can't have a go at the town council, nor its officials, without a cast-iron case."

"Jenny McPhee, as well as the lads from Planning, know a thing or two."

"Does she now? And what else?"

He waited, watched, as Don started winding himself up — to tell or not to tell.

"I've come across Bill Ross's name from time to time — in connection with his building contract out west. His was also one of the building firms on Grieg's new mansion, then he gets a contract way out of his territory, across in the west. And although that should be a county council decision, not the town council's, there is talk that Grieg put in a word — at the very least."

"Joanne's husband seems quite a character." McAllister sighed. "Right, tell me
again, in detail. No, wait. Let's settle in."

McAllister went out, came back with a
coal scuttle, banked up the fire, then fetched
two more bottles of beer from the scullery,
poured them. He offered Don a cigarette,
lit up, then proclaimed, "I'm all ears."

The next morning, with the new newspaper
fresh and crisp in front of them, Joanne,
Rob, Don and McAllister sat reviewing that
day's edition. Friday was traditionally a
quiet, tidying-up sort of day and Joanne was
officially not supposed to be at work but
she loved the Friday-morning peruse-the-
paper get-together.

McAllister finished reading, shook his
copy of the *Gazette* back into shape. "Everybody, well done. We're a long way off the
newspaper I know we can be, but we're getting there. Thanks." He rose.

"You'll fill the lass in on the other stuff?"
Don wanted out of that particular task.

"Oh. Aye. Joanne, in my office in five
minutes."

He and Don left. Rob shrugged a "no
idea" and he too left.

Joanne hated that. Why did she have to
wait five minutes, why not tell her im-

mediately? It was like being at school waiting for the interview with the headmistress, knowing you were in for it. Mystified, she sighed, suspicious it would not be good news, fearing it would be one more burden she didn't need.

McAllister had a propensity to sit back and view events with an amused detachment; nothing to do with him, he wasn't a character in the events, just the instigator. In other words, as someone had once said, he was a born editor.

The goings-on with Joanne — her lapses into unhappiness, the way her husband so obviously saw her as a possession, the bruises she tried to but couldn't always hide — he tried not to judge. It appalled him but he had to admit it was not uncommon. A man had a right to do what he did within his family.

And somewhere below the surface of this and other small towns and villages everywhere, he knew there were other visceral tides — dislike of change, anything new, anything, anyone different. Those with a university education, those who were deemed to live above their station, those who spoke or dressed differently, those who didn't go to church, didn't look after their gardens, women who wore trousers or makeup, who hung out the washing on a Sunday, all were victims of the susurration of gossip that permeated the town.

The distrust, even dislike, of outsiders, the Italians, the Poles, the English, all that was spoken of openly. No one saw anything wrong in calling foreigners by belittling slang names. God help anyone with a Germanic-sounding name, even if their family had been in Scotland since the Hanseatic treaties. All this, McAllister knew, would reflect on whether the charge against Peter Kowalski would be dropped and whether the other Polish man, newly escaped from the Russian occupiers, would get a fair hearing.

The interview with the drowned boy's parents also cast a shadow on McAllister's soul. It brought to the surface the bright pain of another boy, another drowning. He shook himself, hearing his mother's voice telling him, often, that too much thinking never did anyone any good. As he aged, he was inclined to agree.

But the previous night's conversation with Don was sharp in his mind.

Right, he thought, Joanne, he had to talk to her. It was only fair to warn her of the gossip. He walked into the reporters' room.

"Joanne?"

The telephone in her hand, she held up a finger in a "one minute" gesture.

"Yes, who? Mr. McLeod? Hold on." She had detected Don's laborious shuffle coming up the stairs. "Who shall I say is calling? Righty-oh." She held out the receiver. "Don, a Mr. Burke for you."

McAllister was decidedly uncomfortable telling Joanne of the rumors about her husband. Bill's name has been mentioned in the gossip about dodgy dealings with the town council, he informed her. She was not at all pleased.

"Typical," she fumed. "All the goings-on over council contracts being awarded to favorites, relatives, those that went to the right school, those with families of influence, 'You scratch my back, I'll scratch yours' kind of thing, and there's Bill, with none of the right connections, trying to make a go of it, fairly and honestly . . ."

She had no idea if this was really so. She just presumed it must be so because that is what Bill had told her.

"Then, when they, those jumped-up, too-big-for-their-boots, favor-for-a-favor, doing-deals-on-the-side councilors think that maybe they've been found out, who gets the blame? My husband and hardworking people like him."

Joanne had to stop to breathe.

"Honestly I could — I don't know — I could wring their necks."

She made a fierce twisting gesture, demonstrating the time-honored way of dispatching a feathered fowl. Certainly not squeamish, was Joanne Ross.

"Finished?" McAllister inquired with a slight smile. He, like many a chicken before him, had been quite intimidated by the gesture.

"It makes me so mad."

"I know. Can't say as I blame you. Don and I thought you should know the rumors and —"

"McAllister." Don walked in. A grim-faced Rob followed close behind, as yet unseen by Joanne.

"What's the matter?" She quipped, "Your friend Mr. Burke, or was it Mr. Hare, from the mortuary got a wee tip for you?" One look at his face and Joanne felt her heart leap. "I shouldn't have said that."

"It's about the boy." He looked straight at McAllister as though this was somehow *his* fault, as though the new editor's wishes for something, anything, newsworthy to happen had brought this upon them.

"He was dead before he went into the

water. It was no accident."

There was nothing Joanne or Rob or McAllister or Don McLean could say. The news stunned them.

That night, the girls in bed, Joanne sat at the fire with her knitting and a play on the Home Service to distract her. Bill came quietly into the room.

"I didn't hear you." She put her knitting away. "Tea's finished. I didn't know if you'd be home."

All this said quietly, casually, trying to gauge his mood. At least he hadn't been drinking — that she could tell.

"It's all right, I had some fish and chips in Eastgate. I was out that way to pick up supplies. I'm off out west soon."

"Again?"

"Aye. A few problems on the site. Nothing that can't be sorted out."

"Did you hear the news about the wee boy? The one that drowned in the canal?"

"Aye, they were all talking about it in the chip shop."

"The news was probably around the town in five minutes," Joanne guessed. "It's so terrible. How could that happen in a safe place like this?"

"It's not the same since the war," Bill

reminded her. "Too many strangers have moved here."

Joanne was uncomfortable. They had had this conversation before. He disapproved of her friendship with the Corelli family. The air was full of static, their conversation fading in and out. Nothing of importance would ever be said, nothing that mattered ever be talked about. Her thoughts were as tangled as leftover wool in a knitting basket, and she rehashed all the well-worn thoughts that plagued her with increasing frequency: What kind of a marriage is this, we never communicate, we have children, we share a house but not much else. And the thoughts brought her back to the persistent nagging voice, the wee devil over her left shoulder, saying, there must be more to a marriage, to a life, surely there must.

But she could not give up; for better or worse, in sickness and in health, she'd made her vows. She'd love, she'd honor, yes; it was the "obey" she had problems with. Within the first year of making those promises she had discovered she'd married a stranger, a damaged man, a Scottish man.

"You have disgraced our family — don't ever expect any help from us," her mother had told her. So much for Christian charity, Joanne thought, and ten years on, her parents had not relented. No, there was no way out of a marriage, no place to go except to further disgrace. She couldn't do that to the children.

Laying aside her knitting and her frustrations, Joanne asked, "A cup of tea?"

"Great."

She brought the tea. The ten o'clock news came on.

"Switch that off." Bill was sharp. "All this Suez nonsense, talk about bringing back conscription, I don't need reminding. Another thing, they're saying some maniac killed the wee boy. You stay at home with the girls till he's caught. You're only a typist. The *Gazette* can easily get someone else to fill in."

"You're right." That surprised him. "I'll ask Don McLeod if I can rearrange my hours and work only when the girls are at school. I'll walk with them in the morning and meet them in the afternoon."

There was not much he could say to that.

Careful, scared, but encouraged by his silence and by the fact that he was there, at home for once, sitting by the fire with her, Joanne decided that it was now or never.

"That Don McLeod in our office" — she tried a laugh — "a big gossip he is and no mistake." She also knew better than to use

McAllister's name. Bill had vented some bitter remarks about the new editor-in-chief. "Them strangers from down south think themselves the bee's knees," Bill had remarked. Often. It was one of his mother's favorite expressions too. He folded the paper to the sports pages, only half listening; he was not in the least interested in her work.

"Aye, he's heard that Mr. Grieg the town clerk is up to some shenanigans with council contracts."

Immediately alert, Bill tried not to look up from his page. "What did he say?"

"Not much. Just that Mr. Grieg had better watch his step, that he was being talked about more than usual, and Don McLeod said he was onto Grieg's tricks, and if Grieg doesn't take care, he'll get found out this time, for sure."

"That'll be the day."

Joanne was pleased; she'd successfully tiptoed around the subject, given Bill the hint without him blowing up. To her amazement, Bill started to explain some of his business dealings.

"Thon Mr. Grieg, you're right, he does throw his weight around. He makes it hard for small contractors to make an honest living. But it's always the way when you take council contracts, they cut you to the bone, and that's what they did to me with this job I have on over in the west." He folded the paper. "But it'll all work out, you'll see." He was sure of himself, something she had always admired. "Come over there with me, next time I go. The weather's usually terrible but it would be a wee break."

Her eternal optimism drowned out the past few weeks, few years, of unhappiness. We'll give it another go, she thought, another chance, it'll be different this time. She had said this so many times before, it was getting harder and harder to persuade herself, but what choice was there? She was married — till death do us part.

"Aye, I'd like a break. I'd like to get away from all this sadness."

This Sunday morning in churches and chapels and gatherings throughout the town was a time for fear and a time for reflection. This Sunday's sermons were all on a common theme, the death of a child in their midst. This Sunday Joanne, along with many another parent, had faced the enormity of what had happened in their quiet community. But with other parents, Joanne had also felt a twinge of guilt as she counted her blessings, saying a quick prayer of thanks to God, who had spared her children.

"Suffer the little children to come unto me . . . for of such is the kingdom of heaven." Duncan Macdonald quoted the scripture at his powerful, commanding yet comforting best. The prayers were for the dead, yes, but mostly for the living, those frightened, bewildered, at the very idea that something so terrible could happen. The minister, reminding them that faith and love would see them through, finished the service by leading the congregation in the singing of that ancient song of comfort, the Twenty-third Psalm. "The Lord's my Shepherd, I'll not want . . . ," welled up to the ceiling, sung with spirit and the occasional tear, then a subdued congregation walked home, tightly holding on to the hands of their children, home to the Sunday lunch.

Sunday lunch with the Macdonalds was always cheerful. Joanne loved visiting her sister and her daughters loved playing with their cousins. Taken around the ten-seater table in the most agreeable room in the house, the kitchen, where big sash windows looked onto the garden, lawn, fruit trees and vegetable patch, lunch was a family ritual. The children had been asked to gather the leaves off the lawn into a pile, but instead, they were playing, chasing and throwing handfuls and armfuls of the crisp autumn leaves. Thrown high into the cerulean blue, they fell from the heavens in gold and red showers onto dancing, cartwheeling children. Orange and gold and bronze leaves and leaf skeletons and earth-smelling dust clung to their jumpers and hair, making the dancing figures look like little leaf creatures from an illustration in a child's book of Faeries.

Granny and Grandad Ross very occasionally joined in these family gatherings and somehow it seemed right that they were here, that the whole family was together today. Except Bill Ross. It would have been most unusual if he had been at the table. At the sight of the children enjoying themselves, forgetting the solemnity of the day, Granny Ross couldn't help herself. She rapped on the window. "Stop that. This minute. You're in your Sunday best."

The children took no notice, pretending they couldn't hear her.

Elizabeth Macdonald set the pots with the homegrown vegetables on the Aga top, occasionally opening the slow oven to baste the lamb. They were awaiting the arrival of Duncan from his greeting and hand-shaking duties outside the church. Duties that could take a good half hour or so, as there was always someone who wanted "a wee word." Joanne set the table, chatting with her sister, usually about her new job and the people she met. Joanne loved these conversations. Her sister, and her sister's family, were the only relatives she had left.

Although Granny Ross disapproved of Joanne, her sister Elizabeth and her brother-in-law Duncan, him being a minister of the church had ameliorated her initial opinion of her daughter-in-law. "Not good enough for my son" was code for "brazen hussy." Now it was "Too big for her boots" and that other expression, common throughout the land, used to describe any woman who thought for herself, who did not conform, who tried to better herself: "Who does she think she is?"

Mrs. Ross senior expressed these opinions to no one but Grandad Ross, and he filtered his wife's monologues as he filtered the background chatter from the wireless, only tuning in when his sixth sense told him that an "oh really?" or an "uh-huh" or a "grand" was needed.

Granny Ross could stand it no more. She turned to Elizabeth.

"The bairns are filthy. Look at them."

"They're having a lovely time, aren't they?" Elizabeth beamed. "Grandad, could you ask them to come in and have a good wash before lunch? Granny, could you look at the lamb for me? I think it's about right."

She knew full well Granny Ross would sniff at the lamb, "Underdone," she'd mutter, but that was how the minister liked it. The vegetables were almost raw, the tatties still had their skins on and Duncan insisted on draining the curly kale water into a mug, adding a good pinch of pepper and drinking it. Then he, a minister of the kirk, would serve himself and her husband, George, a glass of stout. He even offered some to the womenfolk.

Duncan's Ford Prefect crunched up the gravel driveway. The ordered ritual of the Sunday lunch began.

Church first, Sunday school for the children, family lunch, then the Sunday Afternoon Walk, that was the time-honored ritual for most families. Unless they were Wee Frees. To Granny Ross's eternal shame, her son refused to join them, hating church. Usually it was back to the house for dinner (she would have nothing to do with calling it lunch), where Granny Ross cooked; Grandad Ross read the *Sunday Post;* the children read the comic section of the paper starring Oor Wullie and the Broons;

Grandad would check the football pools, listen to *Two-Way Family Favorites* on the Home Service and snooze in his chair.

Then, early afternoon, come rain or shine or snow — maybe a blizzard would stop them, but nothing else — they would set off, dressed in their Sunday best, hats and all, on the Sunday Walk. The girls knew that sulking or complaining would get them nowhere, "fresh air makes children big and strong."

The Rosses' route never varied. So, once out the garden gate, across the road, along past the rows of neat, tidy, identical bungalows, Granny Ross would start her monologue on the state of the neighbors' gardens. The children had to be restrained from skipping too high or chatting too loud, and a shriek or a shout would result in a slap from their grandmother. It was Sunday, after all. Soon they reached the imposing iron gates of the cemetery.

Granny Ross always read the *Gazette* in unchanging order. Births, Deaths and Marriages first, though in her case the order was Deaths, Births and Marriages. Who died, their age and where they were buried was of great importance. The volcanic plug and its surrounding acres, densely wooded, deeply mysterious, was *the* cemetery, Tomnahurich.

On each side of a narrow spiral path winding to the top of the plug were the graves of previous centuries. Newer graves spread outward along wider gravel pathways on the flat. But the only place to wait for the Second Coming was right here. Granny Ross knew that and pitied anyone who had to lie in lesser grounds. There were burying places where others went to wait for the Resurrection. For Catholics, as they are going to hell for their popery, there was no need for a burial at all as far as Granny Ross was concerned. Religion for the north of Scotland was tribal. Ecumenical causes and the Iona idea of a loving Christianity were mostly ignored. The answer to "What church do you go to?" told more about a family than their profession or trade. The river was not the only divide in the town.

Once through the gates, Annie and Wee Jean ran to the start of the climb. Up the winding paths, past lichen-covered gravestones, some staggering, some fallen, some placed flat, spiraling round the hill, up through the cold canopy of laurel and cypress and holly and oak, jumping over fallen tombstones, daring to tread on the dead, up to the top, to the panorama of town and firth and canal and river and off in the distance the snowcapped mass of Ben

Wyvis, the children ran. Grandad, using his walking stick on the steeper parts, followed steadily, slowing to tip his hat to ladies and his betters, his wife following in his wake. The grandparents reached their favorite bench in their favorite spot, with a great view of the town gasworks, a good five minutes after the girls.

"I'm fair peched," Grandad said, as he said every Sunday.

"That's 'cos you're old, Granda." Wee Jean cooried into the old man's side, hiding from the North Sea wind.

"Where do we go when we die?" Annie started.

"Heaven," Granny sighed.

"But maybe I'll go to hell, like the Bible says."

Grandad said immediately, "Of course not," but Granny secretly thought that there was something about this child that would lead to no good.

"Good girls go to heaven and bad girls to the other place." Granny had to get her bit in. She was ignored.

"Grandad, tell us about the faeries," both girls begged. They had heard the stories many times before and never tired of the telling.

"Once upon a time there was a faerie

queen. . . ."

"And she lived in the woods on the hill called Tomnahurich," they joined in.

"And one day . . ." He continued with one of his many versions of the legends that added to the mysterious allure of the hill that physically and psychically dominated the town.

Annie tried to pretend that the story was for babies like Jean but, as always, she too became absorbed in the tales. A girl who lived in her imagination, she often wondered if she was adopted or, more likely, kidnapped by the faeries and returned to the wrong family. But no, that couldn't have happened as she was too like her mother; tall, skinny, thick brown hair with a curl and passionate green-gray eyes. But eyes that betrayed a suspicion of people.

"Time to go," announced Granny Ross. "My old bones are feeling the damp."

At the bottom of the hill they passed the new graves.

"Will the faeries look after Jamie?" Wee Jean asked Grandad.

Granny Ross grabbed the girl's hand to hurry her out of the cemetery and continue the walk to the Islands, and to evade the question, scolded, "If you want your Sunday treat, we have to hurry."

It was most unusual for Mrs. Ross to forgo the pleasure of checking the new graves. Examining the wreaths, counting their number, reading the cards, this was the highlight of her week. Family wreaths were judged by their cost, others by the importance of the sender. The usual morbid questions from her eldest granddaughter were not what she needed, today of all days.

The Islands were just that, a group of small, scattered islands in the middle of the river linked by a series of footbridges. Tunnels of trees, waterfalls, rapids, birdsong, benches along the sandy paths leading to the Island Café, serving Italian ice cream and teas, this was a favorite place for the Sunday walk and for courting couples.

Annie and Wee Jean waited in the queue clutching their threepenny bits for an ice cream. Granny Ross settled on the veranda of the café with a group of lady friends, each surreptitiously eyeing up any new hats and all trying valiantly not to be the first to broach the subject on everyone's thoughts, the death of the boy. Grandad stood outside the café raising his hat to a passing stream of acquaintances. He was a well-known, well-liked man, champion of the local bowling club and member of the British Legion and a singer of renown. And he had once had a reputation as a bit of a ladies' man, so Joanne had heard.

Ice cream in hand, Annie ran ahead and was now jumping on the suspension bridge, finding the exact spot to make it sway up and down in a caterpillar motion. Granny Ross and her friends were regathering on the pathway about to go their separate ways, still chattering away like a gathering of rooks at twilight. "Oh really?" or "Oh I know!" they cawed from time to time. Grandad and Wee Jean waited patiently. Between licks on her cone the wee girl was explaining about her friend Jamie.

"My friend Jamie, he's dead." She started in a matter-of-fact six-and-a-half-year-old way.

"Aye, it's very sad." Grandad held on to her free hand, treasuring the contact.

"We saw him," she explained, "me and Annie, we saw this great big black hoodie crow. He opens the door, all of a sudden like, an' he spreads out his wings" — she flung her arms up and open in a wide circle, splatting ice cream like seagull poo down her Sunday coat — "and he picks up Jamie in his wings and takes him to Heaven an' now baby Jesus'll play with Jamie an' when he's in the hole in the ground in the cemetery the faeries'll be his friends too, so he won't be lonely and he won't be feart of the water nor the dark like he used to be."

Grandad stared down at the child. At first he was confused, then astonished, then a little worm of concern started to burrow its way into his subconscious; what on earth was the child on about? Granny came up from behind. He jumped. His first conscious thought was relief that his wife hadn't heard the child's ramblings.

"I hear Joanne's friends, they foreigners, have got themselves into a right pickle."

There was a note of satisfaction as she explained what she had heard about Peter Kowalski sheltering a fugitive from justice. She got no answer but was used to that. There had been other, much darker rumblings on the subject of the two Polish men, but she judged that now was not the time to raise the subject.

"Those Italian friends of hers, the ones with the café and chip shop, they've done well for themselves." She jumped from subject to subject like fleas on a dog, but Grandad Ross was used to this and never made any attempt to follow his wife's logic. All would be revealed in due course, this he knew only too well.

"Aye, they come to town with nothing,

straight out of the camps some of them. And look where they are now — taking over the place."

It would be a long time before there would be any Christian forgiveness for the former enemy. Midwar, released from the camps where they were interned, quite rightly as she saw it, some had just walked into cafés and chip shops throughout Scotland, so she said. No matter that no Scotsman knew how to make ice cream, nor coffee, no matter that the men and women had spent years in cold windswept camps, laboring in fields trying to turn the tide of stones that appeared after every plowing, planting potatoes, working the land. Some were farmboys from another impoverished region, albeit warmer and with no midges; some were fellow Scots detained for being of Italian ancestry. The hard work, the loss of their businesses, their land, and country, and language, the death of their families; that meant nothing to Mrs. Ross. To be fair, Grandad thought, the Scottish regiments suffered horrendously in Messina, Monte Cassino, all through the Italian campaign. Their son, their only bright laughing boy, had come home from Italy a haunted, damaged man.

Granny Ross's rant came to an abrupt

halt. She had spied the pale pink and white splats on Wee Jean's coat.

"Will you look at the state of you?" she cried.

And, dragging the sniveling child by one hand, nagging her husband over her shoulder and calling to Annie to keep up, she marched them past the war memorial, past the municipal flower beds with only the sad remains of fading wallflowers and chrysanthemums showing, marched them over the suspension bridge, past the infirmary, home, to a cup of tea, the wireless and a rest.

They were sitting comfy by the fire in the study, Joanne's feet resting on the fender, Duncan's opposite, a cup of tea and Dundee cake on a tray between them. Elizabeth was snoozing on the sofa in the sunroom; the children were out in the garden again, enjoying a late burst of autumn sun.

"That was a nice sermon today. A comfort." They reflected on the subject never far from anyone's mind that day. "Those poor parents."

Duncan nodded, then started cautiously on his mission.

"What's happening with Bill? We never seem to see him these days."

"What's happening? I'd like to know that

myself."

The bitterness in her voice made him deeply sad.

"Joanne, I'd like to help; I'm uncle to your daughters so I feel I have a right to speak. The girls are being affected by all this tension."

She looked down. The criticism hurt. Wee Jean was having nightmares, Annie had started wetting the bed again — at nearly nine years old — but Joanne had no idea that the cracks in her marriage were so visible.

"I hate seeing you unhappy . . . in my job I see more of it than I care to. But that is what I'm here for, to listen, to help if I can." He sighed. "It's over ten years since the war ended, but it's not ended for some. Men scarred by war, yes, but families scarred too, women, children, parents, all affected to a greater or lesser degree."

"I'm trying my best with a husband who never talks, never shares, never shows his feelings. I don't even know if he loves me. I feel sometimes that he resents me and the children for tying him down. We were too young to be married. He can't forgive his daughters for not being boys. And why does it always have to be me, the woman, that's in the wrong? What am I supposed to do, pray tell me?"

This silenced him. It was all too familiar.

"I know, I know. I've made my bed and all that. That's what my father, my parents — your in-laws — said. No Christian forgiveness there!" Like a hole in a dam, Duncan's concern had penetrated the carefully constructed wall around her emotions. Enough, she chided herself. She took in his concerned expression and smiled.

"My friends, they keep me going. And my job, it's exciting, a challenge."

Joanne knew the expression "Confession is good for the soul" but had never quite believed that. Confession, she thought, was plain embarrassing. But she couldn't stop herself.

"I need the work at the *Gazette.* It's not the money, though that helps, but the escape, the company, using my education, having others respect my opinions. What I get at home is 'A husband and children not good enough for you?' Bill can't take the disgrace of having a wife who works. He says it shows him up. His mother makes it clear she's on his side."

"Perhaps he's jealous."

"What of?"

"Your abilities, your education, the way everyone likes you."

"He's told me in no uncertain terms that he thinks I'm above myself. The list of my deficiencies is long indeed, according to him; love of classical music, books, plays on the wireless, fancy food — by that he means coffee — foreign friends, and he goes on about me wearing slacks to work. If men wore the kilt to ride a bicycle they'd soon understand." She tried a wan smile. "But that's his mother talking."

There was a comfortable silence for a moment or two while they both pondered the dilemma.

"It's just that . . . I'm tired," Joanne started again. "I'm tired of Bill's anger."

To Duncan, no matter how sympathetic he was, leaving an unhappy marriage could never be countenanced. For the sanctity of marriage, there could be no compromise.

"I'm going to talk to Bill." He was decided.

"Please, don't."

"You are my parishioner as well as sister-in-law, I have to try."

"I'm the one who will suffer if you do." She rose. "It'll soon be dark, I must away and fetch the girls." Her neck was stiff from tension. She needed to walk. "Bill's asked me to go on his next trip out west, a wee break on our own. I'll try to talk to him then, tell him how I feel. Give it a try anyhow." She turned in the doorway. "Thanks for listening." She gave a little wave with her fingertips, leaving Duncan fixed in his chair by a weight of sadness and outrage and helplessness and admiration.

And they had both entirely forgotten about the little boy.

Six

Monday morning, not his favorite time of any time, McAllister woke to a sky that seemed to have dropped from the weight of unshed rain, so low he felt that if he reached up and poked it, the hole would never be plugged. The day did not improve. Watery gray light persisted; a fitting shroud for the horrifying news that leaked through the town.

It had been confirmed midmorning by the procurator's office; the boy had been dead before he went into the canal lock. It was now a murder inquiry. The police would have summoned the parents for questioning; McAllister knew that family was always first in the suspicion stakes. He believed their story. It had to be checked, probably had been already, but they had both been working, on a public bus, so they were probably covered.

Wait, he reminded himself, see what

unfolds, no use speculating; an unexplained death is seldom simple, often a combination of events, and McAllister knew how to wait.

Rob was busily typing the football news; Joanne was trying to decipher the handwriting of a contributor who reported on the state of the Gaelic-speaking nation of the Highlands and Islands, a report that seemed to be a list of roadworks and ferry delays and not much else. Don was dealing with all the "fiddly bits," and proofing the cricket team's annual report was one of the more tedious jobs. In his view, the only reason the town had a cricket team was solely because they had an Anglican cathedral that had a cricket pitch, and you couldn't have one without the other. It was in the bylaws of Anglicanism, he declared. The three worked steadily, comfortable company.

Joanne kept returning to the chat with McAllister, wondering if she should broach the subject with Don, ask what he had heard. Rob had no such inhibitions.

"What did McAllister want, the other afternoon?"

"None of your business," Joanne snapped. Then she felt guilty. She typed somehow louder than usual.

"Serves me right for being nosy." Rob was

incorrigibly cheerful.

"I heard a certain WPC is keeping you company," Joanne said to get him back. Rob always brought out the wee girl in her.

"A coffee, that's all. Besides, she's too old for me."

"She's younger than me." Joanne knew as soon as she said it she'd walked into it and grinned.

"That's what I mean." He licked his finger and marked one in the air for him.

Rob wondered, should he risk another question, should he ask her about her daughters' weird story? A murder inquiry was so unusual, a child murder at that. So what if the girls *had* seen something?

Woman Police Constable Ann McPherson had been adamant she wouldn't talk about her job. "I'll be fired on the spot if Inspector Tompson thinks I've been talking to you." She did tell him, to share a laugh she said, the story of Joanne's daughters and the hoodie crow. He hadn't laughed. Something about a hoodie crow sent shivers through him — it was the kind of thing his Gaelic grandmother would talk of, or sing about, scare him with, as a wee boy. He had often laughed with Joanne about his paternal island grandparents' collection of stories and songs about murders, drownings,

treachery, bastard bairns, young girls betrayed, endless heroic defeats at the hand of
the English and of course witches, spells
and the faeries. And hoodie crows.

No. Wait. In poor taste. We're still in
shock, he thought, caution winning for
once. Rob looked across at Don. "What will
happen next with the hunt for whoever . . .
you know, the wee boy?"

Don looked up. "This is a rare event for
the Highlands, so they will probably get an
expert detective from down south to take
charge."

"Has this *ever* happened here before?"
Joanne asked.

"No, lass. Not that I know."

And since he knew everything, that meant
not in living memory.

Inspector Tompson was in a vile mood. He
was being replaced as head of his first and
only murder inquiry. That made him all the
more determined to arrest somebody before
an outsider came waltzing in to grab all the
glory. He was the man on the spot. He, who
had put up with years of slow-witted, silent,
stubborn Highland folk, he who was from
Glasgow, who had been somebody in the
army, who had reached the rank of sergeant
by his own merits before accepting promo-

tion and a transfer to this cut-off backwater, he would show them. He knew who had done this, stood to reason, he knew as soon as he had heard it was a murder. No, he had no proof, none whatsoever. But he'd find some.

As for Mr. Angus McLean . . . Inspector Tompson fumed as he remembered. The solicitor might think he had gotten the better of him with Peter Kowalski and the Polish sailor, but no, not this time. And last but by no means least, he'd somehow see those tinkers charged with something — anything.

"WPC McPherson," he yelled out his office door. "Here. Now."

"You'd think I was his sheepdog," she muttered. But being only a WPC and knowing, never mind her five years' service, that she was only allowed to work on a high-profile case because no one else wanted to work with Tompson, she was wise enough to keep this thought to herself.

After the long distance between them, Keith was delighted that his mother, Jenny, was on visiting terms with himself and Shona. His brother Jimmy had ignored their mother's prejudices and had been a frequent caller.

Keith, Shona, Jenny and Jimmy had been going over the old family stories, all afternoon they had been, with much laughter and an occasional somber "Aye," followed by a silence, then back again to more mirth and the occasional burst of song from Jenny. Karl, still staying in Keith and Shona's spare room, was watching, enjoying but unable to understand most of the time. Even their English was incomprehensible to him. Jenny, speaking in Gaelic most of the time, would start, "Do you mind when . . . ?" singing, "Oh rowan tree, oh rowan tree . . . ," sitting back dreamily. "I mind camping up near Ardgay one summer. . . ." They were gathered to help Keith. Compiling the legends, the sayings, the superstitions of the Traveling people was his new-found passion.

"Why you want to know all this is beyond me," Jimmy teased, but he too enjoyed reminiscing on times past. The McPhee family still traveled, but these past three years, they had camped in benders by the river in Strathconnon for the winter months.

"I know." Keith laughed tolerantly. "When we were wee, you couldn't see the sense of joining the Dingwall library, far less getting an education, and as for going to university . . ."

"We even had to get the doctor in Beauly to stand guarantor in case we used the books to wipe our arses," Jimmy told Shona. He laughed, but he regretted that his reading and writing were of the basic, learned-in-prison level. Still, he could read the form guide and that was enough. "But Ma is certain you're the first tink to graduate from Glasgow University."

Keith was notoriously backward in coming forward, but this pleased him. Now he was a schoolteacher, collecting the lore and the songs — "tinkers' tales," as some would have it — from his mother, her mother, the old folk, black tinkers so-called, the river pearl fishermen, the itinerant farmworkers, and around campfires, in the back of wagons, picking the berries, at the tatties, at the agricultural shows, at the horse fairs, he asked questions and he listened.

"Who better to record tinkers' tales than a tinker?" he told his brother.

"Who will be interested?" Jimmy replied. "All that stuff is for bairns — faerie circles and clootie wells and what time o' the moon the lassies collect dewdrops to wash their face. Anyone who buys a book on that must be awfy keen on nonsense."

The banging on the door brought the cheerful blethering to a halt.

165

"Polis," Jenny sighed.

Shona was about to ask "How do you know?" but thought better of it and went to the door. Before she could even say "Come away in" the inspector had pushed past her, followed by an apologetic WPC Ann McPherson. She was only there because she had to be, and to take notes.

Inspector Tompson went over and over the same points for a good hour, getting nowhere.

"Who picked up the Polish man?" He didn't even glance at Karl. Spoke of him as though he wasn't in the room. Who had taken him where on the night of his escape? He was in the camp by the shore, wasn't he? And they had hidden him from the authorities, hadn't they? And who had told Peter Kowalski?

The "no" and the "don't know" and the "no idea" and the "no I never" or the shrugs and the silence and the looking down or away or up at the ceiling should have had the inspector in an apoplectic fit. But WPC Ann watched carefully as each refusal to give information, instead of infuriating him, drove him on, made him more sure of himself, leaving her puzzled, then deeply worried.

How did the man know about them? How

166

had he gotten here? Why had they hidden him in this very house? Didn't they know they were harboring an illegal alien? Didn't they realize that if Keith McPhee was charged, the education board would be the first to find out? He himself would make sure of that. Shona was the only one distressed by the barrage. The idea that Keith could be reported and lose his job, his reputation, terrified her.

"It wasn't him, it was me, I gave him shelter," Shona blurted out.

"Lass, lass," Jenny sighed. "Never say anything to anyone. Now you see why I'm feart for you. Marrying into a Traveling family is no easy."

"Enough." Tompson stood. "Jimmy McPhee, with your past record, the sheriff would no look kindly on a charge of helping a fugitive. As for you, Keith McPhee, be grateful I'm not charging you either. But don't think this is the end of it."

He pulled himself to attention and announced in his best parade-ground voice:

"Karel Cieszynski, I am arresting you on suspicion of murder. You do not —" The rest of his words were drowned out in the uproar from the McPhees. Karl looked around, bewildered, with no idea what was going on.

Tompson produced his handcuffs. Ann McPherson stood gaping and wondered, What on earth is that idiot of an inspector up to? But she had no choice. She helped her boss rush the arrested man down the stairs and into the police car before a riot erupted.

Joanne got the story from Chiara — the phone had rung in the reporters' room in the late afternoon just as she was about to leave. As ever, no one else was about to pick up the phone.

"Gazette," she sighed. "Chiara." She listened. "Slow down." She held the receiver out, flicking her hair from her ear. "I can't. Not tonight. Tomorrow?" She listened again. "What?" Then a sound like the chatter of a flock of starlings came out of the phone in a long burst. "Never!" By now the other three in the room were interested. "I can't believe it!" Joanne sat down. "Aye, I'll tell them. And if we can help, call" — she looked around — "McAllister." She put down the phone. "Chiara Corelli."

She shook her head, not knowing what to think. "They've arrested Karel what's-his-name, Karl — the Polish man. He's been arrested for murder."

That afternoon, a larger-than-usual gathering of mothers waited outside the school. Shifting and re-forming, restless, chatting in that hushed tone reserved for funerals or really meaty scandals, they stood in a herd waiting for the bell. In a place where five-year-olds walked to and from school unaccompanied, where children played, alone or in small groups, in streets and parks and fields and woods, their only fear being bullies or bogeymen or ghosties, where everyone knew everyone, strangers were not a danger because they hardly ever saw anyone they didn't know, or know of.

Bill was the only man waiting. He hated that.

"Where's Mum?" Wee Jean stopped still when she saw his van outside the playground gates, anxious. "Is she a'right?"

"Course your mum's all right," he snapped, irritated that Joanne wasn't there being a proper wife and mother and annoyed at the implications in the question.

"You're going to Granny and Grandad's. Mum'll be there by teatime."

Mum and Granny and Grandad all having tea together cheered the little girl. Annie knew better. First her mother's questions, then their dad picking them up from school, all the other mums at the gate, teachers quiet, and a special assembly tomorrow morning — it had to be about Jamie.

As though sensing the mood of the town, dark came early that day. Joanne, pushing her bicycle, walked home from her in-laws' with the girls. She was pleased the fear was over. An arrest coming so quickly, that's a relief, she thought. Chiara's worry that she, Peter, all foreigners, would be somehow blamed, Joanne dismissed. Watching her girls running on ahead, leaping from pool to pool of grub-white street light, trying not to stand on the lines between the paving stones, chanting out the childhood rhymes, just as she and her friends had done, she convinced herself that life would soon be back to normal. Except for Jamie's family. Poor souls.

Annie sat at the kitchen table, hands black with Brasso, polishing away at her brass imp. She had even ironed her Brownie uniform herself.

"Mum, next year, when I fly up to the Guides, I get a much nicer uniform, blue, not yuch brown, and you go camping in the

Guides." She kept polishing, her tongue sticking out in effort.

Joanne had said nothing to the children about Jamie, the arrest; she had not mentioned the subject to them. She had sometimes thought that they would be fine hearing of such things, but it just wasn't done.

"I'm going for another badge tonight."

"Oh really, which one?"

"Storytelling. Brown Owl asks questions on a book you've read, then next, she gives you three choices an' you tell a story on one of them for five minutes."

"So that's why you can't put down *Kidnapped.*" Joanne smiled at her daughter's excitement. "Then you'll have seven badges altogether."

"An' if our six get two more badges tonight we beat the Bluebells."

The Bluebells, led by Sheila Murchison, Annie's sworn enemy, were archrivals to the Snowdrops. Secretly, Joanne agreed with Annie. Sheila at nine was exactly like her mother: a snob, a gossip and a pillar of the community. Mrs. Murchison had somehow found out the date of Joanne and Bill's wedding anniversary, put two and two together and shared this information with all who would listen.

Wee Jean and Joanne enjoyed being on their own by the fire, Jean coloring in her *Bunty* comic, Joanne knitting, Annie out, and Bill not yet home.

"That was Jimmie Shand and his band with a selection of jigs and reels. Next we have Kenneth Mackellar with some favorites from Rabbie Burns." The sweet tenor floated from the wireless — "My love is like a red red rose" — when the doorbell made them jump.

Joanne had no idea who the short round brown creature was, wispy gray hair escaping from a brown hat squashed down low on the forehead, round National Health glasses and, with that myopic glare of the shortsighted, squinting in the bright light from the open door.

"I'm Tawny Owl."

Half-owl, half-busybody, Joanne thought, so she had to suppress an involuntary giggle when the woman introduced herself. "Oh, yes. I'm Joanne Ross. What's wrong? Annie, are you hurt?" Annie didn't answer. "Come on in — er, Tawny Owl."

"I have to talk to you, Mrs. Ross. It's serious."

"Jean, up to bed with you." She shooed the little girl out the room. "Can I get you a cup of tea?"

The woman refused tea, wouldn't sit down, her outrage, like a topsail in a storm, carrying her onward.

"I'm not stopping long, Mrs. Ross. Brown Owl asked me to bring Annie home. The child has been telling lies, she was rude, she talked back, refused to listen to Brown Owl. We had to fail her in her storyteller's badge. We can't have that sort of behavior in the Brownies."

Annie, by the side of Tawny Owl, the woman gripping her thin arm, was cowering like a mouse snatched from a field of stubble. Instinctively Joanne sided with her daughter. Brown Owl, a good friend of Mrs. Murchison, was someone Joanne would nod to in church but had never wished to make a closer acquaintance. "Tell me exactly what happened."

The back door slammed. Bill walked into the middle of the confrontation, took one look at the ensemble and gave a dangerous grin. "What's she done this time?"

Annie tried to make a break for the safety of her mother.

"She cheeked Brown Owl." Tawny Owl had a sudden insight as to how ridiculous this sounded. "It's serious."

"Cheeked Brown Owl, eh? What did you say?" To Bill, his eldest daughter was trouble. Had been even before she'd been born.

"She told the most fantastic tales."

"She's always havering, that one," Bill informed her.

The woman, put out by Bill's attitude, by Joanne's lack of contrition and most of all by Annie's lack of apology, scolded him as though he was the nine-year-old.

"It's no a laughing matter. A child is dead."

"We are all well aware of the tragedy," Joanne said coldly. "But what has that to do with this?"

Bill, irritated, rebuked in his own house, sat in his chair by the fire and waved at the woman to explain. "All right, all right, what happened?" He was beginning to scare Joanne. She prayed their visitor would not smell the alcohol on his breath — the gossip would be all over town by tomorrow.

"For the storytelling topic — for a badge — Annie chose 'my biggest fright.' She then proceeded to use the tragedy of that poor wee soul's death to tell a ridiculous tale of a hoodie crow taking the boy off into the sky, she said, then dropping him in the canal.

Brown Owl had to give her a good telling-off, pointing out how ridiculous, not to say distasteful, her story was. The child wouldn't be told — she shouted at Brown Owl and refused to stand in the corner."

"She said it was a big fib," shouted Annie. "It isn't, and she said I was telling lies." She wailed: "But it's true. A hoodie crow *did* get him."

Wee Jean, eavesdropping at the top of the stairs, clutched the banisters, shivered in fear and sympathy.

"Don't shout." Bill glared in warning. "Of course you were lying. You're always making things up."

"Bill, can I have a word?" Joanne whispered.

"It's true," Annie persisted. "I did see a hoodie crow. He wrapped Jamie up in his wings."

"Enough o' your lies."

Joanne tried to shoo the woman out the door. "Thank you, Tawny Owl. Leave it to us. We'll speak to her."

"That child and her lies. She has to learn. She has to apologize or else she'll be asked to leave. And then she'll never be allowed to fly up to the Guides."

Annie let out a howl at that. Then her father grabbed her by her wrist, dragging her toward the stairs.

Joanne pushed the startled Tawny Owl out the front door, slamming it behind her.

"Wait. Bill. Please. Listen."

"You always stick up for her. No wonder she gets in trouble." He was halfway up the stairs, dragging Annie, who was desperately clinging onto the banisters.

"Let go." He smacked her hand free. "It's time you learned a lesson."

"Mum, Mum!" The child reached out for her mother. Wee Jean shrank into a corner of the landing, sobbing. Joanne stood helpless at the bottom of the stairs, unable to intervene, her own pain still fresh.

"It's true, Mum! I didn't lie. I saw it." Annie wouldn't give in. "Mum, I'm telling the truth. You promised. . . . Mum!" She wailed the accusation.

The sound of leather on bare flesh, once, twice, not stopping, cut through Joanne. Still she stood still for too long, an eternity, half a minute, paralyzed.

"Enough. Stop it." She was up the stairs and into the bedroom, grabbing the army belt in midstrike.

Bill had done enough to satisfy his anger. He threw the belt to the floor and yelled at Joanne, right in her face, "See what you've done! See what happens when you go traipsing off to your precious job! You can't look after your own bairns properly." With a growl of "I'm sick o' the lot o' you" he pushed past her. The two girls and their mother stopped breathing for a long second. The back door slammed.

Joanne picked up Jean and put her into her bed, surrounding her with her rag dolls, trying to soothe her sobs. She then crept into Annie's room, where the child gave an occasional heaving sob and hiccup, tears all cried out. The girl lay on her tummy, a pillow over her head, too sore to turn over. The injustice and betrayal burned deep and would take a long time to dim, if they ever did. Her mother had lied. Her mother hadn't protected her.

When Joanne, her own tears dripping onto the bedclothes, tried to stroke her daughter's shoulder, an arm lashed out, a leg kicked her away.

"I told the truth." The child could barely get the words out. "You promised. You said I'd no get into trouble if I told the truth." She sniffed deeply, wiped her nose on the pillow slip. "I hate him," she said, and turning to her mother, "An' I hate you too."

The weight of Abraham settled on Joanne; she had sacrificed her child to protect herself.

SEVEN

Rob was furious.

"The Aberdeen paper has stolen my scoop. All I'll get published is a few lines stating that Karl unpronounceable has been arrested. Six days after the event. Their wee worm of a reporter has someone inside the procurator's office feeding him information."

"What do you expect? They're a daily and this is big news." Don didn't look up; he was stabbing away at Rob's prose with a stub of pencil. "Maybe the troll at the typewriter filled him in on more than the essentials."

Rob smirked at Don's description of the legal secretary.

"I recall there was talk of you and the lady in question once walking out together."

Don snapped. "Who told you that? That was twenty years ago."

"Oh, so there was something?"

"Never you mind, and never believe all you hear. Especially not in *this* office. If you want to find out the leak, start with a certain inspector who has no time for foreigners, nor smart-alec boys wi' a well-connected father."

Grabbing his corrected proof sheets, Don made for the door.

"Don't forget. They are a daily — they're all about headlines. We're a weekly, we do more judicious, considered pieces."

"I'm not sure I know how to do deep articles; you always cut them to shreds."

Before they could continue, Joanne walked in. Don looked at the clock. "Not like you to be late." Then he peered at her drawn face. "You're right peely-wally, are you no well?"

"I'm perfectly fine, thank you."

He made for the door but not before Joanne heard him mutter something ending in ". . . women's troubles."

Rob took one look and he too made for the door.

"Gazette." Joanne had been hoping for some peace in the empty office but the phone had not stopped ringing. The only topic of inquiries was the Polish man. Some wanted more information, some wanted to give

information, some knew it had to be him because he was a stranger, others said it was because he was a foreigner, and others still said they had seen a strange man hanging about — not up the canal, just a strange man hanging around the town. Joanne told everyone to call the police station.

Strange men — ha, plenty of them around, was her conclusion as she hung up on one particularly verbose caller.

Ten seconds' peace and the phone rang again.

"Gazette."

"You sound as fed up as me," Chiara said.

"Aye, well, things are not easy right now."

"Can you come over later? I really need to talk."

"I'd love to but it's hard right now. And I can't get out of the office this dinnertime." She could but she wouldn't. The thought of facing anyone, even her best friend, after last night, made her shake. "Then I have to take time off to meet the girls from school. Bill insists." She couldn't say that now that Karl had been arrested, the girls would again walk home alone — a sixth sense stopped her. But the fib felt uncomfortable. "Tonight is out." She didn't explain. The look Annie had given her as she said cheerio outside the school this morning would haunt her for a long long time. "Tomorrow's out — press day. And now Bill insists I keep my promise to go out west with him on Friday." Though how they would get through a whole three days together she could barely imagine. "I'm sorry, Chiara, I —"

"Joanne, I'm really worried. So are Papa and Aunty Lita. Peter is absolutely shattered by the news. We've had phone calls, an anonymous letter, and this morning, as he walked to work, someone spat at Papa. The chip shop will open as usual but the café is closed for today at least."

"Why on earth . . . ?"

"Because some people think we hid a child murderer, that's why." Maybe even you, Chiara thought. "But you're busy, so I'll catch you later."

Joanne was left with the phone in her hand, feeling even more wretched, when McAllister walked in.

"Where is everyone?"

"Out."

He too retreated; his office was safer than facing a woman in one of her moods, he thought. Or was there something more?

Half an hour later, remembering past barbs about not informing McAllister of any and every piece of information that came

181

her way, Joanne walked across the landing and knocked on the half-open door.

"Chiara Corelli called," she reported. "They are being bothered by anonymous phone calls. She says people think they hid the Polish fellow, Karl, the one who killed wee Jamie."

"Hold on." He waved her to a seat with his cigarette, like a magician's wand, making smoke circles in the air. "First of all, the man, Karl, *has* been arrested, but that doesn't make him guilty. . . ."

"But it stands to reason, he must have done it, the police wouldn't arrest him otherwise."

"No, it doesn't stand to any reason. Let's see what evidence the procurator presents. Just because Karl is a stranger in the town, just because he is *not* Scottish —"

"But he went missing the night the wee boy vanished."

"— just because there was the coincidence of them both going missing on the same night —"

"Nobody in this town could possibly kill a wee boy."

That was Joanne's firm and final reply.

Aye, McAllister thought to himself, why bother with a trial? They would, the whole community, have him hanged, drawn and quartered out on the castle forecourt at dawn, if they could.

"Joanne, we newspaper people, we're supposed to be unbiased. Let's wait and see, shall we? Innocent until proven guilty? Now, tell me what Chiara Corelli said."

Cycling home after work, Joanne was past the corner shops before she realized what she had seen. Or not seen. The chip shop was in darkness. A recent institution in a town where ration cards and war were a not very distant memory, it stood in forlorn darkness, large pieces of board crisscrossed with battens of two-by-two covering the wide window space. Usually, the shop was lit up like an oceangoing liner, the scenes in the windows a tableau of town life. Through the fogged-up glass could be seen customers sitting at a long bench, waiting patiently, chatting to each other or reading the paper. On the high counter stood large jars containing pickled onions and pickled eggs in dark brown vinegar, which always reminded Joanne of anatomical exhibits of some obscure animal brains. At this time in the evening there were usually at least half a dozen people sitting at the small group of tables with salt, vinegar and sauce in large bottles on red-and-white check oilcloth.

Fish suppers were posh, served on plates, with a knife and a fork; tea came in a cup with saucer and orange cordial, bright as a traffic light, came in a glass.

Single men still in their working clothes, families out for a treat, courting couples, eating before making for the La Scala to see the latest Hitchcock film or *Oklahoma!* that seemed to have been running for forever — soon to exchange long passionate fish-and-vinegar-flavored kisses — ate at the tables. Young men in small groups, about to take off for the billiard rooms, hanging around the wondrous purple-lit jukebox, searching for Bill Hailey or Frankie Lyman — never Perry Como — also congregated in the comfortable, humid chip shop. But not to-night.

She wheeled her bike to the door where, attached with a single drawing pin, drooped a hand-lettered envelope saying CLOSED. She remembered the phone call and was appalled. Too wrapped up in the stifling, walking-on-eggshells truce that was her own home life, she hadn't been to see Chiara. She hadn't even called back. And now it was too late for a visit; she had to collect the girls from their grandparents'. This was the one time she wished they were wealthy enough to have a telephone at home. She spoke a promise to the stars. Tomorrow I'll call first thing. Tomorrow.

The phone call to Chiara did not go well. Joanne offered to meet for coffee.

"Joanne, the café is shut. And now the chip shop has to shut too; someone chucked a brick through the window. Peter has had a couple of nasty phone calls, clients cancel meetings, one contract has been postponed, and people he's known for years cut him dead in the street." Chiara's voice faded in and out as though there was something wrong with the line. "So perhaps it's better if we wait and you come over when all this has died down."

There was little Joanne could think of to say.

"Chiara, you're my friend," she started, "none of this matters to me and I'm sorry I haven't called in but . . ."

"We'll talk when you come back from the west coast. Maybe things will have calmed down by then." Her voice went very faint. ". . . 'Bye, Joanne."

Rob was sitting across the table trying not to notice but taking in the gist of the conversation from the way Joanne hunched her shoulders, adding ten years to her age.

"Chiara?" he asked after she had hung up.

Joanne nodded.

"Aye, I saw the chip-shop window." He was never one to pretend. "It will get worse, I think. This is such a terrible crime. The waiting, the trial, and Peter Kowalski charged with being an accessory, all this will be very hard on the Corelli family. And every other foreigner in town."

Don came in on the end of the conversation, took one look at Joanne and ordered her out. "Off you go. Right now. Go see your friends. They need you."

"Chiara said not to bother, or words to that effect."

"Saying it and meaning it are different things." He shooed her out the door.

"Now you, young Robert McLean, I want you to first check up on the damage to the chip shop, find out what you can about this jiggery pokery, put an article together." Don continued with his suspicions. "There's something no right about this arrest business. Too convenient. Thon Inspector Tompson is jumping the gun — again."

The grumbling terrier-like growl coming from the sturdy terrier-like body made Rob smile. He could almost see the hackles rising on the back of Don's neck.

"You're beginning to sound like McAllister." Rob agreed. There *was* something not right about the arrest. "If you think about it logically, what with what the watchman said about that night, and the tinkers . . ."

"Aye, that's what I mean, logic, there's not a lot of that around."

The curtains were drawn in the deep bow windows that faced the street, as though announcing a death in the family. Joanne reached for the bell. As she followed Chiara through to the kitchen, she felt that the light of the house was diminished. The sense of sun and warmth and earth and orchards and olives and flowers and friends all seemed a memory. Their home was once again a respectable Victorian-Scottish-solid-Sunday-go-to-church, hard-to-heat house.

The visit was a very long half hour. Aunt Lita had disappeared upstairs after greeting Joanne. Gino Corelli was nowhere to be seen. As they sat together at the table, Chiara filled her in.

"We know very little," she started. "Mr. McLean the solicitor will call us when he knows more. Peter is still out on bail, thank goodness, but he was questioned endlessly."

"What evidence have the police got against Karl?"

"He didn't do this, Joanne. I don't know the man, but Peter's word is good enough for me."

They were silent for a very long thirty seconds.

"What happened at the chip shop?"

"Idiots with bricks." Chiara went silent again. "I'm sorry, Joanne, I can't think straight. But thanks for coming." They both stood. She reached up to give her friend a hug. "Not like me to be lost for words, eh?"

As they parted at the front door, Chiara asked, "Are you all right? You look a bit down."

"I'm fine." Joanne knew she would never share last Monday night with anyone. What would she say? Oh, by the way, I betrayed my daughter?

"Chiara . . . you know, if you need me . . ."

"I know." She smiled back. "I know." She nodded fiercely.

Next afternoon in the office, the whole of the editorial staff, all four of them, were sitting around the reporters' table putting the final touches to the edition.

"I like this." Don had proofed through McAllister's editorial without one stroke of his pencil, cutting not a single word of the piece.

"Can I see?" Rob snatched the piece of paper out of Don's hand. "Oh, right." He read it, then passed it to Joanne. "A bit hard, aren't you? And not many people know what *xenophobia* means."

"Exactly." McAllister knew that ripping up the typewritten words, scattering them in the river and chanting some ancient Gaelic curse would be equally as effective as his editorial. "But we have to try. Remember the lesson of the silent majority."

The war was not that long over, so his words hung in the air.

"Rob, when this story becomes clearer, you write it up and I'll see if I can get an article placed in the Glasgow press."

"Great. Can you really swing it with the editor? Aye, sorry, course you can." Rob jumped up, so excited at the idea of writing for a prestigious newspaper that he fell over his words as well as his feet.

"I just wish that my girls had it right. That it *was* a hoodie crow that snatched the wee boy up." But Joanne said this quietly. McAllister registered her words, heard the touch of despair in her voice, but before he could take her up on her comment, Don announced, "Finish up, everyone. One hour. Can't keep the presses waiting."

Peter Kowalski sat in his tiny sanctuary, hands clasped behind his head, staring at the scudding clouds. The outer office was a large square room with drafting boards all around the edges. The inner office was small and round, set in a turret sticking out to the corner of the street with views of church spires and a glimpse down an alley of the river. It had reminded him of an illustration from a childhood book of the tower in which Rumplestiltskin had spun straw into gold. He loved it. It was his. He had reinvented himself in this distant land through determination and hard work. And, as Inspector Tompson had told him repeatedly, he was about to lose it all.

So, sitting in his sanctum, Peter went over and over the interrogation, trying to see how the inspector's mind was working, where his questions were going, questions that had become stuck in Peter's mind like an endless annoying tune picked up from the wireless, and the more you tried to banish it from your mind, the more it went round and around.

Yes, he, Peter, alone, had picked Karl up that morning.

No, he didn't know who put the mysterious note under his office door.

No, he didn't have it anymore.

Yes, he had picked Karl up near the canal bridge.

No, he had no idea how Karl had got there.

No, he had no idea where Karl had spent that night.

Yes, it was the town side of the bridge.

No, Karl wasn't wearing a coat.

Yes, he took him up the glen to give him a place to stay.

No, he wasn't hiding him; Karl had wanted some peace and quiet.

No, nobody else was involved.

No, Gino Corelli had nothing to do with it.

No, he didn't know Jimmy McPhee.

Yes, he did expect the inspector to believe him.

EIGHT

Joanne thought of people's lives as books; books she remembered, books she was yet to read, books she had read and returned to the library to a shelf marked biography or history or fiction or even romantic fiction. Remembered characters and fragments of a novel's plot were often more real to her than actual events in her life. But the tantalizing possibility of a new chapter in the story of her life, even of a new book, was a recent idea.

Of her own story, she would have written it thus: beginning — childhood; middle — the war; ending — marriage. I need a subcategory, she thought; romantic fiction — failed. For too long, she had been waiting for the scene, toward the end of the book, where he would turn to her and say, "I'm sorry. Forgive me. I've been to hell and back. But the war is over and now . . ." She almost put "and with the help of a good woman" in her imaginary manuscript but could hear Don's chortle as he edited out the cliché.

"Journey to the West" was to be the next chapter heading. This is it, Joanne kept telling herself, a last chance. This time we have to *talk*. Then again — the thought would sting her like a paper cut — how many times have I said *that*.

Sitting beside Bill, in the noisy, shaky, damp, smelling-of-fresh-wood-and-old-socks van, not much passed between them as they drove out of town in the dark. Not that they had spoken much all week. A driving rain accompanied them along the shores of the smelled but unseen firth. Their spirits matched the gloom. Dawn broke very gradually through dank cloud. On the higher passes between glens the water vapor was so dense it was as though they were driving into perpetual dawn like an airplane flying into perpetual sunset.

The van reached the top of the pass, and Bill stopped in a passing place before the drop into the faultline that led to the west coast. A biblical shaft of sun shone down on a distant shepherd, his dogs working a flock of blackface sheep, bringing them to lower pastures.

They had left behind the sepulchral cloud and the unease that hovered over them like a golden eagle sizing up a newborn. The paper was finished and would be, by now, scattered throughout the Highlands and Islands, the girls were with their grand-parents, and she was going on a holiday — three whole days. Joanne was determined. This was what they needed, this time she would make it work. And her mood lifted with the elusive sun and the sense of the distant Isles. She started the song. Bill joined in. They used to sing together a lot, in the days of the war. Everyone did. But the habit had died out. Joanne still whistled, but less and less.

By yon bonnie banks and by yon bonnie
    braes,
Where the sun shines bright on Loch
    Lomon',
Where me and my true love were ever
    wont to gae
On the bonnie, bonnie banks of Loch
    Lomon'.

Following the railway track, the van rattled along with the singing, westward to the sea. Giant boulders and scree scarred the hill-sides. The distant navy-blue peaks, jagged as in a child's drawing, were outlined against a sky-blue sky. Clouds scudded, their shadows racing each other, making the fern carpet flicker from dirty rust to brassy gold.

The road up to the pass could be seen in the distance, sharp zigzags cut into an almost vertical hill. Passing places, marked by signs that would show in deep snow, protruded out over sheer drops with no soft landings in the rocks and heather below. Joanne was uncertain that the van could make it. It did, in first gear and at a walking pace.

At the top, the Bealach na Ba leveled for a mile or two before a slightly less steep descent. A small slate-dark tarn seemingly with no edge hovered at the brink of the drop to their right, a perfectly formed mirror for the clouds to admire themselves. The sea that took up two-thirds of the moving picture dazzled bright one moment, dark silver the next, and the islands big and small, some only oversized boulders, disappeared to then magically pop up in a seemingly different spot. Joanne felt that she would not have blinked if a sea dragon had landed across the bay.

Below, a sheltering of buildings and small clachans followed the curve of the shore.

With a shop, an inn, a post office, a school, a harbor and twenty or so houses, the habitable land was a narrow strip squeezed between mountain and sea. Whitewashed but-and-bens, some still with thatched roofs, punctuated the slopes. A patchwork of tiny fields hemmed in by stone walls alternated with strip fields following the lines of the land. Breughel painting the countryside of the Middle Ages would have recognized the scene. But this is the land of the clans, of the Clearances, the land of the ever-diminishing Gaeltacht. And God.

Bill had nursed the van up the pass with one eye on the temperature gauge. It was on the red. He decided to rest before the downhill stretch.

"Five minutes before I can fill her up again."

"Right you are."

They waited to the gurgle and hissing and burping and sighing of the radiator and the smell of rusty water. A dark hairpiece of heavy cloud descended abruptly, and the light vanished; out here, weather changed by the half hour, seasons by the hour.

The sound of running water got to Joanne. Tammy and scarf pulled tight, she stepped out into the mist, scouting around for bushes. There were none, only occasional tussocks of thin grasses and bog cotton and lichen-covered rock. A few steps and the van vanished. She crouched down. A cough from a spectral blackface sheep startled her, then the sun broke through a hole in the cloud. Caught squatting in the spotlight, half a dozen curious sheep for an audience, she saw the edge a few yards off, falling away to the shore hundreds of feet below. She burst out laughing.

"Mind how you go," Bill called out. "It drops away over there."

"Thanks. I've just worked that out for myself."

By the time the radiator was cool enough to refill they were chilled and damp, and Bill was impatient to get down the mountain. He had had enough of scenery. Joanne took a last look over to Skye, the cloud already a story tucked away for later. Or to share with Chiara.

"When we reach the village, leave me at the inn and I'll explore. We'll have tea when you get back."

"Aye, it's getting on and I'm to meet this man about the houses," Bill replied.

They freewheeled down the last of the hill, a bump, the engine caught and they motored into the village.

■ ■ ■ ■

She stretched and shook the cramps of the journey from her bones before going inside the hotel. A bar ran through to a small parlor where a brass ship's bell hung above a handwritten notice, *Ring for attention.* She did.

"I'll be right with you," a voice called out, and almost immediately Mhairi was there. Both women started, then stared. What startled Joanne into recognition of a girl she had barely met was her bright rosy red apple cheeks. Joanne collected words and clichés and was always pleased to come across an exact illustration, to be mentally matched to her list of favorites. What Mhairi felt when confronted with the guest was panic.

"Don't I know you?" asked Joanne.

"I don't think so." The girl went bright pink. She was a hopeless liar.

"I phoned about a room for tonight. Mr. and Mrs. Ross."

"Aye, I'll show you up."

Mhairi seized the bag and hurried up the narrow steep staircase, Joanne following.

"This is the room." A pretty bedroom, the dormer window looking directly onto the harbor. "I'll light the fire."

198

"Thanks," said Joanne. "This is lovely. What's your name?"

"Mhairi."

"Mhairi, now I remember. I'm Joanne Ross — you worked for my sister Elizabeth Macdonald and Reverend Duncan Macdonald."

Mhairi turned from pink to red.

"Och, I'm sorry. Me and my big mouth. Not another word. Promise."

The relieved look on Mhairi's face said it all.

"Will you be wanting supper?"

"That would be lovely."

Joanne changed her shoes for wellies and set off in what was left of the afternoon light to explore the harbor and village.

Mhairi MacKinnon worked away in the kitchen, the door to the bar left open in the unlikely event of guests arriving. With black pudding-basin haircut, white white skin and blue blue eyes, she could have been a Celtic beauty if only she had an awareness of herself.

The owners of the inn were from Easter Ross but now lived over the mountain. The steep miles across the pass made this place another country. Mrs. Watt, her employer, knew most of Mhairi's story but was only too glad to have someone reliable, willing to work with the "demon drink," as the minister never failed to call it in his three-hour Sunday sermons. The water-into-wine parable had been passed over by the congregation of the Free Church of Scotland, or Wee Frees as they were commonly known.

A lass already lost was how Mhairi saw herself, so one more sin, the serving of alcohol, wouldn't matter. But the shock of meeting Joanne Ross, the shock of meeting someone from the town where her tragedy had played out, the very thought of someone who knew the truth of her secret and that very someone lodging at the inn, was worrying.

Not that most in the parish didn't know; it was more a matter of acquiescence to an age-old convention: Children born out of wedlock were given away, sometimes to the tinkers. Failing that, especially if the lass in question was young, the child was passed off as a sibling. Everyone knew, everyone accepted the lie; it was just the way it was done. To most, Mhairi's family had done the decent thing. To others it was a disgrace and the whole family was made to feel the shame.

Tales of girls told never to darken the door again, cast out into the proverbial storm, were many and ancient. Songs of betrayed lassies, kidnapped babies, babies being stolen by the faeries or lifted up by golden eagles, all those tunes, words, poems, were part of Scottish folklore. Mhairi was just another story, and a not uncommon one at that.

Bill shifted uncomfortably in the driver's seat, engine running, heater blasting hot to the body, freezing to the feet, waiting for the foreman to turn up. He stared at the unfinished buildings, his forced optimism seeping away. His picture of himself was that of a survivor, and by sheer belief he had often been able to turn disasters around. This time, he thought, we're cutting it very close. The contract, with a clause that he had skipped over, so desperate to sign, stipulated the end of December for completion of the job. Still possible, but where were the men that he needed in order to finish the job?

Unexplained delays, materials not delivered, delivered but to the wrong port, bad weather, bad luck, a badgering bank manager; all this had plagued the project from the start. Then workers left; lack of lodgings, frozen out by the locals, the weather, the isolation and the west-coast Sabbath, so they said. "Acts of God," the previous site foreman had said. Bill recalled the man as a strict Sabbatharian, dour but honest.

"The site is jinxed," another had complained to Bill as he collected his cards.

The almost completed, desperately needed council houses, sitting forlornly waiting to be fitted out, were to have been Bill's financial salvation. He was now certain sabotage was the root of his trouble.

He'd seen enough. He wanted away from the site. A van drew up.

"Mr. McFarlane." Bill got out to greet the new foreman. "Let's get to the hotel."

"They'll no be serving," McFarlane pointed out.

"No. No for a drink." Bill laughed, but he was offended by the assumption. He knew Andrew was a teetotaler. "Tea and a fire is what's needed. It's dreich and there's that much rain over here, I'm thinking Noah would have had his ark built before I get these houses done. Well, no use girning, let's get by the fire and see if we can figure a way out."

Back at the inn, Bill Ross and Andrew McFarlane were the only ones around, apart from Mhairi. Joanne was in their room curled up on the bed with a book, fire blazing. Sheer bliss, she thought, reading in the afternoon. The bar was dim although all the lights were on, the peat fire smoldered, with an occasional blowback smoking the room. Bill had the list of what needed doing to finish the job. The more he and the foreman looked, the more impossible seemed the task of unraveling this fankle.

"I need to hire four men for a few weeks, but there's no one to be had." Bill pointed to the schedule. "But I'm now certain there's something going on. Shenanigans with deliveries, men walking off the site, it stinks to high heaven. And the name Findlay Grieg keeps coming up."

At that, Andrew McFarlane's eyes went greener. "What have you heard?"

"You yourself said the men left the site because there's no materials. The supplier swore the shipment was sent three weeks since, but it's stuck in Kyle, nothing to do with him." And he wants paying, Bill didn't say. "I'm away over to see for myself. And thon local firm that didn't get the contract are passing the word to others, so I hear, to not cooperate with us."

"So, if the job's no on time, the second bidders'll hope to pick up the contract."

"Aye, I've seen it all before. No doubt I'll see it again." And I've done it maself, Bill did not say. "But Grieg? What's thon sleikit manny going to get out of it?"

"I did hear he's building what he calls a lodge, for visitors, with fancy rooms and shooting and fishing and all laid on," Mr. McFarlane contributed, "for the Yanks and suchlike that want to return to the home of their ancestors."

"Done wi' favors for favors, I'll bet." Bill looked dour. "The lady owner of this place is a right gossip, *and* she has no time for Mr. Grieg, so I hear. Maybe I can charm some information out of her."

McFarlane laughed, partly in admiration and partly in disapproval.

"I've no doubt you'll work your usual spell. Anyhow, you'll no be needing me the now. I'll leave you to sort it out. One way or another."

As soon as he said it, he regretted his choice of words. One way or another was exactly what Bill would do. Unlike himself, he knew Bill had few problems with the niceties.

Come to think of it, he told himself on his way home, Bill Ross and Findlay Grieg deserve each other.

The herring were lightly fried in oatmeal, plump and juicy. Golden Wonder potatoes, yellow, fluffy, had a nutlike flavor; the swedes were fragrant, the moist orange flesh mashed with hand-churned butter; a simple, delicious, traditional west-coast meal. Bill ate in silence. He had always liked his food and nothing beat herring. Joanne waited for Bill to tell her of his meeting. He didn't.

"That was lovely, thank you." Joanne smiled at Mhairi as she cleared the table.

"Can I get you anything else?"

"A pot of tea would be nice."

Mhairi was delighted. Someone had noticed her cooking. This was a singular occurrence in her two years at the hotel. She brought them a tea tray, banked up the fire and prepared for closing. The few earlier customers were long gone. Joanne wished her good night and took the tray upstairs, leaving Bill alone at the bar.

"I'll be right behind you," he promised. He ordered a half gill, then another. A third glass was served before Bill felt comfortable.

"What is it about this place? Why does everyone shut you out? What's wrong with the people over here?"

Polishing the glasses while she waited for him to finish up, Mhairi did the barmaid's listen, one ear on the customer, the other on the ticking clock. Bill was becoming maudlin and she wanted to go home.

"I'm being frozen out. They didn't want an outsider on this job. No supplies. Men quit. Foreman quit. A plot, that's what it is. Thon Grieg has got me, no two ways about that."

This disjointed dialogue was between himself and his whisky, that Mhairi knew, but the name made her all ears. "Mr. Findlay Grieg?"

"The one and only."

The third dram and the long day finally won. He bade Mhairi good night and stumbled up the stairs.

Two thoughts stayed with Mhairi from that night and the thoughts burrowed like wee black moles into her nights: Mr. Findlay Grieg, she knew more than enough about him; and Joanne Ross, a nice woman, kind, she'd like to ask her for help, but could she be trusted?

The lintel of the door frame was especially low. Bill hit his head as he came into the room. Cursing, he dropped onto the bed and scrabbled around trying to pull off his boots and clothes. Joanne had turned out the bedside light and lay beneath the eiderdown, pretending to sleep. He pushed his cold body up against her, icy hands running over her, whispered loudly.

"What you need is another bairn. A wee

boy. That's what you want."

A mist of secondhand whisky breath enveloped her, killing desire stone dead.

They left the inn early, the dawn pewter-flat from an absence of light. Bill whistled as he drove, Joanne silent, desperately trying to recall dates. A pregnancy would close the trap.

Up and over the bealach, back down the hairpin bends, a right turn to the sea, and the van reached the fishing port and the ferry crossing to Skye. Sea, sky and land faded in and out on a melting horizon. An occasional distant darker gray suggested an island. Buildings huddled along on the foreshore, shape-shifting in the rain.

Whitewashed terraced houses peered out at the harbor, small windows grudgingly allowing some light in. Seagulls kept up a perpetual screech that periodically rose to hysteria pitch when buckets of guts were tipped into the waters of the harbor. Picturesque in summer, it was bleak the other ten and a half months of the year.

"Mrs. Watt? I'm Joanne Ross, and this is my husband, Bill. We stayed at your lovely hotel last night."

"Come in, come in, the both of you. Mhairi told me to expect you."

They were shown into the front parlor, where they stood around awkwardly until she returned with the tea. She bustled about, a mother hen of a woman. Mrs. Ina Watt saw herself a true Highlander, a hospitable woman, originally came from Dingwall in Easter Ross.

"Bill, you explain." Joanne prayed that Bill wouldn't offend the woman by relating any of his inexhaustible fund of Dingwall small-town jokes. He could safely joke about their football team. Everyone knew they were a disgrace.

She knew that Bill didn't want her here when he talked to Mrs. Watt. It would cramp his style. He would have to tone down the color, stick to the truth, go easy on the waffle. He was not an analytical man, emotions were foreign territory, talking was for passing on information, charming people, telling a story, having a joke. Meaningful conversations were for women. Margaret McLean had once remarked to Joanne that had Scottish men been gifted with the graces of Rudolph Valentino, they might be forgiven, but with a culture of claymores instead of scimitars, what could you expect?

He told Mrs. Watt most of the story but left out the bank, the final, final letters, the missed appointments with the manager. The story was new to Joanne too. This was the first time she had heard Bill put all the pieces in joined up talking. After seeing the ghost of a building site, she had worked most of it out for herself. That the situation was close to desperate was now clear.

Mrs. Watt waited until Bill had finished, then asked, "Do you fancy a wee dram in yer tea? I know it's a bit early but it'll warm you up."

Joanne covered her cup in refusal; Bill held his out. A hefty slug did indeed warm him up and he fancied that Mrs. Watt, as she turned to put the bottle back, did likewise to her own cup.

"What a day." She began, using the convention of a conversation on the weather before deciding how much to tell. "I don't mind the cold. I like the snow. But this dreich mist, it gets in everywhere. If it keeps up, I'll be back to the east coast before long. Drier, you know. There's not much to keep us here this time of year. We do a good trade in bed-and-breakfast but only in the summer. Course we'll no take single men nor seamen, respectable folk only."

She blethered on while Bill sipped his fortified tea and Joanne warmed herself by the fire. The pain from her thawing hands and feet, almost frostbitten on the drive over, was now a warm tingle.

"Willie, my man, he'll be sorry to have missed you, Mr. Ross. He's away over to Skye to look at some cobals. We're thinking of setting up a business hiring them out to visitors as sea loch fishing is getting popular in these parts."

"We just dropped by to bring you the list of the messages Mhairi needs. We must be setting off back home soon, before it gets dark." Joanne was desperate to get the woman to return to the point of their visit.

"How's Mhairi managing? I hope she looked after you? More tea?" Mrs. Watt tucked the list into her apron. She continued to blether, a burn on its way to the sea; restless, relentless, determinedly tumbling over any object in its way.

"Thon man from over your way, Mr. Grieg, Mr. High and Mighty I call him, he's going into the fishing business too. It's a whatjemaca'it, a lodge. Rowan Lodge. I ask you. Like in Canada, he says."

Bill had been sitting there, a glaikit look on his face. It took him a moment to realize what Mrs. Watt was on about as he had shut off many sentences earlier.

"And the midges over there, they're that bad, thon peat bog's no place for visitors. Well, I says to him, with all the money you've put into the place, I hope you get something back. It'll be fine, he says, as bold as brass. Got my contacts, he says. I know all about his contacts. Disgraceful. And my Mhairi says he's no playing fair wi' you neither. The man's got no shame. More tea?"

There had been no need for Joanne's intervention; wait long enough and Mrs. Watt would tell you the antecedents of every family in both the shires.

"I'm in trouble, Mrs. Watt." Bill needed to keep the conversation on his concerns. He switched the charm back on. "I need someone who knows about these things to put me straight. I might end up losing everything."

"You poor soul. It's no about thon council houses is it?"

Bill nodded.

"Aye, I thought as much." And she was off again. "Now I'm no a gossip, but I can't stand that manny. An' the builder, a local man as you know, nice enough fellow but no much of a thinker, Grieg has him in his pocket. All the work done on thon lodge thingy is at cost price or nearly, so I hear, in the hope of council work to come. County council work, but Mr. Grieg is only town council. Queer that! And it all must be costing a pretty penny. All swanky inside, so I hear, tartan carpets and the like. Rowan Lodge, I ask you!"

"But what's Grieg up to exactly?" Bill was dying of curiosity.

"Exactly?" That stopped her. "How should I know?" She realized her tongue had got the better of her. "I'm no a gossip."

Joanne turned to Bill. "I could look up the planning notice in the *Gazette* archives."

"The *Highland Gazette*?"

"Aye, I work there."

"You have a job?" Mrs. Watt looked at Joanne again. "Now I know why you're so anxious about this contract. It's aye hard to make ends meet when you have bairns. My man has always been able to look after me but I won't pretend that he could run our wee B and B business without me."

All this did not go down well with Bill.

"But tell me," she started up again, "tell me about the wee boy that drowned and thon Polish sailor, you being in the know and all. How could he do that? Kill a bairn? Mind you, them foreigners —"

Bill raised his arm in an exaggerated arc and looked at his watch. "We haven't time to sit around and gossip."

"Gossip? Me gossip? I don't know anything about anything. I'm no one to gossip."

"But I thought you said Grieg —"

"Thought's a fine thing. I've said nothing. Nothing at all. Look now, there's a wee gap in the weather. See? Best take advantage of it. It's a long drive back and it'll be dark by four thirty. Nice to meet you. Cheery-bye."

Before they could get a word in, they were out the door, out on the pavement, in the fine misty rain. Joanne looked at Bill and rolled her eyes before making her way back to the van.

The fine mist and rain made visibility poor. As they slowly followed the road south along the sea loch, the peaks of the Five Sisters were only a memory, a mark on the map. After about fifteen miles a painted sign appeared at the bottom of a rough track. Lurid pink and silver salmon were leaping over the lettering that proclaimed *Rowan Lodge.* And in the space of a few minutes the mist evaporated, the sun shot through the breaks between clouds, the mountains appeared again to take up their usual positions as a backdrop and there on a small rise perched a building. It looked painted onto the landscape. With 360-degree views to the sea, the islands, the mountains behind and beyond, the size of the construction made Bill whistle.

"Some lodge!" Joanne too, was awed.

They drove up and parked. The long two-story building, with a grand entrance and reception rooms plumb in the middle, was in local stone with a slate roof. A grand stone terrace big enough to turf over for a bowling green was almost finished. Sounds of hammering on stone and wood echoed around the grandiose foyer and up the elaborate wooden staircase.

A painter, previously contracted to Bill's project, was varnishing the wood paneling that covered the lower part of the walls. No doubt his colleagues were around. At least the workman had the decency to look shamefaced.

Bill walked around the building site, taking his time, estimating the square feet of it, checking everything. And running his hand over the oak banisters, admiring the hand-forged railings, estimating the amount of slate and of stone, noting the expanse of glass and stained glass windows fit for a cathedral, and gilt-framed paintings of stags at bay or highland cattle, Bill was all the while making a mental calculation on the cost of the project. And when he reached the conservative side of a breathtaking total he knew he had been outfoxed. Yet in some part of him, he was full of admiration for the gall of the man. And jealous.

Their journey home was quiet. Through the light of an almost full moon, the final stretch, before the road descended to the east coast, had the added danger of wandering sheep suddenly appearing in the middle of the road. Broken walls of deserted crofts showed up as dark shadows on the hillsides. During the Clearances, this drovers' route from the west came to be known as Desolation Road, the evicted and often starving clansmen herded to the emigrant ships or to the poorhouse. The very rocks of the drove roads had witnessed and retained the sorrow of the desperate human exodus, sending the Highlanders to form diasporas in Canada and America and New Zealand and Glasgow, Joanne remembered, and the stories, the history and the mountain ridges seemed to press in on the passing van. Bill too felt the weight of the day, but he put it down to the weather.

On the final miles along the shore back into town, Joanne insisted on calling in to Bill's parents to kiss the girls good night. But they were asleep.

"How was the trip?" Grandad Ross asked

as she came into the sitting room.

"Grand, but the weather was winter one minute and summer the next."

"I'll put the kettle on." Granny Ross put her knitting aside and rose.

"I'd love to but Bill's waiting."

"He's outside?" Grandad Ross was not happy. "Well, if he can't be bothered coming in to see his own mother and father, he'll just have to wait."

"He's tired after the long drive." She was too tired to come up with the usual elaborate excuses for her husband.

"He needs a good talking-to, that son of mine."

"How were the girls? Did they behave?"

"Wee angels they were."

Granny Ross rolled her eyes at this.

"Saturday matinee, Wee Jean wanted to go home early," Grandad told her, "frightened by the big boys shouting." The sound of her shrieks still echoed around in his head. "Mind you, the film *was* a bit scary and she has such an imagination."

"That's more Annie's trouble than Jean's." Joanne laughed.

She managed to extricate herself after five minutes, knowing that Bill would be furious at being kept waiting but even more furious at his own cowardice, his own shame whenever he had to face his father. His mother might forgive him anything, but his father saw everything.

"See you in the morning at church. Night." She shivered, pulled her coat tight against the cold and walked down the path to her husband and a decision. Standing at the front door, the sight of his son's van annoyed Grandad Ross yet again. We've all been through some things that don't bear thinking about, he thought, we all have had to put behind us the death of friends, the horror of the past; there are two generations of us with memories we have to live with, it's no excuse, he thought, fuming.

"George, shut the door, there's a terrible draft," Granny Ross called out from the sitting room.

That son of mine, I despair of him, he thought as he took a last look at the Milky Way. He admired Joanne, a grand lass, he told everyone. But something was not right in their household, he knew that. He also knew to hold his tongue. Look out for the girls, he told himself, that's all I can do. Then, for the thousandth time, the memory of the morning's outing to the cinema came back to plague him.

Grandad Ross was a practical man. He

worked at the iron foundry, a good steady job. After surviving the First World War all he had wanted he now had — a quiet life, a shed and a bicycle. His escapes were the weekly trips to the library to satisfy his unquenchable thirst for cowboy books — Westerns was the only section he ever visited — and a regular outing to a film at any of the three cinemas in town that were showing Westerns, especially John Wayne films. His idea of America was in shades of red and yellow. Not like the Highlands, where he pictured everything in shades of gray and brown and green with occasional flashes of brightness breaking through.

The Saturday-morning children's matinee at the Palace he enjoyed as much as his granddaughters did. Probably more than Wee Jean, he acknowledged; she found it intimidating but loved going anywhere with her grandad. The Lone Ranger was his favorite, followed by Zorro, the Masked Avenger. He liked Charlie Chaplin but loved Buster Keaton. The adventure serial made especially for children he didn't mind but he couldn't abide *Lassie*. Not that he would ever say so — it was Wee Jean's favorite.

This Saturday morning it was the usual bedlam. The front rows below the screen was a no-go area; a seething tangle of wrestling boys lit by the ghostly flickering of the black-and-white film on a worthy topic, or a topic of interest to adults and girls, they ignored, waiting for the action to resume. At a distance they seemed indistinguishable from a freshly landed catch of giant squid.

The noise, like the keening of a storm at sea, made it difficult to hear the dialogue. The entrance of a well-known character, particularly a baddie, made the noise swell to hurricane force. Banging the seats up and down in time to the cowboys chasing the Indians, screaming out to a character to "mind yer back" or "kill him dead" or yelling "eeugh" when the hero smiled at the heroine, all swelled the racket loud enough to be heard across the river.

Running, scampering, scuttling like rats in a pack, up and down the aisles, dodging the outstretched arms of the usherettes, the boys would make a break for the toilets in small groups, off to sneak a fag bought in packets of five or to open the safety doors to let in their chums who didn't have the sixpence to get in. But first they had to evade the clutches of the manager as he patrolled the aisles. An ex–military policeman, he was nicknamed Ping after the Elastic Man, but he was Elastic Man with a moustache and a terrifying sergeant-major bellow, which he used at close range to yell right into the eardrum of any boy whom he managed to snare. His ability to reach out and trap a boy by an arm, an ear or the elastic of their shorts was legendary. In the town, he was known as a nice man. He gave a generous discount to members of the British Legion, showed popular, not-quite-first-release films, with good old-fashioned British war films a specialty. Parents liked him too. The sixpence it cost to be rid of their children, particularly on dreich winter Saturdays, was money well spent.

The girls, they were altogether another story. The older ones, around twelve or thirteen, Annie watched with envy. She memorized the moves; the flick of the hair, the smoothing down of the starched-petticoat-full skirts, the sashay up or down the aisles guessing, no, *knowing,* that when *she* reached that age, she would never quite make it into a clique. At nine she just *knew* she had that hidden mark, that unquantifiable air about her that made her not quite right to join in, to belong. Arm in arm, two by two, went the girls sneaking a look to make sure of an audience, floating down the aisles, off to the toilets, never alone, as being best friends meant coordinating your bladder clock, and there they would meet up with other best-friend couples, to then stand in front of the big smoked brown mirrors, to practice blowing bubblegum. They had not yet reached an age where they were clever enough to talk about other girls. But their silence toward someone outside their group was just as eloquent.

This Saturday morning seemed more subdued than usual. Grandad left Wee Jean in her sister's care, told them he was going out to the foyer to rest his ears, promised to bring back some sweeties, and while he had the chance, he had a sly cigarette. Two puffs later, the heavy swing doors flew open, letting out a blast of noise and an anxious usherette. The doors opened out a second time. Annie emerged dragging a shaking Wee Jean, who was mewling like a sackful of kittens sensing the river.

"The hoodie crow! It'll get us. The hoodie crow. I saw it!"

Annie was shaking her sister, hissing in her ear, "Don't tell! Don't say anything! Don't!"

Seeing her grandad, the little girl ran to him, clutched him around the legs, taking great big gulps of air between sobs and heartbreaking, keening wails.

"There, there." Grandad did his best. "There, there, ma wee pet." Wee Jean was exhausted with fear. Her cries were now hiccoughing sobs. "Grandad, Grandad."

The usherette hovered helplessly flapping her hands. "It's all right, dear, it's just a fillum."

"Sorry 'bout that," Grandad apologized.

"Not at all. She's a bit too young, that's all."

Annie said nothing. But she was as white as Zorro was dark. That was the villain of the piece, that was who had set her sister off, Zorro.

They walked out to a darkening sky and a darkening river.

"We'll get an ice cream. But don't tell your granny. Ice cream is a Sunday treat."

"But can we still have ice cream tomorrow?" Jean managed to get out.

"Of course. But mind . . . sssh!" He held a finger to his lips. "Our secret."

Grandad Ross, a grandchild's hand in each of his, crossed the main road to the café.

"What was that all about?" he muttered, furious at himself for leaving the child. His wife was right, his stories of hoodie crows and trows and witches and faeries *were* too frightening for wee ones. His favorite rhyme, "At the Back o' Bennachie," sung with great gusto, was about a mother who had lost her two sons.

Oh, one was killed at Huntly Fair,
And the ither was drowned in the Dee,
    oh.

What was he thinking of, he asked himself. He knew Jean had not been herself, nor Annie, both of them had been subdued, nervy as spooked horses when they sensed the Indians surrounding the corral. They had been like this ever since their wee friend, the wee boy, Jamie wasn't it, since he had drowned. And again, Jean was harping on about a blasted hoodie crow. All his fault.

"Grandad, it was nothing." Annie looked up at him. "Really. It was just Zorro, in his mask and all. It scared her." She didn't mention that it had scared the life out of her too. She too saw what her sister saw — the hoodie crow.

And when they reached the other side of the road they saw that the café was closed, firmly shuttered; the usually bright happy corner of light and cheer and ice cream was as dark as the rest of the day.

NINE

Rob was running up the lane toward the *Gazette* office when he saw McAllister up ahead. He caught up with him but instead of going inside, McAllister took Rob by the elbow and led him to the entrance of a close that ran between and under the building in the three-story terrace built circa 1680. The smell of damp earth put Rob in mind of a grave. The door at the far end led to stairs going down into the basement and sub-basements where the machinery was housed. It baffled Rob how the machinery got down there; he half-believed Don's story that the building had been constructed around the printing press. And the printers came with it, Rob had quipped, only to be hit on the head with a rolled-up *Gazette*.

Back against the wall, legs crossed, McAllister produced a packet of Passing Clouds, offered one to Rob. Rob refused.

McAllister struck a match on a patch of stonework, pink with enough phosphor to blow up the building. Generations of journalists and printers had sheltered in this exact spot, to smoke, to contemplate the weather and the state of the nation. This same refuge had probably been used to discuss the progress of the battle of Culloden or Waterloo, or to form the elaborate union rules, zealously enforced by the father of the chapel, that were a bane to journalists everywhere.

"So. Tell me." McAllister blew the smoke through his nostrils like the proverbial dragon. "Hoodie crows?"

"Big, black and scary," Rob shot back.

McAllister made a fair impression of Robert Mitchum squinting down the length of the cigarette.

"Actually," Rob continued, "I was thinking on the same thing myself a wee while ago. Joanne said the girls were adamant; a hoodie crow picked up the boy and took him off. But now, for some reason, they won't talk about it. Don thinks it's all wee girls' havers. But my mother is not so sure. And I got to thinking. . . ."

"A conspiracy of crows," McAllister muttered. "Is that the collective noun? I know it's a parliament of rooks." He threw the butt into the gutter. "What else have you heard?"

"Best ask Joanne."

"Aye, probably best." Though he wasn't certain that it was. Joanne had been uncharacteristically unpredictable lately. The usual cacophony of bells struck nine. "We've thirty seconds to get to the Monday meeting on time."

"Race you up the stairs."

Rob was off before he could see the expression on McAllister's face.

Me? Race? he thought. Me — the Grand Panjandrum of the *Highland Gazette*? *And* a two-pack-a-day man?

"Let's get started." Don was in the chair at the head of the table. Rob was perched on the edge of the table. Joanne was slumped on a stool, elbows on the table. McAllister was leaning back, the chair balanced on two legs and at that delicate angle where a degree or two more and he and the chair would go tumbling.

"McAllister?"

"I've nothing that's fit to print — yet."

Don rolled his eyes. "Well, whatever you write, can you make it more relevant? No more xenophobia stories. Most of our readers had to look that one up in the dictionary

— if they could be bothered, that is. As for your lecture on Suez — putting the prime minister in his place, your diatribe on Hungary, your campaign on Scottish independence and I don't know what else besides, I've told you, we're a *local* paper, we report on *local* news. We don't investigate, we don't write about stuff that's none of our concern —"

"So tell me, where do *you* go for a fish supper now that the local vigilantes have targeted the Corelli business? All the way across town to Eastgate?" He didn't get het up, he didn't raise his voice, but the passion swept the room like a sirocco from the Sahara. "Isn't this how it started on the Continent? Isn't this what we fought against?"

"Aye, all right, all right, you've got me." Don held his hands up in surrender. "But please, no words of more than two syllables. And no being a cleverclogs wi' your quotes in Latin."

"I did Latin," Rob volunteered.

"So did I," Joanne added.

"Aye, but can you box the compass or calculate the odds for the three thirty at Ayr? Or do anything useful with all your learning? No. So, what next?"

"Follow up on the Polish gentleman in gaol?"

"Enough of that for now." Rob looked disappointed. "Leave it with me, though, I'll fish around," Don promised. "I've heard that the detective from down south has arrived. Maybe your contact in the polis" — at the word *contact* he wiggled his eyebrows — "maybe she can tell you more. For now, get the sports done and check if there's anything other than drunk and disorderly at the sheriff's court. Joanne?"

"The usual. There is one thing, though . . . but it's not news."

"Let me be the judge o' that," McAllister interjected.

"Well, when Bill and I were out west, we came across the new scheme that Mr. Findlay Grieg has going. It's a great big hunting and shooting and fishing affair with at least twenty rooms. Mr. Grieg calls it a lodge. Bill says it would cost a mint to build."

McAllister whistled. "That *is* news. Has anyone seen the planning application?"

"I was going to check at the county council." Joanne was slightly hesitant, assuming that one of the others, the professionals, would take over the story, if it became a story.

"Good thinking. You do that. Get a copy

of the planning application. I'd be very interested in whose name the application was made. Don here would certainly have noticed if it was in Mr. Grieg's name."

Joanne sat up straighter than she had done for a while.

"Another thing, Joanne: hoodie crows?"

Don groaned. "You're off with the faeries again. Hoodie crows! I'll leave you to it. Some of us have real work to do." He waved a pile of copy at them and left.

"He thinks it's all wee girls' havers," Joanne told McAllister.

"I love the story of Annie ringing the doorbells." Rob reached for his motorbike jacket. "I'm off to collect the football reports. See ya."

"Right, Mrs. Ross, from the beginning, doorbells, hoodie crows, the lot."

Joanne smiled. "Well, that afternoon he disappeared, my girls were coming home from school with Jamie, the boy that drowned, or was killed, well . . ."

McAllister was back in his office, feet up, cigarette in hand. He thought over Joanne's story. He didn't agree with Don. There was something that bothered him about the girls' story. He reached for the phone. Mr. Frank Clark the headmaster; if anyone would know anything, it would be him. He put the phone back in the cradle. Better to talk face-to-face. He'd walk over to the school.

Hoodie crows; thoughts of them accompanied his walk down through the old part of town, past churches and shops and bars, past the back of the market and the auction rooms, left at another church, to the stone stairs, the treads of which were bow-shaped by centuries of people making their way down to the river. The vista to the north of the town was framed by the buildings, and the resemblance to a Victorian etching was made all the more authentic by the churchyard and moss-covered gravestones that lined the stairway to the right. Farmland covering the distant hills formed the backdrop of the picture. Friesian cows were mere specks in this landscape. McAllister could visualize them; heads down, obsessed with the rich green grass, occasionally looking up, they would ruminate to the spectacular views of the firth and the town and the distant haze of moorland and history.

The pedestrian suspension bridge across the river not so much swayed as buckled, wind blasting into his right ear. Walking the short distance to the school he kept shaking his head, trying to dislodge the evil vacuum where the wind had managed to penetrate right through the eardrum.

The school was the usual intimidating late-Victorian Gothic of the 1880s but seventy years later, mature wild cherry and sycamore trees softened the gaunt structure. Their roots had escaped up through the tarmacadam in many places; covered by fallen leaves and the propellers of sycamore seeds, they tripped the unwary. They scared Wee Jean; she thought of them as tree fingers, tunneling their way up through the earth, searching for the rapturous light, like the illustration of the Resurrection in her Sunday school picture book.

During the day, the school echoed to the ebb and flow of five hundred children. The smell of generations of pupils, of damp wool, forgotten gym shoes, of stale milk and school dinners and carbolic soap, reminded McAllister of his own primary; the same high windows you could never see out of even when you stood on top of your desk, the same school hall, where the morning assembly, with obligatory prayers, reading of announcements and the occasional public belting of the worst offenders, took place. And the same feeling that no matter how clear your conscience, you might be picked out and punished for an offense you couldn't remember committing. Or worse, you could be nominated for some mention or award or prize, the result of which was at the very least a Chinese burn from the other boys come playtime.

He walked through the hall that doubled as the gym. Supervised by their teacher, following the instruction sheets, children would exercise to the music broadcast on the Home Service of the BBC. In thousands of schools, tens of thousands of children jumped as one to the fruity voice of the announcer, setting the kingdom all atremble, the calisthenics and marching done, out of time, to the tune of "The Grand Old Duke of York." He was swamped by memories, and he shuddered.

"Hello. Can I help you? Oh, Mr. McAllister, it's yourself."

Frank Clark's voice cut short the reverie. McAllister had met the headmaster through the committees and social functions that their respective positions condemned them to. They liked what they saw and what they had heard of each other.

After the handshake and social niceties, McAllister began. "I wanted to talk about the boy."

"Jamie."

"Not for publication, just to try to understand."

Mr. Clark looked closely at his visitor. He was not about to give information for the gratuitous delight of the morbid. He'd already had the tabloids onto him.

"Such a tragedy. I've never come across the like before." Frank Clark started. "Of course the children are distressed, as we all are. The Ross girls in particular."

"Joanne Ross? Her children?"

"Sorry, none of our business. But I thought she'd have said, you working together."

McAllister rubbed his face with both hands. "Of course, her children were the last to see the boy." He shook his head, trying to settle the mind shift. He was uncomfortable with the way the conversation was heading. "Mrs. Ross told me about the interview with Inspector Tompson and the hoodie crow story."

"Annie lives in a fantasy most of the time. But that's typical of children in her situation."

McAllister could not quite fathom what that meant but let it go.

"Mrs. Ross has gumption," Mr. Clark continued. "The job at the *Gazette,* I get

233

the feeling that gives her the lifeline she needs."

McAllister had the feeling the conversation was at cross-purposes.

"Do you think her children know what happened?" He brought the conversation back to the point of his visit.

"No. But with children, they may not talk directly, but read their stories, look at their paintings, you soon see if there are problems, fears. In wartime, children draw planes dropping bombs, soldiers, guns, blood, all the usual catastrophes. Normally, in a town like this, they paint their family, nice houses with flowers, cats and dogs, blue skies with a big sun. Lucky them. But some show a darker element. Dark skies, rivers colored red, fire, and people standing apart, no hands joined like in most family portraits. I'm no psychologist but even I can see the effect that violence in a family can have on children. The girls walked home with Jamie, he disappears, and because they are already disturbed, they make up an explanation."

"And what's that?"

"That he, Jamie, was grabbed by a hoodie crow. It's an explanation for the unexplainable. They can't fathom that he disappeared into thin air, then was found in the canal, where he would never go of his own free will, so they rationalize, fantasize. That's my explanation. But, who knows?" He paused. "Look, I can't discuss my pupils' family matters, but you know Joanne Ross, you know her situation . . ."

McAllister was not about to reveal that he had only recently realized something was amiss and had ignored it as not his business.

". . . all I can say is, I'm used to Annie Ross being a storyteller. Her sister is a timid wee soul, but she too says she saw a hoodie crow. Whether she is following her big sister or not, I don't know. But you know how children are, and I don't know about you southerners, but here in the Highlands the hoodie crow as a metaphor for evil is a common tale."

"Aye, I've heard something of that."

"It was, is, a tale used to scare children. Like ghosts and bogies and faeries, our children are brought up with all these nefarious creatures hiding under the bed. For all our television and brave new world, this place still has its Celtic roots. Stories of crows pecking out the eyes of newborn lambs, well, it's not that long ago that this town was fringed with working farms. And then there are all the other superstitions used to scare wee ones —"

"Jamie's parents say he would never go near water."

"Terrified. He wouldn't even walk across the suspension bridge to swimming lessons. He also had bad asthma, the chlorine at the swimming baths set him off, so he was excused."

"I'm not trying to do the job of the police but there is something here that feels wrong. Or rather, the arrest of the Polish sailor feels too convenient."

"I did have some terrible suspicions myself," Frank Clark confessed. "So I was relieved that the sailor was arrested, relieved that my worst nightmares were unfounded."

McAllister always found that the best way to elicit a story from those he was interviewing was to say nothing. Or at least look slightly perplexed. The explanation would surely follow.

"I know you know the situation —"

McAllister didn't but he gave a slight nod.

"— and I can trust you to be discreet —"

Another nod.

"— but at the time, well, I thought Annie Ross knew a lot more than she was saying." He paused, considered whether to continue but knew he must, if he was to get a good night's sleep. This thought had been gnawing away at him, asleep and awake; he needed to talk it through, if only to be laughed at. And he had no fear of McAllister's mockery. He instinctively knew that the man sitting before him would give his fears due consideration and a measured opinion.

"I was terrified Annie Ross might have pushed him into the canal."

"So you're not one of those who is scared to think the unthinkable." McAllister posed this less as a question, more as an observation. He too had been so accused. He too had dared to think the unthinkable, to accuse an untouchable.

"Well, I'm not sure *how* involved the child is, but she certainly knows something." Frank Clark gave a grim smile. "It's quite a relief to know I am not the only one who can suspect even the most innocent in our society."

"I was with the International Brigade in Spain," McAllister simply said. "And, I'm from Glasgow."

On his walk back to town, McAllister watched a gang of boys, newly released from school, swarming like ants over a half-demolished house, searching for firewood. Halloween was only a week away. It was the time of year, as much as the conversation with Mr. Clark, that added to his sense of foreboding. The ever-present image of another boy, another poor soul, drowned, this time in a river, not a canal, a boy whom McAllister had had to identify, came welling up like bile.

The talk of ghosts hadn't helped. The stairs he was walking up, the lanes where he took a shortcut, the Town House, the castle, the very cobblestones; like every place in Scotland they were soaked in history and ghosts.

"You're getting maudlin, McAllister," he chivvied himself. "Time you took a break, a trip home, a few days, take the train, back to my own ghosts, aye, and a beer or two in my own pub."

"Mrs. Ross, a word before you leave?"

He never quite knew how to address her. "Mrs. Ross" was normal office etiquette but the intimacy of that dance at the Highland Ball had him thinking of her as Joanne.

"Certainly, Mr. McAllister."

Her reply and her smile turned it back on him. Joanne it would be.

"Joanne, I've been thinking on what your girls know about the disappearance of the wee boy." There was never any need to say which boy.

"I know. But they'll never say anything now." She offered no more of an explanation.

"I had a talk with Frank Clark. He worries about Annie in particular."

"Oh really? You were discussing my child with the headmaster?"

"No, well, not really," he said, floundering. "I was trying to find out more about what happened that day."

"Why? You have as much of the story as anyone. Besides, it's all over. The man who did it is in jail."

"Look, Joanne —"

"Look yourself, Mr. McAllister. You and Mr. Clark have no right discussing my daughter." She caught his flush. "Or my family. I work here. That doesn't give you the right to stand in judgment."

"It wasn't like that."

"No? You have no idea what it's like in this town. You have no idea what I have had to go through. The talk, the snide looks, the pity. That's the worst of it — pity. And this job, a job I love and a job I think I could be good at —"

He nodded. "Of course you're good. You're —"

"— you have no idea what I go through to

keep working here." She was standing, back to him, holding on to the windowsill, not seeing the rolling clouds and darkening sky. She took a huge breath. "I get enough from my mother-in-law and the fishwifies I live amongst." She breathed out. "I hear it all the time," she said quietly, "a woman working, a woman not suffocating at the kitchen sink, it's just not done." She turned. "I've even had to stop wearing slacks to placate my mother-in-law." She leaned on his desk and looked straight at him. "I put up with enough without you gossiping about me."

She left his office, she left the building, she collected her bike, she pedaled across town and she kept up her anger, almost all the way home, before giving in to despair on the final hundred yards.

"I can't leave him. I can't walk out. If they talk about me now, think how much worse it will be. And where would I go? I can't put the girls through the disgrace. I can't leave. I can't put the girls through any more. I must stay. For their sakes. I can't leave. For their sakes."

It was a strange and strained week. Even Don noticed the distance between Joanne and McAllister. Rob used it as an excuse to stay out of the office as much as possible.

He now dutifully sat in the courtroom attempting to pay attention; drunk and disorderly, assault (fighting after the football), drunk in charge of a horse, cycling without lights. One charge, stealing fishing nets, broke the monotony, as no one in court could understand the Peterhead accents.

His mind wandered, remembering Don's suggestion that he quiz WPC Ann McPherson on the detective chief inspector newly arrived to oversee the investigation. He also remembered that Sunday at the seaside.

"Seaside in October, we must be mad," Ann had laughed. She was not happy at being seen with Rob around town, scared that Inspector Tompson might spot them. He was happy for the excuse to take the bike to the seaside town of Nairn, with a good seventeen miles of flat straight road to open up the throttle on the bike and stretch the speed limit with only the level crossing halfway to slow them. The wind, straight off the North Sea, gave them a good excuse to shelter in the dunes beneath his jacket. But Ann kept complaining of the sand getting in everywhere.

"Next case." The shout of the court usher made him jump. He had missed the verdict. A fine, and bound over to keep the peace, the fishermen would no doubt sort it out themselves and be back in court next week.

"Driving whilst incapable" was next. Rob was too young to find a wooden bench uncomfortable, and the courtroom kept reminding him of the case that was on everyone's mind. But Karl unpronounceable would not be tried here, Rob reminded himself; no, that would be in the full panoply of the High Court; the peripatetic advocates and judge from Edinburgh would preside over the theater that that trial was sure to be.

Don was not convinced that Karl could have killed the boy, didn't like the timing nor the geography of it, he said. McAllister found the arrest too convenient. But no one quite knew the details of the case that Inspector Tompson had made to the procurator fiscal. Rob had asked, but Ann McPherson was not telling.

But who else could have done it? Rob reasoned. Nothing really bad went on in a cut-off place like this, so it has to be a stranger, he rationalized.

A general shuffling and rearranging and the next case, a boundary dispute between crofters, a dispute that had been simmering for forty-seven years, now started.

Half listening, practicing his shorthand, or hieroglyphics as Don called it, Rob went off into another dwam. I'll be out of here one day — of this he was sure — off to the big city, and then . . . He turned to a new page of his notebook, but instead of following the case before the court, he started to write like an automaton at a séance. He printed the boy's name, JAMIE, at the top of the page. Start at the beginning, write down what you know, wasn't that what McAllister was always harping on about? So . . .

The boy — on his way home from school — disappeared down the road from the McLean bungalow. Hold on, Rob told himself, start again — the boy — walking home — with his friends Annie and Jean — playing at ringing doorbells. Next morning — first light — he was found drowned. No, that's not right. Rob added a line — dead before he went into the water. He printed BEFORE.

Another page. CANAL LOCK, he headed the new page, half a mile from where he was last seen. Right, what next? Rob pictured the track leading to the canal towpath and the locks. Lined with elder bushes, and stands of whin and gorse, there was not much cover there. The stretch of road where the boy had disappeared was a much more likely place to grab a small child. The Victorian and Edwardian mansions sat in large grounds, the curved driveways hiding the houses from passersby, quiet, ideal for the setting of a Sherlock Holmes or Agatha Christie mystery. When he was little he had thought of one of them as a Scottish version of Bleak House. The mature sycamores, the oak and the beech trees, one magnificent copper beech, a holly tree or two, a stand of firs where he used to collect cones for the McLean household fire — his mother loved the scent — chestnut trees, at this time of year thick with conkers and after school, thick with boys collecting said conkers, this veritable urban forest would provide great cover for nefarious deeds.

Then there were the rhododendrons, a favorite of Edwardian gardeners, which with the soil of Scotland, not much different from their Himalayan home, had flourished. High roundels of dark green, with dark dry caves under the thick glossy leaves, it took a very heavy rain to penetrate the earth underneath. This enclave of middle-class respectability where Rob had grown up he now saw differently, changed by the knowledge of a terrible event. A great location for a horror film. Rob could see it. But a horror really did happen, he reminded himself. So . . .

A policeman had rung their doorbell, that

night, late, asking after the boy. No one had seen anything, his dad told the constable. Ringing doorbells — he smiled. His mother had tried to be cross with him, when he was wee, when a neighbor complained. He said he would stop ringing doorbells in their street, and he had. Just moved on to a street further away. A few nights ago his mother laughed, telling him about Joanne's Annie. First time he had heard of a girl playing the game. Good for her, he thought, I like her, she's brave, has a mind of her own. I wonder if she knows anything at all about what happened to Jamie. Says she doesn't, but that doesn't mean much. Except . . . Rob remembered the story of the hoodie crow — where did that come from? Maybe Annie will talk to me, her uncle Rob. I'll bribe her with a shot on the bike.

The gavel banged hard and loud. Rob switched back to the here and now; twelve o'clock, Monday, October, the sheriff's court, the mid–nineteen fifties, the Highlands of Scotland, the world.

"Twenty-eight days this time," the sheriff pronounced. "I'm sick of the sight of you every Monday morning."

The drunk looked aggrieved. "Can you no make it three months? I'll miss out on ma Christmas plum duff otherwise."

■ ■ ■ ■

They were alone in the office; the others had left a good hour since.

"I'm thinking I'll go back down south for a few days. After we've got this edition to bed, of course."

Don grunted. He wasn't not listening to McAllister; he was flicking through a sheaf of rejected copy trying to find something the right length to fill in a hole left by an advertisement dropping out — and it was five minutes before the presses were due to roll.

"It's time I saw my mother —" McAllister continued, but the phone interrupted. He reached across the reporter's desk. "*Gazette*. No, he's busy." Don was shaking his head. "No. Can you call back? All right, I'll tell him. Hold on." He put his hand over the mouthpiece. "It's your man, Mr. Burke, says it's important."

Don looked up at the clock, three minutes. He reached over for the phone.

"A bit late for you to be calling. Aye. Aye. What?" He sat abruptly. "You must be very very certain. You are?" He listened. "Christ!" More tweetering came from the receiver. "No, of course not. Not a word to anyone."

He put down the phone. McAllister waited.
  "The boy was interfered with before he died."

TEN

The glass-domed Victorian fancy-cake cathedral of a railway station never failed to impress McAllister. Platform after platform of puffing hissing engines resembling the starting gate at the racetrack, the nervous animals waiting for the off, was the first sight of the city for many arriving from the towns and villages and clachans of the Highlands and Islands.

McAllister jumped on a tram and with a lurch it clanked off through the city. The Bank of Scotland, Royal Bank, Clydesdale Bank, Corn Exchange, all the monumental edifices around George Square, were familiar landmarks. He had passed them every day as a scholarship boy off to the Glasgow High School for Boys. The glories of wealth and history were pockmarked by bomb craters, bright pink with fireweed; daytime playground for children and dogs, nighttime territory of drunks and prostitutes. The tram trundled on up Duke Street. Glimpses of the cathedral and the necropolis flashed by up the steep side streets, marble angels silhouetted against the sky, wings outstretched, awaiting a photo opportunity.

The tram halted outside Duke Street jail. The high walls as daunting as ever, songs and stories of the inmates, the executions, hung in the air; McAllister felt a frisson of childish fright that never quite went away, even in middle age. He walked swiftly up the hill to home, never lingering, never looking to left nor right, another habit from his school days, his body remembering the many kickings on these steep pavements. The uniform, especially the cap, was a shining invitation to those he'd left behind, betrayed, the high school badge marking him a traitor. And his being a Catholic in this Protestant stronghold was another reason for the terrors he had suffered as a small boy.

He rang, waited. A faint shuffling came down the hall and the door slowly opened.

"John." The flat voice revealed no surprise, no emotion.

"Mother," he replied to the woman he had not seen for over a year.

She shuffled back to her warm kitchen with the gas oven lit, the door left open.

"It's easier than fetching in coal." She nodded to the cooker.

"I'll get some. Light the fire if you like."

"Suit yerself."

McAllister left his bag and coat in the hallway, took the battered brass coal scuttle outside to their coal hole in the back green, crouching under the scant city stars to fill it. He remembered the fights with his dad about his jobs.

"I have to do my homework, Dad. It's too dark, Dad. I did it last night, Dad. And the night before. It's his turn, he never does anything."

He never ever won the argument. Never would now. His brother never made sixteen and his dad was another statistic of the fire-bombing of Clydeside; firemen, fire engines, a shipyard, all gone in one night.

The coal caught slowly. The kindling, a splintered crate, sparked blue.

"So, how's it been, Ma? Did you get my letters?"

"I'm no one for writing, you know that, John."

"I wish you'd let me get a phone in for you."

"Nobody in our street has a phone. What would the neighbors think?"

No point in arguing; he knew he'd never win.

"I'll catch up with some auld friends at the *Herald* before I go back up north."

"Oh aye." Huddling into herself, tugging her old cardigan tight, the tweed skirt wrinkled around her knees, she looked like a refugee.

A refugee from life. McAllister sighed under the weight of the thought.

"Will you be biding here long?"

"Just the two nights, if that's all right?"

"It's your home, John."

His home; from where he went to school, served his cadetship, left for a war and emerged the sole survivor of the family tragedies.

"A pint and a half."

McAllister looked around. His pals from the news desk would be in for the mid-evening break any moment. The double swing doors let in a rush of damp cold air and two roly-poly middle-aged men so alike, they looked like a pair of wally dugs off the mantelpiece.

"Mac, how's it going?" Smiles and handshakes all round. "How's the teuchters treatin' you?"

"Grand, just grand. What'll you have?"

251

"A pint an' a half for us both. Still got a paper to get oot."

Both men poured their half gill into the pint in the traditional manner and gave a simultaneous sigh of satisfaction as the first sip relaxed them into their evening break.

"What brings you down here, apart from needing to visit civilization now and again?"

McAllister laughed. "There's not many would think 'Glasgow' and 'civilized' fitted into the same sentence. No, I came to see my mother for the anniversary."

"Oh. Aye. Must still be painful for her. You don't get over an accident like that. Burying a child — it's no right."

It was no accident, he didn't say; they, his friends, his colleagues, thought him obsessed. The memory hanging, they all stared into their glasses for an awkward second.

Willie Graham, the shorter and rounder of the two journalists, glanced at the big wall clock.

"Time for a half-pint, then we must be getting back." He signaled the order. "See you've a wee bit of bother up your way. The Polish man must be feart for his safety in the local gaol."

"It's certainly a shock in a small town where everybody knows everything."

"No like here, then. You'd be hard-put to

252

run all the bad stories in this place."

"The gangs still about, then?"

"In control, more like."

A clock's chime cut through the buzz of the bar. They downed the dregs of their drinks, held out a farewell hand, then hurried back to the late shift on the news desk, John McAllister's former life.

He had returned to the tenement soon after closing time, a couple more beers and whiskies closer to the wind. Opening the door to the front room, a small lamp of the religious variety lit up the family shrine. He picked up the solitary photo of himself on the china cabinet; thirteen he was, in his brand-new school uniform that had cost his father three months of overtime. A wedding picture of a strangely solemn bride and groom and a formal photo of a group of firemen, indistinguishable in their uniforms, were to left and right. He put on the main light, too tired to sleep. He picked up a photo with his father and friends smiling out through the years. A good man, so everyone said, and McAllister agreed, ". . . the best." He put the picture back.

The mantelpiece and piano top were reserved as memorials to his brother. At least twelve pictures of Kenneth stood in polished silver frames: a skinny wee boy in baggy shorts with oversize gloves dangling on the ends of sticklike arms; with different opponents facing off against each other; with a group shot of equally skinny boys in the ring; with all the club members on the annual ferry trip down the Clyde. He picked that one up. Kenneth was wild with excitement; it was that obvious even in a group of thirty or so boys. There was something about one of the other boys, one of the ones leaning over the ship's railings smiling down at the photographer, that made him stop. . . . No, couldn't be, it was just that Scottish, cheeky, eye-squinting grin and freckles that made you certain his hair was carrot red; the kind of a face that made him seem familiar. Possibly.

The photos of his brother had all been taken at the club, costing sixpence for the group shots, a shilling for individual ones — not expensive. His mother had never missed a year. Then dead at fifteen, verdict suicide. But his mother was right, it was never suicide. And the church had agreed, so she got her funeral. He may have killed himself, wee brother of mine, but something, someone, had pushed him into drowning himself in the river. McAllister believed that then and still believed it now.

Interfered with — a ridiculous idiom to his writer's way of thinking. Kenneth may have been spared that, but mentally?

Over a breakfast of tea and a cigarette he chatted to his mother of his new life. Whether she heeded or not didn't matter; he felt the need to fill the vacuum of a house empty of hope. He told her of his first six months, of the town itself, of the people and the newspaper. Then he ran out of steam.

"Can I borrow one of the pictures from the boxing club?"

"As long as you bring it back."

It broke his heart that she hadn't even the energy to ask why.

"I'm away now to the *Herald*. Can I get you anything whilst I'm out?"

His coat already on, picture in his pocket, hat in his hand, he turned, hesitated.

"Something happened in the Highlands. It reminded me of what happened —"

"He fell. He drowned. Nothing more happened, John. That's the end of it." Her voice, harsh as a seagull's squawk, left no angle for argument. "I don't need you harping on again with your wild theories. You've more imagination than sense, I've always said."

He patted her shoulder. They were not people who touched.

"Would you like some fish for tea? I'll be down that end of the town. I'll call in to Tommy McPhee under the bridge. You always said he has the best fish."

"If you like."

"Anything else? Maybe some stout?"

"I'm fine."

"I know, Ma. I know you're fine."

He gently squeezed her arm; it felt like the carcass of a scrawny hen. He walked out into the city morning, a time of day he had seldom seen when a reporter on the late shift, and, rounding the corner into a cold easterly, his eyes were watering. He blamed it on the wind.

McAllister needed a favor. Sandy heard him out.

"It's still about Kenneth, is it?"

"It's always about Kenneth." McAllister was grim. "But something I came across, I'd like to check. Probably nothing. Most likely me off with a bee in ma bunnet — again."

The *Herald* never changed; the news desk, the subeditor's desk, the copyboys lurking behind anything that they could lurk behind. It had been a year but many there hadn't noticed, presuming that McAllister had just returned from a long lunch. Sandy Marshall had kept in touch. A talented reporter, like many before him he had made his name as a journalist only to be kicked upstairs to become a frustrated editor.

"So no hope that you've come here to rescue me from all this shite?" Sandy gestured to the pile of papers colonizing his desk.

"I'm here to see my mother. The anniversary again." He was going to say that he was here to support her, maybe be of some comfort, but he had no idea if his arrival made any difference at all.

Sandy focused on the previous "probably nothing." He'd had experience of McAllister's understatements. Cadets together, both bright working-class boys, they were escaping the destiny of going down the pits of Clackmannanshire, for Sandy; following his father into the fire brigade, for McAllister.

"Here's a pass for the archives." He scribbled a signature. "Any developments on the child's murder?"

"Not yet, but the story is yours when I have it."

"The usual place in Buchanan Street the-night?"

"Aye. But I've got to get back north soon.

A newspaper to run."

"Is that what you call it? The classies still on the front page, are they?"

The search in the archives was tedious. He had read, almost memorized, the articles — brief mentions really, often. But now he thought he had a new tack. The date, and more important the place, was on the back of the photograph in his mother's even writing. He eventually found the file. There were far more references than he could ever have imagined. It took all morning, and after reading and trying to make sense of what he had found, McAllister needed air, needed to walk and to smoke.

Out in the streets and lanes and back-courts of the city, he wandered without any particular direction. In between needle-sharp showers, heavenly searchlights of sun highlighting turrets and gargoyles and statues and ironwork, then returning to rain before anyone got their hopes up, he walked, thinking, not looking.

He stopped at the fish shop under the bridge, then the fruit barrow. The tingling in his feet, like the sensation of defrosting after a walk in the snow, came from the underground railway vibrating the pavements and cobblestones. The air too was vibrating from the constant stream of trams and buses and overhead trains grumbling as they left the station, and civilization, bound for the wilderness beyond. Tollcross, Glasgow Green, the Clyde, legends and stories and songs mapped every part of the city. Or so McAllister fancied. He passed Barrowlands dance hall; he never noticed the squelch underfoot as he crossed the sodden turf of Glasgow Green. The route that he was walking, his private Via Dolorosa, hadn't registered. He was stopped. The gunmetal-gray river, flowing endlessly, barred the way. His internal compass had brought him to within a few yards of the infamous footbridge.

By daylight the bridge was busy with old men, bairns on bikes, mothers with prams laden with washing, shopping and babies. By night, the elegant suspension affair, the demarcation line between the Billy Boys and the Fenians living across the Clyde, had seen more skirmishes than Londonderry. He walked to the dead center of the bridge and stared unseeing down to the water below. A brass plaque, he thought, that's what's needed, a memorial to the mostly young men, his brother included, who had died between the cables of this Glasgow landmark. He turned and walked swiftly back the way he had come.

If I was writing this up, he told himself, I'd put "He fled the scene."

His weak attempt at humor didn't help, so he made for the nearest public house.

That same night, in the same pub as the night before, a neutral pub, no allegiances, round the corner from the Athenaeum, with an odd mix of students, workingfolk and that lost tribe of Glasgow, Partick Thistle supporters, and, for reasons no one could explain, folk from Kilmarnock, gathering together, drinking together, singing together in this oasis of alcohol, a Glasgow bar. There's none like it, McAllister remembered. Settling into a table under the window, McAllister and Sandy Marshall supped companionably with not much said.

"Another?"

McAllister stood to get in his round when the doors swung open, letting in a gust of wind and rain and an imposing figure in black. At the sight of him, a memory, the same memory buried deep in the collective unconsciousness of all Catholic boys, made McAllister shudder.

"Over here," Sandy called out.

Leaving a much-mildewed golf umbrella by the door, the man joined them. He requested a Guinness. McAllister looked furtively at the newcomer in the bar mirrors. The next Great White Hope with a good resemblance to Spencer Tracy, was McAllister's first impression. He waited a while for the Guinness and his heartbeat to settle, then, balancing three glasses, returned to the table.

"Michael Kelly. You must be John McAllister." The priest stood, holding out a massive ham of a hand.

McAllister returned the handshake.

"Sandy has told me some of your story. I'm deeply sorry about your brother."

"It's been eight years, nearly nine."

"But it doesn't go away."

"No. It doesn't." A strong pull on his beer, then McAllister laid the photograph on the table. "I'd like to ask you about this."

"The Boys' Boxing Club." He turned the picture over. "But this picture was before my time. The club closed. But we reopened. There is a huge interest in boxing ever since a Scot won the Lonsdale belt." Father Kelly kept staring at the group photograph as though searching for something or someone. "No, I can't place this picture. But I think I recognize one of the boys. If you'd like to visit —" He laughed at McAllister's expression. "No, no strings. Sandy told me you've

261

forsaken the faith."

"Aye, lost it somewhere between the Gorbals and Guernica."

"But this fella here" — Father Kelly placed his finger below a skinny larva-white boy in boxing shorts pulled right up to his oxters — "if it's the same person, he volunteers at the club, I'll introduce you."

Five o'clock in the afternoon, almost dark, McAllister again made his way to the river, then across St. Andrew's bridge to the club that was a recurring setting in his recurring dreams. As he opened the door the smell brought the nightmare from sleep to awake; plimsolls, socks, disinfectant, sweat, terror. The bilious institutional green of the walls was the exact color of fear. And the never-changing noise: grunts, moans, shouts, commands, shuffle-shuffle of feet, tick-tock, tick-tock of a big boy in the corner with a skipping rope, the repetitive pounding on the punching bags, the *oomph* of a man on the huge medicine bag swaying from the ceiling, the sound for all the world as real as a blow to the belly. And every sound was distinctly Glaswegian.

"Mr. McAllister, is it?"

A short man with mouse-brown hair in a lavatory-brush haircut, narrow eyes and a narrow mouth, stepped forward. His grin expiated his looks, making anyone in range of his searchlight smile feel that they were interesting to know.

"I'm Joe Brodie. Michael Kelly told me to expect you."

McAllister noted that he didn't use the honorific "Father."

"I knew your wee brother Kenneth."

Straight to the point; McAllister liked that.

"I'm happy to talk about him with you, all you want."

On the train journey back to the Highlands, he thought over his visit home and laughed at himself. In the eight years of his quest — the matter of the Gorbals Boys' Boxing Club — he'd found, like any true Scotsman, the key to it in a bar. And no, he hadn't been mistaken; it *was* Jimmy McPhee in the photo with his brother. As for the elusive object of his obsession — he wouldn't give him the dignity of a title — he was no further toward finding his whereabouts.

"No idea what happened to him," Joe Brodie had said. "All I remember was that he was here one minute and gone the next." Aye, Joe had replied to McAllister's question, Father Bain knew Kenneth. "Kenneth was aye his favorite. But there was no harm in the man — not like *some*." He continued: "He was a dab hand at the photography, he was the one who took all the pictures" — he gestured to the hundreds of framed photographs lining the walls — "probably took this one an' all," he said, handing the photo back to McAllister.

"Gone," was all Michael Kelly could tell him. "I don't know where."

The train sped northward, snuffling and snorting through the empty snow-speckled landscape, racing the rivers and burns and waterfalls and rapids of gurgling whisky-peat foam that ran alongside the tracks, making their way to distilleries downstream. Remnants of ancient pine forest appeared and disappeared as the train chuffed joyously through the dramatic backdrop.

They stopped at the edge of the high plateau to uncouple the dining and sleeper cars and to water the two steam engines needed for the descent to the sea. Once through the Drumochter Pass, a distant Ben Wyvis flaunted a covering of pink snow that changed to blue as the dark navy of evening crept upward from the firth below. The earthly stars of villages scattered along the shoreline were soon being reflected in the clear northern sky. Home? thought McAllister. Aye, maybe. He smiled to himself.

■ ■ ■ ■

It was hard to resist the warm lights of the Station Hotel as he alighted into a blast of icy air. Fellow passengers had scattered into the dark, but McAllister hurried for the bar. He'd never liked drinking nor eating on a train; too afraid of being trapped with someone who recognized him, just wanting "a wee word," usually a libelous wee word. There were not a few in the town who felt it their duty to tell him what to write and how to run the newspaper. No anonymity in a small town.

He settled in a quiet corner behind a pillar, having decided on a pint of the best before going to the dining room for supper. Turned to the sports pages of the Aberdeen daily — "Only thing worth reading in thon rag" was Don's comment on the rival paper — he settled down to peruse the results of the tribal warfare that was the Highland Football League. Figures came and went, footsteps hushed by the thick carpet; midweek, but the bar was busy. The lonely and the anxious from the outposts of the county came for the sheriff's court or to the county council or to check on their looming coronary or some such in one of the two hospitals that served the far reaches of the shire. Commercial travelers from the south, lodging in a bed-and-breakfast that shut the doors by nine o'clock, came for a drink and company. Those waiting for the sleeper to Edinburgh, furtive lovers or wheelers and dealers buttering up their local government representatives, all were here, all used the Station Hotel, for this was the place where the *respectable* folk of the Highlands met. McAllister — he came for the wide selection of single-malts, the food, the quiet and the short walk home.

"John McAllister. What can I get you?"

He looked up, distaste a momentary flicker across his face.

"I'm fine, Mr. Grieg. Fine. Just off. Still got things to see to."

"Just a quick word."

Little deflects a bully, certainly not subtlety. The town clerk proceeded to lecture McAllister for a good fifteen minutes on what stories to run to "improve the paper," all the while waiting to be asked to take a seat.

"I really do have to go, Mr. Grieg."

Seeing his time was up, the town clerk went straight into his backstabbing best.

"Donnie McLeod still with you I see. Aye. Used to be a good man. A right shame he's so fond of the bottle."

He said this while clutching what must have been a double at least, McAllister noted. "As for his betting . . . some very unsavory characters in thon game. Not that it's any business o' mine, but I'm surprised you've kept him on."

McAllister said nothing, waiting for him to put the boot in, and Grieg was true to form.

"He's been poking about in town planning affairs, asking ridiculous questions. I've had to warn him. And stirring up those tinkers, poking his long neb into things that are private council business."

"But if it's council business, how can it be private?"

McAllister was deliberately mild, holding back an urge to head-butt the pompous plook of a man.

"And my dear lady wife was most put out about that sneering wee piece on the Highland Ball. No call for that tone at all. I don't know who wrote it, but I have my suspicions."

"I take full responsibility for all that appears in the *Gazette*."

"The council puts a lot of advertising revenue the *Gazette*'s way. It needn't. There's more than one paper in these parts."

McAllister, in his short time as editor, had come into contact with Grieg a few times and had always regarded him with amused contempt, as one of a type — a puffed-up popinjay who thought himself God's gift (another of McAllister's mother's favorite phrases).

"I think we both know that that's not the way of it, Mr. Grieg." McAllister, icily polite, stood. "I must be off."

He picked up his hat, his newspapers, and strode out the bar, peeved and hungry.

Eleven

McAllister's return to the Highlands and the office brought him back to the unquiet of the other death, the other boy. An uncommonly subdued Don McLeod nodded as he came in for the Monday meeting. A terminally cheerful Rob McLean grinned through a thatch of hair that badly needed cutting. And Joanne? He couldn't make out her mood, but then, he reminded himself, understanding women had never been his strong point; hence the life of a bachelor free, he joked sadly.

"Any news whilst I've been gone?"

"The funeral is the day after tomorrow." Don looked tired. "I know it's taken a long time to release the body, an eternity to the parents no doubt." Don gestured with open hands. "It doesn't bear thinking about."

McAllister was fascinated to note the nicotine stains that covered the center of his deputy's left palm, remembering that Don had spent his boyhood at sea. Smoking with the cigarette turned inward to protect it from the wind was an ingrained habit. Don McLeod, once he had been around the world twice, had forsaken merchant ships and taken up journalism. To him it was not a highfalutin occupation; it was a trade. A job where you did an apprenticeship, worked your way up the ladder, to produce a newspaper in the same format as time immemorial. Police statements, reports from the procurator fiscal, news from the councils were run verbatim. Occasionally he would do a rewrite in reported speech to present a smatter of variety. And if Don knew there was more to the story than was published in the local press, he would say, in private, usually in the Market Bar, of course there's more to it than that, and tap his nose, and wouldn't reveal what he knew, just allow the remark to hang there in the smoke, adding to his reputation for being the man in the know.

"It's a crime that's cracked a faultline as deep as the Great Glen through this whole community, a faultline marking the before and after. We're innocents, McAllister. Stuff like this is for the big cities."

"I know." McAllister changed the subject, weary of thoughts of death. "Any news on

Councilor Findlay Grieg's grand schemes?"

"Not yet," Joanne answered.

"Any more on Karl the Polish gentleman?"

"Still locked up." It was Rob's turn.

"The Corelli family?"

"A bit upset but fine." Joanne again.

"So nothing, no news." McAllister was becoming exasperated.

"Oh, aye, some great news."

McAllister cheered up.

"The chip shop's open again. Must have been your brilliant editorial."

They busied themselves divvying up the rest of the routine. Joanne reached for the bundle of illegible handwritten reports from contributors, the typing of which made her consider profanities. But she was too well brought up to even think of a swear word without blushing. Rob left on mysterious Rob business. McAllister signaled to Don.

"A word?"

In the editor's office, the door firmly shut, McAllister didn't have to ask.

"No, it's not got out. Though how long the news can be kept quiet in this place . . ." He lit up. McAllister took one of his own; he couldn't manage the Capstan Full Strength that Don smoked.

"And aye, you're right. Things like this

can go on anyplace; although it's usually kept in the family hereabouts, well hidden. We know our own perverts and we keep an eye on them. But this? An assault on a wee boy by a stranger?"

"And the Polish man Karl will take all the blame?"

"Who else?" But Don looked uncomfortable. "He may have done it; on the other hand . . . Let's just say I'm yet to be convinced. Inspector Tompson has never, in the eight years since he was posted to the town, been this efficient."

McAllister couldn't bear talking about the matter a second longer.

"I need to find Jimmy McPhee."

"Join the queue. Peter Kowalski is desperate to find him. The polis too. Anything I can help wi'?" Don took McAllister's shake of the head in his stride. He'd find out why sooner or later. He always did.

Joanne walked back to the office after her break, still stunned.

"He gave me permission, permission to work." She was disgusted with herself, not Bill. "How did I get inveigled into that weekend away? I might just as well have hoisted up a surrender flag."

She dawdled down the hill. "I'll bet that

brother-in-law of mine had something to do with this; he said he'd talk to Bill. Till death do us part indeed! All very well for a minister to say, but we could do with an extra commandment, 'Thou shalt not drink and hit thy wife'!"

Back at the desk she attacked the typewriter. That felt better. But she couldn't type accurately. The rendezvous with her husband had left her completely flummoxed.

"Why on earth do I always give in?"

Bill had phoned her at the *Gazette* office, unusual, asking to meet for a coffee — most unusual.

"I can't get out right now," she replied. Fearing he would come round and drag her out of work, she suggested, "How about the Castle Brae Café at twelve?"

"Right you are."

Replacing the receiver all she could think was, I wonder what he wants.

Sitting at a window table, watching the town pass by, she spotted Bill coming up the brae. She studied him as he strode toward her, taking the steep hill as though it was a stroll across a football pitch. She had loved him. She had married him. They had had good times — but too far back to remember. The weekend away had been good in parts but now came the negotiations for her surrender. What choice did she have? The girls had been through enough already. And why oh why, she asked herself, why can't you be like everyone else? Why can't you accept your lot? Her mother's words echoed around her head, echoed as they had done on and off for ten years or so — "You've made your bed. . . ." The sensation of being run over by an emotional steamroller had her almost forgetting to breathe.

Bill told the waitress to hurry. He had an appointment, he said. The woman rolled her eyes but took the order. Joanne leaned forward, speaking in that hushed voice reserved for ministers, doctors, bank managers and public places, and asked, "Have you talked to Mr. Keir at the bank yet? He's called a few times to ask where you are."

"That's my two o'clock meeting." Bill was strangely confident. "I told him about your job. He liked that." He had doubled the amount of her wages when the subject was discussed. That had done the trick. "But still, he has no right to call you at work. I'll have a word about that."

"Mr. Keir was only trying to find you." Joanne was aware that she was once again placating her husband. "Like you said, an extension on the loan is the best idea." It was a habit, a necessary habit; she had to keep the peace after all. "It's good, though, isn't it? The bank agreeing to the extension on the loan? You'll be fine financially now, won't you?"

"Of course. You leave all that to me."

Enough, Joanne told herself, don't push it.

"Guess what?" he went on. "I found out that thon firm, the one that came in second in the bidding for the contract out west, that's the firm doing the work on Grieg's lodge. So, if I don't finish on time, the second bidder can take over. That's the way the contract is worded. So maybe that's what the other crew has been promised."

"Councilor Findlay Grieg! The rat," Joanne exclaimed.

"Rat or no, he's got me. All legal too. But no if I finish on time. I have a wee scheme." He explained his plan to get a couple of caravans and some workmen from the town to go over to the west coast to finish the job.

"But it'll mean spending cash to get ahead. And spending time over there. I can work seven days a week even if those west coast Holy Joes can't." He finished his tea.

"Most of the joinery on thon houses I've done myself already, some plumbing too. So, since I'll be away for a while, you can keep your wee job — seeing as how it makes you happy."

He patted her hand across the table. It was like she was his pet.

"You'll let me keep the job," she stated.

"So long as it doesn't interfere with you looking after the house and the girls." He was pleased with himself, everything settled, no deep discussions like she usually wanted. "I've got to be off. Can't be late for the meeting." He leaned forward, hand on her arm — "See you tonight, eh?" — and winked, leaving a pound note on the table.

Joanne sat, registered him turning left instead of right toward the bank, and continued to sit as the waitress cleared up around her. All her intentions, all the discussions about their life, their marriage, practiced over and over in her head, vanished when confronted with the reality of Bill. Her optimism, that lifebuoy of hope that kept her floating above the reality of the marriage, seemed insubstantial in the face of the force that was her husband. Disgusted with herself, she recited her internal chant.

"I am a person, not a possession."

■ ■ ■ ■

Bill was not on his way to the bank, had never had any intention of going to the bank, cap in hand. He was not on his way to the council works department, cap in hand, to ask for an extension on the contract. He was on his way to meet his savior. The money to see him through the winter and more besides, in five minutes hence, would be his. No questions asked. More than you could say for the bank manager. He recalled the earlier meeting with barely suppressed fury.

"What security can you offer, Mr. Ross?"

"May I remind you, Mr. Ross, that your current loan is way behind schedule?"

"I need more than just your word, Mr. Ross."

Bill couldn't be doing with the doubting Thomases of this world; he would pull this off all by himself. Cash to settle his suppliers, two caravans and some time, that was all he needed. It wouldn't do for Joanne to find out, though. He turned down the lane to the bar near the station. With Joanne, he thought, he had won. She'd never leave him. She couldn't take the shame. She'd never go against the Church. Touch and go though for a while, he knew. Good that he'd taken her out west. And that idea, he remembered, was all thanks to that brother-in-law of hers — first time a minister's ever been useful, he thought with a smirk. He pushed through the swing doors and looked around.

"Over here," a voice called out in a Glasgow accent.

That evening, Bill Ross was at home. Slumped in his armchair, a newspaper open, foot tapping to the Strathspey on the wireless, he was in a rare good mood.

"Now another from Jimmy Shand and his band, this time a Shetland reel — 'Hens o'er the Midden . . .' " The music started up.

Annie was furtively eyeing her father, assessing his mood. She instinctively knew the time to strike. This was big, though. Her mother said they couldn't afford it. But his foot was tapping.

"Dad, Mum, can I go round to Sheila's house to watch television?"

"No you can't," Joanne replied.

Bill and Joanne knew that Mrs. Murchison pumped the girls for information.

"It's no fair. I'm the only one in my class doesn't have a telly," Annie lied, directing her protests to her father.

"I've told you before, we can't afford it," Joanne shouted from the kitchen.

The child was not about to give up.

"Everyone else's dad bought one," Annie persisted, exaggerating as usual. "Everyone thinks we're poor 'cos we don't have one."

That got his attention.

Joanne, peeling tatties for supper, was half listening in.

"We'll get a telly." Bill was definite. "I'll have a look first thing tomorrow. I'll get you one before I leave for the west coast."

"I want to look too, but I'll be at school," Annie wailed.

"I'll pick you up. We'll look in the shop window and you can help choose."

"Me too, me too." Wee Jean was thrilled. She desperately wanted to watch Muffin the Mule.

Annie danced into the kitchen. "Dad says we're getting a television."

"We'll see about that." Joanne frowned. Maybe they could manage to pay for a television on hire purchase. Then again there might be a problem getting the loan. "Christmas is coming up, so if you do without a big present, maybe we can manage it. But no promises, mind."

"But Dad said we're getting one tomorrow."

"I said, we'll see. Now into the bath with you both — we'll play dominoes later."

The girls ran upstairs, no squabbling for once, excited by the magical news — a television. Joanne came into the sitting room, wiping her hands on her apron.

"Bill, what's this about a television?"

"It's high time we got one. We'll be the first in our street. Besides, it's good for the bairns. Educational."

"You yourself told me to go easy until the contract paid out. I could only afford one bag of coal last month. The girls need winter coats before anything else."

The first sign of anger appeared on his cheekbones, a hint of a flush that she knew all too well.

"Here, take this."

He reached into his back pocket and peeled twenty pounds from a big roll of cash and thrust it at her. "Don't let anybody ever say I don't look after my family."

She stared at the banknotes.

"I won it on a horse."

And I'm Grace Kelly, she wanted to say. But she prayed that, even though the last thing she wanted was a television set, he would not let the girls down, he would keep his word this time. But she doubted it.

TWELVE

Wednesday at the *Gazette,* two days before Halloween, the building and all who voyaged in her hummed to the weekly prepublication countdown. A deadline had never been missed and, as McAllister often reminded them, was unlikely to be missed until they put some guts into this piddling wee paper. But the smell of print and paper tinged the pervasive cigarette smoke haze and adrenaline haar in the reporters' room. Joanne's Wednesday-night ritual was to wash her hair twice or the stink of tobacco would permeate her dreams.

Much had been left to the last afternoon. As always. Don, up and down stairs from the stone to the desk, would argue, often for form's sake, with the compositor over late changes. Rob was late, as usual, with a sports report on an intercounty shinty game. As he typed, his toes throbbed at memories of playing in the Camanachd Cup against Kingussie. The memory of the frozen, granite-hard pitches, the shin-shattering knocks, the chilblains and perpetual defeats, still hurt.

McAllister was putting the final touches to his editorial, then he was off to the funeral. A fervent plea for Hungary, a plea that a drop of sanity in an ocean of political stupidity may prevail, was his topic for the week as there was nothing he could write on the subject shaking the town. Maybe after the funeral, he thought. For now, Hungary. Don would take his red pencil through much of it, Joanne would retype it, two, three, four times, they would argue about the relevance in a local paper of news that was unconfirmed, only a whisper, from a country no one cared about, and yet, yet . . . he knew he had to make a stand — if only for himself.

McAllister finished and left without a comment.

Joanne, looking up from the typewriter, blew a strand of hair from her face, stretched her shoulders and saw the cobblestones gleaming wet on the lane below.

"Oh no! It had better clear for Saturday night. I couldn't bear guising in the rain and the bonfire a fizzler." She was also praying that Halloween would be a great success as, just as she had feared, there was no further word about the television. She couldn't bear the girls to be disappointed yet again.

Rob was confident of bad weather. "I remember once" — he took a break from pounding the Underwood so they didn't have to shout — "we went guising in sleet. I was nine and I came down with pneumonia after and my mum was *not* sympathetic."

Joanne laughed. "Why not?"

"I insisted on going as a Roman gladiator. A belt, a sword, bare legs, sandals, a wee kilt thing and two bits of cardboard for armor. I turned from a Roman to a Pict — blue all over."

Don came in with a flurry of paper. "Come on, come on" — he grabbed copy from Rob — "less o' the gabbing."

They got back to their typing.

The service, conducted in the rituals of the Free Church of Scotland, was traditional. Rain was also traditional for a funeral. No women, no children, no outsiders could take part in the final rites, but outsiders had been allowed into the pews on a balcony overlooking the body of the kirk. The singing of the ancient psalms, the haunting plea for comfort and acknowledgment of God's will, was sung in Gaelic, the sound not dissimilar to the Aramaic of the Apostles. The words, unchanged in seventeen hundred years, and sung in Scotland for more than a thousand years, sustained these austere Christians.

The service over, a plain wooden box was gently carried through the doors of the kirk as though it were a cradle, not a coffin. McAllister, the headmaster Frank Clark and a few other men, not of the faith but wishing to show support for Jamie's father, followed at the end of the procession, then hovered discreetly inside the lee of the high stone wall that surrounded the burying ground. Assembled around the open grave, the congregation of black-clad men put McAllister in mind of a gathering of hoodie crows. He shook the image away. The sonorous voice of the minister declared the last funerary rites, his strong cantor's voice uplifted into the wind, sending Jamie's spirit westward, along the glens, back to his ancestral home. "Over the sea to Skye" indeed.

McAllister knew of the psalmody of the Free Church but had never before been immersed in the eerie sound. On the walk along the riverbank back to the office, the chanting from the presentor, answered back and forth by the voices of the mourners, a sound more like the ocean breaking rhythmically against the shoreline than singing, had become imprinted on his brain. Any effort on his part would not rid him of that sound, this he knew, and would always, any and every time heard, be the anthem to this time, this place, this tragedy.

They were almost done, the final proofs all that was left. McAllister shooed them all off with "I'll finish up here. See you in the Market Bar in half an hour or so."

Don needed no encouragement. Rob neither. As he was halfway out the door, he turned back and asked Joanne, "Join us for a drink?"

She looked doubtful.

"Come on, we can smuggle you into the back bar."

"All right, just this once. I've a night to myself, the girls are with their grandparents and Bill has gone out west. But if I'm seen, there goes what's left of my reputation."

"Blame it on me."

"Always," she solemnly promised. Then she stopped, lifted her head, stretched her neck and stood for a second, like a stag at bay, and sniffed.

"Burning toffee."

Rob laughed, "Halloween," and tucked

her arm under his to walk down the rain-slick cobbles of the brae.

That week, the last in October, the town smelled of toffee and turnips. Treadle sewing machines clunked as children changed their minds a dozen times on what to wear but settled on whatever their mothers could produce, old clothes being at a premium, cloth and clothes rationing a not-too-distant memory for most. In Annie's case, it was less what to wear than who to be. And that Wednesday night a final decision had to be made.

"Now you be careful with that knife. It's sharp. I don't know what your grandad's thinking of."

Granny disapproved of everything, thought Annie, but Wee Jean ignored the warning, continuing to carefully, messily, carve out the insides of her turnip, chewing a chunk of the raw neep as she worked.

Grandad had taken over the kitchen for turnip-lantern carving. Granny Ross stood over the boiling sugar for toffee apples. Carved turnips covered the sideboard and the top of the pantry and were all over the draining board. Another group of grinning gargoyle faces, finished except for the candles, were waiting in the galvanized washtub.

The lanterns were one-upmanship on Annie's part. She had not been chosen for the Halloween concert, although she was by far the most theatrical of the troupe. The Brownies and Girl Guides, the Cubs and Scouts, were part of the entertainment for the night. Joanne knew why Annie had been left out of the Brownies' concert group. Her grandparents had no idea, her father neither. Annie knew, cared, would never show it and would never forget the slight.

There was still a lot to be done, two days before Halloween night. Fabric, cut and ready to sew, lay on the sitting room floor. A crown, or a hat and bow and arrow, were yet to be made.

"Will you make my crown next, Granny?" Annie kept pestering.

"I keep telling you, Maid Marion didn't wear a crown."

"She did so. She's a princess."

This conversation had been going on for about two and a half weeks. Grandad intervened. "I'm sure she was a princess."

Annie looked up triumphantly.

"Aye," he continued, "a princess all right. Mind you, didn't she have to disguise herself as one of they forest folk so the bad king wouldn't know she was a princess? And of course, princesses don't have bows and arrows."

It worked. One crown forgotten, one set of arrows to be made. At least it stopped her questioning him about the funeral. And took his granddaughter's mind off the infernal topic of a television set.

Television! That's for those with more money than sense, was Grandad Ross's opinion of the newfangled device.

McAllister walked into the Market Bar twenty minutes later, his hair and coat damp from the fine persistent rain.

"All finished." He looked at Joanne. "A dram?"

"Why not?" She had been drinking ginger beer.

Now, settled deep into a chair, the leather of which looked and felt like it had been tanned from the hide of a mastodon, Joanne propped her feet up on the fender of the stone fireplace, once part of a forge, and warmed her toes. Cozy, she thought. I could get to like this. Don and Rob were in the public bar, forbidden to women by custom and fear of public denunciation as a harlot.

She accepted the drink from her boss, thinking herself a very modern woman — first a job, now a whisky.

"Right. Hoodie crows?" McAllister settled deep into the chair with his whisky and a cigarette.

"I can't believe you're still interested in that wild fancy."

"I was reminded of them again this afternoon at the funeral."

They both looked into the fire for a moment.

"They get all this from their grandad." Joanne explained. "He's a known storyteller, has a great reputation at the ceilidhs, and he's always filling the girls' heads with tales of faeries and bogies and hoodie crows pecking out eyes, golden eagles snatching babies. Not that I mind; it's good for them to know the old legends. I just wish they weren't so bloodthirsty."

"That's the Scots for you." McAllister raised his glass.

"In the Highlands, there are so many superstitions I can't keep track. But if I spill salt, I always throw some over my left shoulder to keep the devil at bay." She laughed at herself.

"Aye, I do the same. Can't get out of the habit." He smiled. "And Halloween, only two nights away, is another of our fine traditions. I loved going guising as a boy." Next day is All Souls' Day, he remembered, but

289

didn't say. That was an anniversary of another funeral. "So all the ghosts and ghouls and lost souls will be out in force and the devil will be on horseback. Woe betide poor *Cutty Sark*." They laughed, enjoying the whisky, the fire and the company.

"But surely you must have a feeling as to whether your daughters were telling the truth — or the truth as they saw it?"

But Joanne had an instant flash of that awful night, of Annie's sobs, her accusations and the unhealed wound still between mother and daughter. Joanne knew that the common belief was that when your husband hits you, you must have done something to deserve it. When a parent hits a child, it's for their own good; a teacher hits a pupil with a leather belt, it's to teach them a lesson. A dispute over business, a bet, an altercation of any kind — there's nothing that can't be fixed by a good fight. And she knew that she could no longer hide her disgust at these accepted conventions. There must be a better way.

"A penny for them."

Joanne shook herself back to the present, to the novelty of breaking all the rules, of being a working woman, wearing trousers, having a drink at the end of the day, in a bar, with a man who's not her husband.

"Sorry, I was away in a dwam." She finished her glass, refused another. "The hoodie crow — well, for them, the bird stands for anything nasty, anything that can't be explained." She glimpsed the clock through the serving hatch.

"Heavens, it's a quarter past nine, I have to go."

Joanne cycled home through a very dark dark, no moon, no stars, the rain alternating with sleet. She seldom drank, and whisky was not her tipple — too many bad associations — but tonight it fortified her from the worst of the weather. Wheeling her bicycle around the back of her house, she was surprised to see a light on in the kitchen. Maybe her father-in-law had come around to collect something for the girls, left it on to help her in the dark. She struggled with the key, having trouble finding the lock. The door opened.

"Oh, it's you." The outline of Bill stood in the doorway. "I thought you'd be out west by now," she continued blithely. "I didn't see the van."

"Where the hell have you been?" Followed by, "You stink of whisky."

"That makes a change. It's usually the

291

other way round." The whisky had lessened the extra fraction-of-a-second gap between brain and tongue that, through the years, she had cultivated, to avoid riling her husband.

He slapped her straight across her left cheek, catching the corner of her eye. Dizzy, face burning, ears buzzing, she stumbled backward into the kitchen, hands held in front of her. But his anger was spent. Or maybe he had heard an until-now-unheard outrage in her yell. "Don't you dare!"

She leaned into the sink. A wave of nausea rose. It passed. The stale taste of whisky coated her tongue. She turned on the cold tap, full force, lapping the crystal-cold water from her cupped palms, splashing in her eye, over her face, feeling it running down her arms, cold sobering water. The nausea evolved into plain simple heartsick; sick of violence, sick of the contempt and sick of his need to control and humiliate. But he had heard right. Her overwhelming emotion was new, as fresh and cold and clear as the water she splashed on her face. Defiance.

"I will not put up with this anymore," she shouted at the closed sitting-room door. "I'm sick of it. Do you hear me? I've had enough."

Silence. Then she surprised herself. I am

not going to say sorry. I will not grovel. I will not take any more of this shite. It was probably the first time in her life that she had used a swear word — even though it was said to herself. This time it was she who slammed the back door, she who stormed out of the house. It was not until halfway down the street that she became aware that one eye was closed, that she had forgotten her coat and that she had no idea where to go.

Pedaling half-blind through tears and rain and a throbbing headache, she found herself at the river. Pedaling across the bridge, pedaling hard up the hill, on through the empty town, past the closed bars, the shuttered shops, struggling over the wet cobblestones, she could pedal no more. She lugged the bicycle up the brae, pedaled past the Academy, round the crescent, arriving at McAllister's house. Why here of all places? She flushed in humiliation. But the bonechilling, wet-right-through cold, and a shivering she couldn't control, and a headache so bad she could hardly see through the one good eye, left no other option. She rang the bell.

No lights showed at the front of the house but in answer to the ring, a dim light came on and footsteps came to answer. He stared

at her, standing there on his doorstep, trying to hold on to her dignity and her bicycle.

"I don't suppose a nightcap is on."

He took her arm and led her through to
the kitchen. He asked no questions; she
didn't explain. A towel, aspirins and a drink
later, a suggestion of a hot bath refused,
directions to the spare room given, still he
asked no questions. Then alone in the dark,
toast-warm under an eiderdown, safe,
exhausted, humiliation dismissed until the
morning, she slept. And the tears that
soaked the pillow didn't wake her.

THIRTEEN

McAllister rose at eight o'clock and it was still dark, being October. He presumed their first encounter would be awkward so he raked the still-glowing cinders in the kitchen range, added coal, found the heavy plaid dressing gown that his mother had bought in a sale on Sauchiehall Street seven years ago and that he had never worn, left it neatly folded outside the spare bedroom door, wrote Joanne a note saying he would be back later, left it on the kitchen table, and using his key instead of banging the door to, he left as quietly as he could, then, feeling strangely cheerful, he strode off into a watery dawn, down the brae and along the High Street to the *Gazette* office.

For the first time ever, he was the first in the reporters' room. Mrs. Smart from downstairs brought him tea. He paused to smell the new edition of the newspaper before reading it. Hands around the mug of thick peat-brown tea, he went through the *Gazette* page by page and was reasonably satisfied with what he saw.

Don arrived about an hour later, saw McAllister at a typewriter and heard Rob clattering up the stairs whilst still carrying on a conversation with Mrs. Smart downstairs. But no Joanne.

"Joanne won't be in today."

Don read between the lines of McAllister's frown and didn't say a word.

"Not too bad, this." McAllister waved the paper, then rose and tucked it under his arm and left with a "Catch you later."

He and Rob jiggled around each other in the doorway and Don folded onto a chair, staring at the vacuum left by the departing editor.

"What?" Rob stared at Don.

"McAllister. He said he liked the paper."

McAllister walked down to the covered market, to the butcher with the best bacon and the baker with the best rolls. He fetched the milk in from the doorstep, glad to see it was not frozen and that the birds had not attacked the gold foil top. He opened the front door, again making as little noise as possible in case she was till asleep, and made for the kitchen. It was the smell of frying bacon that awoke Joanne. He heard the toilet flush and poured another cup of tea. She came through wrapped in the dressing gown.

"I didn't know what to do with your things," he started, "soaked through, so I put everything to dry on the boiler, but they'll probably be a mess."

He kept his back to her as he spoke, busy with the frying pan.

"That's your tea on the table." He shoogled the pan to coat the eggs with bacon fat. "One roll or two?"

"I couldn't manage a thing." Even the smell made her queasy.

"Fine, have a plain roll instead, they're still warm."

He kept busy. She kept still. But sooner or later they would have to look at each other. He made up his own rolls, put them aside and went over to her.

"Here, let me see." Confront it straight on was the best way. "That's a real keeker. Purple, shot through with delicate shades of black, red and green, as a poet would say. Just as well I gave you the day off or you'd never hear the end of it in the office."

She tried to smile but it hurt. "McAllister . . ."

"Only tell me if you want to. No need for

297

explanations."

"Thanks." And that was that.

McAllister left after tidying up the kitchen.

"Pull the door to. I hardly ever lock it."

Joanne felt that she had no right to ask, but Chiara was the only one she could call. Shivering in the drafty hallway, she picked up the phone.

"I'll be right over."

No hesitation, no demands for an explanation; the reaction made Joanne deeply ashamed of the neglect she had shown her friend.

When they were settled together in McAllister's kitchen and after Chiara had whistled at Joanne's black eye, Joanne began to apologize.

"I am so sorry, I didn't heed you when you called, when you needed a friend, I . . . Chiara, I feel so terrible I didn't help you, I was so caught up in my own problems. I am so sorry."

"No, it's fine. I was hurt. But looking at you, I understand. And I have Peter."

This was not said to offend Joanne. Chiara was just stating a fact. Joanne hugged herself in envy, the prickly plaid of the dressing gown making her eyes water.

"I don't think walking out to my car in

your boss's dressing gown is a good idea." Ever-practical Chiara smiled. "Think what the neighbors will say." She said this in a pretend-shocked broad Scottish voice. "Give me your keys and I'll fetch something from your house. It'll only take me half an hour." She held out her hand. "I'm presuming Bill's at work?" She didn't fancy running into him. She thought she might kick him in the goolies. Not that Joanne had told her anything.

"He's gone to the west coast for a few weeks." I hope.

"Good. When you're ready, come back to our house. Papa always says ice cream is the best remedy for falling off your bike."

That did it. Joanne started to cry. She put her arms on the table, leaned over and sobbed and sobbed. Chiara stood by, patting her on her shoulders crooning, "I know, I know," almost in tears herself.

"I'll make you tea before I go." Chiara waved the kettle at her. "I don't suppose there's coffee in this heathen household." She was banging the cupboards open and shut. "Tea it is then."

In the warm solitude of the kitchen as she waited for Chiara to return, she understood what her friend had meant. It doesn't really matter what story is told, it's a matter of saving face. Everyone knows but no one wants to confront a battered wife; look the other way, pretend it isn't happening, sweep it under the carpet, and worse, worst of all because this came from women, and usually from the woman herself, "She must have done something to deserve it." But her complicity in her own fate was shifting.

She looked around, aware of the silence and the warmth and the clean sparse kitchen. She got up and wandered into the sitting room. Again, there was little furniture besides a deep comfortable armchair and a reading lamp, but hundreds and hundreds of books. No bookcases, but books stacked all along the walls at a height just below toppling point, leather bound, cardboard bound, Penguins, manuscripts, notebooks, an atlas open on the floor at the map of countries surrounding the Baltic Sea, the *Oxford English Dictionary* — the complete set making its own stack — bird books, nature books, paleontology, history, philosophy (at least that was what she thought, because she only recognized a few of the names), journals, magazines, old newspapers. She examined the titles, picked up a volume here and there; she had never heard of most of them and many were in French, some in Spanish.

John McAllister, I hardly know him. She was grateful to and fascinated by the man. He was an enigma. And she wished that long ago, in another lifetime, she had had the chance to meet a man like him — a man who could be a friend, whom she could respect.

When Chiara returned it took almost an hour for them to sort everything out, to make their confessions, to make amends, to forgive and then recover from the rift in their friendship. Chiara was never one to hold on to a grudge. Not like us Scots, Joanne thought, we hold on to grudges as though it was character forming never to forget a grievance.

"The worst thing for me," Chiara told her, "is watching Peter. He is so confused. He can't bring himself to believe his fellow countryman, Karl, could do something so awful as to kill a child. Even accidentally."

"The worst thing for me will be facing McAllister in the office," Joanne confessed.

"Tell him you were drunk and fell off your bike, that's what everyone else does." They giggled.

"Don't make me laugh, Chiara, it hurts."

"Stop fussing," Chiara commanded as her

father rushed hither and yon, getting in everyone's way and exasperating his sister, who was trying to serve brimming bowls of soup to the gathering around the table.

"But I like fussing over two such bonnie lassies," Gino protested. The Scottish phrase sounded so funny in Gino Corelli's Italian accent that Joanne didn't mind. Normally she hated it when non-Scots put on a cod Scottish accent. It made her cringe.

"Peter, you help. Gino, you sit," Aunty Lita commanded.

Although not yet married to Chiara, Peter was a full-fledged member of the household, so Aunty Lita could boss him around as much as she did the others. For which Peter was grateful.

"Maybe I fetch your wee girls from school, no?"

"Thank you, Mr. Corelli, but they can walk home by themselves again. It's quite safe now that this maniac is locked up." Joanne caught the wince on Peter Kowalski's face. "I'm so sorry, Peter. I've put my foot in it, haven't I?"

They all turned to their soup and for a good few minutes the only sound was of spoons chiming on china bowls and slurping.

■ ■ ■ ■

Peter thought about Joanne's assumptions as he walked back across the river to his office. He had spent some considerable hours at Porterfield Prison with Karl. They had conceived of the simple strategy of Karl's pretending his English was almost non-existent and for some reason, Inspector Tompson had allowed Peter to act as interpreter. Now that Detective Chief Inspector Westland had joined the inquiry team, the inspector had become almost amenable. The senior detective was watchful but quiet. The new turn in the questioning had Peter extremely perplexed; questions about Karl's past — his marital status, his sexual habits, did he like boys, distasteful questions, nasty, murky, insinuations that worried Peter, as he had no inkling what the policemen were referring to. This particular piece of information had somehow managed to remain secret.

"Papa! Delivering Halloween lanterns in an ice-cream van. Honestly!"

"Grandad and the girls loved it," Joanne told her. "Mind you, Granny Ross looked as though she'd swallowed a soor ploom when she looked out the window."

"Then the chimes going off! And all those wee ones coming with their pennies, and no ice cream." Chiara rolled her eyes.

Oh my papa, to me he is so wonderful
Oh my papa, to me he is so wise.

They sang in unison the van jingle that Chiara had insisted her father install. When Gino played the chimes, children came running as though summoned by the Pied Piper of Hamelin himself.

"It is good to see you laugh again, my beautiful Scotch friend." Gino beamed.

"Scots," Joanne said automatically.

"Scots, Scotch, *sì, sì*. Beautiful all the same. But we got all the lanterns delivered — twenty-eight of them."

Joanne stopped laughing.

"I'm sorry I won't be there — no party this year for me, not with this great keeker."

Chiara looked straight into her one open eye and the other, half-open.

"You'll have to be more careful and not go falling off your bike in future."

Aunt Lita broke the awkward pause. "Do you dress up for Halloween, like the little children?"

"Every year, except this year . . ."

"I have an idea." Lita always wanted everything to be perfect. "We make you a . . . I don't know the word, a man in a boat, from old times, with one eye and a big sword and a hat and feather."

"A pirate."

"*Sì, sì.* Wonderful. We make a frilly for a shirt and I find a hat and — a one-eye mask?"

"An eyepatch. The sword?" queried Joanne.

"I've my Highland dancing sword," Chiara offered.

"Perfect. Now all we is need a big feather," ordered Lita.

"Margaret has feathers," cried Joanne, "but I'll have to hurry, there's only a few hours to the party."

Leaving the chatter and laughter of the Corelli household, Joanne realized what a good idea it had been to invite them to the Halloween party. Gino so wanted to be back as a member of his adopted community. As she neared the double-story council semi, to see the girls before dashing off to borrow feathers from Margaret McLean, Joanne remembered again the look on her mother-in-law's face when the ice-cream van had arrived. Hilarious. And at the sight of her

305

son's handiwork — Joanne's eye was still purple in parts, shaded with a bilious yellow green — at least she had the decency to look embarrassed.

Joanne had not been back to the office. Yesterday, a quiet day at home, no work, no husband, children at school, had given her thinking space to wrestle with two puzzles in urgent need of resolution; a Fair Isle pattern in twelve colors for a jumper for Annie, and the perennial dilemma of her marriage. The knitting had resolved itself. The soft bright shades of Highland Glen wools, now unfankled, were framed in their traditional rows, formed a clear pattern. The puzzle of her marriage was harder to sort out. Leave? If I could, I would. Of this she was now sure. But where *to?* There was no solution to that.

Grandad Ross was taking Annie and Wee Jean to the party. He loved all the Halloween rigmarole. Granny Ross was delivering baskets of tablet and toffee apples, as well as lending a tin bath for dooking apples. She was waiting for her church friends to pick her up in their car. She greeted Joanne's news with a face like a disapproving duchess. But the girls had cheered.

"You can't come. Have you no shame,

showing your face in public?" Granny Ross glared at her. "What will people think?"

Joanne bit back the retort, "If your son had any shame, I wouldn't need to hide my face," and said nothing. As usual.

"Don't worry, I'll be in disguise."

The girls cheered again and Grandad joined in.

The feather stuck out from the pirate hat at a rakish angle and with one shapely leg extended, Joanne thanked her hostess with a principal-boy bow.

"Thanks, Margaret. These feathers are the very dab. This sword, though, it's impossible to sit down. I'll have to be careful I don't poke anyone anywhere sensitive."

Rob sauntered into the sitting room just as his mother and Joanne burst out laughing.

"What's the joke?" He stopped, stared, transfixed, then he wolf-whistled.

"Less of that," the pirate retorted.

"You look smashing."

"Joanne is as lovely as always," Margaret scolded, "but you don't usually notice."

"She's married."

Raising her sword above her head Joanne turned on him in mock anger.

"So, married women are not allowed to

be attractive, eh?"

"Sorry, I surrender, Captain Blackheart. Or is it Long John Silver? No, no parrot."

Joking he may have been, but he sneaked another look. In a man's white shirt, cinched tightly at the waist with Chiara's best, bought in Edinburgh, wide patent leather belt, with handmade Madeira lace cascading at collar and cuffs, tight black trousers, and black riding boots that made her legs look even longer, she was indeed smashing. Lita had taken in the trousers so much, Joanne had had to lie down to pull them on.

"The eyepatch looks great." Rob chattered away in blissful ignorance of its real purpose. Joanne had had two days off with a cold, or so McAllister had informed him. "I almost wish I was coming to the hall."

He didn't mean it. He was off to a much more sophisticated evening at the Pavilion in Strathpeffer. The new band had all the latest from America, and he had a date. With a policewoman.

"Not so fast." His mother handed him baskets of apples and sweeties.

"I have to go soon, Mum. It's a cold long drive on a motorbike."

"If you take us to the church hall, your father will give you the car for tonight."

"I will?" Angus looked up from *The Scotsman.*

"Unless *you* want to come to the Halloween concert instead?"

At the very idea of sitting through endless turns by other people's children, Angus readily agreed.

"Avast, me hearties!" Rob picked up the baskets and led them in procession out to the car before his father changed his mind.

In Scotland, Halloween was a Celtic festival with the night promising a delicious frisson of fear. The evening star hovered above the horizon, the starting signal for the annual visitation from the undead. Ring the doorbell, pretend to frighten the occupants, sing a song or recite a poem, then hold out the bag for the Halloween treats, that was the ritual. The guisers were well prepared for their task of fending off the lost spirits out and about on their annual night of home leave. Ghoulish lanterns, fiendish disguises and fire were tricks from time immemorial to confuse the undead and discourage them from overstaying their welcome.

This year, Margaret and Angus McLean noted, but didn't mention, that there were fewer guisers calling at their door. Jamie's disappearance, on this very stretch of street, the children didn't yet talk about; it was too fresh. But instinctively, when the small gangs of witches or elves or ghosts or Vikings came to the beginning of what they judged to be the stretch where the boy had vanished, they ran, ran as if the devil or a hoodie crow was after them, about to swoop, to pick one of them out, to gather the victim up and take them to join wee Jamie. They ran and ran until they had turned the corner, then gathered to get their breath back, the girls laughing, clutching each other, the boys jumping around, kicking a fence or a tree, yelling out to the stars and the unknown, in a defiant display of bravado.

Outside the church hall, a newly built rectangular construction of no architectural merit whatsoever, men and boys, like a stream of worker ants, were adding branches, off-cuts of wood, anything that could burn, to a dark tepee shape. This bonfire would blaze well into the night. At a clearing well away from the building, a trio of former soldiers was readying fireworks on frames and posts and mounds of earth. A bottle of fortified lemonade did the rounds of the men. The colored lights and bunting that transformed the hall on every festival throughout the year were supplemented by dozens of expertly carved ghastly grinning lanterns that sent dancing shadows across the walls.

Fierce competition between the ladies of the Women's Guild meant cakes galore, decorated in a Halloween theme, usually in green icing. Pyramids of sandwiches, crusts cut off, were served on large aluminum trays. Bowls of nuts were closely guarded, to stop boys sneaking handfuls of walnuts and hazelnuts for ammunition. Industrial-size teapots with industrial-strength tea and sticky, artificially bright Kia-Ora orange squash were served in the plastic cups that made all drinks smell and taste of plastic.

At the far end of the hall below the stage, children jiggled and shrieked, impatient for their turn, mocking their friends as they had a go at dooking for apples. Scones dangled on strings from a clothesline, treacle dripping in dark gelatinous globs onto the painters' drop cloths and the unwary, and hands behind backs, mouths open like baby cuckoos, the children would try to bite through a scone as it swayed in front of them. Invariably a passing prankster would jerk the rope, sending the treacle-soaked scones slap into someone's face or hair or down the back of a neck, to shrieks and taunts of "I got you, I got you!"

A small crowd surrounded their minister, Rev'rnt Mac as they called him, as he knelt down, hands behind his back, to dook for an apple. A passing wee lad jerked the clothesline and treacle droplets rained down on the minister's dog collar.

His mortified mother grabbed the boy by his ear and was about to skelp him on the backs of his knees, but the minister's roar of laughter stopped her still. "That's a good trick, Neil, and no mistake."

"He's a good man, our minister," she told her friends later, "not stuck-up like some. Did you see him laugh? All covered in treacle an' all?"

"Ladies and gentlemen, boys and girls."

The microphone let out a banshee wail. Duncan caught the look of panic from the Boy Scout in charge of the electrics, switched the microphone off and continued in his Sunday sermon voice.

"Ladies, gentlemen, children, we will now have the judging for the best costumes."

Boys on one side, girls on the other, the children lined up. One faerie, only three years old, wouldn't join in without her mother. Duncan, his wife, Elizabeth, and Margaret McLean, with the surprise addition of John McAllister, began the judging. Children, wriggling around as though itch-ing powder had been poured down their backs, watched the judges going up and down the rows inspecting the costumes, sometimes asking what the guiser was meant to be, occasionally conferring with each other.

Annie was as excited as the others but refused to show it. She had a sneaking suspicion that she had no chance of winning because two of the judges were her uncle and aunty and they would never show favoritism. Just the opposite. A short whispered conference and the judging was finished. Duncan climbed back onto the stage, and not risking the microphone again, he announced the judges' decisions.

"Best turnip lantern, Jock Maxwell." Everyone cheered. The best boys' costume prize went to a boy in a box addressed to Australia, second prize to a Viking. Everyone cheered and stamped their feet.

"Best costume, girls. First prize, Amy Wilson."

The young Mary Queen of Scots was the obvious winner. With her natural flaming red hair and a costume her mother had worked on for weeks, she deserved her prize, a beautiful illustrated book of Bible stories.

"Second prize, Annie Ross."

At first it didn't register. Next thing she knew, Granny Ross was poking her. "Go on." She rushed up to collect her book. John McAllister gave her a big wink as he handed over the prize. "The bow and arrows look as though they're for real."

Annie tore off the paper there and then — her very own copy of *Kidnapped*. She'd heard it serialized on Children's Hour, she'd read it from the library, but her very own copy! She was so glad she hadn't won first prize. A whistle, applause and laughter made her look round. There was her mum, standing onstage, looking embarrassed. And there was Mr. McAllister with the microphone.

"Of course, this prize must be fixed seeing as how I'm Mrs. Ross's boss. Still, won fair and square, first prize, ladies' best dressed, dinner for two at the Station Hotel."

He handed her an envelope to oohs and aahs and cheers and applause. All Joanne could think was, What on earth will I do with this?

"I'd also like to add that Mrs. Ross is welcome to come to work dressed as a pirate anytime. Maybe she can frighten the accounts department into a pay rise."

More laughter and applause. Annie watched, so proud of her mum and glad her dad wasn't there. The child knew this small scene would not have gone down well.

The stage and games were cleared, supper was served, then cleared, tables were folded and chairs stacked, all tasks done with military precision.

Margaret decided to stay on for the dancing. McAllister had offered her a dance and a lift home.

"How can I refuse?" she replied.

Joanne overheard the invitation and was amazed. Margaret, she knew, loved nothing better than a swift Strip the Willow, but McAllister?

The crowd cheered through the concert, clapping everyone indiscriminately. After a sketch from the Girl Guides, Sheila Murchison, representing the Brownies, gave a recitation of one of the most maudlin of Sir Walter Scott's heroic poems. Annie didn't even notice her sworn enemy; she was engrossed in her book. Just when John McAllister thought he could take no more unintelligible recitations nor out-of-tune singing, Margaret motioned him to pass his cup.

"No more tea, I couldn't stand it."

"Wheesht." She put a finger to her lips.

He really liked that she was one of the few women of his present acquaintance who

315

wore deep red nail polish. He liked it even more when, out of her voluminous handbag, she produced a slim silver flask. McAllister held his cup below the table and she topped the tea up with a generous tot. Grinning like pupils up to no good behind the school bicycle sheds, they had a quick squint around, lest some harpy from the Women's Guild, or an elder of the kirk, might be watching, then knocked their cups together.

"Slàinte mhath."

The concert ended, the audience trooped outside for the next event. There was no wind, no moon that night, but millions of stars. The bonfire fired quickly; the gallon of paraffin helped. A circle formed, fronts toasting, backs freezing. Cheers, squeals and the howling of dogs accompanied the whiz and bang of the fireworks. The rockets were best, Joanne and her girls agreed, and she hugged them, one on each side, to keep herself warm. As the fire shifted and fell, sparks flew up to meet the constellations. The primitive enchantment of the blaze made even the most prosaic of Scottish souls lift in joy. When the flames died down to a dark red glow, the embers would be perfect for baking tatties. People had come prepared. Wrapped in silver foil, laid around the edge of the fire, the oversized potatoes would be ready for eating or as hand warmers on the walk home.

A chord from the accordion was the signal for the final episode . . . the dancing. Joanne left the fire reluctantly but the opening chords of a Highland reel she could not resist. She stood at the edge of the crowd, clapping and swaying to the music. She waved and laughed as John McAllister and Margaret went swinging around in a hectic Strip the Willow. The past weeks dissolved in a joy of music.

Grandad Ross joined her, Jean slumped over his shoulder.

"I'll take the wee soul home now. She's exhausted."

"Are you sure, Dad? Don't you want to hear the music?"

Joanne knew how much he enjoyed the fiddle.

"Call thon music? Seagulls following the plough'd be better than this lot." Her father-in-law shouted to be heard above the band.

"I forgot, you're not overfond of Kenny Macbeth."

An unknown grievance between him and Kenny Macbeth had lasted all of thirty-odd years. She looked at him fondly and smiled.

"Thanks, Dad, that would be great. Where's Annie? And Granny Ross?"

"Mother's finishing up in the kitchen, Annie's stuck in yon corner with her book, but she'll come home wi' us."

Annie looked up as though she'd divined her name through all the noise and started pushing through the crowd. Granny Ross appeared, laden with empty baskets and the washing tub. A sleepy Jean raised her head briefly from Grandad's shoulder to give her mother a kiss. Joanne turned back to the dancing. She had not gone three paces when a scream sliced through the music. The band played on. The shrieks didn't stop. The music faltered. All eyes turned to the bewildered old man and the terrified child writhing in his arms.

"The hoodie crow!"

Struggling and shaking, Jean tried to hide in her grandfather's coat collar, sobbing over and over, "Hoodie crow, it's a hoodie crow." Annie clutched Grandad's arm, trembling, staring, defiant, transfixed. Granny Ross was lost for words. For once. The Reverend Duncan looked at his sobbing niece. He too was lost for words. At his side stood Father Morrison in a shiny midnight-black cassock and outdoor cape, the collar turned up high against the night. With a huge smile he walked toward an astonished Joanne, hand outstretched.

"It's very good to meet you, Mrs. Ross, I've heard so much about you."

FOURTEEN

"What can I do for you, Mr. McAllister, sir?"

PC Grant seemed to take up all the front desk at the police station, leaving not enough room for anyone else either to sit beside him or squeeze behind.

"Have we met?" McAllister was sure he'd have remembered an elephant masquerading as a policeman.

"No, sir. But I've heard a lot about you. I'm friends wi' Rob McLean." He suddenly realized his gaffe. "Please don't let on to Inspector Tompson, though."

"Wouldn't dream of it. Is he in?"

"Oh no, *he* never works a Sunday."

"Good. Who I really want is Detective Chief Inspector Westland."

"He's no in neither."

"Constable . . . ?"

"Grant. Willie Grant."

"Constable Grant, I need to see the DCI.

It is extremely important that I see him immediately. Urgent, in fact." McAllister was still not sure he was getting through. "It's a matter of life and death."

"I suppose I could phone his landlady."

McAllister waited.

"Yes, uh-huh, could you go get him? Yes, it's important. Aye, police business."

They both waited a good five minutes.

"Yes, sir. No, sir, he didn't say but he says it's life or death. Aye. I'll tell him."

PC Grant put down the phone and pronounced, "Fifteen minutes, sir, he'll meet you here."

McAllister chose to wait outside — more room to pace. It was a ridiculously early hour for him to be out on a Sunday, but then, he had been up most of the night. DCI Westland appeared within ten minutes. They shook hands and went inside. McAllister mentally prepared himself to put his case. He in no way underestimated the task. He knew the accusation would be regarded as an impossibility. But he had to. . . .

"Mr. McAllister?"

"Sorry. I was trying to gather my thoughts."

"Right then." He gestured to a chair and they sat. "Life or death. Which is it?"

"A man's life, a boy's death."

321

"I don't need to ask who the boy is — was."

For all that McAllister was concise and articulate, and for all his pride in his ability to be detached, unemotional, the drowning of the boy had raised the ghost of his own dead and overwhelmed him.

"Have you looked at the possibility that the local priest, Father Morrison, might have had something to do with the boy's disappearance?" The shock on the policeman's face made McAllister charge on. "You've no doubt heard the story from the girls." McAllister could see he had lost him. "About them seeing a hoodie crow pick up the boy and fly off with him?" No, that was not well put. "You know how in Glasgow there are rumors of some of the priests being involved in, well, interfering with boys and suchlike?"

"I don't know Glasgow, Mr. McAllister. And I would like to know how you got the idea that the boy was interfered with, as you put it."

McAllister heard the warning in his voice.

"I know. You're right. I don't know. But I'm convinced you should look into this man."

As the words came out, he felt an immediate pang of regret. McAllister himself hated others telling him how to do the job. How he hated it when someone would say to him, newspaper in hand, What you should do is . . .

"Are you saying that rumors, circulating around Glasgow, about priests of the church . . . are you saying the same thing is being talked of around here?"

"No. No, that's not being said around here — not to my knowledge. But I know, or at least suspect, that there is some truth in the stories. . . ."

"Aye. Stories," Westland repeated. "And tell me, Mr. McAllister, how have you made the leap from stories, unconfirmed rumors, in Glasgow, to here, in the Highlands, to Father Morrison, as far as I know a respectable cleric? And, what did you say, the children saw hoodie crows kill the boy? I've got that right, haven't I? Hoodie crows?"

McAllister walked out into Sunday in despair.

As she cycled to the Monday-morning must-not-be-late-for meeting, she was steeling herself for the first real confrontation with McAllister. Every time Joanne remembered the night of her flight, which was often, she burned in shame. The fine drizzle of chill rain that penetrated every nook and cranny of her coat cooled her cheeks, but the memory of standing — no, swaying — on the doorstep of McAllister's house made her cringe down to her damp boots.

McAllister knows, was all she could think — he knows. And the blame was all hers, of that she was certain. I let this violence happen to me, was how she now saw it.

Joanne was barely in the office door when the phone started.

"Am I the only one who answers the blooming thing?" It was a rhetorical question.

Gazette." She sat on the edge of the desk. "Chiara! How are — ? Slow down — tell me again. . . . Never!"

"What was that all about on Halloween night?" McAllister strode in and was looming over her.

"That's terrible!" Joanne, trying to concentrate, flapped her hand, shooing him away as though he was a swarm of midges.

"I went by your house yesterday," McAllister informed Joanne. "No one was in."

"Chiara, say that again."

"Do you mind getting off the phone to your female friends?"

"I can't believe it. It's just so . . . Uh-huh, right, I know, unthinkable! That inspector is mad! Aye, I'll be by as soon as I can."

She turned on McAllister. "That was Chiara Corelli and —"

"Why was your wee girl so terrified of that priest?"

"It was Halloween. She was exhausted." Joanne was distracted, didn't pick up that McAllister was serious.

"You yourself said she saw a hoodie crow when the boy disappeared! She was terrified because he is what she saw!"

"McAllister, what on earth are you talking about?"

"He's the hoodie crow!"

"Don't be ridiculous. He's a priest!"

"What's that got to do with it?"

"McAllister, have you lost your mind? I told you, it's all havers. Sure, they saw something, shadows most likely, but there is no hoodie crow."

He glared at her. "Your daughter said — no, she screamed — he's the hoodie crow. She was pointing straight at the priest."

"She sees the hoodie crow everywhere, in the street, at the pictures, in her dreams . . . and, in case you hadn't noticed, it was Halloween — all the children were working themselves up to be frightened."

"You're ignoring the obvious."

"Is this a private fight or can anyone join in?" Don appeared.

"He's off his head." Joanne jumped off the table and out of reach of McAllister's rage.

Rob, not far behind Don, last as usual for the Monday meeting, joined in.

"What's going on?"

"McAllister thinks Father Morrison is the hoodie crow and . . ." The logical connection to that, she couldn't make. But the fierceness of McAllister had Joanne completely flustered. She had never seen the man emotional about anything.

"That's it? You're taking bairns' fancies seriously?" Don shook his head.

"That's daft." Rob was laughing. "I've known Father Morrison for years."

"You know him?" McAllister practically pounced on Rob.

"He's our next-door neighbor. A nice man. Maybe a bit too fond of a drop, and he's forever taking photographs, but harmless."

"Your next-door neighbor, he lives on the street where the boy went missing, and you didn't think to tell me!" McAllister was cold with anger. "Don't you get it?"

Rob had his mouth open to speak but didn't have a hope of a chance to say anything.

"The girls saw a hoodie crow take the

boy." McAllister pointed a finger at Rob's face. "A priest, in a cassock, looks like a great big hoodie crow. And that is what they saw."

They were all three staring at the editor. Joanne was the first to move. She hadn't had time to take off her hat nor scarf. She grabbed her coat and made for the door.

"I'm away out. If you need me I'm at the Corelli house. And instead of shouting your unbelievable, your *mad* accusations about a *good* man, a priest, how about this? The procurator fiscal is accusing the Polish man — Karl — with sexually interfering with the boy." She was shouting now. "Did you hear me, McAllister? Someone did something unspeakable to that boy. Now, *that* is unbe-lievable!"

"There goes your theory, McAllister." Rob pointed out, "Priests are celibate."

Don had to look away at that comment.

"Tell me, Mrs. Ross, what exactly is so unbelievable?" McAllister knew he was pushing it but couldn't stop himself. Joanne stood silhouetted in the doorway, desperate to be anywhere but here. Don and Rob, invisible onlookers, were also wishing they were elsewhere.

"I . . . it's unbelievable that anyone could do that, to a child, to a wee boy. . . ."

"It's not unbelievable in the real world," McAllister retorted. "It's not unbelievable that a priest —"

"It's unbelievable in *my* world."

"So you're going to bury your head in the sand? Ignore the fact that perverts live amongst us? Pretend that children don't get assaulted? Pretend that men don't beat their wives, pretend that —"

He stopped and stared at her in horror. She stared back. There was absolute silence — except for a phone ringing downstairs and footsteps clattering down to the print room and a distant bus straining up the steep brae and a flock of gulls swooping by the window.

"How about a cup of tea before we start the meeting?" Don broke the spell.

But Joanne had fled, so there was no one to make the tea.

It was Elizabeth Macdonald who answered the door. Monday was her husband's day off and she guarded his free time like a mother hen with a newly hatched chick.

"Mr. McAllister." Her surprise at seeing him turned to concern when he took off his hat. ("A face of thunder, now I know what that means," she remarked after he had left.)

"If you'd like to see the minister, he is at

the end of the garden cleaning out the hens and I don't think he'll be in for a half hour or so. But you're welcome to wait."

"Thank you, no. I'll go to see him." He set off down the path, leaving her with the thought that such a wounded soul might not notice the stench of fresh chicken manure.

Duncan Macdonald closed the gate to the chicken run and walked to the middle of the lawn to converse with McAllister. His guest had refused all offers of tea or of waiting until the minister had cleaned himself up. This wouldn't wait, he could see that, but he was astonished when McAllister told him of his mission.

"Mr. McAllister, I know my nieces. They are a bit unsettled just now, what with their friend dying and everything. They are lovely children but with vivid imaginations. What happened at the Halloween party was understandable. In fact, a few other of the wee ones were scared too when Jean called out 'hoodie crow,' but it's children, they don't mean anything by it." He talked in this vein for five minutes — and got nowhere.

"Mr. McAllister, I know Father Morrison. We have worked together on some committees and suchlike. I know him. He is a good, hardworking, compassionate man.

"Mr. McAllister, you can't say that. It is wrong to make such absurd and unfounded accusations.

"Very well, Mr. McAllister, I will take you at your word. I know you don't spread rumors and I trust you to keep these allegations to yourself.

"McAllister, if you ever need to talk to someone, I'm always here."

This offer Duncan Macdonald called out to the retreating back of John McAllister, who was fast disappearing into the drizzle that intermittently drifted in and out of the Monday morning in the first week of November, striding out on his mission, off to plead his case with anyone who would listen.

"Do you have an appointment?" Angus McLean's secretary asked the question knowing full well the answer. "Please take a seat, Mr. McAllister, I'll see if he is available." She also knew the answer to that but liked to observe the formalities. Or demonstrate her power, as Rob would have it.

"I see." He didn't, but Angus McLean interjected this and other such platitudes throughout McAllister's diatribe, growing more and more perplexed as he heard the wild conjectures from a man he had always regarded as the soul of reason.

"I hear what you are saying, McAllister,

but it's very farfetched.

"Now, hold on, McAllister, you are on very dangerous ground there. You can't make inferences like that, especially not on the word of two little girls.

"McAllister, the best I can advise you, as a solicitor and as a friend, is to think very carefully on what you are saying.

"No, McAllister, all I am saying is that you seem overwrought and perhaps you need to think through the conclusions you have come to. You have absolutely no proof of what you are saying."

"Aye, I hear you, but this needs a dram, if not a bottle, before I can get my head around your thinking."

Don stood in McAllister's office watching him sitting in the chair, knee jiggling, hand flicking a pencil in a frantic rhythm on the desk, fever-dark eyes staring out into the two o'clock semidarkness of dank cloud. He looks as though he's waiting for the executioner to appear, Don thought.

"Go home, McAllister, you're no use to us here. I'll be by your house when we've finished up. You supply the bottle though; one o' your single malts would go down a treat."

Seven o'clock but it could as well be

midnight, for the town had shut down against the weather; Don and McAllister were in the sitting room, which could have been mistaken for a stockade made from books, deep in chairs on either side of a fire. A solitary standard lamp in one corner cast a jaundiced yellow light, the blazing fire the only other source of illumination. The bottle, but no water, sat on a side table and with glasses charged, McAllister told Don why he had come to thinking what he thought.

"It was on Halloween, eight years, no, nine years now, that my wee brother Kenneth was found in the Clyde. . . ."

Don was a good listener. He listened without saying a word. He listened between the lines. He listened until the story was completely done.

"There was ten years between us — a lifetime at that age," McAllister started. "I didn't really notice my brother — I was too busy being a wee big man. I started at Glasgow High School, where I won a scholarship when he was a baby. I was a cadet on the *Herald* when he went to primary school, and when he too went to the high school, like many another Glaswegian, I was in Spain with the International Brigade. Terrible times that was, but the best of times.

When war broke out with Germany, I ended up writing propaganda for one of the ministries, as well as being back on the *Herald*."

Don knew he would never hear more than this, the bare bones of McAllister's life. And he would never ask.

"And all the while, I never noticed. I never knew that, to my brother, I was a hero. I was straight out of the Saturday-matinee films he loved, I was a character from the Biggles books he read, I was a bona fide *Boy's Own* hero. There I was in the school uniform with thon stupid cap, which he loved, there I was a cadet, on not just any old newspaper, but on the *Herald*, then there I was with all the Glasgow heroes — the intellectuals, the Union men, the poets — in Spain. And him, though only a wee boy, he followed and fantasized over my every move. Aye, I was a right hero and I never knew.

"So, the war was on, bombing at full tilt in Glasgow, especially around the Clyde shipyards. My father died in the Clydeside Blitz, 1941. It was a terrible time for all of us, and Kenneth, he was only ten. But still I never noticed my wee brother. I was living away from home, I was busy, I had my own friends, I had a woman in my life — I had endless excuses, but in truth, Kenneth

333

McAllister was the boy who lived with my mother and who was mad keen on boxing, which I loathed.

"Anyhow, when he was fourteen, the war was ending, he started coming to visit me, usually on a Saturday afternoon. I didn't mind. We didn't do much, just mooched around, occasionally went to the football, sometimes to a matinee, and it didn't matter even when it was foreign films with subtitles, he just wanted company. He seemed a bit quiet. Not that I really took notice, as I didn't know him. My mother asked me to talk to him. She thought he was too quiet. She said he was quite the chatterbox before. And, she said, he had stopped going to his boxing club — which was his passion, all he was really interested in, outside of books.

"Next thing, so it seemed, but really it was almost two years, he was found in the Clyde. The police said he had jumped, but the priest, the one that ran the boxing club, agreed to agree with my mother. He fell. That way, they could all do their hocus-pocus funeral flummery. Then all would be fine and dandy. Except for my mother. And for me."

The sounds of the wind, driving a horizontal rain, trying every trick to penetrate windows and doors, was providing the sound effects to the story. Now the fire added to the atmosphere, the wood construction collapsing in on itself, sending showers of sparks dancing up the chimney.

"My mother used to say that these" — McAllister poked the fire, setting off another display — "the sparks, they were souls flying up to heaven."

"And the hoodie crow?" Don broke another long silence.

"Aye. That." McAllister's bark of laughter made Don shudder in sympathy. "It reminded me, that's all, brought it all back."

McAllister topped up their glasses and was surprised to find the bottle almost empty.

"Aye, the sight of them, the priests and the brothers from the boxing club, huddled around his grave, made me think of a congregation of corbies — and you know how evil those birds can seem. So since then, I've always seen priests as crows. Corbie, hoodie crow, priest; it doesn't seem far-fetched to me." McAllister got up. "I've got that poem here somewhere, Edgar Allan Poe, he knew the power of ravens. Where did I put it?" He fumbled around the walls of books, gave up, sat back down, holding an empty glass, back to staring into the fire.

Don waited. Ten minutes was it? No, more

like five. But time seemed elastic by the fire, in the half light, on a night between Halloween and Armistice Day.

"I know something happened to my brother. I slowly came to realize that whatever it was, it had been happening for a while, over a few years. That really shook me. I tried to find out. I started, and ended, at the boxing club. I began to get an inkling of what he had been through, but it was like trying to hold down smoke. Black, stinking, noxious smoke; I could smell it but never find the source. They could teach the Intelligence Services a thing or two could that lot." He reached for a log, dropped it onto the fire, sending forth more souls.

"McAllister . . ." Don sensed that there was nothing more would be said that night. So he did what he did. After all, wasn't he the man who worked out the priorities, assigned the tasks, who would précis a story into digestible chunks? It was what he did best and this was no different.

"You're a journalist to the bone, McAllister," Don started. "And you're up here in the Highlands to show us teuchters a thing or two. But remember, for us, this is about the wee boy Jamie."

He held up a hand for his turn on the floor.

"I know this has stirred the ghosts. I'm not saying a word about your wild ideas, although I think you're off yer heid, no, what I'm saying is, we have to do what we do." He instinctively reached behind his ear for his pencil. It wasn't there. "Paper, McAllister, pen, pencil, anything, I can't think without scribbling."

McAllister took a deep breath and forced himself back to now. His quest, his nine years of guilt, he could nurse another night. They went into the kitchen, sat at the table and started.

"Right. Where are we? The Polish manny, Karl." Don made a heading. "Did he do it?"

"The tinkers are his alibi."

"And most of them are scattered the length and breadth of Ross and Cromarty and maybe into Sutherland." Don wrote FIND JIMMY MCPHEE in block capitals.

"Jimmy McPhee." McAllister leapt up and came back with the photograph and laid it on the table. "This is Jimmy McPhee" — he pointed to the wee face with a closed-eyes grin in the third-to-back row. "And this is my brother, one row down."

"Well, well." Don reached for his specs to examine the picture. "I know Jimmy was a champion boxer. I know he trained in Glasgow. This gives you another reason to find him. Next — see if you can find what really happened to Karl between jumping off the ship and him appearing back in town. Now . . ." Here Don stopped to think.

"This business of a person unknown interfering with the boy, was it done to him by the person who killed him? Had it been happening on a regular basis? Do we know of anyone who does this to boys?" Don looked over his glasses at McAllister. "We must do this fast, for when word gets out the Polish man may not survive prison. Right. What else? Father Morrison." Don printed the heading and yawned. "It's late. But see, this is — what was it you called it? Investigative reporting? You're aye hammering on about it to Rob, now *you* show us how it's done."

He pointed the pen at McAllister. "This obsession of yours, priests and hoodie crows, that's your affair. This" — he tapped the paper — "this is about the boy, not your boy, I grant you, but the wee boy here, in this town. Find out what happened to him, then maybe . . ."

Maybe you can lay to rest the other ghost, he thought but didn't say.

He rose to go. He gathered his coat and his hat. McAllister went to the door with him. And Don being Don, he couldn't leave without a parting shot.

"McAllister, one thing more. I'll no have an atmosphere in my newsroom. You owe Joanne an apology."

Although there was three-quarters of a bottle of best Highland single-malt in Don — for it was he who polished off the bottle — he pulled his hat down over his forehead, belted his coat tight, and with a wave good night, he trotted off into the wind and the rain and the black as though he was off into a sunny day at the races.

McAllister shut the door. As he went about switching off the lights, damping down the fires and closing out the night, he felt grateful to Don McLeod; grateful he had stayed the course of a strange evening, grateful that Don hadn't asked if he had read all the books — McAllister had had to drop an acquaintance for asking such an inane question — and most of all grateful that Don hadn't said "sorry" at the end of the monologue on his private catastrophe.

Maybe it was a hangover from Halloween, maybe it was the looming Armistice ceremonies, or perhaps it was the persistent drizzle, but in the quiet, by the fire, in other households in the town, more soul searching was taking place.

Rob was still shaken by the scene in the office that morning. So he dealt with it the only way he knew how; he joked. That McAllister has some daft ideas, he told his mother, but this beat the lot. Hoodie crows, he laughed. Margaret McLean smiled at her son but said nothing. The child's screams still rang around her head. She hadn't a daughter, nor sisters, she couldn't remember her own childhood, but in her limited experience, little girls screamed at everything and anything. So she tried to let the absurd idea go. But couldn't.

With the resident next door, Margaret had had only one quibble — the rhododendron forest. Like Burnham Wood, she had told him, it was preparing to march across their lawn and take over. Father Morrison smiled his friends-and-neighbors smile, nodded frequently as she explained how little light her sunroom was receiving, and did nothing.

Rob thought the man harmless but . . . He remembered one unusually sunny summer — right after Father Morrison had arrived. Rob was eleven or twelve, and with two school friends, they were romping on the lawn in their swimming trunks, having water fights with the watering-can and buckets, playing at pulling each other's trunks down, when they caught a glimpse of a figure lurking in the same, but shorter, rhododendron bushes. They spotted the camera. All three boys stopped their games, uncomfortable but not alarmed, and without a word being said either then or later, they went indoors. It was nothing.

Angus McLean informed no one of McAllister's visit. The passion behind the accusations had startled him. He heard McAllister out, made very little comment, thought about it for the rest of the day and then placed a phone call to an old friend, a former colleague who was now a distinguished member of the church hierarchy.

And Chiara. She told Peter and she told Gino. Unlike Chiara and Joanne, they could allow that perhaps a rare rogue priest could commit offenses against God and the Church. But Father Morrison? No, he was a good man. They knew him for a caring, charitable parish priest — better than many they had come across in different times and places.

Duncan Macdonald, visiting his parishioners, attending the sick in the hospital, the infirmary and the asylum, or sitting by his fire trying to compose next Sunday's sermon . . . in between, in the still moments, the memory of his niece's shrieks echoed in his head. He knew of abominable practices in all walks of life — why not amongst the clergy; we are men after all. He had no time for the notion of celibacy — how could such a person understand the everyday pressures of family life? The pressures on the celibate, and the loneliness; a recipe for disaster was how he saw it. But Father Morrison? The Reverend Macdonald was certain he was a good man; kind, caring, with a rare under-standing as well as compassion for some of the unfortunates that he helped.

And Joanne; she was sitting alone in the newsroom, hoping to avoid McAllister and deep in thought. She did believe her girls, yet she still found it impossible to fathom their story. But the hoodie crow a priest? Never!

"Can I have a word?"

Joanne jumped.

"McAllister, you scared the living day-lights out of me."

She had her hand on her heart as she spoke. The room was empty; Don and Rob were doing whatever it was they were do-ing.

"I owe you an apology. I wasn't thinking. Too many things get covered up was what I was trying to say. I didn't mean *you* when I —"

"Apology accepted." She rushed on to cover her embarrassment. "I've been thinking about what Annie and Jean saw. The idea of a priest being involved is so ridiculous but what if it was something like that, something similar, that they saw?"

"What exactly?"

"I don't know, McAllister. I've been thinking on it till I'm dizzy."

"Can't you ask them again?"

"No, it's impossible." She shivered. The distance between her and Annie was as wide as ever. "Peter Kowalski is convinced Karl the Polish man did not do this. To prove where he was at the time, he needs the tinkers to come forward. But Karl will never give them up to the police, especially after they saved his life. And he says that the night after he jumped ship, the night the boy disappeared, he went back down the harbor to try to get his belongings from the ship's captain. But the captain wouldn't let him on board."

"Really? Tell me more."

"Ask Peter Kowalski. Karl told him what happened that night, no, two nights it was. Then Peter picked him up the following morning, near the canal bridge on the road north." She frowned as she faced the possibility. "But if it wasn't Karl, if it can be

343

proven he couldn't have done it, who else, what else, could have killed, and done *things* to, a wee boy?"

FIFTEEN

Don took over production of the *Gazette.* McAllister shut himself in his office, sitting at his desk like a hen on the nest, doing the jobs Don gave him, writing a perfunctory editorial, smoking enough to warrant a visit from the fire brigade, going over and over, again and again, the few facts that he had gleaned about the crime.

McAllister had talked to Peter Kowalski with no mention of his alternative theory on the fate of the boy. The notion of a priest harming a child would be met with ridicule, he now knew that, and Peter and the Corellis were Catholic, after all. Peter said the charge against Karl was based on his being in the vicinity of the canal the night the boy disappeared. Also Karl's greatcoat, the coat he had tried to retrieve from the ship, had been found on the canal banks. That, Karl couldn't explain. Peter didn't know why he believed him, but he did. Right time, right place, he had told McAllister, convenient at best, a witch hunt at worst, was how he put it. The coat was worrying, but there was bound to be an explanation. The tinkers, they could back up Karl's story — but would they? Peter hadn't been able to find any of the tribe that had rescued Karl from the river.

Don pointed out that there were enough holes in the fugitive's version of events to make it all very suspicious. He even told McAllister that it was possible that Inspector Tompson had it right. After all, they didn't know the whole story. Time and place, yes; motive? — Fear of capture. Don had listed the points. Death an accident? Maybe. Involuntary manslaughter a possible verdict.

"And the assault on the boy? Can you explain that away?" was McAllister's objection to this scenario.

The *Gazette* was out. Joanne was still wary of McAllister; she couldn't bear the haunted figure he had become of late. His obsession with the boy's death was raw and obvious. All her education and upbringing had taught her to leave such things to the police. They know what's best, she reasoned, that was their job. She wanted the cynical Mc-

Allister back. She liked that version better.

She liked the single Mrs. Joanne Ross much better also. With Bill away she was beginning to open herself up to possibilities. Her daydreams would start, One day I'll . . .

"Get ahold of yourself," she muttered as she walked down Union Street, "a life of my own is as likely as . . ." She crossed the road trying to find a simile that, if written down, wouldn't be deleted by Don with his stubby wee pencil.

Joanne was on a mission. Six and a half weeks to Christmas and she hadn't started baking — I'm not much of a wife and even less of a housewife. Christmas in Scotland did not reach the Dickensian fervor displayed by the English. Christmas was quiet, a time for church and children. New Year was another matter. The distillery lorries were already out delivering throughout the county. Market stalls were busy taking orders for fattened geese and hens. The grocery shop on Union Street was frantic with women buying ingredients for Christmas puddings and New Year black bun. Shiny elfin-sized shovels poked out from open sacks standing on the floor displaying flour (four kinds), lentils, barley, peas (two kinds), and gleaming butter beans big as river pebbles. In drawers behind the counter were raisins, sultanas, currants, spices, crystallized fruit and all kinds of nuts. Male shop assistants were expertly measuring out and weighing the brown paper bags before tying them with a neat double handle of twine and writing on them the name and address of the lady of the house, ready to be put on the afternoon trains or to be delivered by the emporium's distinctive vans with the coat of arms proudly painted on the side. The store was an institution in the counties of the north.

"Cash or charge, Mrs. Ferguson, or Lady Fraser, or Madam?" came the question as the orderly queue of ladies took their turn at the counter.

"How are you, Mrs. Ross? The bairns keeping well?"

"Fine thanks, Mr. Malcolm. Could I have a pound of currants, half a pound of raisins, some glacé cherries and some whole almonds?"

"Baking a Christmas cake are we?"

"Not a chance. I could never compete with my mother-in-law. Just a Dundee cake."

"Mrs. Ross senior finished her baking long since, I suppose?"

"Aye, ten weeks she gives it, sitting in the

larder, sooking up their daily dose of brandy. Black bun and Christmas cake take at least six weeks, so she tells me. I contribute the silver threepences for Christmas pudding, that's all she'll trust me with," Joanne joked as she got out her purse. "What do I owe you?"

Payment was placed into a small screw-top barrel that whizzed around the shop on a system of pulleys conveying the money to the cashiers, lording it in an office that looked down on the shop floor.

"Hello, Mrs. Ross." A blushing Mhairi stood with a list in one hand and a small case in the other. "Do you mind me?"

"Of course, how could I forget? Mhairi from the inn on the West Coast. What brings you over here? Oh, I see, the Christmas list. Of course!"

"I see Mr. Ross most days," Mhairi told her. "He's fine." I see him every day and he's usually well away, she thought. But she would never say that. "Aye, I had some business to see to. Then I've to get all these messages for Mrs. Watt. I hope I can find time to look for a present for wee Rosemary. The train leaves back at four o'clock."

Joanne had finished her shopping and wasn't due back at work for an hour.

"Tell you what, let's have a cup of tea.

Coffee maybe? My treat."

Mhairi blushed. "I couldn't."

"Nonsense. Give Mr. Malcolm the list. Come with me whilst the order's being made up." She took the girl's arm and marched her off.

To Mhairi, the noise, the coffee monster, the jukebox, the steamed-up windows, the unfamiliar menu, the casual way Rob McLean appeared and sat down to join them, were exciting and scary and bewildering all rolled into one.

"A cappuccino for me," Rob ordered.

"Same," said Joanne.

The waitress licked her pencil, taking in Mhairi's country face and clothes, waiting.

"My friend will have the same." Rob to the rescue.

They drank their coffee, they chatted, then Rob told them he must dash.

"Where are you off to in such a rush?" Joanne asked. "It certainly can't be work."

"I'll let you in a wee secret, Mhairi, I have a rock 'n' roll band."

"A what?"

"You know, the new music from America. I get the records from the airmen at the Lossiemouth base and I dance to it at the Two Red Shoes in Elgin."

"I've heard a wee bit o' that," Mhairi

contributed, "on the wireless — Two-Way Family Favorites. But I really like Doris Day — 'What will be, will be.' "

"Not quite my cup of cappuccino." Rob laughed, and he went into an uncannily accurate takeoff of the radio show using his spoon as a fake microphone. "Next up we have a request from Sergeant Donny Douglas, BFPO 69 in Germany, for his sister Fiona in Ecclefechan — Bill Haley and the Comets — One o'clock, two o'clock, three o'clock rock." He jiggled off, leaving Joanne and Mhairi in fits of giggles. "Great meeting you, Mhairi," he called. "See you next time you're in town."

She watched, awestruck, as he left in a rush of scarves and gloves and motorbike jacket. "Is he your friend?" she asked Joanne.

"Well, he's a good ten years younger than me, and we work together, and I'm friends with his mother, but yes, he's a friend."

"I know his dad," Mhairi said. "He's a nice man too. Not at all stuck-up."

"Oh really? Do you know him from the hotel?"

"No, from here. He helped me out when I was in trouble. I saw him again this morning. He's been right good to me."

Joanne was curious by nature. That would

make her a good reporter. She also knew when not to ask questions. That would make her an even better reporter.

"Mr. McLean helped me," Mhairi continued. "Your sister and her husband the minister, they were kind to me, and Father Morrison, he helped me the most." Joanne, clearly astonished, had no idea what Mhairi was talking about.

"He, I mean Father Morrison, helped me to stay in a place where lassies like me have to stay when they're no married and then they have their babies and the babies are adopted and they never see them again." Mhairi continued speaking without pause, without breath, getting it all out before she changed the two-years-or-more habit of keeping her secrets nursed close to her heart. She needed to say this. Once only would be enough. Then she could go back to pretending.

"Then I said no. I said I've changed my mind. And I was told I had to. I had to give up my baby when it was born. I ran away. Your sister's husband took me in and I stayed with them for a whiley."

"That's when I first met you." Joanne smiled.

"Aye, I was as big as a bus by then. Reverend Macdonald spoke to Father Morrison and he made it all right with the nuns at the home. The father, he said I didn't have to, if I didn't want to, and he said it was good that a baby knew its mother, and he made the adoption people go away, and he talked to my father, and he writes to me sometimes, just a wee note now and again, and he always asks after Rosemary, and he said he wished he had a mother like me, who kept her baby, because he never knew his own mother."

"Rosemary is your baby." Joanne could think of very little to say.

"Aye. Well, I know *you* know. At first my dad thought it best to pretend we adopted her. But that never fooled no one. Now, I'm not going to pretend anymore. I promised no to tell, that was the agreement, but I want a name on her birth certificate. It's not right — father unknown, that's not nice on her birth certificate. I'll still keep it a secret but his name should be there. Mr. McLean is going to help me."

"Yes. I agree." Joanne admired the girl's bravery.

"I don't think her father will agree, though. He wanted nothing more to do with me after I fell in the family way. Nor with wee Rosemary. He's never even seen her. Too feart of what folks will say. Feart his wife'll find out, an' all that." She took a sip of cold coffee.

Joanne watched the determined face and fierce eyes and was reminded of Celtic warrior women keeping the English Redcoats at bay.

"But he said, Rosemary's father that is, that if I kept pestering him, he would see to it that she was taken away from me. Mr. McLean says he can't do that. And Mr. McLean said he has responsibilities to his child. But I don't care about that, I don't want his money. I like my job. Mrs. Watt is good to me and she knows about my situation and she says it doesn't matter. My mother and father, they worship the wee lass. They're real Christians. Not like some. And they've always stood up for me, unlike Mr. High and Mighty Findlay Grieg."

She caught the bus to the house. It had some funny name next to the door — Latin, Father Morrison had told her, but Mhairi always called it the Big House. She walked through the gloom of the rhododendrons emerging into the early afternoon light. She rang the bell and when the door opened, Father Morrison, in a soutane large enough to double as a tent, loomed over her. He bent down to her, wrapping his prehensile arms around her, almost lifting her off the doorstep in a hug. On tiptoes, laughing, wriggling, she exclaimed, "Father Morrison!" Hugging, touching, showing emotions, wasn't the done thing in Mhairi's way of life.

"My dear, dear girl." He put her down, stepped back, looked her up and down, smiling into her heart.

"You look grand. Apples in your cheeks. And so grown up. Your mother and father must be right proud of you."

"You look just the same." And he did. Still the same ginger giant, with the same sparse, see-through-to-the-scalp sandy hair, the same ginger wire-brush hair on the backs of his hands and knuckles, with a smattering on and in his ears. She had a pig on the croft that had hair just like that, and she loved pigs, loved their great friendly nosy natures, just as she loved Father Morrison.

"A cup of tea first, then all your news."

He strode to the back of the house calling his questions in his booming voice, over his shoulder as she trotted behind him.

"How's your mother? How's your father? And how is wee Rosemary?"

He put the kettle on the stove.

"I keep all your letters; I love hearing about the wee lass. Is she as bonnie as you?

You must get some pictures done."

Mhairi sat beaming as Father Morrison fussed around, searching for the tin with the shortbread, placing on the table the mismatched cups and saucers, instead of the best china — which he hated — putting the milk bottle out instead of using the jug, and finally pouring the tar he called tea, which Mhairi had acquired a taste for when she had stayed with the big bossy priest, who treated her as family and who had stood by her, giving her the encouragement and the courage to change her life.

"And Mr. McLean, what did he say? Will he be able to sort it all out?"

"Father" — Mhairi was laughing — "I'll tell you all about it if you give me a chance. I can't get a word in edgewise."

Father Morrison reached across and touched her gently on the head as though bestowing a benediction on the young woman whom he thought of so dearly.

"You know how proud I am of you, don't you?"

"Aye, Father, I do. But I would never have found the courage to keep wee Rosemary if it wasn't for you." She beamed at him. "And I'd never ever have found the courage to stand up to thae nuns if it wasn't for you!" She giggled at the memory.

"A child should know his mother," he stated simply.

"I'm right sorry you never found your mother."

"Aye, well, what's done is done."

"I know. But to never know your own mother, to be an orphan . . ."

"In that orphanage . . ."

She barely caught what he said but she heard the pain.

"It was all a long time ago." He recovered. "What matters is to forgive and get on with life. And now, dear child, I want to hear all the news about you and yours."

"I think Rosie's finished teething. Well, she's sleeping sound every night now."

And for the next hour, before Mhairi had to leave to catch the train home, they drank more tea, and reminisced, and laughed about the times they had had together when Mhairi was expecting, when she was in despair, and they laughed about the time when the nuns from the adoption agency came to collect the baby, and she was cowering in terror in the kitchen, with her coat on, hiding the baby under it, waiting to run out the back door, and he was holding them off at the front door, and they remembered when her parents came over from the west, and she told them she would never

357

ever give Rosemary up, and Father Morrison persuading her mother, who didn't need much persuasion, and her father, who needed even less when he had the wee thing, his first and only grandchild, in his arms, and they both — Father John Morrison and Miss Mhairi Mackinnon — agreed that those were heroic times, times to laugh about now that it was all over and wee Rosemary was settled with her mother and her family.

"The birth certificate? Has that man agreed to his name on it?"

"Mr. MacLean is seeing to all that," Mhairi told him. "But he'd better agree, else Mrs. Grieg might find out what she married."

Don had heard that Jimmy McPhee was in Ross-shire, arranging the wedding of the eldest brother, Keith. Later that day, through the mysterious McLeod network that operated on a bar-to-bar basis, the word got through to Jimmy.

"McAllister," he barked into the phone. "Mr. McPhee . . . Fine, Jimmy, just the man. Uh-huh, aye . . . If you give me directions I'm sure I'll find it. Tonight? Right-oh. Seven it is."

The drive to Ross-shire took McAllister a

good hour and a half through the dark. In the beam of his headlights he spotted the caravans, the lorries, the ponies tethered to silver birch trees and, further down the river meadow, one bender much larger than the other three. He switched off his engine. The river-running, tree-rustling quiet lasted a fraction of a second before a chorus of fearsome-sounding dogs made him stay in the car, the door shut, waiting. Someone arrived.

"McAllister?"

He wound down the window.

"Aye."

"Over here."

It was just above freezing outside, but inside the bent birchwood and tarred tarpaulin covering, the bender was spacious and warm from a potbelly stove. What with the carpets, the wireless in a walnut cabinet, the gramophone and crammed-full china display cabinet, McAllister thought he could be in an Edinburgh sitting room, though without windows. Jenny McPhee sat regally in her armchair, tea service at the ready.

"Tea or a dram or both?"

"Both."

He took off his coat and hat, settled down, comfortable with these strangers. They reminded him of the Romany families he had encountered in Spain and the south of France. He wouldn't have blinked if someone had produced a guitar and struck up some flamenco and Jenny McPhee had joined in on castanets.

"Thank you for agreeing to talk to me," McAllister started.

"No," interrupted Jenny. "We will listen, then . . . we'll see."

"It's about Karl, the Polish man who jumped ship in the harbor and who was rescued by your kinsmen."

"Now, did we say he was rescued by one of us?" Again Jenny broke into the conversation.

"Who was *supposedly* rescued by your kinsmen."

"That's the way." Jenny laughed.

Jimmy grinned at his mother, grinned at McAllister and sat back to enjoy the contest.

"Karl, the Polish man who jumped ship and who was rescued from the river by persons unknown" — McAllister looked across at the blackcurrant eyes, received a nod and continued — "was aided and sheltered by a number of souls, identity also unknown, for a night or two; that part is unclear. A note was delivered to Peter Kowalski, by a boy, whose identity is also unknown, informing Peter of the fugitive's plight, and his whereabouts, with instructions —"

"Written in Polish by the man himself," Jenny said, butting in again.

"— with instructions on where to meet."

"By the canal bridge, on the road north, at eight in the morning, when it would still be dark," Jenny informed him.

"So." McAllister paused; Jimmy topped up his glass. "So, if nothing is done or said, this Polish man Karl will be prosecuted and most likely found guilty of the murder and sexual assault of the boy —"

At that, Jenny winced in shock. "Surely no?"

"That's what happened and those will be the charges, Mrs. McPhee." McAllister spoke gently, seeing even in the dim how shocked his hostess was. "Unless something can be done to prove Karl couldn't have done it."

"This changes things," Jenny muttered, looking straight at her son.

There was a hush in the room, if you could call this canvas-covered space a room. McAllister knew better than to ask for help.

Jimmy McPhee spoke. "Or else it can be proved that someone else did this filthy crime."

There was a pause in the discussion as the

three mulled over this thought.

"You do understand our situation, Mr. McAllister."

It was Jenny who needlessly reminded him that the plain fact of being a Traveling family of the north — of anywhere in the country — made it almost impossible for them to be witnesses in front of a judge and jury, even more impossible when the accused was a foreigner.

"As Jimmy says," she pointed out, "the only thing for it is for the real murderer to be found."

And that, McAllister knew, was that.

He next reached into his inside pocket and produced the envelope with the photograph and handed it to Jimmy. Jimmy stared at it, grinned and passed it on to his mother. She examined it, then handed it back to her son, who examined it again more closely. Neither of them commented; they were never in the business of handing out information, they just sat and bided their time.

"My brother, Kenneth, second row on the right."

"I did wonder," Jimmy said.

"You knew him?"

"Barely. But aye, I did see him around the boxing club. I was a boarder wi' the brothers so I never got to know him properly."

"You heard what happened?"

"Aye I did, an' I'm right sorry."

With no introduction nor thought, McAllister went straight to his and his brother's story.

"In those days I thought I was the bee's knees; working on a prestigious newspaper, new friends, breaking away from my background, going up in the world, my own man. I had my own single end, but I still had my dinner with the family most Sundays. I met up with my brother now and then for a Partick Thistle game. But the ten years' difference was too much for me to have a real relationship with him."

Jenny and Jimmy McPhee listened without interrupting as McAllister told them the rest of his family's story. But when McAllister reached the subject of the boxing club, Jimmy became restless.

"My mother still has all his photos and cups, keeps them in her cabinet. That's where I found this picture." He looked down at it, although there was no need, it was imprinted on his brain.

"Anyhow, he became silent, moody, wouldn't get a job. But as I said, I really didn't pay much notice."

He faltered.

"A dram." Jimmy placed a tumbler in his

hand. McAllister tipped it down. "He came to see me one Saturday, late. I'd been out wi' the lads and had had a few. All I was fit for was my bed. He tried to talk. I fell asleep on the couch. The next week, he gave it one more go. We met for a Partick match. I was on late shift, I had to go to work after the game, so I only had one beer. When he needed to talk, I let him down, too drunk. This time I was too sober, so again, he couldn't say anything."

McAllister stopped, caught Jimmy's intense gaze, took another gulp of whisky and continued. "He drowned in the Clyde. Jumped off the suspension bridge, the one from the Glasgow Green to the Gorbals. My mother has never believed he killed himself. But he did."

"What did you think?" Jenny asked.

"I didn't think, I was too shocked, too guilty. Later, I came to accept that he jumped," McAllister replied. "I also realized that something made him kill himself, he was trying to tell me what, and I hadn't taken time to listen.

"Then months later, a story came through on the boys' boxing club. It was to be closed and a presentation was to be held marking the end of an era. It wasn't my job to cover local news, a cadet did that, but for some reason I went. I stood through the usual boring speeches and was about to sneak off when a mention was made of a former instructor, a pillar of the church and club so the speaker said. I didn't catch the fellow's name but I did catch the curse from the man behind me. He said, and I quote, 'May he rot in hell, the bastard.'

"A woman wheeshed him and he left. I tried to follow, but by the time I'd pushed my way out he was gone. I never did find that man."

"Tell me, John McAllister, what's this about?" Jimmy queried.

"An obsession of mine." There was no joy in his self-mocking laugh. "Let's just say I'm not overfond of priests." Then he told them of the children and the hoodie crow.

"They were playing a game, right?" Jenny asked. "The boy rang the doorbell, the door opened and they say he was lifted up by a hoodie crow, right?" Then Jenny thought, "Maybe they saw the idea of a hoodie crow." She smiled at the skeptical face.

"You're too educated, McAllister. But think on it. The hoodie crow — the Baobhan sith to us Highland Travelers — can be an evil spirit."

"A crow that feasts on dead flesh, pecks out the eyes of newborn lambs, is a harbinger of bad luck — yes, I see that." McAllister continued, "What you're saying is, they saw something, something big and black that they couldn't make out, and their friend disappears, so they make up the idea of a hoodie crow."

"But why can it no' be for real? Bairns can see what we canny see, or what we have had bred out o' us."

"Maybe." He sighed. "The boy's body being found in water, the same as Kenneth, brought it all back for me. . . ."

"Find who did this, McAllister," Jimmy ordered. "Find who killed the boy. And any help you need, just ask." He stood. The audience with Jenny McPhee was over. As he walked McAllister to his car he made a promise.

"The other matter, we'll think on it. Any man, even a foreigner, at the mercy of thon eejit Inspector Tompson, has my sympathy. He has my double sympathy when he's locked up in the town prison. Not a nice place that." Jimmy shuddered at the memory.

The next morning, McAllister sat in his office contemplating the previous night and the phone call from Sandy Marshall. His friend had used all the resources of the paper, not to mention a few favors and a bit of cajoling. Nowhere in the labyrinthine administration of the church was there any information on a Father John Morrison. His last posting before being sent to the Highlands was a church orphanage; that was all Sandy had been able to find out.

A very irate Inspector Tompson had told McAllister not to call again. "Father Morrison is a respected member of the community. I know him personally, being one of his congregation, and a fine man he is too."

"For God's sake, listen to me," McAllister cursed, then apologized for blaspheming.

"For the final time, it's none of your business but yes, we *have* questioned Father Morrison. Yes, the boy disappeared near his house and yes I've had his background checked and no, there's nothing to make me doubt his word. He's a man of the cloth, for goodness' sake."

McAllister got in his final question.

"For the last time . . . the tinkers aren't talking. They've not-so-conveniently disappeared into the wilds of Ross-shire. As for them being an alibi for a Polish DP — who would trust a tinker's word anyway?"

McAllister slammed down the phone, threw his head back and, looking for all the world like a wolf baying at the moon, he let out a string of curses, never heeding that they might be heard in the reporters' room or the office downstairs or through the town and out into the wind to be funneled down the faultline to all of the Highlands and Islands.

SIXTEEN

"Get your jammies on, you two. Hurry up, or the cinnamon toast'll get cold."

Sitting around the fire, Joanne was deep in her worn womb of an armchair, the threadbare arms covered up with off-cuts of tartan, knitting. Annie was sprawled on her stomach over her beloved red pouf with Egyptian motifs stamped into the leather, which she bought at the church jumble sale with her pocket money. Jean was lying on the hearthside rug playing with a doll. The three of them were deeply content. Joanne had a fleeting shadow of guilt for not missing her husband. Annie was relieved that her father was away. And Wee Jean did not think about it at all, too busy enjoying the happy household.

"Half an hour to bedtime," Joanne told them as the news ended on the wireless. "One of you, fetch the dominoes."

By the third game, Wee Jean was half-asleep and taking ages to lay down a domino, driving Annie crazy.

"Play your five." She nudged her sister.

"How do you know I've got a five? Muum, she's cheating, she's looking at my dominoes."

"Right, let's call this game a draw." Joanne winked at Annie and for once she didn't argue. "Upstairs, girls. Brush your teeth and call me when you're in bed. Then one story each."

The girls asleep, a concert on the Third Programme; Joanne was in her nightie and dressing gown, curled up in the armchair. She loved a quiet house, a good fire, a good book, a cup of tea and the wind outside. She occasionally laid the book aside to stare into the flames, remembering the encounter with McAllister. She was half nodding off, when footsteps outside gave her a start. Someone rapped on the front door. She went into the freezing hallway.

"Who is it?" No one she knew would come to the front door.

"Is Bill Ross there?"

"He'll be back in a minute."

"Can I have a word?"

"Who is it?"

"Jimmy Gordon. A pal of your husband's."

"I'll tell him you called by."

Joanne talking through the locked door, was now shivering.

"The thing is, Mrs. Ross, or can I call you Joanne" — he continued the conversation through the door — "I heard he's still out west and I have a wee bit o' business wi' Bill. It's urgent. Some financial situations to work out. An' I've got tae get it settled out afore I get back to Glasgow."

"I see." She didn't. "Financial situation, you say."

"Aye, a wee business arrangement me and him have. Mrs. Ross, I'm freezing ma' arse off oot here. An' I dinnae want to discuss delicate matters what wi' the neighbors listening an' all. Maybe we could discuss this inside?"

That did it. She unlocked the door. But not just one Gordon stood there. There were three, three peas from the same pod. Joanne was mortified when she realized she was in a nightie in front of strangers. And they were strange indeed. They went from first brother to third brother in eighteen-month intervals, all three the same Glasgow-short height, all three round and solid with greased, slicked-back, black hair. Brothers two and three had that blank, numpty, brought-up-on-chips-and-pies-and-Irn Bru look about them. Brother number one obviously was the boss. "Sleikit" was the only word for him, but with menace added. He grinned at Joanne, his whiter-than-white full set of false teeth beaming out as bright as the Channory lighthouse.

She took them into the kitchen.

"As I was saying, me and Bill have a wee business arrangement going and I wanted to make sure he understood a' the terms and conditions. If you get ma drift."

"Terms and conditions," repeated brother number two.

"Ye know," contributed brother three.

"No, I don't know." Joanne didn't invite them to sit down, so they all stood in a circle. She was cautious but curiosity won. "Why don't you tell me what this is about?"

"Tut, tut, lads. He's no told the wife." Jimmy Gordon made great play of looking shocked. "An' they say there's no meant to be ony secrets between husband and wife. Whit's the world coming to?"

Joanne had had enough.

"Mr. Gordon, tell me what this is about, then leave. It's late and I'm tired."

He told her. All one thousand pounds of it. It sent her head reeling.

"So I just wanted to let you to know that my brothers'll be the ones to collect. I have to go back to see to business in Glasgow.

They'll be keeping an eye on things for me, making sure the payments are on time. Since you'll be seeing quite a bit of them it's good we've been introduced. Right?"

"Right." Anything to get rid of them. "I'll see you out." She opened the front door. "I'll make sure Bill gets the message."

Brother number one turned, his grin up to full wattage.

"I'm sure you'll make sure he gets the message." He looked around. "Nice wee house you've got here. Sorry I was too late to meet the lassies. Annie and Jean, isn't it?"

He shooed his brothers out into the night, gave a cheeky tip to his hat and followed them to the car.

Joanne slammed the door, locked it, ran to the back door, locked that too. Standing in the kitchen, caught between rage and terror, she started to shake. Finding themselves beholden to Glasgow gangsters was one thing; them coming to her house, mentioning the girls, was quite another.

"Dear heavens above! You idiot man! What have you gone and done this time?"

Huddled at the top of the stairs, listening in to every word, Annie was wondering the same thing.

■ ■ ■ ■

Ben Wyvis loomed white in the pauses between weathers. Snow had settled on the tops of the lower hills. The town stood granite-still before the horizontal sheets of rain coming straight from the North Sea. Cyclists were the main victims, malevolent gusts trapping them on the bridges, intent on whisking bike and rider up into the cloudscape and suspend them in a painting conjured up by Chagall's Scottish cousin. Joanne had pedaled hard through all that the heavens could fling at her, trying to forget the picture of the malevolent gleam in the eyes of the eldest Gordon brother. No use. Neither wind nor rain nor cold could shake it loose.

Sitting at the reporters' table alone, she worried. Too much was happening, her foundations were shifting and the nocturnal visit from the Glaswegian brothers had shown her a circumstance and set of characters encountered previously only at the pictures.

McAllister sat in his office nursing his gloom. With a theatrical sigh, he unfolded himself from the chair and took himself to the reporters' table, looking for something, someone to distract him. Joanne looked up through a wing of hair. Both hesitated; the easy familiarity had not yet returned. She was about to tell him of her strange encounter when Rob charged in. Exhilarated by his brilliant idea, he strutted over and perched himself on the edge of the desk.

On wakening, he had called asking for an interview, he told them both.

"Hello. Oh, it's yourself. Really? Aye. No, nine's not too early. Friday morning it is then. Grand," was the reply.

Father Morrison then asked after Rob's father and his mother before signing off with a cheery "Bye-bye."

"So I've set up an interview with Father Morrison." Rob was well pleased with himself.

"You're daft."

"Thanks for your confidence, Mrs. Ross." Rob turned to McAllister. "It'll be fine. He's known me a long time. He thinks of me as a boy. Who better to do an interview?"

The editor nodded. "Aye. Who better?"

"Besides, he'd never talk to an old man such as yourself."

"Oh dear, I'm kicking myself for not thinking of such a brilliant idea. Satisfied? But no mention of anything about —"

"Hoodie crows. I'm not that daft. Then

you can buy me a drink after."

"You're too young to drink."

Atmosphere lightened, Rob grinned cheerfully. He couldn't abide gloom.

"I'll do it as a good-luck-and-farewell piece."

"What?" McAllister stared.

"Didn't you hear? He's been given a promotion. He's off to take charge of a school in Lanarkshire."

"Why the hell didn't you tell me?"

"I've only just found out. And besides, you're not exactly approachable these days."

"Right, lads and lasses." Don walked in. "When you've all finished righting the wrongs of the world . . ."

McAllister turned to leave, but Don, rolling his eyes in exasperation, shoved a pile of copy paper into his hands, telling him to have it done by the end of the day. "Then you can be off chasing shadows and crows. In case you've all forgotten — we've a paper to turn out."

"Yes, Mr. McLeod," chorused Joanne and Rob.

They all settled down to grapple with the controlled panic of another deadline.

It wasn't until late in the morning, alone with Don, that Joanne decided he was her only hope. She had first thought of Chiara — but she had enough worries of her own. She thought of Rob — but he was too young to take it seriously; he would probably get excited at the thought of meeting real live gangsters. She thought of McAllister — but she was still wary of getting close to him; he was her boss, after all. And Don? He knew life. He wouldn't pity her. Or judge her. And he could keep a secret. So Don it was.

"Don, if you wanted to borrow money in a hurry, where would you go?"

"Just ask, I'll always help out."

"No, but thanks anyway. I mean, if a person in the town was in real trouble, and needed a lot of money in a hurry, is there a moneylender or something like that you could go to, apart from the pawnbroker in the market, that is?"

"Maybe. But you'd be a fool."

"How so?"

"Interest, lass. Compound interest, starting at twenty percent, more if you're desperate."

"You're kidding!"

"What's this about? Yer man?"

"It's a long story."

"Right you are. It's nearly one, we've time for a pint and a chat — on me."

Arm-in-arm down the slick-wet cobbles of

Castle Wynde, off they slithered to one of Don's favorites. It was a long narrow place, nearly all streetfront, in a lane opposite the station. High smoked-glass windows, cut-glass mirrors, like the inside of a Gypsy wagon except for a bar, with brass railings and spittoons, running the length of the room. This was definitely a "men only" public house. Joanne didn't care anymore. She was a journalist.

They sat in a corner. She told Don. He whistled.

"The three Gordons." Don was taken aback by the whole story. "Poaching on McPhee territory. What a nerve." He was dumbfounded by the amount of money. "That much?" He was furious when she told him that they knew the girls' names. "This is serious, lass."

"I know. Bill has big problems with the terms of the contract; he can't wriggle out. Councilor Grieg's has somehow got a hold on him. But going to these men, that's not a solution. I wish I could do something." She stopped. She thought it over for five seconds. May as well, was her decision.

"Maybe I *can* do something. I have an idea to help Bill. A not-very-honorable idea, but . . ."

By now Don was thoroughly intrigued.

"You're talking to the right person then."

"It's very, very hush-hush."

"That requires another pint."

He came back.

"Right, tell me all. I'm the keeper of the secrets of this town, going back centuries. Besides, you should always have a sneaky unscrupulous person in your corner."

"And that sneaky unscrupulous person is yourself." She pretended to hit him, made him swear that he would never tell, then she let him have the whole story.

"My God. The bastard. How old was she when she had the baby?"

"Sixteen."

"Then she was fifteen when he had her."

"She was the housekeeper. First job, straight out of school."

"So what are you going to do?"

"Blackmail him."

"I like the sound o' that."

"I'm going to blackmail him into doing something completely legal, something completely within his power, something that any decent person would have done already."

"That's ma girl."

"One thing though, Don." She stared at him. "If I can fix it, I don't want Bill to ever hear of my part in any of this."

"Aye, I can see that. Bill couldn't take any more of your being better than him."

"What?"

"It's no your fault." He saw that he had offended her. "And I'm not saying you do it deliberately . . . all I'm saying is, he must feel inadequate around you. I mean, look at you, you're bright, a daughter of the manse, and let's face it, you'd never have married him if you hadn't had a bun in the oven." She went bright pink at that. "I know everything, remember?" He nudged her with his elbow. "No, what I'm saying is, he's not the kind of man who takes kindly to interfering women."

"You don't pull your punches, do you? And I'm not interfering, just helping. It's my family too."

"I know, but that's not how he sees it. He's the man, breadwinner, the boss, and he has his pride." Don shook his head. "You're too good for that man, Joanne, and he knows it and resents it."

"Aye, so I've been told, and he's been told the same often enough. That's the trouble. But that's not how *I* feel."

Felt, she realized with a jolt, that is not how I felt, past tense. And now? That, she hadn't yet worked out. She had been feeling that her anchor was slipping for quite some

380

time now. Even though it was a poor excuse for a marriage, she was tied to it, it was what she had chosen. Over the past few weeks, though, it felt like the wind had changed, that a new direction maybe, perhaps, might just be possible — a life on her own. How to do it, that was still problematic. She felt Don watching her. She smiled, shrugged a what-the-heck, then told him, "Back to the office, Mr. McLeod, I've an appointment to make before I lose courage and change my mind."

"Come in, sit down. Would you like some tea?"

Joanne sat in front of his desk, knees pressed tight together to stop her shaking. She wouldn't be here if Don hadn't said he'd do it himself if she backed down. Grieg filled his executive chair. He needed it; born big, he was now gone-to-fat big. He smiled ingratiatingly at Joanne but was unable to disguise his dislike. Over the years, they had met at one function or another. She had never bothered to hide her contempt at his pawing and his passes.

Bill Ross made a bad match there, he thought. Look at her. For all her posh ways of speaking and her airs an' graces, look at her in a tweed skirt, lace-up shoes and for goodness' sakes, a knitted tammy.

"So, to what do we owe the pleasure of your visit? Naturally, I'm always happy to help the ladies and gentlemen of the press."

She smiled politely at the condescension, picked up her prop, her notebook, and began at the beginning, not stopping nor pausing at any of his snorts of protest. Finished, she closed the blank notebook and sat back, quietly waiting for the response.

"Let me go through this again. Let me see if I've got this clear. You want me to fix a council contract for your husband. You want me to use my influence to get a payout of money on a half-finished job."

"Ninety-five percent finished."

"It's not possible."

"It is. I've read the contract and in amongst the gobbledygook is a clause that allows you to authorize payment for work done but not completed due to exceptional circumstances. The remainder of the work can be completed in a few weeks, but you could persuade them to authorize an extension."

"And what are these exceptional circumstances?"

"The weather."

"This is Scotland in winter, my dear."

"I'm not your dear."

"Oooh, touchy are we? Well, well."

"It would be a good idea for you to agree to this."

"Oh really?"

He is enjoying this, Joanne thought. Well, here goes.

"It would be a good idea to agree to my proposal because, if you don't, I will write up the story on your 'Rowan Lodge' project stating that there are irregularities in the planning permission process, you also have a conflict of interest and I'll write anything else I can dig up."

He roared with laughter.

"Dig away all you want. Everything on that project is aboveboard. I have nothing to do with the development company. It belongs entirely to my wife and her father. There is nothing for you to dig up, as you put it, so I think it is time for you to leave."

It was his self-satisfied leer that did it. Joanne would otherwise never have stooped to using the private life of others.

"You won't want your wife, a company director and pillar of the church, to go through the pain and disgust and humiliation of finding out that you seduced a fifteen-year-old girl who was in your home, in your care, and then, when she had your baby, you refused to recognize the child."

Absolute silence. Joanne waited.

"And what proof do you have for this preposterous story?"

"I'll just have a wee word with your wife, point her in the right direction, let her find out the truth. If she asks, I'm sure she will be told."

"I've done nothing to you," Grieg protested.

"Yes you have. You set out to destroy my husband and his company so you could get work and materials on the cheap for your Rowan Lodge scheme."

"Why would you want to save your drunk of a husband? He has nothing good to say about you." This felt like an ice dagger to the heart, but she would never give him the satisfaction of a reaction. She sat, immobile.

"You can't prove anything." His agitation, desperation Joanne thought, deflated him and he floundered down to reality like a huge collapsing dirigible.

"You're right. I can't. Not without compromising a lovely young lass who doesn't deserve any more trouble. But I am prepared to tell Mr. McAllister and Don McLeod and your wife, Mrs. Grieg, and my mother-in-law, and all my women friends and" — she'd run out of names, then inspiration struck — "and the whole of the

Kyle Women's Institute."

"Fine, fine. You've made your point." He stared at her, reappraising her. "I can hardly credit that a minister's daughter would scheme like this."

"I can and I will, Mr. Grieg. Just like you."

"Tell me what you want." He was attempting to be all business and took out his fountain pen, unscrewing the top, but he could not disguise the shake as he went to write.

Joanne knew it; he had folded. Always stand up to a bully, she reminded herself.

"I've told you. It's simple. Bill will put in an application for an extension to finish the contract, citing delays due to weather." He wrote. "All work already done will be paid for by the end of December. That has to be put in writing to Bill. You can keep your own wee scheme going; nothing will change. The local firm can finish Bill's contract along with yours, but you must use your own materials, paid for by yourself, not Bill's supplies."

He nodded agreement and sat back, deflated but relieved.

Joanne, realizing she was winning, continued. May as well grab the chance, she thought.

"Secondly, I want a council house. In my

name only."

That made him stare. "And may I ask why?"

"No, you may not."

"It's not so easy. The council waiting list is very long, and you've already got a house, a good one."

"I'll have one of those prefabs you've been going to pull down the last five years. No one wants them."

Joanne knew it would take them at least another five years to demolish those houses. If ever.

"I'll see to it. But it'll have to be a swap, your bigger house for a prefab."

"Agreed. Finally, I want you to acknowledge your daughter, even if it's in secret."

"Now hold on. That's none of your business."

"Mr. McLean is a fair and discreet solicitor. Mhairi doesn't want a fuss either. Just do it."

This is too easy, thought Joanne. "One final thing."

"What now?" Grieg was exhausted. No one had ever turned the tables on him before.

"I want an absolute promise that you will never mention this conversation to anyone. Ever. Otherwise you know the consequences."

"I promise." The look of relief on his face made Joanne want to laugh. "You have my word of honor on that."

"That's not worth much, is it, Mr. Grieg?"

And with that Joanne left the room, shut the door behind her and stood shaking in the corridor outside.

"Oh my goodness me!" She grinned, amazed at herself. She ran down the stairs, skipped along the corridors, fairly dancing along the riverbank, full of glee and desperate to catch Don McLeod, to recount the whole interview, in every tiny detail.

Then she stopped. "What on earth possessed me?" She grabbed the railing on the riverbank, her heart racing. She had asked for a house, had made the decision — she was leaving Bill. That hadn't been her intention. She turned back. Then stopped. It didn't have to be a final, final step. She would not put her children through the disgrace. But it could be a bargaining chip when she spoke to Bill. She tried to laugh; I've been spending too much time with Don McLeod. The river went out of focus. She shook her head, blinking rapidly. A voice, a well-modulated, bitter voice, came down through the years, her mother's voice, You've made your choice, Joanne, it said, and forever more you will have to live with it. "*No,* Mother." This she spoke aloud, then quickly looked round to see if anyone overheard. But the wet, cold pavements were empty.

Scared but terminally optimistic, she went over the possibility of a new beginning, of living up to her own expectations of a single life with two children. There would be the condemnation from town and kirk, the challenge of working on the *Gazette* and keeping house, her mother-in-law's reaction, and her sister and brother-in-law and how hurt they would be. And how would she tell the girls? And tell Bill and get away safe? And a new house, her very own, how would that be?

"Well, at least it will be exciting," she told the cherry tree beside her.

SEVENTEEN

Eight-thirty-November-morning light was only one or two notches up from dark. Four-thirty in the afternoon and dark would return, leaving the counties of the north shut in under an immense blackout curtain. The MacLean household was lit up like the *Titanic.* Rob felt the need for brightness before tackling his morning. Digging with gusto into the full Scottish breakfast of eggs, bacon, black pudding, white pudding, tattie scones and toast with homemade whisky marmalade, Rob greeted his father with a full mouth, a grunt and a gesture toward the frying pan.

"If you're offering, then yes."

His father had just come back from his morning constitutional. His face glowed in the heat of the kitchen.

"So, to what do we owe this banquet? A promotion? An engagement? Last request before the scaffold?"

"I felt like cooking," Rob explained. "I'll be going into work later but first I've an interview next door with Father Morrison. He's off to a new job down south."

"Mr. McAllister put you up to this?"

"No, it was my idea." Rob was pleased with himself.

His father looked over his spectacles at his son. He was confident in his boy but uneasy just the same. Rob caught his father's frown and was grateful.

"Don't worry, if he turns obstreperous, I'll yell for Mum. That'll put the fear of God in him."

"A fear of God appears to be distinctly lacking in this case."

"Dad, you surely don't agree with McAllister's wild theories?"

"No, I don't. It is an impossible thought." He hesitated. "All the same, call me when you're finished."

The doorstep of the Big House took up more space than most people's kitchens, Rob reflected, and the house was as welcoming as a vault. Hand poised on the bell, the realization that this was the last place wee Jamie had been seen alive chilled him. Ridiculous. McAllister had two and two making thirty-nine. Rubber footsteps came

squelching down the linoleum in the hallway.

"Here we go." Rob prepared a Cheshire
cat smile.

Father Morrison filled the doorway,
cheeerful as ever. "Come in, come in. A
dreich day. At least you didn't have far to
walk."

Rob followed him into the sitting room,
where a freshly lit fire was struggling to stay
alight against the frequent blowbacks. A dim
overhead light, with a parchment-colored
shade, sent out a watery custard light.

The house and the room were far different from Rob's childhood memories of
when his grandparents lived here. Ornate
sideboards, bookcases and a desk were still
in situ — too large to move. Some of the
original carpets and runners had also been
left behind — too old to matter. What *was*
different was the general air of shabbiness
and the faint institutional smell of boiled
cabbage and disinfectant. Close up, the
priest too had an institutional tinge; boiled-
tattie complexion, musty soutane and a
home haircut. He was big, granted, but
frightening? No. Up until now, Rob had
always thought of Father Morrison as a nice
man — if he thought of him at all. Now, in
his newfound role of investigative journalist,

he furtively examined the man. He searched for the right word. Gone to seed, like a former sportsman down on his luck; that was it. That is how he would describe him — if Don didn't cut it out.

Exactly one hour later Rob scurried down the driveway, turned left to his own house, walked through to the kitchen and dropped into a chair.

"That didn't take long." Margaret was ironing. Rob sat silent. She made tea. She let him be. Waited. Elbows on the well-scrubbed, well-worn table, he cradled the cup, taking slow sips.

"Mum, you know I love you."

Margaret was shocked. A normal Highlander did not say such things beyond the age of six.

"My dear Robbie. Tell me about it."

Shaken, embarrassed, a wee boy again, he told her.

"I don't know what to say." She started. But she did. "Rob, we have always taught you to believe in goodness and in kindness and honesty. So we must suppose that the reverse exists. Look at what's happened and is happening in Europe. Your father and I went through two wars. We know evil exists. I try not to see it, but it is there, in big and small ways. And always balanced by good."

Rob nodded.

"This morning, in Grandma McLean's old house, for me a happy house, I felt something that made me feel sick." He looked up at her. "The trouble is, well, it was nothing really. It just gave me the creeps, that's all." He shook himself like a dog after a dip in a swamp. "I feel such a fool for overreacting."

She listened, didn't say much, just murmured reassurances. But Margaret was seething inside, feeling that her only child, her sunny boy, was losing his innocence.

Rob left for work, having told her a simple version of what had happened. Yes, Rob assured her, he was fine. And no, Margaret assured him, she wouldn't say anything to his father about Rob being upset; she would just give him the facts. Then, after waving him and his motorbike out the gate, she called her husband. She didn't know what to think. Rob assured her again that it was nothing. It was only some photos, he said. But her first reaction was the same as Rob's; there was something unsavory about the obsession with young boys. Dozens of photos, Rob said, and sheets and sheets of negatives, all of boys.

She phoned her husband. She told him.

Quickly, quietly, no drama in her voice, she related the bare facts. No need to worry, she said; it's probably harmless, she said. She put down the phone, leaving Angus McLean to draw his own conclusions, to exercise his eminent sense of right and reason. She then went round the house locking every door, every window, closing curtains as though death had visited. She switched on every lamp in the house, banked up the fire and even then, she still felt chilled. She remembered. She could now see for herself how the idea had come about; a hoodie crow indeed. But the step between a distasteful hobby and the killing of a child, that was a step she could not contemplate.

Don walked into McAllister's room, a cup of tea in one hand and the layout in the other.

"Am I interrupting?" He nodded to Jimmy McPhee.

"Yes," McAllister told him.

Don was not in the least offended — he knew he would find out what was going on eventually.

"When you're done here, a word?" he asked Jimmy.

"Aye, I'll see you after," Jimmy agreed.

McAllister closed his office door.

Jimmy McPhee went straight to the point. "I didn't tell you everything when you came to our place. But ma mother thinks you should know." He left McAllister in no doubt that if he had had his way, this conversation would not be taking place.

He told his story straight, in his harsh, crackling voice, speaking in the local dialect with the local speech pattern of glottal stops and swallowed words and sentences spoken on an ingoing breath. He dropped in the occasional Glasgow swear word, picked up from his time on the boxing circuit.

McAllister kept his head down through most of the monologue, allowing Jimmy McPhee a private space to remember.

"We were at the berries one summer, in Blair, I was eleven, but small, still am, and runnin' round, driving everyone daft. And I was always in fights.

"Ma, she had this notion to get at least one more of us educated and she had heard of a place in Glasgow where you could go to a good school for free if you were any good at sport an' if you were poor. We definitely made it in on the poor bit, an' I wasnae a bad boxer neither."

Speaking with the ease of a natural story-teller, he told it as a tale from a distant past, a story that had happened to someone else.

"So there I was, a tough skinny wee tyke, boxing and training and trying to put on a bit of weight. We had some good instructors, fathers or brothers, mostly Irish, mostly fine fellows, tough but fair. And school, a boarding school it is, it wasn't so bad. I could read and write a wee bit, but I was a dab hand at the numbers. Helps me work out the odds." He grinned.

"But you know how, as bairns, you just *know* some things. Not much is said, you certainly don't discuss it, and it's just a word here, a curse there, a warning or two. So, it wasn't long before I heard the talk about one of the fathers. Watch out for him, dirty old B, and they all laughed. But not as bad as that other manny, the one that was supposed to be a teacher, the one that left, said one of the boys. Aye, *him,* said another. I was right confused. The warnings, I had no idea what it was about, I thought it meant that some of them were a bit too rough in the ring, nothing I couldn't deal with, me being tough an all. It was not like some of the stuff the boys from the orphanage had to put up with. That was a ferocious awful place."

They simultaneously lit a cigarette.

"So not long after, I met this father they

had warned me about. He was a big man a'
right. Cheerful, smiling, Glasgow through
and through. I ended up on his dormitory
wing. The boys were no scared o' him, but
they didn't like him. Me, I couldn't see the
problem. He loved all his "innocent wee
souls" as he put it. There were the photos,
right enough, that was his hobby and he
was a dab hand at it. He liked doing the
private portraits as well as the usual group
shots. You were in your boxing drawers and
gloves and you did the poses. It all seemed
harmless enough. He did harp on a bit
about nasty wee boys with dirty habits. I'd
no idea what he was on about.

"So all was fine, until you started changing — you know. Then, when we had the
weekly bath night, it was — all scrubbed
clean are we? I'd better check. That was the
inspection to see if you were clean, everywhere. He'd peer in yer lugs, inspect yer
fingernails and yer hair for nits, then, making a game of it, he would check your willie.
Touch it. And he'd go on about keeping yerself clean in mind and body, about how
filthy thoughts and filthy habits was how
the devil got into you.

"Now, I'm a tinker an' I was that wee bit
tougher than those boys, but the real difference was this; I knew my brother would

397

listen. Keith, fifteen and strong, wi' a good heid on him, he'd help. So one day I told ma brother. It took me a while. The man was doing nothing wrong, not really. He was a decent fellow, mostly. We all liked him, sort of, but I knew it wasn't right."

Jimmy looked straight at McAllister and grinned. "Us tinkers are brought up with the stallions an' mares, we know all about nature. This wasn't natural. So, next thing I know, Ma comes down tae Glasgow to take me back to the Highlands. We're off on the road for the summer, she said, needs my help with the horses, she said."

He stopped, remembering. "Aye. And that's no all she said. She said I was a grand lad." He grinned again. A picture of his mother as she marched off to the office of the school's headmaster came into his head. He never knew what was said. He had no need. He never doubted his mother's capacity to put the fear of God or of the devil into anyone. And if that failed, Jenny McPhee would blast the culprit with a string of tinker curses — in Gaelic.

Jimmy wasn't finished.

"What he did, see, Father Bain, was built you up when you were young, 'specially the ones who were good boxers, made you feel so proud, someone special, he was like a real father to the boys, and many of them had no one. Then as soon as you started to become a man, he made you feel like shite. So it was nothing really, he didn't hurt you or harm you. There were others who were right sadists, and worse. No, he was one of the good ones. But he made you feel so dirty."

Jimmy stopped. "That's it. If it helps."

It took some moments for McAllister to recover.

"Jimmy, this Father Bain, was he the man who took the photos of my brother?"

"Aye, the same."

"And have you seen this man since then? Maybe up here, in the Highlands?"

"No, I haven't. But that doesn't mean anything. I don't recall bumping into any priest since I came back up north."

"Jimmy, would you do something for me?"

Half an hour later, McAllister was still off in some distant void, but returned to the here and now by the clatter of Rob running up the stairs, banging around the reporters' room, asking for the whereabouts of the editor. He roused himself and yelled out the door.

"In here!"

Rob blew in, still in his motorbike gear.

"So?"

"Well . . ." Spiral notebook in one hand, drawing pictures in the air with the other, Rob started to describe the interview with the priest.

"It was all very civilized, chummy really."

McAllister took a second look at his junior reporter. For all his brave, look-at-me-I'm-grown-up air, the lad was shaken.

"Sit."

Rob did as he was told, then started again.

"I asked about his past assignments. He told me; very proud of his boxing club and community work in Glasgow. But the war put an end to the boys' club."

McAllister stared. Then even before he heard what Rob had to tell him, he began to feel better. These shadows of coincidence, he thought, I've not imagined them.

"Next, he described his heroic service spent helping the bombed-out families in Dumbarton-shire. Then, after the armistice, he was running a church adoption and foster care agency that was also some kind of home. An administrative post, he says."

"Involving children?" McAllister asked.

"Aye, all ages; babies, up to school-leaving age, orphans mostly. Then eight years ago he came here to the "retreat" next door to us. Only a few other people have stayed there as far as I know. He keeps himself to himself, never goes out much.

"So, all the while I was sooking up to him. You know, Father this and Father that and 'Oh how interesting.' He lapped it up. Then when I'd got my notes for the article, I decided to play a wee game so I could have a look around.

" 'Father Morrison,' I says, 'I'm sorry, we don't have your picture. Do you still have that big camera of yours? You could set it and I'll push the button. I remember you being a dab hand with photos.'

"The silly old fool fell for it. Off he went to get his camera, me following behind. When he turned round and saw me in his studio, as he calls it, he didn't look too pleased, but I turned up the charm a notch. Told him how professional it all looked. He switched on a big lamp, showed me the big professional camera on a tripod. He fiddled with his light meter, the settings, then showed me how to take the picture. He posed against a white sheet. Pleased as punch he was. Vain too, combing over the baldy bit on his head in that stupid old man's way, you know, tramlines across his skull.

"Then I told him we didn't have anyone to develop the film. Could he suggest anyone? And could we have it soon, as I wanted the piece in the next edition? And the fool, just like that, says, 'I'll do it myself,' he says, 'won't take long,' and did I mind waiting? Mind — I couldn't have suggested better myself. 'No problem,' I said, 'I'll wait in the kitchen, write up my notes.' Then off he went into the darkroom and I had the house to myself."

Rob paused. "You know it used to be our house?"

McAllister nodded.

"Well, when Grandma McLean lived there, my cousins would come to stay and we played hide-and-seek or Swallows and Amazons or Sardines. It's a big house, lots of cupboards and attics and the darkroom, that was once a dressing room, off what was my parents' bedroom.

"So there I was, alone, and naturally, I had to have a poke around. I looked in the bedrooms; all empty except for his one. I checked his bedroom. A very large, very gory, very dead Jesus hanging above the bed gave me a bit of a fright. I checked the stuff on his table, his cupboards, his chest of drawers, and there, underneath his drawers, I found photos."

Rob was so engrossed he didn't even laugh at his own joke.

"There was a pile of them. Negatives, contact sheets, and lots of photos. Photos of boys. I stood like a stookie staring at the pictures. That was when Father Morrison called out he'd finished. I barely had time to put everything back."

Rob stopped. He sniffed. He looked out the window, then continued.

"I made a big palaver of looking at the time, told him I was late for work, grabbed the photo of him by the corner, it was still wet, and said I had to go. I made for the door, blethering nonsense, and had to stop myself running down the drive, straight home."

"Did you take any of those other pictures with you?" McAllister asked.

"I couldn't. I knew he'd be on to me if I did." Rob was miserable.

"But you have the photo of Father Morrison?"

"I gave it to Don."

"We must take this to the police." McAllister could feel the man slipping away again.

"How? There was nothing in the pictures really. They were just" — Rob searched for the words — "not nice. They were pictures of boys at the boxing and group shots and photos taken on excursions and stuff . . . but there were lots of pictures of boys in a big bath . . . you know . . . it was just that . . . the way they were posed, it made me feel . . . well, dirty." Rob was staring at the carpet. "And I searched his drawers; that's illegal. My dad would go spare if he found out."

"Morrison would first have to make a complaint," McAllister pointed out.

"I didn't steal anything, but if we tell Inspector Tompson, he's just as likely to arrest me. Attempted burglary or some such."

"The chief inspector from Aberdeen, Westland's his name, he's in charge and he's a dammed sight more on the ball than Inspector Plod. At least I hope he is."

McAllister, looking out of the casement windows through rain that was now turning to sleet, remembering other photos, photos sitting on the mantelpiece shrine, his mother's pride and joy, knew that there was too little, in fact none at all of the solid evidence needed to connect the priest to any crime. But that was not his job; he was a reporter, reporting the facts. He thought about his brother, his mother, Jamie, all the young lads who had been tainted and tarnished by men like Morrison, and he knew he couldn't ignore what he suspected.

"I'll get to the heart of this. No matter how long it takes me."

And Rob, at the same time, in his own way, was making the same promise.

McAllister and Rob walked the very short walk to the police station. At the front desk, the editor asked for Detective Chief Inspector Westland. The desk sergeant told them he was out but would be back soon and invited them to go on up and wait.

A tall narrow window giving out onto the Castle Wynd dimly lighted the detectives' lair, which lay off an equally narrow winding stairway. Handy for the courts, which were in the castle proper, but cramped with three desks, the door to the room was left permanently open to all the comings and goings on the stairs.

"Tompson will let Morrison know what I did. They're in the same church," Rob whispered. He was desperate to get out of this meeting.

"Wheesht. Leave it to me."

Inspector Tompson appeared. He didn't even greet them, just glared.

"What now?"

"We're waiting for Westland." McAllister was determined to ignore the inspector.

"Detective Chief Inspector Westland to you." Tompson then poked a finger at Rob. "His time is too valuable to waste on

405

speculation and innuendo from the press. Not to mention libel."

McAllister, using his height and his formidable voice, stated, loud enough for everyone in the police station to hear, "I shall be letting the chief constable know that his officers are not interested in receiving information from the public. And furthermore, no more help will be forthcoming from the *Gazette,* not whilst I'm the editor."

Halfway down the stairs, McAllister's furious progress was halted as he ran into DCI Westland. Rob, at his heels, almost fell on top of the editor.

"I heard that." The policeman held out his hand. "Would you care to come upstairs again and give *me* your information? In private?"

So they did, leaving nothing out.

Joanne had not seen Chiara for nearly a week. They arranged to meet during Joanne's lunchtime break and have a sandwich at the coffee bar.

Gino waved as she came in, beamed at her, shouting a hello above the roar of the coffee machine, and pointed to where Chiara was waiting. The friends had this part of the café to themselves. No one mentioned it, but custom was still slow.

There were some in the town who would always believe there was a link between the Italian family and the stranger awaiting trial for killing the child.

Stands to reason, some said, they're all foreigners. Aye, others said, and I heard the Italian girl is engaged to that Polish man who is protecting thon murdering bastard.

And so it went.

"Long time no see." Chiara smiled.

"There's been so much happening." Joanne smiled back.

"You look different." Chiara examined her friend. "It's not the hair. No new clothes — you're still in that disgraceful old tweed jacket you love. So . . . your husband is away . . . is that it? Nope. A man? Ah hah! A hint of a blush. Tell me all."

Joanne was laughing by this time. "You know, if I didn't know you better, I'd say you've grown up."

"Thanks a bunch."

"No, I mean that as a compliment."

Their sandwiches and coffees arrived. Chiara thanked the waitress and when she was gone, they started the real conversation. Anyone watching would have seen two heads leaning close, one with raven black hair, the other bright brown. They would have noted an occasional touch to the arm, a hand placed on a friend's hand. Anyone listening would have heard a constant murmur coming from one, and exclamations of "Never!" or "Get away!" or "Oh my goodness!" and muffled bursts of laughter and moments of quiet and a final "You never!" coming from the black-haired woman before they hugged, then ate their sandwiches and drank their cold coffee.

"Look at the time." Joanne was up and grabbing her scarf and hat.

"Please say you'll come." Chiara, pleased again.

"I don't see how I could manage it."

"Ask McAllister for a lift. He'd never refuse you."

Joanne gave Chiara a mock punch and tried to get out the door before her friend could see the light in her eyes.

"Friday night then?" Chiara called after her. "And if you don't ask him, I will."

Joanne sat in the visitor's chair in McAllister's office. Then stood up. She offered to make tea. He refused. She looked at him. He stared back. She started, her tone formal sounding.

"I don't know how to say this. I don't know where to begin. McAllister, I'm determined to make something of my life. I know, I know, hard for a woman, especially in this place, in these times, but I will." She took a deep breath. "Can I have a full-time job?"

He looked surprised. Then nodded.

"Can I have a raise?" Again he nodded.

"Thank you. I suppose you want an explanation?"

He shrugged.

"Thank you so much," was all she could manage to say. She stood.

"One thing more . . ." She hesitated. "Would you take me to a dance in Strathpeffer on Friday night?"

It had come out all wrong, she realized that, but before she could clarify the request, McAllister smiled at her and asked, "Are you asking me for a date, Mrs. Ross?"

"No, never, I mean, no." Chiara had *that* wrong, she thought, I can't be grown-up if I keep blushing all the time. "No, what I meant was . . . Rob has got this band —"

"So I heard."

"And Peter Kowalski plays guitar and there's a drummer and someone else and they're playing at a party to celebrate Keith McPhee marrying Shona Stuart. So Chiara wants us to go. To support Peter." She dared a look and he seemed interested. "So I thought maybe you could give me a lift and we could all have some fun, because it's all been so serious lately."

"I think that's a fine idea. I'll be happy to take you."

"You will? Great."

And he watched as she fairly skipped out of the room.

"I hear we're going to a party."

"Aye." McAllister continued to work without looking up.

"For heaven's sake! Make an effort, man!" Don stalked back to the reporters' table.

McAllister was there ten seconds later.

"Sorry. I'll explain, but not now. How about supper, my place, tonight?"

"I'll bring a bottle."

McAllister was gratified when Don asked for seconds. The cock-a-leekie soup was his culinary magnum opus. And the tattie scones were not bad either. But he'd cheated and bought those at the bakery.

"So," Don said as they stretched out either side of the fireplace, feet on the brass fender. "Might as well tell me because otherwise I'll have to find a way to get rid of you." He waggled his glass at the editor. "You're no much company at all these days."

"You showed the photo to Jimmy?"

"Aye, you were right, it's the same man. That must make you feel vindicated."

"No, I feel strangely flat. I thought I would feel triumphant — to be proved right on a matter that has haunted me for years — but, no. Until we know who killed the boy, I won't be celebrating the fact that I was right."

"Taking smutty pictures doesn't make him a murderer. Even Jimmy doubts he would do that." Don spoke slowly. "Then there's the matter of getting hold of some of the photos Rob saw, to support your theory. We're back to the same problem; who would listen to wee girls, or the lad or to Jimmy McPhee, against the word of a priest?"

He looked across at McAllister. McAllister sank in his chair, defeat showing in every part of his body.

"Killing the boy," Don continued, "frankly, I don't see it, unless it was an accident. What does Jimmy say?"

"He doesn't believe Morrison, or Bain, as he knew him, would interfere with a child, far less kill him. He told me he was one of the better ones at that school he went to. There were others far worse is what he told me."

"And DCI Westland?"

"I don't know. He listened. He'd already talked to Morrison. He couldn't find anything amiss. He noted what he called an innocuous collection of photos of junior boxing groups. He also told me that he is convinced Tompson arrested the right man. The case against the Pole is circumstantial, but his greatcoat being found on the banks of the canal clinches it for him. The procurator believes he can get a conviction."

"I know you won't thank me for saying this," Don went on, "but it's still all speculation on your part. And, as I said, it's only photos, lots worse has happened. You know that, you having been a war correspondent. But cheer up, he'll be out of our lives by Christmas."

"Aye. And what havoc will he wreak on other boys' lives?"

"That's just the way it is, John, it's just the way it is."

Eighteen

Cars, vans, motorbikes, bicycles and three large charabancs, as well as those on foot, filed along the narrow winding road that was shaped by the river. Their destination, the small spa town, was hidden in a fold in the glen. Although early, six o'clock, it was well past dark. Every star in the heavens was visible in the still cold air. Silver birches lived up to their name, the trunks marking them out in the forest like squads of soldiers in ghostly livery. There was no moon; starlight alone was enough to light the way.

The stream of guests meandering across the football field to the hall didn't give a thought to the venue, the commandeered Scout hut; the Spa Pump Room and Ballroom, where the gentry held their functions, was intimidating. This was a night for letting the hair down.

Fiddlers warming up sent their chords into the night, summoning the stragglers.

Colored lights around the porch and windows made a rainbow beacon for those farther up the glen. New arrivals were enveloped in a thick warm mist of laughter and light as they stepped over the threshold.

Two shepherds from up Strathconnon way had been banished to the porch to suck their reeking pipes. Arguing amiably, their conversation occasionally faltered as one or another hawked, then spat into the grass with great relish.

"Tonight. Mark my words, tonight."

"Naw. The morn. First thing, likely."

Jimmy McPhee chipped in.

"And what are you two auld boys blethering about now?"

"The snow, laddie. The snow."

Jimmy looked around.

"Don't be daft. It's a beautiful night. Look at thon stars and no a cloud in the sky neither."

"Aye, I grant you. But smell. Can ye no get a hint o' it? That's snow in the offing for sure."

"Well, five quid says no snow the night," Jimmy said. "No snow on the lowlands afore December."

Spit in the palm, a handshake, they accepted the bet. "You're on."

The hall was overflowing. At one end,

below the stage, a long table was set for the wedding party. Along the sides, trestle tables with borrowed tablecloths, posies of flowers and mounds of sandwiches and cakes were set for the guests. Tea urns operated out of the kitchen. This was the women's territory.

The male guests, with boys running through and around and under their heels, milled outside like cows awaiting the call to the milking shed. One or two would break off from their huddle, then re-form with another gathering. In their wedding and funeral best, faces shiny from a fresh wet shave, a dent around the skull from the ubiquitous flat cap, they gave off a whiff of Brylcreem and carbolic soap.

A table by the kitchen door was set up with ginger beer and Irn-Bru and sickly-sweet orange squash. Despite the hall's strict no-liquor policy, beer was handed out from underneath the table and the men added a sly splash of whisky from the hip-pocket half bottle. Some were already well away, but as yet quiet, slightly swaying, still coherent. Ritual greetings were exchanged.

"Archie."

"Donald."

"Aye" — said upward on the indrawn breath. "Aye." The greeting returned downward on the outgoing breath. Silence followed. Talk of the farm, of neighbors' farms, of distant rumors of farming in other counties, would come soon enough. Conversations needed oiling.

Inside, the women caught up on family news and eyed each other's outfits. All were in their bonnie best. The treadle sewing machines had been busy, new dresses specially run up for the rare outing. The eye-watering smell from home perms canceled out the tang of Pears soap and eau de cologne. Babies expected, babies born, news of offspring grown and gone, along with intimate details of real or imaginary medical complaints, were the topics for the isolated, gossip-starved women.

Mothers and grandmothers occasionally broke off to shout at the children skating and sliding across the wooden floor, liberally scattered with chalk dust to enhance the swing of the dancing.

"Mind yer good dress, Morag."

"Watch yer best breeks, Hector."

All spruced up, hair stuck down, the boys ignored the warnings and continued to pelt around the floor. The girls promenaded around the edges, preening themselves in their full frilly dresses and sugar-starched petticoats. But too soon they were sucked into the whirlpool of sliding and gliding and pulling and chasing.

Into this melee plunged McAllister. He was amazed that he had agreed to be here. Joanne rushed off to find Chiara, Ann McPherson went searching for Rob, and Don had just plain disappeared.

The drive over to the Strath had had McAllister holding his breath on every bend. The drive back would be worse. Don could never be persuaded that driving with a few beers and as many whiskies in him could possibly affect his judgment. I've been driving like this for forty-odd years and never had an accident was his reply. Why he had agreed to go with Don McLeod was another decision that puzzled him, but McAllister was in Don's car, at Don's mercy, out of cowardice. An hour and a half, there *and* back, alone in the car with Joanne; he wouldn't have known what to say. He suspected she felt the same. He had been glad of the other passenger, WPC Ann Macpherson. The two women chatted in that way that women do, warm and comfortable in each other's company. He envied them. But he had to stop himself cross-questioning the policewoman, and he had to order himself not to ask Don to pull in at every roadside phone box so he could call DCI Westland to ask if he had made an ar-

417

rest yet. Not that Don would have stopped.

A microphone whistled. The MC, his dinner jacket as shiny as his slicked-back hair, stepped to the front of the stage.

"Ladies and gentlemen, will ye take your partners and form yer sets for Strip the Willow."

The stage was jam-packed with at least a dozen fiddlers, and the five accordions were marking time as the dancers frantically searched for a partner. The night had barely started, so most of the dancers were women chummed up with their best friends. A reluctant lad was dragged determinedly to the floor by a lass from a neighboring village who fancied her chances. A cheer from his friends got the blushing boy to his feet. In formation, a frantic dance began. Up and down and around and around they swung, changing partners, forming and re-forming into circles, arches, young girls with their fathers, women with women, lads and lasses gradually joined in, with the audience clapping and shouting encouragement.

The skirl of "whee-eech" came more and more frequently as the dancers twirled faster and faster. The couple in the middle of the ring almost flew to the rhythm of the snare drum. Then a final chorus, and the dancers collapsed in panting exhilaration.

They were replaced by the next shift, readying themselves for the Dashing White Sergeant.

McAllister glimpsed Joanne going in and out of one of the sets through arches of upheld arms. Her laughing eyes were a sight he had not seen in a long time. He smiled, happy for her. The music finished. The bandleader and head fiddler, Archie Stuart the old ghillie, took the microphone.

"Can I have a bit o' hush now?" He drew a cat's wail across the strings of his fiddle. "Hold yer wheesht out there." Slowly the noise subsided to a murmur.

"Whilst we all get our breath back and some of us avail ourselves of the light refreshments" — that got a good laugh — "I'd like to introduce a lady who needs no introduction. A big hand for the singer, Mrs. Jenny McPhee."

Hearty applause and a whistle or two greeted Jenny as she took the stage. She stood in a single spotlight, her tiny frame in a Stuart tartan taffeta skirt and white blouse, her indomitable presence drawing the audience into her web, with no musical backup, no microphone, rock-carved form mountain-still, she started.

"I give you 'The Berry Fields o' Blair.' "

A round of applause rose and faded to a

respectful hush. The opening stanza filled the hall. Her clear true voice rang full and powerful. She sang out the verses, the gathered family, clansmen and friends joining in the refrain:

The berry fields o' Blair

McAllister was enjoying himself immensely, joining in as heartily as his neighbors. From the corner of his eye he saw Rob making his way toward him.

"Later, Robbie, enjoy the song."

Rob whispered back. "I have to speak to you. Now."

McAllister followed. Every eye was on the stage but the crowd parted and regathered around them as naturally as a burn diverting round a rock. McAllister, still entranced by the music and singing, hadn't yet caught Rob's anxiety.

"Dr. Matheson has driven over from Beauly with a message from my mother."

"Is she all right?"

"Aye, she's fine. Look, it's probably nothing, just getting herself worked up, but she thought you should know."

"What?"

"Mother saw Father Morrison leaving the house. He left in a taxi."

"Where is he off to?" McAllister shouted, his voice drowning in the applause from inside the hall. He jiggled from foot to foot as he tried to think, the frost creeping through his thin soles and chilling his bones. Echoing out into the still cold night came the haunting refrain of Jenny's second song, "Aye Fond Kiss." It was McAllister's favorite but it didn't register.

"My mother thinks he may be off on the night train south."

"But why leave for the station so early?"

"Scared DCI Westland might be around to arrest him? I don't know." Rob watched as McAllister peered at his watch in the light leaking out of the hall door.

"An hour and twenty minutes." The editor had come to a decision. "I should just make it."

"To the station? You're mad. Apart from black ice and the likelihood of snow, you hate driving a car."

"Give me your bike keys."

Rob obediently handed them over without thinking. In shock, he watched McAllister stride over to the bike and start the engine, well in control of the machine. Rob grabbed the handlebars.

"Here, have this." He handed over his scarf. "Wait. My hat and jacket are inside,

421

you'll freeze without them."

"No time," McAllister shouted, already on his way.

"Shall I call the police?" Rob yelled at his departing back.

"What for?" cried his editor over a shoulder.

"Aye, what for indeed?" Rob stared morosely at the taillight disappearing into the dark. "And mind my bike."

Then the sound of the fiddlers, and accordions with the skirl of the pipes worked their magic, and Rob turned back to the serious business of having a ball.

Ten minutes or so later, the children burst into the dancing crowd, shrieking in excitement.

"It's snowing! It's snowing! Come and see!"

Some of the children regretted telling their parents; they were made to leave the party early. Families from outlying glens and those from the Black Isle had a way to go to reach their homes and were worried about the possibility of being stranded. The locals would have a trudge through the cold, but what did that matter when they were at the best gathering in years? And two old men were on the hunt.

"Have you seen Jimmy McPhee? Any

chance he's in the kitchen?"

"He's around."

"He owes us five quid," they chorused.
"Apiece." They grinned at each other, tooth-
less grin from one, his dentures having been
removed to facilitate easier drinking.

The party had mellowed. Tired but happy
bunches of guests sat around, catching their
breath for the next round. Rob found
Joanne sitting with Ann, watching the crowd
clearly enjoying themselves.

"We're up soon," he told them. "Pity
McAllister won't see us."

"Really? Have you scared him off without
a chord being played?" Joanne teased.

"It's not that." Rob blithely told them the
story.

Ann stared at him incredulously.

"And you've told the police about this,
have you?" Her tone was icy.

Rob squirmed. Joanne looked away.

"Well, McAllister seemed sure . . . and I
thought . . ."

"You both thought you'd play the dashing
heroes," Ann finished.

"It's not that, Ann. It's your inspector;
he's not interested. He made that clear
yesterday. A priest can do no wrong."

"I know, I know, and I'm sorry. But this
DCI Westland, he's different."

"Really?"

"And, for your information, I'm certain the detective chief inspector is interested in Father Morrison and is trying to find some concrete evidence. But don't tell anyone I told you." She waggled a finger at Rob. "I must find a phone. I've got to report this."

"There's a box up the road," Joanne remembered.

"Come on," Ann asked, "give me your pennies."

"What about my turn?" protested Rob as he searched his pockets.

"I'm sure I'll get to watch you another time. I have to report this."

Joanne and Rob handed over coins and Ann ran out into the snow.

"Do you think McAllister will be all right?" Joanne asked, "This weather is awful."

"I know. I hope he takes care of my bike."

Chiara came up behind Joanne. "Isn't this fun?"

"Great! Where's your fiancé? I saw all that dancing cheek-to-cheek stuff. Very saucy."

"He and the other lads are setting up." Chiara pointed to the stage. "Peter says his violin teacher would be rolling in his grave if he heard him playing guitar and playing this — I don't know what you call it — this music. But they're really good."

"Really?"

"I think so. But I've only heard one number so far," Chiara confessed.

The two friends grabbed some lemonade and went to the front. The MC came on to announce the band to a small crowd of diehards and drunks, happy with whatever music was provided to prolong the drinking and the dancing.

"Is everybody having a grand time?" The MC was barely standing. "Right ye are. So, friends, let's hear it for the new, the extraordinary, the previously unheard and probably never to be heard again, I give you . . . the Meltdown Boys."

The hall lights went out; a solitary spotlight came on. Rob was center stage with guitar and microphone. The drummer counted them in and off they went with their version of Little Richard's "Tutti-Frutti." The crowd stood momentarily — no one knew how to dance to this music — and then clapping and swaying, everyone under twenty finding their own style, going wild, their elders transfixed by the bacchanalia before them.

The song came to an abrupt end. Cheers, whistles and shouts of "more, more" followed the final chord. Then they were off again into the same song, twice more.

Rob leaned into the mike, sweating, thrilled at the reception and thrilled that no one seemed to notice he knew only three chords. Peter with his musical training had carried most of the band, and his tall good looks were attracting almost as much adulation among the lassies as Rob himself was.

"And for our next number, straight from the U. S. of A, we'd like to do a tune by a new band, Bill Haley and the Comets. It's called 'Rock Around the Clock.' "

No one knew what to expect. Very few had actually heard, they'd only read about, the music from America that was shaking the country awake.

Rob slung his guitar to one side, grabbed the mike and, with Peter striking the chords behind Rob's half-shouting, half-singing, they launched into:

"One two three o'clock, four o'clock rock" (crash of chord with cymbals).

"Five six seven o'clock, eight o'clock rock" (next crash, one chord up the scale).

All the band now joined in and off they went, fast and furious. Chaos ensued. Everyone was up. Jumping, dancing, birling, swirling and skirling, some swinging their partners around as in Strip the Willow, others trying the crazy dance steps they'd seen on the television. And the band played and played and played until everyone, the audience, the players, the onlookers, had to stop, completely exhausted.

"More, more," came the cries. But the band packed up. They were on strict orders to end before midnight. The hall license ran out "on the dot of twelve."

"Besides," as Rob confessed on the journey home, "we only know two numbers."

The drive through the glen was treacherous. Doubly so on a motorbike. Black ice had already formed in the deep bends of the road, which was a mere extension of the riverbank. The tunnel of rowan and birch was claustrophobically dark, heavy snow-bearing clouds shutting out the starlight. McAllister heaved the bike through the twists and turns, praying that no one else was coming the opposite way.

Past the distillery, he shot out onto the main road, terrifying himself. Though wider, the way was still tortuous. With McAllister frozen to the handlebars, the Triumph flew through the night, following the shoreline of the firth he could barely see but definitely smell. The gaps between the flurries of fat snowflakes decreased. Black ice, hairpin bends, short flat straights, corkscrew bends, an abrupt blind corner under the railway bridge, then over the final humpbacked bridge, he shot into the still night of the town. Now the snow was falling straight and steady, thick and lying.

McAllister careened into the station square, skidding past the silver stone *Highlander* from a long-forgotten desert war, indifferent to the snow and the drama unfolding beneath his plinth. Three minutes to go. The train would wait for no one. McAllister stumbled off the bike, landing at the feet of the doorman, in full braided uniform, on the red carpet of the Station Hotel steps. Before he could even tip his hat, a ten-shilling note was thrust into the man's hand.

"Look after this, will you?"

The final whistle sounded. The engine jolted and spat. The coupled carriages, after an initial groan of protest, slowly started down the long platform. McAllister stumbled over the closed ticket barricade, lurching like Frankenstein's monster up the platform, limbs and muscles frozen. He began running, running for life itself, now running parallel to the tail of the train. He grabbed the cold metal bar of the guard's carriage door but didn't have the strength to swing himself up. Any second, he would run out of platform. The carriage door opened, a hand grabbed his jacket from above and someone else shoved him from behind. In he tumbled, landing on all fours. The train gathered momentum, echoing through the railyards, a puffing dragon of light heading for the mountains.

Frozen, exhausted, exhilarated, he looked gratefully up at his rescuer. The train guard, who recognized him, grinned at McAllister.

"We can't be having the editor missing the train, can we now?"

He was shown a seat, the lack of a ticket brushed off as a mere formality. Then a wee silver bottle of spirits, handed to him by a bemused fellow passenger, revived him somewhat.

"Never again," declared McAllister in gratitude, "never again will I complain about being a public figure." The kudos of the newspaper worked wonders in an emergency.

"I have to find someone . . . a friend." He attempted to get to his feet again.

"Wait on a wee whiley. You're drookit and they are no going anywhere." The guard fussed. "Give me yer jacket. We'll dry her on the firebox. Breeks too. I'll fetch you a blanket to cover your dignity."

"I have to find him in case he's gone.

Maybe he was never on the train in the first place. He could've flown already."

"Here, have another dram." The stranger opposite passed back the flask. "You look and sound like you're in sore need of it."

NINETEEN

Joanne dutifully came into the office, even though she had had only a few hours' sleep. No one else was there. It being a Saturday morning, the girls were with their grandparents. She fiddled with some typing; she returned a couple of phone calls; she made tea; twice, she considered phoning Mhairi on the west coast to leave a message for Bill, ask how he was doing, but didn't. He would assume she had a guilty conscience about something or other. She had; she could feel herself stretching, growing, singing inside herself, and not for one moment did she miss him. Her legs ached from dancing, her cheeks ached from laughing; the only thing she needed to know was that McAllister was safe.

When Don walked in looking as though his horse had come in at fifty to one on the nose, she blurted out, "Where's McAllister?"

"Holed up in some hotel bar way out in the wilds, probably. The tracks are snow-bound so no train is getting through. They've probably taken the passengers to Aviemore or Carrbridge." He saw through her. "Don't worry about him."

"I'm not."

"He'll be fine. I do know though that he definitely caught the train."

"Would you like some tea?"

"No, lass, but thanks for asking; I need a hair of the dog and we've to meet Jimmy McPhee."

He looked out the dirty window to a whitescape of rooftops contrasted by a black pearl sky. He had sniffed the air to see if more snow was to come but could only catch last night's whisky and decades of tobacco.

"Come on, we'll shut up shop and adjourn to the meeting room. Jimmy wants a word."

He printed CLOSED — SNOW in his red checking pencil and turned to Joanne. "Pin that up outside and we'll be off."

"I can't keep going into public houses," she started. "If my mother-in-law finds out . . ."

He winked. "But this is an order and Mrs. Ross senior dare not cross me. I mind the time — well before she married . . . no, I'll keep that story for emergencies."

Laughing, they stepped out into the hush of snow, he tucked her arm under his and they lurched down icy pavements to the alternative *Gazette* office.

They made an incongruous couple. He was shorter than her by a head. He had on the proverbial trilby that looked as though there should be a betting slip tucked into the band. Her Fair Isle tammy was set at an angle that was jaunty, just short of saucy. He had on the polished brogues that had lasted fifteen years and would last a good many more. Joanne's zippered sheepskin boots stopped short of her skirt, revealing International Brigade Red socks. His tweed jacket had leather elbow patches — with a Masonic badge that he wore for all the wrong reasons. She had on an olive green belted raincoat that was ten years out of date and made her look like an extra in a louche French film where people made love to people they were not married to. Neither carried an umbrella. Umbrellas are not favored by Scottish people, despite the precipitous weather. And if you chanced to see these two walk by, and were asked to guess who they were, what they did, where they worked, you would guess newspapers.

They settled in, in Don's corner table.

Joanne looked around. Multiple customers, reflected in the multiple mirrors, gave quite the fairground atmosphere to the drinking haven. The swing doors opened and closed with a one-o'clock-Saturday, half-day-at-work frequency.

"Don't look now," Joanne murmured, "but those men that have just come in, that's the Gordon brothers."

Don looked. The eldest brother, spotting Joanne, waved.

He came over. "How's it goin', Joanne?"

"It's Mrs. Ross to the likes o' you." Don, alert as a sheepdog when the wolves were on the prowl around the fold, fairly growled at Jimmy Gordon and his brothers.

"Get away, we're old friends."

"Not the way I heard it."

Jimmy Gordon looked closely at Don, dismissed him as an old nobody and pulled out a chair. His brothers did likewise.

"And who invited you three wee nyaffs to the table?" Don demanded.

"Who's gonny stop me?"

"I am."

Jimmy McPhee appeared from nowhere and stood behind Joanne.

"Well well well. Jimmy McPhee."

Jimmy looked them over. "The gormless Gordons." No one took offence. They'd been called it often enough to make it a double-barreled surname.

"So what brings you up here?" Jimmy McPhee's cheer radiated menace.

"Just a wee visit. Old friends, you know."

"Old enemies an' all." Jimmy kept up the rigor mortis grin. "I never knew you had Highland connections. Remind me of yer family ties."

The barman was polishing the glasses, pretending nothing untoward was happening but watching it all in the mirror above. The other drinkers, agog, watched the protagonists in the wall mirrors where they were half obscured by the advertisements etched into the glass for beers and whiskies. Joanne watched the two Jimmies face up to each other, trying not to make a move nor breathe too loudly.

Gary Cooper, *High Noon,* popped into her head, except Jimmy McPhee was facing down three instead of four. She had trouble suppressing a nervous giggle.

"I think you'll find it's more a business visit." Don knew what he was doing.

"And what kinda business would that be?" asked Jimmy McPhee, knowing exactly what the Gordons' business entailed.

"I did hear they've been fishing," Don offered.

"Poaching, more like," Jimmy McPhee responded.

"Aye, that's my drift."

"We're no too keen on that up this way."

"Penalties are high, was what I heard." Don again.

"Families don't take kindly to other families camping on their grounds." Jimmy.

"It's not as though you or yours would go fishing down south." Don.

"Heaven forfend." A mock look of horror from Jimmy McPhee.

"Will ye look at the time, boys." The eldest Gordon turned to his brothers. "Oor train leaves in ten minutes. Great to see ye again, Jimmy." Handshakes all round.

"You too, Jimmy."

"Say hello to yer ma and yer brothers. Nice to meet you again, Mrs. Ross. We'll be away off the noo. Chilly in these parts."

The doors swung shut. There was a momentary silence, then a buzz ran up and down the bar.

"But the trains aren't running," Joanne started.

"My round." Don rose.

"What on earth was that all about?" Joanne looked at Jimmy McPhee.

"I could ask you the same thing, Mrs. Ross."

Jimmy sat down and looked her over. She looked away. He didn't know how much Joanne knew. He himself knew almost everything of Bill's affairs.

"That late-evening visit they paid to Joanne, when pretending to look for Bill Ross, they asked after the girls." Don was back.

"That's against the rules," Jimmy stated flatly.

Joanne said nothing.

"Aye. Well." Don knocked back the dram. "Much obliged, Jimmy."

"Not at all. Good to know about the poachers."

"Thanks for the party last night, Mr. McPhee. We all had a great time."

"Aye, it was grand, wasn't it? Not sure about some of the music, though. Any word on McAllister?"

"Not yet."

Jimmy shook Don's hand and left.

"Thanks again." Joanne waved cheerio as he pushed through the doors.

Walking back up the narrow lane, back through to the High Street and the office so Joanne could collect her bike, she put the question.

"Don, what on earth was that all about?"

"Went well, didn't it, my wee scheme?"

He grinned and kept walking. Exasperated, she poked him in the ribs.

"You set all that up, didn't you? For your own delight?"

If he weren't a man nearing sixty, Joanne would have sworn he was sniggering like a schoolboy.

"Aye, magic wasn't it? And for your information only, that was the biggest bunch of heavies you're ever likely to meet, getting their comeuppance."

Joanne was none the wiser.

"You *will* explain, Don McLeod, all of it, or I will never cover the Highlands and Islands Women's Institute AGM for you, ever ever again."

He raised his hands in mock surrender. She listened in astonishment. Bill's involvement with the Gordons was one thing, but to find out that her encounter had been with one of the most feared bosses in Scottish crime was something else again. How dare that husband of mine endanger their girls, how dare he? But she kept this thought to herself.

"So that's that?"

Don thought for a moment. "There's still the matter of one thousand pounds."

"And we still don't know what has happened to McAllister," she added.

■ ■ ■ ■

McAllister woke. Everything was white. He tried sitting up and roared like a wounded bear. That really hurt. His face and head and ribs and knee hurt like hell but not as much as his face. Out of the window, snow, calm and deep, covered everything, every tree and shrub and distant mountain. The horizon blurred as sky merged with snow and the whole scene was framed by the glittering magical patterns made by frost on windowpanes. A row of humped shapes not far from the windows made him think, Cars? Car park? Then he remembered.

He wanted to shout for the nurse but knew he couldn't. He found a bell.

"My clothes?" A low-pitched moan was all he could manage.

She gave him a pencil and paper clipped to a board.

Clothes. The coat. Where are they? he wrote.

"You'll not be needing those today."

Envelope. Inside a railway coat. Ask guard. He scribbled frantically, then handed back the clipboard and attempted to swing his legs over the side of the bed. The waves of nausea were worse than the worst hangover he could remember.

"The coat was taken off to dry along with your clothes. I'll find it. But only if you promise to stay put."

McAllister waited. He kept feeling he was going to be sick from the pain, or the drugs, or the fear that a stranger would pick up those photos. Maybe they were lost; the thought made his stomach turn. Footsteps squeaked up the polished floor, the person invisible to McAllister, cocooned as he was behind a hospital screen.

"Is this what you're looking for?" DCI Westland held up a thick brown envelope as though it were an unexploded bomb or a lump of shite, distaste showing on every pore of his snow-ruddy face.

The policeman sat on the bedside chair, speaking quickly and quietly.

"The doctors say you'll be fine but you need rest. You've done a great job, Mr. McAllister. Now leave the rest to me." He looked at the gaunt man, at the white bandage around head and jaw that seemed to meld into the white skin and the pillow, emphasizing the eyes, dark and dead as the coals on a snowman's face.

"I hope these photos will help to put this man away." The chief inspector was unsure that this would happen but now was not the

440

time to say so.

"Hoodie crow." The words came out as a groan.

"I give you my word, as a father of two fine lads, I'll do all in my power to catch this man. I promise the pictures will be kept locked away, authorized persons only to see them. Does that help you rest more easy?"

Hoodie crow, McAllister scribbled, held up the paper.

"He'll be found. Rest assured, I'll track him down. If he had anything to do with the boy's fate, I'll make sure he's locked away for life."

McAllister closed his eyes. If, the chief inspector said. If. And if the priest escaped, he would continue to desecrate young boys' lives; of that he was sure. But a vivid scene flashed before him; photographs of his brother and others, all being shown, passed around, in a crowded court. He felt an overwhelming sense of helplessness. He needed reassurance. He struggled to reach out for the policeman's arm but was exhausted, drifting in and out of consciousness.

"I'll be back, McAllister. You sleep, then you can tell me all that happened."

He had no choice in the matter; there was nothing McAllister could tell him in the state he was in, not being able to speak. Westland, policeman, father and realist, knew there was no evidence linking Morrison to Jamie. As for the photos, they only proved that the man had an unhealthy liking for young boys, nothing else. A complaint would have to be made for an investigation into the matter. And who ever would come forward to complain, never mind stand up to a court appearance? Who could prove that they were anything more than unsavory pictures? Who would believe that the experience might hurt a boy? Embarrass? Maybe. But harm? And the improbability of anyone's listening to a child, taking their word against the word of a priest; he was back to the same old conundrum. The next leap, from priest with an obsession to priest as a killer, of that there was absolutely no proof. The chief inspector walked out of the white world of the hospital into the white world of the mountains at a loss as to where to turn next.

Willie Grant waved to him from across the cleared entranceway, gesturing to the Land Rover.

"Sir, the snowplough has been through but the roads are still bad and there's more weather on the way."

The chief inspector kicked the wheel of

the vehicle. He knew nothing could be done.

"Sir, I've booked you into the Carrbridge Hotel. It's famous for —" Willie stopped. Me an' ma big mouth, he thought.

"For what, Willie?"

"Well, they do say, or so they tell me, that it's got the best selection of single-malts in the Highlands."

"In that case, lay on, Macduff." Westland gave Willie a grin, reaching up to pat the lad on his broad shoulders. "Well done, Constable Grant. Well done on everything."

McAllister slept five hours or so, then started to drift in and out of half dreams and images of the previous night. He still felt chilled to the bone despite the warm hospital bed. What had happened? He must remember. Where was he? The station square. Falling off Rob's bike. Running for the train, frozen through. A hand pulling him up. Another pushing from behind. Aye, that was it.

"In the nick o' time, eh? Och, it's yourself, Mr. McAllister. Soaked through, too. Here, give me yer jacket an' have a loan o' this."

His rescuer took off his heavy railway-issue overcoat, putting it over McAllister's shoulders. "We'll get these dried out on the engine's boiler. Won't take long."

A fellow passenger poured a generous tot into the cap of his flask. McAllister knocked it back. The heat went all the way down his gullet and lit up his vital organs, melting the ice block that had settled in his innards. The ticket inspector appeared with a large white mug embossed with the royal coat of arms of the train. It contained tea with yet more whisky. His eyes watering, he cupped his hands around the mug. His knees started to shake. The railwayman reached up to the overhead rack. He placed a blanket over McAllister's legs. . . . In his hospital bed his knees started to tremble at the memory; now it was all coming back to him. . . . Stripped off his wet jacket as he was bidden, handed them over to the guard, hands and feet and face hurting as the circulation came back . . . yes.

The train labored up the long hard haul, up the Drumochter Pass. McAllister was desperate to find the priest before the train stopped on the high plateau, where the sleeping and dining cars would be attached for the journey south. It took him a good half hour before he could stand and when he did, he realized that what little strength he had was whisky strength. He buttoned the overcoat, set off, checking every carriage, until he reached the first-class section. There, seated in splendid comfort, sat Father Morrison, hands clasped around his belly, feet stretched out, dozing, comfortable as a cat on a hearthside rug.

He started when the door slid open. A shadow crossed his face as McAllister came in, sat opposite him, and nodded, too tense to talk.

"Mr. McAllister, what a surprise." The man recovered quickly. "Are you off south on business too?"

"I'll not call you Father, you've disgraced that title."

"Oh really?"

"You know what I'm talking about."

"No, I'm afraid you've lost me. Are you cold? Let me get you a rug," the priest offered.

"I want nothing from you!" McAllister sounded petty even to himself.

"I don't think that's so, otherwise, why are you here?"

Outside, in the pitch-black dark, swirling snow danced in the spill of the carriage lights. McAllister sat silent for a moment longer, taking time to control his anger and disgust. He studied his nemesis. He saw a big man, middle-aged, a pale face and pale skin with fading freckles. The eyes, washed-out blue, were so pale that in certain lights, the sockets could seem empty. The sandy hair, thin on the head, thick on the wrists and hands, made McAllister realize he would never again be able to face a pork-knuckle dinner. The man's heavy body, and forever to McAllister he would be a man, not a priest, was shaped by years of rugby and boxing but was long past its glory days. The man's projection of calm innocence, his smile, his air of reassurance, incensed McAllister even more, making it hard for him to control his shakes. The quest for an answer to his brother's death had been with him for almost a decade and now, with the man he sought sitting opposite, a lassitude descended over him, deep as a bank of sea fog. His ability to think, to reason, to judge, faded. The unexpected air of kindness and concern had cast a spell.

"Let's drop the charade. You take an unhealthy interest in young boys."

"Not so. I'm a father to them."

"It's much more than a fatherly interest!"

The priest raised his open palms to protest but McAllister persisted.

"I believe, no, I *know,* you have damaged, sometimes beyond repair, the lives and souls of those young children in your care."

"That's a monstrous lie."

"Tell me your version, then."

"I have no version. Only the truth."

He linked his hands together on his lap before starting. He told his history, and as he spoke, it slowly dawned on McAllister that the priest sincerely believed his own truth — that he was helping to save the souls of the young boys in his care.

"I have devoted my whole life to the care of young people. I've run youth camps, sports clubs, cared for orphans and unwanted babies. I have an unblemished record. Check for yourself. If there are those who don't understand my mission, that's not my fault."

He was starting to get worked up. "And you, an experienced journalist, you would take the word of little boys as gospel, you would take their word against mine?"

He leant back, wriggling his shoulders, calming himself.

"Why would they make stories up, these boys?"

"I had to point out their sins. They don't know what their dirty filthy habits will lead them to. They don't have the discipline it takes to be pure. One minute they're innocent wee souls, next, when their bodies start to change, they become impure, with no control. They have to learn. Their unfortunate backgrounds and lack of a good

Christian upbringing makes them little liars. We cannot always overcome our blood. But some do."

He sighed theatrically. "I was a good priest and a good friend to them." He spoke passionately, explaining, justifying. "I tried to instill discipline, cleanliness, pure hearts and minds and bodies, into their corrupted little lives. I tried to give them a chance to make good." He paused for a moment and looked out the window into the storm. "There was a time, some years ago, when I erred." He said this quietly, before turning back to McAllister. "But God is my only judge and I promise you, I do all in my power to look after those in my care."

"And the photos?"

"So Rob McLean *did* go poking about in my private affairs. Yes, I take pictures of innocent pure boys. I capture the essential good in them before their fall from grace."

He really believes all this shite, McAllister realized. "What about wee Jamie?"

"The boy who drowned? I had nothing to do with his death."

"Are you trying to tell me you know nothing about what happened to him?"

The priest turned his face back to the swirling snow. "Anything that happened to that wee boy was purely an accident."

"You killed him."

"I did nothing of the sort." His indignation made him turn red, starting at the nose.

"And years ago, my brother, Kenneth McAllister?"

"Well, well. The great John McAllister; it took you long enough to realize I knew Kenneth." He smirked. "And you the star journalist, you the famous war correspondent too busy going places to bother with your own wee brother." He was enjoying stirring the guilt. "Aye, he told me all about you. Worshipped you, you the big shot. And look at you now. On a miserable wee publication that doesn't mean anything to anybody." He smiled. "Besides, it was all a long time ago."

"Not for my mother it isn't."

"I'm sorry." His Dr. Jekyll persona returned. "You're right, your poor mother. I'm really sorry for her." His hands were up in an apologetic benediction.

He's good at this, McAllister thought, he's convincing, and he believes himself.

"John, your brother's death was unfortunate. It's always unfortunate when someone dies by his own hand. And so young. But there it is."

"Jimmy McPhee, you remember him?"

"McPhee? I remember him well. I was

always glad that our paths didn't cross in the Highlands — quite a temper has Jimmy McPhee." He leaned toward McAllister. "But he is a liar and a rascal. Him and all his family."

"The photographs." McAllister persisted. "Can't you see that they could be construed as disturbing? Can't you imagine how some boys might feel abused to be photographed naked?"

A momentary flicker crossed Morrison's confident features.

"Healthy minds, healthy bodies — you're no doubt a man who knows his classics, it has been part of many cultures from the Greeks onward."

He sat back, smug and satisfied, his hands again clasped over his belly, as though he had delivered a final unarguable case for his perversion. But McAllister caught a tiny flicker of an eye toward the suitcases on the luggage rack before Morrison settled back in the seat.

"I've always taken photographs. I could have been a professional, so I'm told. As a matter of fact your old paper has published a few over the years. Some of the photographs in my private collection may not be understood by the ignorant. But they are beautiful portraits with nothing untoward

450

about them. Nothing wrong at all."

"Fine, then, we'll be stopping shortly so you won't mind checking with the police to see if it's all right for you to be off to the city without a word to anyone — just in case you're wanted to help with inquiries, as they say. You won't mind that, will you, Mr. Morrison, or is it Bain?"

McAllister was near the end of his strength when the thought flashed before him.

"Hang on. You said the death of the boy Jamie was an accident. But the police think it was the Polish man, only they have no proof. So if you had nothing to do with it, you must know something, you must be protecting —"

The blow was sudden and fierce. McAllister was completely unprepared. The big man brought his clasped hands, a double fist, swiftly upward. McAllister instinctively jerked backward, but not quickly enough. The left side of his jaw caught the full force. The right side of his face hit the window and he slid down, leaving a streak of blood and snot, before crumpling onto the carpet. Distantly, he heard the compartment door open and close.

"The communication cord." He couldn't move, couldn't reach up. But he dragged himself along the floor and half-upright, clutching onto the seat, the compartment door handle, he lurched into the corridor. Morrison was by the carriage door. He had opened the window. He was leaning out with his hand on the handle waiting for the train to slow. Like a wounded beast, McAllister found the adrenaline he needed and threw himself at the priest, gripping him around the legs. The big man had endured many a tackle in rugby. He shook McAllister off easily and with an added kick to the ribs sent McAllister tumbling backward into the man's suitcase. The door opened; the train slowed to walking pace. The priest was poised to take flight. Then a tremendous lurch, as the engines pulled hard, sent a shock wave through the couplings. The carriages concertinaed into each other. John Morrison Bain went flying. In a flash, into the whirl of wind and snow, arms windmilling, he tried to grab anything but found nothing. He tumbled into the deep soft drifts, careering down the embankment. The hoodie crow had taken flight. It would be in a series of black-and-white images that McAllister would always remember the last sight of his nemesis.

His face hurt, his ribs hurt, he was lying in a puddle of melted snow and his senses were rapidly shutting down. A stop was coming up soon. They'd find a doctor, or at least a dram. They'd find the man. Had to. Then he saw it. Or rather, felt it. On the undamaged side of his rib cage, the metal corner poked into him. The suitcase. The photos. They must be there inside. Were there any of Kenneth? Or Jimmy? Or of wee Jamie? This was the evidence. It took all his willpower to stay conscious. But he had to know.

Get a grip, McAllister, he thought, moaning. He shifted over and leaned against the wall. The carriage door had slammed shut but the snow blew in through the open window, creating a miniature snowdrift on and around him. The suitcase catches flicked open — not locked. He scrabbled through the contents, tossing clothes, boots, robes to the floor — no photos.

The pain was coming at him in waves. A purple light filled his head when he shut his eyes — the doorway to oblivion, that he knew. Inside pockets; empty. Zipped pocket on the lid — spare socks. Another lurch of the train sent a shockwave of pain from head to toe. The suitcase was lying on its side, empty. Along the bottom, the metal strips were held together by black electrical tape. He clawed a corner, pulled at an end. Then another. And another. He ripped a fingernail and the flesh on his thumb. His hands were so cold he didn't notice. He reached inside. He eased out the cardboard envelope and shook it open. Photographs spilled around him, slithering and sliding onto his lap, the floor and into the melting snow. One look was enough. He scrabbled frantically for the pictures, stuffed some back into the envelope, others into the greatcoat pocket, his hands barely able to obey his brain. Lying there, eyes shut, amid the strewn wreckage of suitcase and clothing and papers and rolled-up socks, he struggled to keep himself in this world but failed. As he descended, the thought of all this shame being exposed in police stations, in the procurator's office, before a jury in a court of law, sickened him; the thought of unknown eyes poring over images of defeated boys decided him. And, decision made, he hid all the photos as best he could, then he let go.

The train drew alongside a platform lined with storm lanterns, sending out wavering pools of light into the fast-falling snow. There was much more than the usual activity outside. Railway officials and policemen, muffled against the storm, moved like marauding bears through the carriages. The carriage door opened.

"Mr. McAllister sir, what have we here now?"

Constable Willie Grant came to the rescue like the proverbial St. Bernard. And like the dog, he too had a flask of alcohol. He spoke to the comatose figure as he would to a lost boy, not bothered that there was no reply.

"You'll be a' right, sir. The doctor'll be along soon." Willie Grant had his arm around McAllister, easing him up to a sitting position, tenderly brushing the snow from his hair. He put the flask to McAllister's lips and though most of it trickled down the side of his mouth, the fumes were enough to bring him back to semiconsciousness. McAllister's first thought was, What kind of nasty cheap blend is this stuff?

"Best go easy on the whisky, sir." The policeman put the flask away. "Mr. McAllister, have you seen yon priest fellow? I've had word that I have tae hold on tae him."

McAllister tried to speak, tried to nod his head, but everything hurt.

"Mmm-mm, gone." It came out as a groan but Willie Grant got the message.

"You just hold on, sir. I'll be back in a tick."

But he had passed out.

An ambulance arrived. McAllister was

taken to hospital, patched up and put to bed. Just as the shot of morphine was taking effect, Willie appeared again.

"I'm right sorry about this, Mr. McAllister sir, but I need to get the search party going and there's a fair bit of snow the night. Can you tell us anything?"

Big galoot that Willie Grant sometimes seemed, this initial impression hid a kindness and a courtesy. He handed McAllister a pencil and his spiral notebook. Drugged and speechless, the journalist's instinct kicked in. He scribbled down the gist of what had happened, finishing with "Find the bastard!"

Willie stopped at the nurse's station as he left. "Can you figure this out?" He handed her his notebook. "I canny make head or tail o' it."

The sister squinted at the spidery scrawl.

"After the doctors' handwriting I've had to put up with, this is easy."

In the dark, they tramped along both sides of the tracks where the priest was thought to have flown the carriage. The snow was now horizontal, driven by a fierce whistling wind. An arctic hour and a half later, PC Grant called off the search, concerned for the safety of his helpers.

"Daylight the morrow, lads. Meet at the car park of the Carrbridge Hotel."

Willie Grant went back to the police station to discover one more problem; the phones were down. So he did the only thing possible. He went to bed.

It was only a few weeks to the solstice. Dawn came about eight o'clock. Willie Grant had been up for some time preparing a huge breakfast, his recipe for a successful day's work. And today was looking to be very hard work. Not the least of it would be shoveling snow. Then there was the matter of no phones. Added to that was the sole responsibility of finding this man. But Willie still made time for breakfast.

Snow chains on, he backed the old Land Rover out onto the main road. Crews spreading salt followed the snowplow and with a vehicle like his, PC Grant had no problem getting to the hotel. The early sun laid a pink glow over the snow, the mountains, the lochs and the tarns. Along the horizon, the pink quickly turned deeper and deeper to a pure blood red, shot through with shimmering, shifting pink, orange and violet. The high sky was deep cerulean blue, the air still and calm and crisp and cold. And dangerous.

"Red sky in the morning, shepherd's warning," Willie muttered.

Other Land Rovers, some locals on foot and two men with ponies met up in the hotel car park. One volunteer, a shepherd, had brought his dogs. The black-and-white collies were more used to digging for lost sheep but had shown a talent for finding other lost creatures. Maps were consulted, opinions solicited, options agreed on, then off set the raggedy band, each with a section of track to scour with a rail crew on a push-and-pull track-maintenance bogie at the ready to relay information up and down the tracks. Willie Grant and his team, including the dogs, were to cover the downward run toward the pass of Drumochter. They searched for signs of disturbance in the snow, but the storm had continued most of the night, masking everything. A scant hour later the men began to look upward as often as downward. The sky was closing in.

"Keep at it, lads. As long as possible." Willie passed a flask of tea among the crew as they continued their search. He squinted his eyes against the brightness of the snow. Coming down the tracks toward them was the bogie.

"Constable Grant," came the shout. "We've found him."

The vehicle came to a halt on a long screech of brakes. The men crowded around, eager for news.

"The receptionist at a guesthouse in Kingussie says a big man, soaking wet and covered in snow, came looking for a taxi. Said it was important he got to Glasgow and the train was no moving. No one local would risk the journey, but another guest, in a hurry to be away before the storm set in for good, he offered the fellow a lift. They went off thegither on the main road south."

"When was that road closed?" Willie was anxious.

"Not till a whiley later. The weather was nor'easterly."

"Was the road further south snowed up?"

"No knowing, Willie." One of the men thought about it. "Sometimes it's all this side o' the hills. Sometimes it's worse o'er yonder."

"So he could have got through, you're saying."

"Aye, mebby."

A few big soft flakes began a gentle dance. It was time to give up. The rail crew offered everyone a lift back to the station on the bogie. Most of the searchers clambered aboard. The shepherd, deciding to walk back along the tracks, whistled for his dogs.

One came immediately. One didn't. The big collie bitch started to sniff at the snow farther along the search area, toward the main road. Then she sniffed in tight circles, running around a clump of gorse. She started to dig with happy snuffling grunts, slowly at first, then faster, certain, her companion circling her, making small encouraging yelps.

"Leave her be," said her master to the watching team. "Stand back and let her do her work."

They were well trained, these collies, barking only in an emergency. A small piece of black cloth was uncovered. The dog sat back, satisfied. Now it was her master's turn. Willie and the shepherd crouched down and continued to widen and deepen the hole with their bare hands. He pulled. A bundle of cloth came out of the snowdrift. A neatly rolled cassock.

"He'd have taken that off — all the better to move in the snow. Keep digging, lads, make sure there's nothing else. I'll put markers around the area so's we can find it later."

"Well, no much later," the shepherd told him. "Fifteen minutes or thereabouts and it'll be another day before we can come back. If that."

"Oh aye?" Willie asked.

The older man stared at the constable with steel gray eyes.

"Aye," apologized Willie. "You're the local."

No more was discovered. The men left, glad that their efforts had yielded something, if not the man himself. Willie set back out to check the progress of the snowplows and to catch any more news from the surrounding villages. There was still no telephone, no messages. He didn't hold out much hope for finding this priest fellow.

"Long gone," he was convinced. "Back to his protectors."

TWENTY

"Ouch! That hurt!"

Chiara fidgeted, impatient to get down from the dining table, where she was standing so Aunty Lita could adjust the hem of the heavy satin wedding gown.

"Well, keep still. You're jumping around like a circus flea."

"But, Aunty, I have to meet Peter. I'm already late."

"Cara, he loves you — he'll wait."

"Whose crazy idea was it to get married in December anyway?"

"It means a lot to Peter, to marry you on his mother's birthday. So romantic."

A week to go; Peter had absolutely refused to cancel or postpone the wedding. Karl is in prison, there is nothing we can do but wait, he told her when she had raised the question. Peter was shaken, even humiliated, by the reaction of some in the town. He had assumed that after all this time he was one of them, a citizen of the Highlands. But no more; he now knew there would always be those who would look closely at him when a scapegoat was needed. The Corellis had also suffered — they were outsiders, accepted, but still outsiders and always were, always would be. The attitude of Inspector Tompson shocked him; his logic was that Karl, as a stranger *and* a foreigner, must be guilty. The policeman's attitude that he, Peter Kowalski, fifteen years in the town, was guilty by association was, to the inspector, a logical conclusion. Karl's imprisonment, his own brief incarceration, had changed Peter. That his place, their place, in this Highland society that he had held so dear was tenuous and that blame for the unexplained, for plagues, famine and pestilence, could be used as an excuse to take away all that he had worked for — that shocked him.

Chiara had shared their fears with Joanne, who had cheerfully informed her that although she was Scottish, she too was an outsider, and that's the way it always will be. "Even when I'm dead and buried," she said, and Joanne had laughed.

Gino walked in. "An angel." He beamed at his daughter. "And so like your mother." He couldn't hide the tears. "But it's no problem, Chiara *mia.* If you want, we have the wedding in summer. You wait another seven months, no? You tell me, I do it. For you, anything."

"Papa, you know I didn't mean it." Chiara was still agitated. "I'm worried, that's all. Peter is still upset, and will our friends make it through the snow? The Edinburgh lot are fine, they'll come along the coast. But everyone from Glasgow has to come over the mountains. I hope they don't get stuck."

"All the families are meeting in Edinburgh, and there's no snow on the East Coast," Gino assured her.

"There's no point in waiting another seven months, I don't think they have summer in Scotland." Aunt Lita was half-joking. "Maybe in a week the snow will be gone. But it would be lovely to have a white Christmas."

They met that evening in the small restaurant and cocktail bar, perhaps the only sophisticated venue in town. It was a last chance for a quiet evening alone, to talk, before being swept up in the wedding drama where, increasingly, Peter felt like an actor in an especially effervescent Italian opera.

In the corner, at a candlelit table, they sat quietly, ate sparingly and looked at each other often. The waiter came and went, as unnoticed as the food. Chiara was immensely glad that Peter seemed to have recovered his good cheer.

Dinner over, he inquired, "Would you like a digestive?"

"No thank you." Chiara was dreamy, slightly inebriated from the wine.

"I have a request." He reached into his pocket, took out a red box and laid it on the table between them. "Would you wear this when we marry? It was my mother's."

Chiara stared at the necklace shimmering in the candlelight, then stared at Peter.

"How on earth did you get this?"

"You know some of the story of Karl. The rest I will tell you, but this, this precious gift, he brought from my mother, and now it is for you. I want you to wear it on our wedding day."

Chiara was mesmerized by the gift and the knowledge that this man, who had brought joy and love and hope to her, her family, their friends, was to marry her. Next week.

"Peter. This is so beautiful. Thank you." In English, it seemed a pitiful, small phrase, "thank you," but she could find no other, and he spoke no Italian. She held it up. He watched the motes of light dance across her skin, her hair. "I will always think of your mother when I wear it."

"I also have this, it arrived yesterday." He handed over a large envelope, an official look about it. It was addressed to himself. "This comes from the Catholic agency in Edinburgh. They help people in Europe find each other, keep in touch. But they must go carefully. The situation is difficult. Look, inside."

There was an official-looking letter from the agency and a letter in a cheap gray envelope addressed with only Peter's name. The letter was in Polish.

"My mother, she wrote this to me. The priest in our village passed it on to someone in contact with the Scottish part of the organization. I can write to her the same way but not too often. It could be risky for her."

He gave one big deep body-shaking sob. He quickly grabbed the napkin and turned the distress into a cough. Chiara reached for Peter's hand and leaned over, and, in pure Scots, said, "If that offer of a digestive is still on, I'll have a cognac."

The weeks leading up to Christmas always brought more advertising than usual, so a bigger paper. Don McLeod, master of the "wee fiddly bits," had three pencils, one behind each ear and one in his hand, as he marked and deleted his way through stories and fillers, penciling in the blank spaces in the layout. Joanne was sorting through her notes to finish a feature on Christmas holiday fare and "wumen's bibs 'n' bobs," as Don so kindly put it.

"I saw McAllister, he got back midmorning —"

Joanne looked across at Don.

"— he's fine, but since he's stuck at home and because he can't shout yet, I'm giving him all the shite jobs. Plus, I get to do the editorial. I'll do it on the state of the roads, that'll annoy the hell out o' him. Our star reporter has promised to deliver a typewriter to him — whenever he gets back from wherever he is."

"Any news on Father . . . on the priest?"

"Still searching."

"Don, do you believe the priest could have done this?"

"I don't know, lass. I've told you I have ma doubts about the Polish man, then again, we don't know for sure he *didn't* do it. But Father Morrison? Let's just say it would shock the hell out of me." He put down his pencil and looked at her. "And very little indeed shocks me. Then we are back to the question, if not one of those two, who, what kind o' monster, would hurt and kill a wee boy?"

She shivered. Every mention of the boy distressed her. "I'll happily deliver the work to McAllister." She handed over her sheets of copy. "I can go now if you like." She needed to get out. She would never let Don know how much she needed to see McAllister for herself. Reports on his well-being were not enough. But before she could get down the stairs, she had to run back to grab the phone. She had given up expecting Don to pick up the receiver when there was a woman around to do it for him.

"*Gazette.* Bill! Hello, stranger. Where are you and how are you?"

"Great. I'm back and at the works," he replied. "You?"

"Oh, you know. Busy. The girls are getting excited about Chiara and Peter's wedding."

"I've good news."

"Oh?"

"Aye, I've managed to sort out that wee hiccup in the business. I've got to put some figures together and the county building department will pay out on work already finished. I told you it would be a' right. You should have more faith in me."

"Yes, *you* were right. That's great news."

She couldn't take his crowing. "Listen, I have to go. I'm in the middle of something."

"Right you are. I'll see you at home the night. See if you can leave the bairns with my ma and dad."

"The girls are at your parents' anyway because it's press night, remember. I'll be out too, I have to try on my outfit for the wedding — I'm matron of honor, remember." She frantically searched for a way out. "But I won't be back tonight. I promised Chiara I'd stay with her, we're having a girls only last-night-of-freedom party. I'm really sorry, I didn't know you were coming home."

Chiara will back me up, she knew.

"Being with your friends is fine. But you be home thenight. You're my wife."

"I promised weeks ago." I may be your wife but you don't own me — goodness, I sound like a wee girl. That gave her courage. "It's all arranged, Bill."

"Unarrange it then. I'll be waiting up for you."

He hung up. Joanne sat staring at a dead receiver when she realized Don was looking at her.

"Were you listening in?" she snapped.

"No, I was not listening in. This is the office phone." He turned back to his work.

"And don't take it out on me, whatever it is."

An engine with snowplow had cleared the tracks, the trains were running, albeit slowly, and McAllister was immensely relieved to be home. The taxi from the station had had to take a roundabout route to his house. Black ice lurked on the braes. His neighbor and former landlady had set the fire, cleaned up, and left soup on the stove. "Just a wee warm-through, Mr. McAllister," she told him. "That's all it needs."

Hands wrapped around a mug of soup, he watched the slow shifting beam from the rising sun stream through his kitchen window, a healing gold-pink light from a William Blake painting of Creation. It brought a sigh of gratitude.

Thank goodness soup is the national dish, McAllister thought. Otherwise I might starve.

Rob was on his way with a typewriter. He would need it. DCI Westland was due later. But the thought of facing questions, commiserations and plain nosiness was more than he could abide. He was heartsick at the priest's escape. But write it he would. All of it; not just the facts, the plain cold he-did I-did, that would never cover the beaming innocence of the man's smile, the sheer effrontery of the man's self-belief. And then there was that niggle, just like the itch under his bandage that he could not scratch, that flea of an idea that kept him from a comfortable doze or a dwam, the idea so disturbing that he couldn't, wouldn't face it. What if I'm wrong?

The bell rang. The door was unlocked. Rob walked in, lugging the awkward machine. Joanne came close behind with newspapers, copy paper and brown paper bag.

"This is great." Rob grinned at the silent editor. "I can say what I like and you can't reply. Christmas is coming, so, in lieu of a goose, I got you this." He produced a bottle of Glenlivet. "I raided the petty cash and forged your OK on the chit. I put it down as a bribe to a councilor."

McAllister took the bag from Joanne, found gingerbread, some scones, half a dozen floury rolls and half a pound of best Ayrshire bacon.

"Ta." He raised his eyebrows in appreciation.

"And for my next trick" — Rob waved the pages of a hastily written article — "whilst you were careering around the mountains having a wee holiday with all thon bonnie nurses to take care of you . . ."

Joanne was pouring tea and almost spilled it as she watched Rob do an impression of a conjuror.

". . . I've been conferring with my source in the procurator's office, and Karl unpronounceable has been let out." Rob was pleased with the reaction. "Aye," he went on, "Jimmy McPhee rounded up some of his many cousins to vouch for the Pole. They gave a statement directly to the procurator — they'll not talk to Tompson — saying Karl was with them on the night the wee boy went missing. DCI Westland and the procurator agree they have no real evidence against the Pole. Apart from finding his coat near the canal, it was all circumstantial. So now, he's out, and Tompson is livid.

"One more episode to add to my masterpiece: Polish aristocrat finds happiness in the Highlands; friend arrives after many heart-rending adventures to bring happy tidings from count's long-lost mother; Polish friend gets caught up in an as-yet-unsolved crime; those outcasts of Scotland, the Traveling people, they come to his rescue; then . . . in the nick of time, he's let out for the wedding of his fellow countryman to an Italian chip-shop heiress, where he will be best man. They'll lap it up."

Rob looked into McAllister's eyes. Weary, defeated; that was what Rob thought he saw. No, can't be, he told himself, not My Hero Mr. John McAllister.

"Aye, you're right. I don't have an ending."

Joanne kept her counsel. She'd heard it all in the taxi to McAllister's house. There was nothing to add. She offered to make more tea. McAllister refused. She stood to leave. She took her coat. She looked at him. He stared back.

"I haven't heard the details, but I'm sorry about Father Morrison getting away. I know it means a lot to you."

His face, what with the bandages and bruising, showed little, but his eyes . . .

Rob picked up on the atmosphere. "Right, I'm off back to the office. I need at least an hour to get my taxi money from bringing the typewriter. Mrs. Smart, keeper of the petty cash, is immune to my charms."

Joanne followed, shutting the door quietly behind them. The sight of her indomitable boss so reduced was disorienting. But the next time she found herself alone with him, the old trust and easiness would return, of that she was certain. We have seen each other raw, open, without defenses, and I like this McAllister better. But I have to work with him, no place for anything more; I'm a married woman and married women can't have single male friends — more's the pity.

"Rob, I need to walk. I'll see you back at the office."

He looked, waved, and left her to her dilemmas.

Joanne walked a roundabout road to the office, adding about one mile to a half-mile journey, not noticing her exact whereabouts. She thought until her head hurt and her nose turned red, and her toes she could no longer feel. Only her hands were still cozy — sheepskin mittens and anger at her husband kept them warm.

This part of the town was all crescents and avenues and walks, too genteel to be streets. Built in solid stone, the occasional mansion and the semidetached houses and rows of terraces hid large back gardens. An occasional beech or oak or sycamore towered high above the solid Protestant dwellings. Low walls along the front gardens were indented by regular pockmarks, where iron railings once stood before being sacrificed for munitions in the first war. The earth was bare now; the fallen leaves had been swept, gathered, and burned. Joanne knew for certain that in spring, there would be careful displays of snowdrop and crocus and daffodil and jonquil. Some gardens were elaborate constructions of glittering granite studded with dormant Alpine plants and varieties of heather. Like a mortuary display, Joanne thought. *I'm* going to have blackcurrant bushes and raspberry canes and rows of cabbages and marigolds and sunflowers in my garden, and I'll plant night-scented stock outside the bedroom windows. My prefab, my very own home, it may be tiny, but the garden is big, I could really make it really lovely. If I decide to take it, that is.

She continued walking through the well-mannered backcloth, then, rounding a corner onto the main thoroughfare, the gardens ended abruptly. The high stone wall of the prison that sat smack bang in the middle of the town began. The menace enclosed within the walls was palpable, especially on gray winter days. She crossed to the other side of the road. Jamie's murderer would be brought here. She had to hold on to the conviction that he would be found. There was a sense that, forevermore, she would see this place, this time in her life, not as a time when she began to find her wings, but more as a time when she lost her innocence. Children could be killed. Children could be harmed. That had never occurred to her before.

Down the steep hill toward the river, holding the iron railing for balance — the paving slabs glistened ominously in parts — she made for the river that cut the town in two, running water being her place for thinking.

I have to tell him. She turned the dogleg of the descent.

How on earth will I manage that? She cut around the back of the church.

He'll never let me go. She crossed the road to the riverbanks.

How can I put the girls through the shame? She was walking away from the town center toward the Islands.

How will I face Bill's parents — and my sister? She reached the war memorial.

I hope I don't end up in hospital again. She was crossing the suspension bridge that led to the infirmary, stopping in the middle, looking down through the galloping flow, now a steel gray flecked with silver, cold blue snowmelt swelling the river to halfway up the grassy banks. The incoming tide added to the flow and counterflow, setting off crests of white horses that pranced in irregular silver ranks across the wide waters.

He is always sorry afterward — so he says. She reached the opposite bank and turned toward town again.

He came to the hospital to visit me that time he broke my collarbone. It was turning to dusk although only two o'clock in the afternoon.

He said he was really sorry. She was shamed by the remembrance of her cowardly gratitude when he walked into the hospital with a box of chocolates.

I stay for the girls. That was ever the excuse.

On her left, the cathedral was melting into the sky, and downriver, the bridges and churches and distant hills, in various shades of a nothing color, made Joanne feel she was walking in a dreamscape.

Passing through the final stone arch of the bridge back into town, the idea sparked.

"One thousand pounds."

She rushed up Bridge Street, hurrying so as not to lose courage — yet again. Panting, she stumbled into the sudden warmth of the reporters' room, her feet painful, protesting against the sudden change in temperature. Don was alone except for the paraffin stove set on full blast, a pile of copy and a cup of tea that smelled distinctly of a distillery.

"Pleased to see me or have you been running?"

Until Joanne had worked with him, drunk with him and begun to know him, Don Mc-Leod would never have seemed a likely candidate for the role of Sir Galahad. A Celtic Sam Spade? That was more like it.

"Don, can you do something for me?"

"Can? Probably. Will? Maybe."

"I need to warn Bill that someone may come looking for one thousand pounds."

He looked her over. He took his time. She could feel the blush spread from her cheeks down her neck.

"Mrs. Ross, one thing I will *not* do is get involved in family matters —"

"Fine." She turned away. "Forget I asked."

"— unless you can give me a very good reason why I should." He finished.

"Well, it might mean I don't come into work covered in bruises and unable to sit at my typewriter," she snapped.

And knowing how much it cost her to admit this, he said, "Good enough."

"Really? You'll help?" He nodded. "Then maybe you could call, or meet, or somehow let Bill know all about the matter of the one thousand pounds."

"Aye, I could." He nodded again.

"Then I want you to help me figure out how I can hold that over my husband and buy myself out of a marriage." Her look, as

478

she said this, was defiant and scared and she suddenly seemed three inches taller to the much shorter Don.

"I've taught you well, lass." He winked. "Leave it to me."

"Gazette."

"Joanne, my dear. How are you?" They were almost finished with the edition and Joanne was weary, so the sound of Margaret's voice was more than welcome. "I'm looking for that scallywag son of mine to see if he will be home for dinner tonight."

"He's not here but I'll get him to call you."

"Thank you." She paused. "I don't suppose you would be free? It's press night; I know the children are at their grandparents', so why don't you join me? There's a delicious supper prepared. Don't worry, it wasn't me that cooked," Margaret McLean gushed on. "I'd love the company. Angus has some meeting or other, and I'm sure Rob will be out chasing some girl. Could you possibly join me?"

"I'd love to. I've to pop into the Corellis' to check my dress for the wedding, but that will take half an hour at most." She hesitated. "Margaret, could I possibly stay the night?" Bill would never find her there.

"My dear, of course. That will be fun."

Margaret put down the phone, pleased Joanne had not seen through her subterfuge.

My oh my, she said to herself. That wonderful young woman is being slowly smothered; we'll have to sort something out.

"Gazette." Rob took the phone call from WPC Ann McPherson.

"We have to talk," she said.

"Uh-oh, it's always serious when a woman says that." He certainly hoped it wasn't serious. I like her, he thought, I really like her. But I'm too young for serious.

They met in the café near the post office. As usual, she took the lead.

"First, can we pretend I'm not a police officer when I ask these questions?"

She didn't wait for an answer, just plowed on.

"I know you, I know what a nosy parker you are, and I get the feeling you know more than you think you do about the goings-on in the house next door to you — if you get my meaning."

Rob hated the way, at nearly twenty years of age, he always looked guilty when caught out. He couldn't do blasé; he'd practiced in front of the mirror and just looked plain glaikit. He couldn't recall anything in particular that he had done wrong. But then again, this very morning, he *had* been

480

considering how to get into the locked mansion again — just for a wee nosy around.

"I want you to think on this — is there anything, anything out of the ordinary, anything at all, that makes you suspicious about Father Morrison?"

She paused, speaking carefully, not wanting Rob to see her dilemma — not yet. As a woman police constable, she was the lowest of the lowly. A glorified typist to most of her male colleagues, someone to bring along when women and children were involved and even then, many of the men thought her presence unnecessary. But WPC Ann McPherson wanted to be a real policewoman.

"Another thing. I want you to trust DCI Westland." She held up a hand. "I know, I know, you don't like the police, but if you do think of anything, tell *me.* I promise it will go straight to him and not to your favorite inspector."

Rob wondered what she was trying to say. The memory of those shots of the defenseless boys, beaming at the camera for the most part but embarrassed to be photographed in the more compromising poses, made him take her suggestion seriously.

"Fine. I'll think about it. If I come up with an idea, I'll tell you. Promise."

"At first I was really excited about working on a murder case. We never get anything like that around here. But now, every time I think of that wee soul, I feel ashamed. I want this solved, but we seem to be getting nowhere and, well, I feel we're letting him down." She was closely examining the swirls of pattern on the Formica tabletop as she spoke. "Rob, we have to find whoever did this."

The silence was about five seconds. And for once, Rob had nothing to add. Ann rescued them.

"Anyway, as per usual, I'm breaking the rules — passing on police information, and especially to you." She had him now. "All I'll say is" — she grinned — "ask Gino about the convoy."

"Convoy?"

"It's driving Inspector Tompson nuts. And it's a great story."

"That's Inspector Tompson. . . ." They sang out together: "Inspector Tompson, without an H, with a P."

"Tell me more."

Ann shook her head and repeated, "Ask Gino."

Joanne had felt a presence — No, she thought, an absence — as she walked down the path to the McLeans' front door. Wee Jamie disappeared from here. She was glad when the door opened and she could step out of the dark and the shadows.

She and Margaret sat by the fire and chatted. No more, no less; no deep and serious discussions, no philosophizing, nor revelations, unless they were amusing. Joanne loved the novelty of a good listener who was genuinely interested in her work at the *Gazette* and her dreams of a career. Margaret in turn enthralled Joanne with stories: Paris in the thirties, Edinburgh society, Highland balls, staying with stuffy relatives in freezing baronial castles for New Year parties.

"I wore woolen underwear — long johns and vest — under a Fortuny gown on one particularly cold Hogmanay in a castle where it was colder inside than out."

The gin and the stories were working well.

"Speaking of gowns, what are you wearing to Chiara and Peter's wedding dance?"

Joanne confessed she was planning on wearing her matron of honor dress or even her Highland dancing dress and sash.

"You may remember, last time I got dressed up, it didn't go down too well with some." The recollection still hurt, but a smidgen of revenge had been exacted. The face of Mr. Findlay Grieg as he peered down her cleavage was the least of the unpleasant memories. And who's had the last laugh, Mr. Grieg?

Margaret squinted down the long slim ivory holder she habitually used, and peering through the cigarette smoke, she sized Joanne up.

"I think it would be about right. Come on, let's see."

The small room, off a large bedroom, was filled down one side with dresses and ball gowns, hidden in protective bags. Opposite, a table was laden with makeup and unguents of the most expensive variety. Lights set around the mirror made Joanne think of a dressing room of some famous star of stage or opera.

"This one, I think." Margaret held up a floating, shimmering dress of pale blue silk, studded with star clusters of beading, looking critically at Joanne, then back to the dress. "No, not that one. Let me see. Aha! This one." She held it up. "This one definitely."

Joanne looked doubtfully at a most peculiar garment. It hung straight. No form, no shape. Delicate uneven pleats ran from shoulder to hemline, with a deep V neckline front and back.

"And this." She threw a cape at Joanne.

The soft, deep, glowing fur made her want to bury her face and hands in the pile.

"I'll be back in a minute. Try the dress on. And put on a pair of the highest heels you can find. Luckily, we're the same size."

Joanne wriggled into the gown. It fitted. More than fitted: it hugged every contour of her body. Her breasts were clearly outlined, the cleavage accentuated. The deep ruby silk set off the red in Joanne's hair. The silver fox-fur capelet, much lighter than it looked, draped gracefully over her shoulders. She breathed in its warmth. She pirouetted. The gown rippled with a soft swooshing sigh. Catching herself in the mirror, she was amazed at the transformation. For the first time, she glimpsed her own beauty.

"Margaret."

Joanne tiptoed through to the sitting room, three inches taller in a pair of snakeskin sandals.

"Oh, my dear." Margaret clapped her hands. "Perfect."

From the sitting room doorway, four other hands clapped in appreciation.

"Rob. Mr. McLean. I didn't hear you come in."

Rob grinned. "You look a complete smasher. Doesn't she, Dad?"

"Absolutely! Couldn't agree more."

Joanne laughed and did a mock catwalk prance toward him. He opened the record player, put on a Viennese waltz, bowed and, still in his leather motorbike jacket, asked, "May I have the next waltz, Princess Cinderella, or are you a Highland Mata Hari?"

"Idiot." Joanne mock-punched him, then curtseyed — "Thank you, kind sir" — and they waltzed around the carpet, Margaret and Angus McLean joining in, laughing, smiling, good friends together.

Later, Joanne snuggled under the eiderdown with the hot water bottle Margaret had insisted on filling for her. Tired, emotional, happy, she was halfway down the spiral to sleep when a stray thought, insistent as a wasp after the jam, dragged her back to consciousness.

"What was it Annie had said about the hoodie crow? Where did she say she had seen it?" But it refused to come to her. Thoughts of new beginnings, a single life with two children, working full-time on the *Gazette,* her mother-in-law's reaction and her sister and brother-in-law's, the condemnation from town and kirk, the challenge of living up to her own expectations, how she would tell Bill and the girls, and what would McAllister think. . . . She heaved the quilt right up to her nose. The frost could be sensed, smelled almost, hard, bright and clean. She smiled. Her breathing slowed again. Her last thought in the strange bed was, Well, I won't be able to say my life is dull anymore.

That same night, across the river, in his own bed again, McAllister was sleeping the sleep of the completely exhausted. Angus McLean had visited and stayed briefly, conversation being limited. The solicitor had brought books, magazines and week-old English newspapers. The London papers were full of politics. The Suez Canal continued to dominate the news. The books included one gem, the new Evelyn Waugh. The magazines brought a vivid variety of writing, especially the *Spectator.*

His incapacity in the speech department had reminded him of his true skill — writing. He started after Mr. McLean had left and remembered how much he enjoyed it. I should write more, he thought. A short story, maybe a color piece for a magazine; this is the twilight of the Celtic race, surely I should be recording the demise of an ancient culture. Keith McPhee has his Scottish history and stories of the Traveling people, I could record the ordinary, the people who still live as they have for generations, never going anywhere, except to war, lives and language and the land unchanged until now; they are the keepers of the lore. Nineteen fifty-six, the winds of change have reached us, he thought, we'll not be able to shelter from them.

He reached for the em rule, laid the large sheets of paper out on the dining table and started to lay out his ideas for a new dummy for the *Gazette*. Local news first of course, two columns of national headline stories, features and in-depth articles, op-ed and letters and the Godspot, a section for women readers, a nature column maybe, the classifieds, then sport on the back three pages.

He penciled in ideas, made lists in the margins, New Year, a new paper — maybe. A *Highland Gazette* fit for the second half of the twentieth century. He hummed a discordant version of "Coming Through the Rye," another favorite Rabbie Burns song. Finishing up, he looked over his work and pronounced, "This is going to be exciting."

Under the layers of eiderdown, drifting off, wisps of thoughts, like mist on a peat bog, floated images of Joanne through his whisky sleep; Joanne frowning over the typewriter, Joanne pedaling her bike against the gale, Joanne laughing and mock-fighting with Rob, and a bruised and subdued Joanne limping up the stairs to work. But the image of her sitting quietly, lost in a daydream, with a half smile, and her humming a tune, that was what accompanied him into his own dreaming.

Rob always fell asleep instantly. A thought flitted around as he got ready for bed. What was Ann trying to tell him? He turned out the bedside lamp, pulled the blankets up to his nose. The faint smell of smoke that he had noticed as he put away his motorbike was still there. Was it coming from next door? Can't be. He turned over. There it was, definitely. An odd smell — burning wool? Singeing blankets? He'd investigate. In the morning. And he was asleep.

Twenty-One

Rob ran into Gino, literally, outside the station bookstall.

"Sorry, Mr. Corelli. I didn't see you." It was on the tip of his tongue to say because you're so short. But he didn't. "I was looking for you, I wanted to ask you about the convoy."

"Convoy? What is a convoy?"

Rob explained.

"I don't know nothing about no convoy." Gino was puzzled. "Maybe you mean about our friends from all over Scotland, and some from England, driving up for the wedding. *Si?* And some, the older ones, they come by the train, that's why I'm here. You come to my house later, *si?*"

"*Si.* I mean, aye, I will."

Rob saw a story in this, and the offer of coffee he would never refuse. In a tea-drinking nation, coffee was a novelty, real coffee a rarity. Rob had had to learn to like the stuff. It was part of his self-education to become a sophisticated man of the world like McAllister.

When he arrived at the Corelli household the final, final finishing touches to the wedding dress were being made. This time, it was the veil that needed adjusting.

"To match the necklace," Chiara said.

"What necklace?" Rob asked. But no explanation was given.

Gino was glad to see Rob. "Come into the kitchen, I'm making the coffee." The fuss over — to him minor — details was exhausting. He thought the dress looked perfect five fittings ago. He was also exhausted by the logistics of accommodating such a large group of wedding guests. Weeks had been spent sorting out hotels and boarding-houses. He had to make sure the landladies understood that locking up for the night, indeed locking the guests out, at nine in the evening would not be acceptable.

"This is a good Christian household, Mr. Corelli. The doors are locked at nine o'clock sharp. No exceptions. No, no keys are available," more than one landlady had declared. That eliminated those particular guest-houses. A NO ALCOHOL sign in the foyer eliminated others. Gino was shocked to find that some landladies were reluctant to take children. Accommodation was found in the string of boardinghouses along the riverbank for most of the guests; the rest would cram into Gino and Lita's house. Gino poured another coffee.

"Rob, my boy, maybe you can help me, you and your motorbike. Maybe you make a convoy, *sì?*"

Rob agreed, even before he knew what he was agreeing to.

"Many guests, they drive here. I tell them to meet you in Nairn, *sì?*"

"Nairn?"

"Aye. They rendezvous for lunch. At the Napoli, my friend's chip shop."

"Best fish and chips in the north. Excepting yours, of course," Rob added quickly.

"That's a right. Mine's is the best. You go, no?"

"*Sì.*"

As he was about to turn onto the bridge to go back to the *Gazette,* he remembered he had forgotten to investigate the smell of smoke from the house next door. "Later." He revved the engine to get up the hill, sending a flock of seagulls screeching skyward.

Next day, Rob wheeled his bike out of the shed to a bright blue sky with not a cloud and only the scent of frost to cause concern.

Snow still lay on the hills and the mountains but the town was dry.

"It's a brilliant day for a bike ride." Margaret tucked in his scarf and kissed his cheek. "I do like a man in a leather jacket."

"Marlon Brando's got nothing on me," Rob yelled back, then opened up the throttle.

Once clear of the town, the road ran parallel to the railway line for most of the way to Nairn. A flat straight seven-mile stretch was interrupted only by a level crossing. The temptation to speed was too great for a young man with a big red motorbike; the Triumph fairly flew. Glorious winter sunshine so bright that it hurt the retinas and dry, still cold made for a very short journey. It was a small, prosperous merchant farming town. A substantial area of Victorian and Edwardian houses, complete with a park and bandstand, enhanced the air of prosperity. On the southern end, a fishing village settled on the river mouth. The Nairn, a clean gentle river, ran down from mountains and moors, waylaid by a distillery and fishermen, and could be added straight into a glass of whisky. Across a wooden bridge was a particularly windswept golf course that followed the clean white sands of a beach that stretched mile upon mile along the shores of the firth and what seemed like mile upon mile out into the firth at low tide. When the sea retreated, the water was barely visible from the high sand dunes. And as long as you didn't mind the biting North Sea winds, and the Presbyterian Sabbath, this was a fine wee town.

The fish-and-chip shop and ice cream parlor stood opposite the high harbor wall in a converted tackle shed. It opened only on weekends at this time of year. In summer it did a roaring trade with day-trippers and holidaymakers staying in one of the many boardinghouses or at the town campsite. Now the only crowds were flocks of marauding seagulls.

Turning off the main road Rob wound his way through narrow streets lined with whitewashed fisher cottages that opened directly onto the pavements. As he came into the cobbled square, he stared at the corral of multicolored vehicles. He hadn't expected so many. Across the river, he spotted yet more vans all lined in a row. Fish-and-chip vans — seven, no, he counted again; eight. With the serving sides closed, and no smoke pouring from the chimneys and without their omnipresent smell, they could have had the forlorn look of a deserted funfair, but the fluttering bunting more than compensated. The brightly painted ice-cream vans, at least a dozen of them in every variety of color, diminished the northern winter. From a charabanc hung red, green and white flags at every window. Along the sides ran the emblem of the Scottish-Italian Friendship Club, Glasgow chapter. Cars, from smart saloons to Ford Prefects and Morris Traveler estates and old jalopies, were flying more Italian flags and at least one Saltire.

"Would you look at thon!" marveled a local, pushing his flat cap back in astonishment. "I haven't seen that many Eyeties since Sicily."

Inside the café, outside the café, seated on the seawall, were Italians; old women in black; young women flouncing by in pairs, their floating dirndl skirts filled out by layers of paper-nylon petticoats, waists cinched in by broad patent leather belts. Like prancing show ponies they tossed their pageboy haircuts in the wind. Others held on to beehives of teased and lacquered hairdos, shrieking at every gust that threatened to collapse the startlingly high edifices. Old men in gaiters all seemed to have bandy legs; young men in tight trousers all seemed descended from storks. Children darted in and out, under and through, winter swallows gathering sweeties and lollipops and pieces of salami. The adults kept talking, with only an occasional swat with the back of the hand being necessary to calm an overexcited child.

Rob walked into the café and introduced himself. He was welcomed by a small round woman in a white apron over a black dress, with olives for eyes and hair in a bun pulled so tight she could have been mistaken for a person of Asiatic lineage.

"Gino told me about you. A fine young man, he says. You must be hungry after the drive. Sit down over here."

"I'll not say no." Rob was always hungry.

"We've no fish and chips. You'll have to eat the same as us."

"Anything's fine, thanks."

She reappeared with an enormous white ashette, heaped high with hams, salamis, sausage, cheeses, pickled vegetables, fish, olives and dried tomatoes. A plate of bread and coffee was placed in front of him with waved instructions to "eat, eat."

"Bianca?" the woman shouted to the back of the café. The waitress — or was it her daughter — came over with the cutlery. A sweet smile and a shy hello were all it took. Rob was smitten.

"Thanks — Bianca, is it?"

She smiled.

"Are you coming to the wedding?"

"Of course. She's a bridesmaid," her proud mother told him.

A shrill whistle stopped further conversation. Laughing, shouting, in Italian of course, the milling groups gradually formed a semblance of order. Rob bolted the last of the food and went to get the bike.

"See you at the wedding, Bianca."

"Aye. See you there." She waved.

Rob, returning her wave, walked backward right into another very short, very round man in a strange black hat with the Italian colors stuck in the band.

"Excuse me, I'm so sorry," he apologized.

"Yes, she is a pretty girl, no?"

"No. I mean yes."

They laughed. They introduced themselves. He was the convoy's commandant. He showed Rob the whistle to prove it. He also had the newest and brightest of the ice-cream vans and, as Rob was soon to find out, the loudest of the chimes. They discussed tactics. Rob would be motorbike scout, escort, navigator and communications officer.

It took twenty minutes for the vehicles to gather their cargo of wedding guests and another twenty minutes of backing up and three-point turns that were often seven- or nine-point turns in the narrow streets, then getting into formation. The commander, a Neapolitan, shouted one final instruction, which was relayed down the line, then they set out of the fishing village, on through the town, out onto the main north road.

The flags and bunting snapped in the wind. The cacophony of jingles from the passing panoply was returned with cheery waves from the astonished denizens of Nairn. Shopkeepers stood in doorways, arms folded over their aprons, amazed. Children and a stray dog ran behind cheering. The police, having been alerted by their colleagues from previous town and county forces along the convoy route, saluted as the vehicles sedately passed out of the town limits.

Slow and steady, they continued on the road they had been on since Arbroath. The logistics of the trip were complicated. Many of the towns they had passed through were a chance for a reunion with friends and family. There were new babies to admire, new chip shops to inspect, many stories to share. Diversions and digressions due to weather, and sometimes wine, meant the journey lasted over a week for the Ayrshire and Clydeside contingent. No one minded.

Edinburgh, Alloa, Dundee, Arbroath, Aberdeen, Forres, Elgin, or was it the other way round, Elgin and Forres, then Nairn; many had lost count of the stops on the road to the wedding.

Rob flitted back and forth carrying messages, checking on the progress of some of the older vehicles, reporting back to the commander that all was well. He tried his best to outdo the children pulling faces at him every time he passed. And somehow he always managed to end up next to the car carrying Bianca. He hoped she was impressed. She was.

Before the last level crossing on the edge of the town, Rob signaled the convoy to a standstill.

"Now; at the town, we go straight through Eastgate, down the High Street, across the river, left at Gino's café and park along the riverbanks. Remember, straight all the way till we're across the river."

"Lead on," commanded the commander.

Entering the town proper, the lead vehicle turned on its chimes, the others following suit. "O Sole Mio" rang out from at least six ice-cream vans. Others played different Italian tunes or opera arias, and one played "Jingle Bells." The chip vans had their own tunes or two-tone klaxons. One played "I've

Got a Lovely Bunch of Coconuts" over and over. The cars and coach joined in, honking the length of the High Street and across the bridge. Rob, proudly leading the procession, slowed at the sight of Inspector Tompson standing on the Town House steps.

He gave the policeman a big wave. It was not returned.

DCI Westland had to share an office with Inspector Tompson. Not an ideal arrangement, he had quickly discovered, but the room the detectives worked from was even worse. Tiny nineteenth-century spaces set off a narrow spiral stone staircase; it was handy for the courts in the castle and the procurator fiscal's office, but not much else. As well as having to cope with the physical limits of the space, he was forced to put up with the limits of Tompson's policing methods. The inspector decided who was guilty, then set out to prove it. His prejudices were manifold. He was incapable of listening. He bore grudges. Detective Chief Inspector Westland was reminded again of the loss of the brightest and best in the war only a decade past. He made a decision. He would talk again with McAllister. The typed report was succinct and clear, but what was between the lines was what Westland needed to hear. It went against the grain to share police business with a layman, but the editor had impressed the policeman. His obsession with the priest was not helpful but understandable. Maybe . . . he thought, maybe I should make my own inquiries about Morrison. Tompson found nothing. But had he looked hard enough? The church had not been forthcoming, Tompson had said, but maybe . . .

What I need is a private phone, Westland decided.

The photographs of the boys, the innocent pictures that Morrison was so keen on hiding, sat on his desk emanating disquiet. The sound of his own boys — chattering, laughing, arguing — was the background noise whenever he looked at the wee faces peering up at the camera. Faces, each and every one different but somehow the same. In shades of sepia or gray, there they were, anonymous boys that only they or their families would recognize. He handled the photos with care, giving each one the respect he would show to his own family snapshots, before putting them into the envelope, then into the evidence locker. Tompson had objected even to that. But at least, thought Westland, I had the sense not to ask him to include the envelope in the file on the boy's murder. That would have Tompson running straight to the chief constable.

Evidence of what, the inspector had demanded when asked to make a file on Morrison's portraits. They are pictures of boys in their boxing rig-outs. What's wrong with that? The images of boys in the bath were equally dismissed. After all, he had said, everyone baths together after any game of sport. Miners bath together after a shift, men bath together after a game of football, what was he, Westland, on about, Inspector Tompson had asked in fury.

"I'll have you know" — and at this he had poked a finger toward his superior officer's chest — "Father Morrison is a man beyond reproach. He's a priest for goodness' sake! We, his parishioners, know him as an admirable dedicated person who gives so much to the unfortunates he helps. Anyone who says different is a Protestant or an Orangeman or a Jew, someone with a grudge against the Catholic Church."

The trouble is, Westland thought, Tompson is right. And even worse, Westland thought for the umpteenth time, we are no nearer finding out who interfered with and killed the boy. The Polish man couldn't have done it — he believed the tinkers' story.

That was another matter. Tompson was livid; he was still convinced of the Polish man's guilt. Who could believe a stranger, who would ever take a tinker's word on anything, he had ranted. What about his coat being found on the canal towpath? Westland admitted he had no explanation for that. I have a good mind to take this higher, Tompson had threatened.

The procurator fiscal was just as unhelpful; no evidence against the man, he has a strong alibi, he had said — and that had set Tompson off again. A heart attack waiting to happen, had been McAllister's observation on the inspector.

McAllister's obsession, the past, was a place Westland decided he would revisit, going over ground the inspector had already covered. He vaguely recalled that a colleague in Aberdeen had been in Glasgow about that time. May as well inquire, he thought, I have to try something. Perhaps the answer, or at least a pointer, *is* in the past.

The only bright part of the day, the chief inspector recalled, was the sight of the inspector's face when asked about the Italians arriving in town for the wedding. That thought sustained DCI Westland as he made his way down Bridge Street back to his icy billet at the boardinghouse to collect a stack of pennies in order to make a long-distance phone call from a freezing public phone box on one of the coldest days of the year.

"Can I do a piece on the convoy for next week?" Rob inquired next morning.

"Ask Don." McAllister didn't look up as Rob poked his nose around the door.

This Friday was even quieter than usual. McAllister sat in his office, infecting others with the palpable feeling of defeat that shrouded him. Everyone tiptoed around him, putting his somber presence down to his injuries. But they all knew it was not that. The ghosts of guilt that had hovered over the editor for many a year were taunting him. The monster is free, McAllister kept telling himself, free to continue preying on other wee souls, protected by the cloth and a church that would always give him shelter and a society that refused to countenance any wrongdoings from a member of the clergy or even acknowledge that such things happened, it was dismissed, wasn't talked about, boys disbelieved if they ever found the courage to mention the unmentionable.

"It's only pictures."

McAllister acknowledged that; it *was* only

pictures. Any connection with his brother and Jamie was a connection of waters, a river, a canal, nothing more.

The frustration that Angus McLean felt with the lack of progress was less than that felt by McAllister; to him, his involvement came about because of his client, Karl Cieszynski, and his friendship with Peter Kowalski. Nevertheless, curiosity and a need for justice aroused him to action. He dialed the long-distance operator for a connection.

"We are both well, thank you. . . . Yes, I know. We are so cut off here that a trip to Edinburgh could well be a trip to the Continent." Angus laughed at his former colleague's teasing. "Yes, I do seem to recall a train that runs south." He listened. "You received my message about the man's full identity? Right. That was good of you. And what did you discover?" He started taking notes. "Hmmm, I suppose we Presbyterians are equally secretive. No point in dirty laundry in public and suchlike." He scribbled some more. "Fine. Thank you. I will pass that on. No, no. It may not mean much, but then again, it is something the police should know."

After many thank-yous and yes-we-will-try-to-make-it-south-when-the-weather-is-better, he hung up the phone and stared out of the casement windows, not seeing the distant Wyvis, a mountain in name, but really only a horizon to the townspeople.

He had to at least consider the unthinkable.

Duncan Macdonald had placed the phone calls some time before, soon after the searing shrieks from his niece at the Halloween party. There had been no response, so he was surprised when the letter arrived.

After the usual preliminaries, the writer came to the point.

I do not personally know the person you mentioned, but I did find a colleague who knew him when they were young. They were both involved in sport. What he does recall is that the priest you enquired about played for a very able, if somewhat fiercesome, team representing his seminary. He was also able to tell me that the priest was a former resident of an Institution for Foundlings and Orphans that has a somewhat questionable reputation for the harshness of their regime. Other than that, I could find no information.

I am sure this is irrelevant but I thought you might like to know, as it gives an idea of how much adversity this man has had to overcome and how far he has risen since his unfortunate beginnings. By all accounts he is a well-liked and well-respected person with a reputation for being a conscientious and caring priest.

The Reverend Macdonald put down the letter and sighed. Poor fellow, he thought, some of those homes for the wayward, as they were often referred to, they made a prisoner of war camp look easy.

Jimmy McPhee had yet to make up his mind. He thought of calling McAllister, many times, but the phone was not a usual form of communication for him. He thought of visiting, but visiting a person in a house was not his way either. A pub was too public; the *Gazette* office was not an option he even considered. No, he would let it go, and if he happened to bump into him, then maybe they would tell him. Then again, probably not. But he would have liked to look at that photo again. He would have liked to look at the faces, count the survivors.

Joanne too was distracted. She couldn't keep avoiding Bill. Tonight, now that all the bridesmaids were gathered, there was a final rehearsal for the wedding. But after that, she would have to return home. As for going to the wedding reception without him, that was unthinkable. Everyone would notice, comment. The excuse of his being out west would not work; this was the wedding of the year. The thoughts churned up her stomach and she began to fear a quick dash out of the church in the middle of the bridal procession. But most of all, a crushing envy of Chiara shamed her. A grand white wedding, *that* she had never coveted, but a marriage to a good man who would love and cherish her, *that* she was deeply jealous of. You are not the heroine of a story in *People's Friend* magazine, she reminded herself; no happy ending for you.

She continued pottering around the office, tidying up, filing, doing the jobs that the men never noticed needing doing before another edition, another deadline came around.

Don, as usual on a Friday, was up and down the stairs, in and out of the office, clutching betting sheets instead of copy paper. He had nothing to say and less to worry over except for the usual quandaries, all to do with horses.

Rob knew better than to ask why Joanne had stayed at their house last night. But he was confident that whatever needed to be fixed, his mother would see to it. He finished his notes on the convoy, dumped them on McAllister's desk without a word, and left. With no luck after driving past two cafés and one chip shop hoping to find Bianca, Rob caught a whiff of acrid smoke from the foundry chimney and remembered. He headed home.

His mother was out, his father at work, the street deserted. He went to the end of their garden, pushed his way through the gap in the shrubbery and went round the back of the Big House to test his theory. Yes, the coal hole was unlocked. He kicked open the low door. He checked around to see if anyone had heard but not even the birds noticed. He found a piece of sack to sit on and slid down the filthy chute, emerging in the cellar. Three steps up and he was in the kitchen scullery. Here the smell was of damp, paraffin and burnt wool. He listened — only a passing car and the sounds of an empty house. He opened the door to the kitchen — nothing, no one. He sniffed. The smell of burning wool was mixed with the scent of paraffin. He opened the door of the Raeburn and, using the poker, he lifted out pieces of blackened cloth. It was wool all right, thick and heavy, not a blanket, a coat maybe. Rob started to put the bits back into the stove but some instinct, which he would later wonder about, made him wrap some of the remnants into an old copy of the *Gazette* lying in a box along with the kindling. A blackened button fell out and that he put in his pocket.

Might as well look around while I'm here, he told himself, and made for the stairs.

The sound of someone unlocking the front door made Rob freeze. The shadow of the person showed clearly through the stained-glass panels. Rob ran to the kitchen door. The key had been left in the lock. He shut the door behind him as quietly as he could and, bending double, the makeshift parcel clutched to his chest, he scuttled along the border of shrubs back to his own kitchen, where he stood waiting for his heart to stop racing, before laughing at his panic.

"Big bairn."

He made tea, then sat at the kitchen table staring out, seeing nothing. It took a good few minutes for his heartbeat to return to normal. Then he began to wonder why there had been no sound of a car in the next-door driveway. He checked. No car was parked in the street. So, who had a key? He had assumed it was the police checking again. But they would have driven in and the noise on the gravel would have been unmistakable. Maybe he should give Ann McPherson a call. The shrill of the phone made him jump. He mocked himself again — guilty conscience!

"McLean residence." He went pink with pleasure. "Gino gave you my number? No, no problem. One o'clock at the café. Great. See you, Bianca."

He looked at the clock — half past twelve; time he was gone. Then he noticed the coal dust footprints on the carpet. In the hall mirror he saw the halo of coal dust in his hair. He saw the black fingerprints on the phone, on the table, on the door and, he knew without looking, it would be a disaster zone in the kitchen. As he told Joanne a few days later, when he heard his mother unlock the front door, he didn't know which sound of which key in which door had scared him the most.

TWENTY-TWO

The first miracle of the wedding day was that it was fine; sunshine, blue skies and a crisp clean cold with so much oxygen in the air, a deep breath brought on a rush of exhilarating energy. Annie and Joanne were to dress and have their hair styled at the Corelli household, so after dropping Wee Jean off at her grandparents', the two of them walked the short distance to prepare for the ceremony. Or rather Joanne walked, Annie ran ahead jumping on the spot at every corner, impatient for her mother to catch up. Granny Ross had refused the invitation to the wedding; she wouldn't set foot in "yon heathen church," so Grandad was bringing Jean to the service.

Joanne rang the bell, and the door opened to a hallway seething with half-dressed girls and boys running in and out of rooms, up and down the stairs, ignoring the yells in Italian from adults, themselves half-dressed, some women with their curlers still in, some of the men, their cummerbunds flapping, all jostling for a place at the hall mirror.

Annie spied one solemn pageboy standing in the bay window. Embarrassed by his velvet breeks and white stockings, praying no one from his school would ever see pictures of him in such sissy clothes, he was trying to distance himself from the mayhem. Annie decided he would be her ally for the day. No giggling girls for her. She stood beside him. In that mysterious way of children, with nothing said, he took one half look and an instant bond was formed.

"Stop running. Line up." Even the adults jumped to it; in any language, Aunty Lita was not to be ignored. She sent them to their various assigned tasks and eventually, all were dressed, all stood in a line down the steps and out into the street. She solemnly walked along the line, basket in hand, handing out corsages for the ladies, buttonholes for the men. That done, she called up the stairs for the bride and her attendants. Chiara floated down, her face pale, her knees shaking. Gino, waiting on the doorstep, offered his arm and with the bridesmaids and matron of honor holding up the heavy train, the procession walked along the riverbank and into the chapel.

Curious onlookers and excited children stood outside for a glimpse of one of the biggest weddings the town had seen. The children knew Uncle Gino from his ice-cream van, knew he would be generous with the pennies, maybe even a sixpence or two, after the service.

At the church entrance an usher handed the other guests a buttonhole of a single rose or a corsage of cream roses and lily of the valley. Grandad pinned one on Jean's coat. The little girl was thrilled. They sat toward the back on an aisle seat. The church was packed.

Peter had arrived a good twenty minutes earlier with his best man, Karl. This had caused a raised eyebrow or two, but Peter and Chiara were certain. He was the best best man Peter could wish for. Both stood proud and solemn, both with a military bearing, picture perfect; no one would have been surprised if they had worn swords at their sides. The organ music filled the church; the murmur of conversation, like waves on a pebble beach, rose and fell in greeting at each new addition to the congregation. The murmurs rose to a crescendo as Chiara, in her wedding plumage, came gliding down the aisle on her father's arm. Gino had looked so comic in a morning suit and top hat that Chiara diplomatically asked that he wear his Italian wedding outfit, "just like at home." Gino had tried to look solemn, but solemn did not come naturally to him. He beamed to left and to right. His white stockings and black pumps danced him down the aisle.

Three bridesmaids to each side supported Chiara's train. The long trailing ends of white velvet cloak were trimmed with white fur and much admired by the ladies of the parish. Two pageboys followed. Joanne knew one of the pageboys and two of the bridesmaids. They were wee horrors. But not today, today they were angelic. Annie was paired with an Italian girl of similar age and height. They had overcome their communication problems — the girl's Glasgow accent was unintelligible to Annie — by nudging each other or hissing "stop" or "go," loving every moment of the long slow walk down the aisle. Annie smiled at her grandad and sister as they passed. Bianca and another cousin followed last and this time it was Rob's turn for a big smile.

The procession reached the altar without mishap. Chiara still looked solemn; this was her wedding day, and, as she confessed to Joanne later, she was freezing cold and terrified she would trip and scared the pageboys would have bubble gum or peashooters or somehow manage to mangle up the wedding train. It wasn't that I was feeling serious, it was a good old-fashioned dose of stage fright, she joked when it was all over. When the bride reached the altar, there was Peter, waiting and smiling and holding out his hand. Then everything around her dissolved and she was aware of nothing except her husband.

The ceremony went perfectly. The couple was married. Joanne cried. So did many of the guests, men as well as women.

The slow walk back up the aisle became a joyful laughing noisy boisterous affair, with the congregation stepping out of the pews to hug and smile and clap before joining the procession behind the family. Outside on the steps the bridal couple stood for the photographs, with onlookers cheering and laughing.

Gino had one more surprise. Right on cue, the church bells ringing out, a coach and four horses all decorated with green, red and white ribbons pulled up by the riverside, ready to collect the bride and her new husband. Where he found them was a topic of discussion for many a month, and Jenny McPhee knew how to keep a secret.

Gino threw handfuls of coins to the children, who scrabbled for them on the pavement and in the gutters. They expected pennies and halfpennies and threepences and a few shiny sixpences but all the coins were silver. Chiara finally made it to the open door of the coach waving at the crowd of friends, looking for one person in particular. Finding her, she threw hard and accurately and Ann McPherson had no choice but to catch the bridal bouquet. She was standing at Karl's side as she caught it. That raised a huge cheer.

As the coach and four clopped briskly up the street, guests scattered. Joanne was joining the family party for lunch; the other guests went to rest before the evening's dinner and dance, some left to see to children or catch up with old friends. Wee Jean dawdled with her mother, waiting for Grandad as he chatted with old cronies.

"Aunty Chiara looked like a princess."

Joanne agreed. For this Italian princess, having made a journey through heaven knows what in the aftermath of war and a devastated Europe, to end up in the faraway Scottish Highlands, there to find the man of her dreams, who had also come through heaven knows what — well, it goes to show there's hope for us all, Joanne decided.

She also realized that the sheer theatricality of it all, the amazing extravagance of the wedding, was not something ever seen among the Scots; their plain churches, their restraint, their respectability were diametrically opposite to everything her friends the Corellis had shown her. Joanne felt that this wedding was not just the marriage of Chiara and Peter; it was a celebration of hope, a celebration of the future and a celebration for all who had survived the dark days of war and internment, and for those who had endured the prejudice and the ostracism of a people who were first enemies, then allies. Now, like everyone else, they were praying for a brighter, better second half to the century.

"Are you coming back tonight, Mum?"

"You and Annie will sleep at Granny and Grandad's house and I'll see you in the morning. There's still snow on the hills, maybe we'll go sledging."

In a rush of happiness, she picked up her little girl under the oxters, swinging her around and around. Like a joyous shaft of sun breaking through the winter bleak, she had a sudden, joyous inspiration that everything would turn out fine. She put her little girl down and crouched beside her and whispered in her ear.

"I've a surprise for you, a very special

present for being such a good girl."

"Really? What is it? Can I have it now?"

"Later. When I come over to say night-night."

When Joanne arrived to say goodnight to Wee Jean, Granny Ross opened the door. "How was the wedding?"

"Grand. It was just perfect."

"You missed Bill, he was looking for you."

"He was invited too."

"Aye, well, he said he'd see you at the reception. He's no big on the church." She gave a smothered snort and muttered, "Heathens," under her breath but Joanne knew that no matter how much she hated Catholics, she held a sneaking respect for the Corelli family.

Joanne held out the basket. Granny and Grandad Ross were in on the surprise. They watched the child as she peered into the folds of blanket.

"It's white fluffy wool, Granny." Then it moved. She gave a little yelp. The fluff ball yawned. "A kitten," Wee Jean whispered. She looked again to make sure. "A wee kitten."

"She's your wee kitten," Joanne told her.

Not daring to speak, Jean slowly reached her hand into the basket to touch the tiny creature. The kitten stirred, yawned again and then went straight back to sleep.

"Can I keep it?"

"Of course, she's yours." Joanne smiled, kissing her daughter's head.

"I have to go now. I'm off to Uncle Rob's house to get ready for the dance. Be good for Granny and Grandad." She bent down to hug her little girl. "You'll have to think of a name for your kitten."

"But Dad said we can't have a cat. He hates cats."

"Don't worry about that. This is your wee kitten, to keep forever."

She gave her daughter a final hug before buttoning her coat to leave the warmth of the house.

"Thanks, Mum. I'll see you later, Dad."

"I'll collect Annie at nine o'clock, right?"

"Right you are. And thanks again for coming to fetch her. See you all in the morning."

Joanne smiled at the older woman, at the picture she made, sitting by the fire with her knitting, her granddaughter and the sleeping kitten. Her mother-in-law rose from the armchair and gave Joanne a pat on the arm.

"Good night, dear. Have a lovely time. You deserve it."

Joanne walked quickly toward the McLean house. There was no moon but every star in the sky and a luminous Milky Way lit the way. She took the gesture from Granny Ross in the spirit in which it was meant and fairly danced along the pavement.

"Wonders will never cease."

Then she slowed to a walk as the realization hit her. Nine and a half years, that's what it has taken for my mother-in-law to accept me. And I am now contemplating a rift that will never be healed. Head down, hands in her pockets, she strode up the street toward the lights of her friends' home.

"May I have this waltz, Mrs. Ross?" McAllister mumbled. His stomach was also mumbling. There had been little to eat at the wedding feast for a man with a cracked jaw, and all the liquid on offer was alcoholic.

"Your husband appears to be celebrating." He nodded toward the bar.

"He's sorted out his business problems."

McAllister was wise enough to make no comment.

"So why so sad?" he whispered into Joanne's hair as they sedately circumnavigated the ballroom. Joanne held herself tightly, careful not to dance too close. The happiness surrounding her had set her off, reminding her of her own failure. Joanne ached from the loss of her dreams, her ambitions, and the end of her marriage. The music stopped.

"Sorry, I have to find Annie, she's going home with her grandad."

"I do believe you're avoiding me, Mrs. Ross." He hoped his smile was in his voice.

"There's really not much I can say to that" — she touched a small unbandaged area of his cheek — "but I owe you a big thanks. The job on the *Gazette* is my life-line."

He watched her weave her way through the crowd, now swirling at a sedate flow, more Blue Danube than the Spey in spate.

"I've not given you the job as a favor." He was muttering to no one but himself.

He found an empty table as far from the dance floor as possible and, cigarette in one hand, whisky in the other, he lapsed into his favorite sport, imagining the lives of passing strangers. McAllister saw before him what he knew to be true but had never articulated. These were his people; the Highlanders, Lowlanders, the Scots. And the Italians, the Poles, the English; strangers diluting the bloodlines of this austere land of mountain and kirk, they were part of the community now, remaking its future.

These are the people who read the *Ga-zette*. The thought pleased him. They deserve better from their local newspaper.

"Is this seat taken?" Joanne reappeared from behind. "Now, where were we? Right." She reached for a glass of Babycham from the passing waitress. "A wedding. So, it will soon be New Year, it's the second half of the twentieth century and I'm going to be in it. I know it will be hard, children, a full-time job, not to mention the gossip about being a working woman . . ." Maybe no husband, but she couldn't tell him that, she still hadn't made the final final decision, the thought of the harm she would do to her girls all that was keeping her bound to a sham marriage. "Also, I have funny foreign friends, even a male unmarried friend." He rolled his eyes in mock horror. "Actually I have three single male friends." Rob waltzed by with Bianca in a tight clinch. "Make that two, but I'm going to do this, I'm going to make a life for myself, I want to use my brain, I want to learn, and I want you to teach me."

"You need a brain on the *Gazette?*" he managed to mumble. As she laughed, he was startled by a fleeting thought: Is there any place for me in her new life?

The microphone screeched. Peter the

groom stood center stage, a guitar in hand.

"In response to many requests, especially from the bride," he announced to cheers and whistles as Chiara curtsied to her husband, "we now have, for your entertainment and delight —"

"Get on with it!" Chiara shouted.

"The Meltdown Boys!"

Peter struck the first chord; Rob stepped forward swinging the microphone stand.

"One, two, three o'clock, four o'clock rock . . ."

Joanne clapped her hands and was up and off, throwing herself into the jiggling throng. The Meltdown Boys were off again, with the same tunes, the same three chords.

McAllister stood. He too was off, but in the opposite direction. Out in the foyer, the noise was mercifully muffled. He fetched his coat, his hat, pulled on his gloves and walked down the broad flight of steps into the street. The music was now a distant rumble.

"I'm all for a bright new world, but if this is the music, God help us!"

TWENTY-THREE

The night of the wedding had been well below zero. The guests leaving the party had not noticed. Next morning the children woke first, delighted at their luck; a weekend and the hills above the town were still covered with a frost-crisp covering of snow perfect for sledging. Amongst the vegetables and fruit bushes and in corners of the lawn, the Ross garden was pockmarked with patches of dirty snowmelt. The snowman too had melted slightly but overnight had frozen again, leaving a ghostly ice-sheen carapace with what seemed a sinister female presence trapped inside. Brown Owl in ice, was Annie's instant thought as she stared at their deformed creation. She also noted that the carrot nose was gone, no doubt stolen by a passing crow.

Grandad Ross put a hand to his brow to ward off the dazzle and scoured the hills. Seeing the snow dotted like holes in a colander with distant figures, he called the girls.

"Let's go sledging now before the snow disappears."

"Really? Now? Great! What about Mum?" They danced around their grandfather.

"We'll call into your house on the way. Go and ask your granny to put some cocoa in a flask for after, and hurry up, we've a hard hill to climb."

"Mum, Mum, come on. We're going sledging."

The girls clattered in the back door, the happy shrieks cheering Joanne immensely. She had slept in till ten and, waking to the clear magic snow light, had made tea, singing to herself, "We're gonna rock around the clock tonight," and had taken a mug up to Bill.

"What time is it?"

"Twenty past ten."

She left the tea on the bedside table, then crossed the room and swept back the curtains.

"Dah-da. Look at that; snow on the hills, a clear sky, a beautiful day."

"Shut the curtains, you stupid bitch!"

He jerked the eiderdown up over his head, sending the cup flying over the linoleum.

She fled, abandoning the puddle of tea and her hungover husband, repeating over and over, "I will not let him get to me, I will not cry."

Grandad was waiting outside, the children having run ahead to join a group of friends making their way toward the canal crossing and the hills beyond. Pulling on her hat and coat and scarf and gloves, she escaped down the path.

"Bill no coming?"

"Having a lie-in. We were late back."

Joanne's eyes were pink. Grandad noticed but didn't say a word. She was silently kicking herself: I wish I'd never helped Bill out with his problems.

"He'll have a hangover when he wakes up." Annie had popped up at Joanne's side as she inevitably did when a subject she was not meant to hear was being mentioned.

"Where on earth did you get that expression from?"

"Well it's true," Annie informed her mother. "Sheila Murchison told me. Her mother says my dad's an alkie." Annie saw the reaction from the adults. What had she said wrong this time? It *was* true. Everyone knew.

Grandad came to the rescue.

"Would you look at the sun. It's getting

low already and it'll be dark afore you know it. March on, ma lasses, hep, one two three."

Crossing over the canal locks Joanne hoped no one would mention the boy. She scanned the skyline. The dense pine forest that hid an ancient vitrified fort dominated the northeastern end. The pines on the northwestern end gathered in ranks around the asylum, now spotlighted in a biblical ray of light. Joanne loved her adopted town.

"Mum, Mum, over here!" Annie rolled off the sledge and with excellent last-minute timing let it career on into the dyke.

"My turn." Joanne grabbed Annie's snow-crusted mitten in one hand, the sledge rope in the other.

"Wee Jean's a fearty-cat," Annie informed her.

"She's only little. I'll take her down with me."

"It's a'right. She's with Uncle Rob. He's got a great sledge."

Wistfully, she looked across the slope. A terrified and delighted Wee Jean, enveloped by a figure in a postbox-red ski jacket, went hurtling down the hill, then veered sharply to the left in a perfect racing turn, stopping just before the drystane dyke. The resultant shriek rattled Rob's eyeballs, switching his hangover back on.

"Rob! Over here!" Joanne shouted and waved.

"How do all girls *do* that shriek?" he asked Joanne. "It's a killer."

"Our secret weapon." She took in the green tinge that a combination of high speed and aching eardrums had resurrected. "Grandad brought a flask of tea and cocoa for the girls." She took it out of her bag, then laid a tartan rug on the wall. "Want some?"

"Absolutely! I'm knackered as well as hungover."

"You're not allowed to say that. Hangover is a rude word," Annie told him sharply.

Rob raised an eyebrow at Joanne. She lifted her eyes to the heavens.

"Listen, why don't you two go and find Grandad?"

"There he is, over there." Rob waved at the distant figure stamping his feet at the edge of a huddle of grandads on sledging duty. "You can do me a favor. Look after my sledge, eh? You can have a shot, if you like."

Annie grabbed the rope with one hand and wee Jean with the other, off before Uncle Rob changed his mind.

"Great wedding." Rob perched beside Joanne on the wall and they shared the tea.

"It was fabulous. It felt like a Highland coronation."

"And you chief lady-in-waiting. I'm glad McAllister could make it." He glanced at her and wondered, not for the first time, if she fancied the editor. Naw, he thought, he's too old. They drank their tea, laughing at Rob's chatter; the convoy, the wedding, the dancing, all safe subjects for a bright winter's day. Not once did Rob ask what was wrong.

"Come on, let's get the girls, poor Mr. Ross looks half-frozen. One last go and then home for me. I'm exhausted."

He held out his hand to help her down off the dyke, then couldn't resist.

"Race you!"

Laughing and pushing, they stumbled and tumbled across the field to join her family for the long walk back. Halfway home, tired and strangely calm given the start to the day, Joanne, giving Jean a piggyback, lagged behind. She nodded and waved at neighbors, acquaintances, all tired and exhilarated by an afternoon in the snow. This is happiness — she smiled to herself — and I like it. A turning point had been reached but she was yet to acknowledge it.

Rob, carrying the sledge over one shoulder, walked ahead with Annie.

"You can borrow the sledge any time there's snow." Annie gave him a Brownie salute to seal the deal. "And, I'll let you in on a wee secret; the hoodie crow — he's gone, flown away. Father Morrison will not be coming back."

"Father Morrison? The minister?"

"Well, he's a priest, same thing really. Yep, the hoodie crow is gone, left town, so no need to be scared anymore."

Annie turned her green eyes on Rob and, staring at him, hesitated a second or two, then burst out, "He's not the hoodie crow! And anyhow, there is no hoodie crow. It's only wee bairns believe thon kind o' stuff. The bad man who picked up Jamie lives at number sixty-four down your street." It was his turn to stare. "I never saw him properly, I just saw a big man lift up his arms" — she spread her arms wide — "and he had on a great big coat wi' a kind o' cape thing like thon detective. . . ."

"Sherlock Holmes," Rob said automatically.

"Aye. An' I told Wee Jean it was a hoodie crow to scare her 'cos she's a wee clype an' my dad would thrash me if he knew we were ringing doorbells."

She stopped. Her whole skinny body went rigid with fury, her fists tight with anger at herself for saying as much as she had.

"An' if you say I told you, I'll say I didn't and that *you're* the one who's lying."

Rob stood in complete shock, watching her run off so no one could see her tears. He knew without any doubt whatsoever that he believed her completely. He also knew that she had said all she was going to say. Ever.

They were invited to the Ross house. I won't be a minute, Dad; I'll let Bill know about supper, she told him. Grandad walked on with the girls. She went in, not bothering to take off her coat. The house was cold. Bill was slumped by the unlit fire, an eiderdown around him, a glass of whisky at his feet, snoring. This is it, Joanne told herself. Bill's outburst this morning is a godsend, she repeated to herself. Everything is as clear and as crisp as the glass ice on the puddles. And as fractured.

He couldn't even strike a match, she observed. Fire all laid, ready to go, and he couldn't even manage that. She stood across the sitting room, with the sofa between them for safety.

"Bill."

He came to and glared at her as she stood, feet together, arms folded as though she was about to dance the hornpipe. It took a while for her words to penetrate. The gap across the room and between husband and wife was wide and deep.

"I've had enough," she started. But she'd said this before so he took no heed.

"I want you out of this house," she continued. "And if you don't leave, I will, and I'll take the girls."

He looked up. It didn't bother him where the girls went, but Joanne giving him orders, that surprised him.

"I don't care what anyone thinks anymore. I will not put up with your drinking and your lying and all your shenanigans and I will not be your punching bag."

He was out of his nest of fabric and feathers and across the room with the speed of a viper strike. His hand came up. She dodged to the other side of the sofa, standing her ground.

"Bill. One thousand pounds."

That stopped him.

"I know all about it, you borrowed one thousand pounds. I have no idea how you are going to pay it back but if you touch me, even the once, I will set your pals the Gordons from Glasgow onto you." None of this made any sense but it didn't matter; what mattered was that he had been found out and that she knew, and that she knew Jimmy Gordon.

He didn't move. Only his eyes in the unshaven face showed the struggle to comprehend how he had lost the advantage.

Joanne waited and as she watched she noticed a tiny patch of gray hairs on the left cheek. No longer the charming soldier boy, she noted, it's time to grow up.

"I could give hundreds of reasons why I can't live with you, but what's the point? You always justify everything to yourself. I don't love you and I don't even like you and I know that's not a good enough reason to leave your husband but I will not be beaten and I know you think it's your right to hit me but I won't put up with it ever again and if you ever try to hurt me or anything else, well, I have friends and, thanks to you, I have met other people who are not nice and they . . ." She stopped. "Well, maybe two of them are not so bad but . . ." What on earth am I saying, she thought, stick to the point.

"Bill. I want you out of this house. I will not live with you anymore." She backed out the door just as he made a move toward her. She saw the raised fist, she saw the fury, and in that second she knew that this was it. It was over. Then she fled.

She tried to run down the street but kept slipping. She walked as fast as she could but kept slowing, slowing to laugh and grin and talk to the rapidly closing day. The air was charged with the smell of newly lit coal, the smoke hanging low; the sky was darkening from pink to red to crimson to purple, the evening star a guiding light on her walk toward the unknown.

"I did it. I did it." She laughed at herself. "You sound just like the girls — I did it, I did it." Good job no one is around, she thought, when she realized she was shouting.

When she reached the corner of the street where the solid unadorned unimaginative council house where her parents-in-law and her girls waited was, she had to stop for a moment. In the dim between streetlights, she felt a not unfamiliar tightening band of panic. Bending over to get her breath, she watched miniature clouds of condensation form and re-form. The warm vapor had a blue tinge. She filled her lungs with cold air and blew toward the light, watching the essence of herself form, then evaporate, another breath, form and evaporate. I feel so light I could fly, she thought, laughing; probably all this oxygen going to my head.

■ ■ ■ ■

"Mum, who lives in number sixty-four?"

Rob stood in the kitchen doorway, still in his damp ski jacket, watching as his mother made tea.

"That's the Youngs' house. Of course Michael Young died in the war, his wife died when she was only forty or so, and they only had the one child, Deirdre, so the house went to her. But she died five years ago. Never had any children, such a tragedy, I know she so wanted to be a mother. Now of course it belongs to her husband, widower I should say. . . ."

"Yes, Mum. And who is her widower?"

"I thought you knew, they've lived there long enough —"

"Mum!"

"Inspector Tompson, of course. What? What did I say?"

The next thing she heard was a motorbike roaring down the street.

"Everyone thinks I'm mental accusing a priest — but a policeman?"

The pain was a throbbing pulse in his jaw and a tight band around the forehead. He shouldn't have gone out last night. Nor drank on an empty stomach. McAllister felt worn down and weary and defeated and past caring.

"I hear you, Rob, but really. Tompson? I don't see it. You will need a cast-iron case and you yourself said the girl won't talk. Even if *you* credit her story, Joanne says her daughter has a wild imagination. The same child who swore it was a hoodie crow, then she let us think it was the priest who took the boy, and now she's accusing Inspector Tompson? No. Beyond belief."

"It was her wee sister who kept changing her story, seeing a hoodie crow everywhere. Annie, the eldest, only said they saw a hoodie crow to scare her sister so they wouldn't get into trouble for ringing doorbells. Look, I know children, I'm nearer to Annie in age than I am to you. . . . The girl blames herself for what happed to Jamie. . . . She is terrified of her father but she *did* see a man, in a big coat, a greatcoat, pick Jamie up, on the doorstep of number sixty-four." Rob started to pace. "I know that house, it's round a bend in the road and about a hundred yards away from ours, it's very like the house next door, rhododendron bushes, stained-glass doors, and the light would be behind him, making a silhouette. Maybe it wasn't Tompson, but it was his house." He was shouting now. "I believe her even if you don't."

"Aye, that's as may be. But with your known antipathy to Tompson, who do you think will listen to you?" Defeat overwhelmed McAllister. "We'll never get Morrison, he's gone. There's no proof of anything other than some distasteful pictures. Nothing more."

Rob couldn't take any more.

"Will you stop being so maudlin, for heaven's sake? I saw those pictures. They are not nothing. They made me feel sick, dirty, unclean. Those boys were used. Those photos were worn, the edges curled, they had been pawed over by some very weird persons. Look, McAllister, I know I haven't seen the things you saw in the war but I *know* this sort of thing can ruin lives.

"And also, there's something going on in that house next door. I went in there, I was in the hallway and someone came to the front door, they had a key, and no, I've no idea who it was, but I bet they were not meant to be there.

"So go on, sit there, tell yourself you were right, that thon bee in your bunnet about it being the priest is the only possibility. But puzzle this out.

"Why was a greatcoat burning in the Reaburn when Morrison was long gone? Here's a button off it to show you I'm not imagining things." Rob ferreted in the depths of his inside pocket, found it, and with it found the key.

"I found this too, it fell out of the remains of the coat."

He laid both on the table and left in despair, realizing that McAllister, his hero, was only human after all.

Barely five minutes had passed when the doorbell rang again. McAllister didn't move. It rang once more. A minute went by, then the visitor came down the hallway.

"The door was open, so . . ."

"Jimmy." McAllister gestured to a chair.

"I came to bring the bottle from Ma. She sez to say, 'Aa the best,' " Jimmy explained, "but you're no well so I'd best be going."

"For God's sake, sit down and open that bottle, that's one of the best single-malts I'll see in a long time."

They sat, nursing their glasses until dusk began to add to the gloom of the atmosphere.

"Jimmy, you didn't come all the way from Ross-shire just to ask after my health. Spit it out, man." McAllister was as direct as a heart attack.

"It was thon photo you showed me," Jimmy began. "I recognized one of those boys, and I started to remember more about those days — and I wish to Christ I hadn't."

Silence.

"I know this boy, a man now, he's stopping hereabouts." He took a sip. "He knew a lot more about the goings-on with your friend Father Morrison — Father Bain as we knew him. He, my friend, was one of the boys from that home I mentioned. And when he was a wee lad, there was an older boy who died there, but it was all hushed up."

"This is the same home where some of the boys from the boxing club were living?"

"Uh-huh."

"Will he tell you what he knows?"

"Aye, maybe, he hates them that much. He knows what went on. He knows Father Bain, Morrison, and he knew the other bastards, the ones who got away with it. Of course no one will ever listen to him, 'specially not now." He paused. "See, there's a wee bit o' a problem — I can't get to speak with him."

McAllister looked the question — why?

"My record means I'm no allowed in. This manny, he's in the gaol. But you can get in, you're respectable."

After Jimmy had left him alone with the bottle of malt, McAllister knew he should phone for Westland. It was only six thirty, the landlady would pass on the message. He was certain he wouldn't be calling the police station. He was uncertain whether he would be calling any policeman, even DCI Westland. And the phone was in the hall, and the hall was cold, and his face hurt, and he was bone weary. Tomorrow, I'll think on it tomorrow he told himself. So he dragged himself off to bed, taking the bottle with him.

With the midwinter solstice a week away, a red-streaked far-north twilight hovered before turning from positive to negative. In those slow moments, every bush, every tree, the buildings, the horizons, shimmered in static. Some nights, when the electricity was so noticeable that the hairs on the back of the neck tingled, when contact with metal gave off static shock, and when the dogs became restless, a splendid light show from the aurora borealis was certain.

Rob wheeled his bike into the garage and as he shut the door, the antics of the rooks in the trees next door melted his frustration, restored his natural state of grace. Cawing, squabbling, scrambling for space on the bare branches of one especially large sycamore that, drooping from the weight of the rookery, looked like a dispirited mother bowed down from the constant squabbling of an overlarge, querulous family. What did you call them — a parliament of rooks? Was that what McAllister had said? McAllister; Rob still couldn't believe he wouldn't listen.

Opening the door to the porch, about to shed the layers of motorbike gear, a smell, in a downdraft of acrid smoke, drifted over the lawn, then was gone. He sniffed. It was that same smell. Rob crept along the lawn, hugging the edge, hidden by rhododendron bushes. The Big House seemed its usual dark and empty self, but Rob sensed that whoever had relit the fire had not left. He looked upward toward the main bedroom, the one Morrison had made his studio. Later he could not recall what had made him certain someone was in there; there was no car around, there were no lights on, no noise, nothing.

It's not that I'm a coward, he told himself as he sneaked back to his own house, I'm not in the least scared. His mother and father were out for dinner, he was just being cautious, being a good citizen, remembering his promise to keep an eye on the house next door, that's what he told himself as he picked up the phone.

"Oh, hello, Mrs. McPherson, can I speak to Ann?"

She arrived fifteen minutes later on her bicycle.

"I hope this isn't one of your stunts to get me out on a Sunday night —" He held his finger to his lips. "It's just that my hair's still damp," she whispered as they huddled by his back door.

A car passed along the road, stopping a few doors further up.

"That'll be Chief Inspector Westland." She spoke softly; the noise of the rooks had settled but there was still the occasional scuffle and indignant caws as a fight for space on the branch broke out. Rob went out to meet him.

"Sorry to get you out, sir. It may be nothing, but I think there's someone in there" — Rob pointed to the house — "and I'm sure I smelt smoke." He didn't mention the previous time he had smelled a fire.

"Can we get in?" Westland asked.

"Ann and I can get in by the coal hole but you're too fat . . . big," Rob amended. "We can open the front door for you. But go through our garden. There's gravel all round the house, so the burglar might hear you.

Come on, I'll show you."

Westland had his police torch, Ann too. She also had her truncheon. Rob was most impressed.

They met up in the hallway and stood at the foot of the stairs, the smell of burning now distinct; the sound of someone moving, opening cupboards, shifting furniture, echoed down the stairway.

"Is the electric still on?" Westland wondered.

"Aye, I think so," Rob murmured.

"Where's the switch?" And in one movement Westland switched on the hall lights, yelled, "Police!" and charged up the stairs followed by Ann McPherson, truncheon at the ready.

It was like a war cry from the clans at Culloden, Rob said later when he and Ann relived the whole episode, but the effect wasn't quite as dramatic as it should have been as there was only one dusty forty-watt bulb for the whole of the hallway and stairs.

Westland burst into the bedroom, Ann following, Rob not far behind.

"Inspector Tompson!" Westland panted. "What the hell are you doing?"

Tompson was shaken but in an instant remembered himself.

"I could well ask you the same thing."

■ ■ ■ ■

He had had a restless night. All the information, the suppositions and the infuriating realization that still there was no real information had sent his brain swirling, the thoughts as dark and as dreadful as water emptying out of a canal lock. McAllister now sat with his morning tea, trying to resist the temptation to add a slug of whisky. He wasn't ready to go into the office for the Monday meeting. They could manage without him. He fiddled with the button. He had scrubbed it with soap. It was a Military Police Service button. He picked it up, put it down, ran his thumb over the raised emblem. He fiddled with the worn metal tag attached to the key. The number on it had been scratched on by hand, probably with a screwdriver. He looked at the clock. Eight. He could call now. He got up, went into the hall, picked up the phone and dialed.

"Highland Bus Station, can I help you?"

"Sorry, wrong number." He replaced the phone, went straight back to the kitchen, poured a dram into a second cup of tea, telling himself it was medicinal. He went back into the hall to make another call.

Before he could pick up the receiver the phone shrilled deep into his hangover. He was regretting the dram already.

"McAllister."

"When are you coming in? I've something to tell you."

"Rob, I've more important things to think about than the *Gazette*."

"No, it's not that, it's —" The shrill briiing of the doorbell gave him a start.

"There's the door. We'll talk later."

He hung up. The shadow darkening the stained-glass door panels was large and ominous. He shuddered; "Someone stepping on my grave," his mother used to say. He opened the door. Looming in the doorway like a specter at the feast was Constable Willie Grant.

"Morning, Mr. McAllister, sir. DCI Westland asked, special like, that I bring the news in person. It's Father Morrison. We've found him."

TWENTY-FOUR

Westland had had enough of the Highlands. He couldn't wait to be on the train home; home for Christmas, home to his family, his city, away from this town and this case. Years in the police had formed his view that no one wanted to know the truth — they only wanted a version of the truth that would fit their preconceptions. McAllister wanted a truth that would relieve him of the guilt of neglecting his brother, the boy's parents wanted a truth showing accidents happen with no fault on anyone's part, the town wanted a truth where no blame could be laid on a native Highlander, the Church didn't want any truth that might reveal priests as mere mortal men with faults and failures and all that that implied, and the chief constable wanted his officers shown as valiant men — he was yet to notice the token women — going about their duties without fear or favor, a bright shining example to the populace of the Highlands and Islands and as good as any police force south of the Grampians.

What the chief inspector hated most of all — and he acknowledged that this was not exclusive to this part of the world — was the denial, the complicity, the hiding of society's ills in order to maintain that all-pervading moral imperative, respectability.

Morrison, found dead in a snowdrift, was a solution to all their problems. He would remain innocent as the lamb but would privately be blamed for any and every sin.

Westland sighed. The meeting with the chief constable had gone as expected. The suspicions that he voiced were met with more than disbelief; he was ridiculed and threatened with an adverse report to his superiors. There was no evidence against this Polish fellow, the chief constable agreed, but the man was not entirely innocent. He has no papers and I have to agree with Inspector Tompson, the senior policeman had said, his alibi is very convenient. The parents couldn't have killed their son, they were at work and seen by half the town, so that theory was gone. The priest is not, and never was, a suspect, Westland was told, and was ordered to leave out the other outrageous, if not downright libelous, suggestion.

No officer on *my* force would ever subvert a criminal case to protect his church. That's me told, Westland thought, sighing to himself, having long ago lost the capacity to be shocked by decisions from senior officers.

Tompson continued in his duties. The fatal accident inquiry into the priest's death would deem it just that, an accident. And still there was nothing, nothing that could show Tompson was covering up for a fellow Catholic.

"I've talked to him," the chief constable had said, "and Tompson explained to me that while he was checking the house, gathering up all that valuable photographic equipment and the rest of Morrison's belongings, he found a greatcoat in the stove and was only finishing off the job to clear out the stove. He is on a church committee that looks after their properties."

"Aye, checking the house in the dark." But again DCI Westland was ignored. He next tried to put a case before the procurator fiscal. They reviewed the photographs found in Morrison's luggage, they tried to piece together any evidence connecting Morrison with the boy Jamie. There was nothing.

"Tompson went to the house to tidy up, as he put it, within five minutes of receiving the phone call that Morrison had been found." DCI Westland pointed out, "He didn't even bother to inform *me* that the body had been discovered; I heard it from the desk sergeant."

"He was only trying to protect the Church from any scandal over Father Morrison's wee hobby," was the reply. "Not that there is anything criminal in the photos. Distasteful as they are, there is nothing that would warrant laying charges. Bring me evidence, and I will make sure the truth is known," the fiscal had promised.

At least he is willing to consider that a priest could be corrupt, Westland thought. But it was of little consolation.

One hundred yards away, McAllister sat in his office, feet on the desk, door firmly shut, lobbing scrunched-up balls of copy paper into the top hat that had mysteriously migrated from the reporters' room. Rob had told him — in great detail and with accompanying gestures and sound effects — about his derring-do confrontation with Inspector Tompson in the Big House, as he now referred to it, having picked up the name from the children.

Angus MacLean had phoned McAllister explaining that his contact in the church had discovered that the demise of the Boys'

Boxing Club was due to the war. There had been talk of an inquiry into some aspect of the club, Angus was told. It was probably nothing more than gossip, his friend had added. So, nothing.

The Reverend Macdonald passed on to McAllister the information that Father Morrison Bain had disappeared for a year or so; on retreat, was the story. He was next heard of as a particularly active chaplain in the Clydeside Blitz. A hero, a friend, a comforter, was the consensus of those who knew him from that time. Again, nothing.

DCI Westland phoned McAllister, relaying the details of Inspector Tompson's explanation to the chief constable for his visit to the priest's home. Westland was livid. He had been forced to apologize for implying that Tompson might be involved in covering up a crime. Not that Father Morrison could possibly be a suspect in the boy's death, the chief constable had added at every opportunity.

Nothing, nil, nada, McAllister doodled in his notebook. The key was on his desk next to the button. No point in informing Westland. He watched clouds, counted passing seagulls, drank four cups of tea, took five aspirins, then, halfway through the morning, his hangover receding, idleness turning to boredom, then instinct kicked in. He was a reporter, so he started with the story. *Maybe I should do as Don does, start with headings. Right.*

First heading: *Key.* Second heading: *Greatcoat.* Third heading: *Big House.* Fourth heading: *Prisoner.* Under *Key* he wrote, *Visit boy's* — he crossed out boy's — *Jamie's parents.* Under *Greatcoat* he wrote, *Whose is it? Why burn? Button?* Under *Big House,* he listed *Tompson's search* — *for what?* Under the last heading, he paused, then reached for the phone. While he waited to be connected he made a decision. He respected DCI Westland, but he was not going to share any information with any police officer, ever.

"Angus? McAllister. I wonder if you can arrange something for me?"

In the reporters' room, they were getting on with a Monday morning not defined by the ritual news meeting.

"You're looking good." Rob examined Joanne. There was definitely something different about her. She looked younger. "New hairdo?"

"Don't be silly, when would I have the time — or the money — for that?"

"It's what I always say to women because if they have had a new hairdo and I don't notice I get into big trouble."

"Let's just say that I'm looking forward to the New Year."

"Talking of which," said Don, "I'm off to chase ad copy for the New Year edition."

"From the liquor merchants, no doubt."

"Cheeky bizzom. No cherry liqueur chocolates for you."

"I'm away out too," Rob said, "and, Joanne, if you need a babysitter, I'm free." He couldn't look at her in case she spotted his guilty conscience — she would not be happy if she knew he wanted to question Annie.

"Oh aye, and where am I supposed to go for a wild night?"

It had been some time since Rob had looked after the girls and now that Bill had vanished, and Chiara was on her honeymoon, there was no social life for her.

"My mother loves it when you come over. Why don't you call her?"

"Well, I have to return the dress I borrowed for the wedding."

"Call her." And he was gone.

McAllister came into the reporters' room five minutes later. In a much smaller bandage, his cheek was down but still swollen, with a shade of light blue-green that gave him a resemblance to a cartoon character — Man with Toothache.

They were comfortable again alone together.

Joanne leaned her elbows on the table, the Glasgow paper open on the features section.

"Is this what you plan to do with the *Gazette?*"

"If wishes were horses, as my mother would say." He half-smiled at her. "No, but I'll steal a few of their ideas. We don't have the advertising to support too many changes and usually not enough material to fill the extra pages."

"You certainly can't say that of the last couple of months."

There was quiet for a few moments.

"So it's all over, is it?" Joanne asked. "Morrison, or is it Morrison Bain, dead in a snowdrift, all sins now attributable to him because he can't answer back? And the chief inspector is off tomorrow, I hear, with no case to be brought over the boy's death. That's it, is it?"

"Aye. Looks like." McAllister fiddled with the button in his coat pocket.

"I never told you," she started, "and it won't affect my work," she was quick to add, "but I've managed to get a prefab. I'll be moving in, sometime in the New Year" — she looked away — "just me and the girls." She couldn't bring herself to say, I won't be living with my husband. "No one knows yet. I want one last peaceful family Christmas with Granny and Grandad Ross, and my sister and brother-in-law. They'll all be very disappointed in me. . . ." She laughed. "Nothing unusual in that!" Her voice dropped a decibel. She shook her head and shook the newspaper shut. "And my husband, along with most of the male population in Scotland, won't notice I'm gone for at least the first two weeks of the year. I'll flit then." When he does notice, then I might need help. Thinking about Bill's reaction was frightening; he would not let her go easily, of that she was certain.

"If you need any help . . ."

"Thanks, but I'll have Chiara plus two Polish gentlemen with a van, plus Rob as babysitter. I'll be fine."

"I've no doubt of that, Mrs. Ross, no doubts at all."

She blushed deep pink and they both turned back to the typewriters and started to clatter away.

Rob hadn't forgotten; the priest may have

perished but it wasn't over. Maybe it was his ambition to be an investigative reporter, maybe it was his nosy nature, but mostly it was plain dislike of Tompson that kept him returning to the same question: What was Tompson really looking for next door?

Rob recalled the picture that had confronted them in the dim light after he and WPC Ann and DCI Westland had burst into the room; drawers opened, linoleum curled up at the corners, photographic equipment stacked up in the center of the room, paper spilled on the floor, negatives scattered everywhere. He had no idea what Tompson's explanation was and WPC Ann McPherson had no idea what was going on at the police station — she was now permanently on foot patrol, Tompson's orders — so, Rob puzzled, what was it he had been searching for?

"Mum? If you wanted to hide something next door, where would you put it?"

"Big or small?"

"Small. I think."

"That's easy."

He was gone before she had finished the explanation.

Rob shuddered. "I hate this place."

The coal hole was the only way he knew

into the house without breaking something, so again, the coal hole it had been. Getting out was simple; he went out through the back door and pulled the door to. Every creak, every scratch of tree branch on windowpane or roof tile, every sigh down the bedroom chimney, had him clammy with fright. The room had been searched again by the police and was in a complete bourach; linoleum had been rolled up, furniture searched, the bed pulled apart. Rob had always been mindful of the taboo of entering another person's bedroom. This time was no different. He crossed the bare floor to the dressing room, making directly for the cupboard behind the mirror that his mother had described. He felt for the hidden catch.

"It's a hiding place where ladies put their jewelry, that sort of thing. Quite common in Victorian dressing rooms, I believe."

You can't see it, his mother had told him; feel for a latch in the top left-hand corner, and push it upward. The mirror will open outward, and the cupboard is behind. If it is locked, I have no idea where the key is, but then the key has been missing for about twenty years. . . . Yes, Mum, he had said.

He pulled the mirror open. The cupboard was unlocked. He put in his hand. It was dim, but he didn't want to switch on a light, not even a torch. He felt around. There was one fat foolscap envelope, nothing else. He closed the cupboard. It took him a few moments to fumble the latch of the mirror into place. He ran down the stairs, let himself out through the back door, pulling it to as quietly as he could, and he sprinted back home to the safety of his bedroom. His father was at work, his mother was out shopping again — Christmas is only four days away, she had reminded them at breakfast. Rob knew he should be back in the office too, Don had told him one hour, no more, we've a lot to do what with McAllister being only half-here.

He opened the envelope. Negatives, large-format, two and a half by two and a half inches, at least a dozen sheets of them. There were also about twenty prints, of varying sizes, some only small snapshots, others larger, professional size. Rob pulled a large one from the pile, stared at it, dropped it, clasped both hands over his mouth, ran to the bathroom and vomited.

Don had given McAllister the same warning.

"Be back here as soon as you can, we have to finish this paper a day early what with

Christmas an' all."

He'd almost said, Yes, Mr. McLeod, then he remembered where he was off to.

This time McAllister drove to the tiny terraced cottage. As he parked the car, he noted that the doorstep didn't shine, the windows didn't glisten. This was not due to the weather. The house itself was grieving.

It took some time for the door to open. At first McAllister thought that the man was Jamie's grandfather come over from the Isles to comfort the parents. It was only when he was ushered into the gloom of the parlor that he realized it was the boy's father.

"The wife, she's gone back home," was the first thing the man said. "Nothing here for her."

"I'm sorry." What a bloody inadequate word, McAllister thought.

"Aye."

They stood. Then McAllister reached for the key. He handed it over. The man held the edges of the tag in two fingers as though it was an exhibit in a trial.

"It's Jamie's key. He keeps it round his neck, inside his vest, in case he loses it." He handed it back. "He doesn't need it now." He turned, abandoning McAllister, not curious, not apologetic, nothing; all connection to the rest of the human race had been buried along with his son in that small coffin, now deep in the dark foreign soil of a churchyard, many miles, then one long and one short sea crossing from their home.

McAllister sat for a while in the car before starting the engine. He felt no triumph in being right. The key; the first item on his list, it could now be ticked off as done and accounted for. He put it back in his pocket along with the button. The coat; why burn it? So no one would connect the owner to a crime? He remembered the greatcoat found by the canal. That belonged to Karl. This button was off a British Military Police coat. What was that all about? He put it aside as too hard. What next? he thought as he drove back to the office.

What McAllister didn't know, but was about to find out, was that the third item, the Big House, the object of Tompson's search, that could also be ticked off of the list.

Don interrupted McAllister and Rob.

"Don't you two worry about a thing — Joanne and me, we'll put the paper out all by ourselves!" But a brief glance at the junior reporter's face showed what he thought might be tear streaks on an alabaster mask. "Oh. Right. I'll see you both later." He turned to go. "I forgot. McAllister, there was a phone call from the prison governor while you were out. The answer is no. He, the man you wanted to talk to, he'll no see you."

McAllister nodded. Don waited. When he realized there would be no explanation he asked, "Is it important?"

"It might be."

"Later then." He left them to it.

McAllister rose, took the envelope, an identical envelope but with far different contents to the one the police now had. He put it in the safe. He spun the tumblers. He handed Rob a hankie. Then he poured them both a whisky. They downed the dram.

"Right, let's get on with it. We've a paper to put to bed."

Joanne glanced at Don when Rob and McAllister took their places at the typewriters. He shrugged. They all worked steadily through the afternoon, all avoiding whatever it was that was still too raw to share.

Rob would never admit it — even to himself — but with his discovery, he had lost his innocence. Normally he welcomed his mother's concern and enjoyed the comfort of her company. He usually shared his triumphs, telling her of his progress on the path to star journalist. But not this time. Mother protects boy, man protects mother, as it should be. What he had discovered in the former McLean family home next door he would never share. The images of those helpless little boys haunted him to the point where he was scared to shut his eyes.

"Joanne will be round soon. Do you want supper before you go?" Margaret was concerned by Rob's silence but said nothing. He'll tell me when he's ready, she thought.

Rob was regretting his offer to babysit. But he had promised, so to cancel would involve too many explanations and he wasn't good at lies. He was certain he could wheedle more details out of Annie; four hours ago he had been a boy, he still remembered how to talk to children.

The girls were in bed. Joanne left. Five minutes passed. Annie came down the stairs for a glass of water. She had her book with her. She sat opposite Rob and they talked about what they were reading. Rob showed her the lurid cover on the new Compton McKenzie thriller; Annie was rereading *Anne of Green Gables*.

"Annie, I need to ask you something but it must be our wee secret."

"You don't want my mum to know."

He looked at her sharply. She replied in such an adult tone, he knew there was no point in being subtle.

"Your mother only wants to protect you, but yes, this must be between us only."

The child nodded.

"I need you to describe to me everything you can remember of what you saw the afternoon Jamie disappeared."

"You're looking for clues? Like the Famous Five?"

"Exactly." Not exactly, Rob thought, the Famous Five didn't have to confront murderous deviants. "So tell me all you can remember and try to describe what the hoodie crow — the man — what he was wearing."

McAllister thought everyone had left so he was startled when Don walked into his office.

"You wanted to talk to an inmate at the prison?"

"Probably a wild goose chase."

"Aye, there are enough geese flying around right now to fill every Christmas table in the county."

"You don't need to know any of this, Don. It's not something anyone should ever have to see."

"Right." He didn't move. "But you'll show me."

"In the safe."

Don took the envelope and emptied it onto the desk. McAllister turned away. Don leafed through the prints, ignored the negatives. He examined them carefully, in complete silence. He looked through them once more, laying two aside. He held them under the desk lamp. He examined the reverse. It was as though he was completely detached from the images, as though they were of the same interest as a corpse on a mortuary slab, fascinating, but with the soul removed. He stacked up the photographs except for two, put the rest back into the envelope and returned it to the safe.

"Firstly," he started, "all these photos are old. Secondly, most of them are not from here. The paper is different. I think they are filth bought on the black market. But these two" — he poked them apart with his pencil — "these two are from someone's private collection. They're not recent either. I need you to look again. Look at the paper, the size of the print, the color tone."

The man in the photograph was shown only from the neck down; the boy's face was in profile. McAllister couldn't bear to see the image, knowing he would take it to his grave, but knew he must. He looked at the borders. He looked at the printing technique. He turned it over and examined the watermark. He calculated the size. Then he nodded.

"I see what you're getting at. And yes, it looks exactly like the others."

"Right." Don handed McAllister a cigarette and went around to the filing cabinet for the whisky. "This man in the prison. Where does he fit in?"

McAllister explained.

"Leave it with me."

It had taken all his guile to arrange the meeting. The prisoner, Davy Soutar, agreed to see the man as a favor to Jimmy McPhee. He had no idea that Don McLeod was in any way connected with a newspaper other than being an avid reader of the racing pages. He knew this because on the few occasions he had seen Don, there was always a copy of the racing pages protruding from the inside pocket of his jacket. A hint that Don might speak up for him on his application for a transfer to Glasgow also helped.

Stepping into the prison, built from the same stone as the castle, and the courts, and the police station, the temperature was colder inside than out. A stench that could never be overcome by the smells of wall-flower and daffodils and buddleia and pine resin and mown grass from the gardens outside the walls made Don shudder.

Naturally, the prison guard knew Don McLeod. When given a nod, he stepped out of hearing. Don leaned across the table, talking rapidly. Davy Soutar listened. He closely resembled a weasel, with the same skinny narrow-shouldered frame and the same beady-eyed weighing-up-his-prey look in his eyes. He stared at Don, and when Don had finished speaking, he lost his feral confidence and instead looked exactly what he was — a victim. He wouldn't meet Don's eye and he refused to say a word. Don then placed a photograph between them. The Glasgow career criminal who had survived many stretches in prison, who ran with the razor gangs and the hard men, who had inflicted and had suffered knifings and beatings and killings and sadistic warders and a sadistic childhood, sat stone still, staring in any direction but that of the photo, his face as weeping wet as the walls of the prison cells.

"I canny," Davy pleaded, "I canny. I canny tell you. No one listens to me, ever. Besides, it's all over with long since, and they got off with everything."

"If I say the name, Davy, just nod or shake your head."

"I canny. He'll get to me. He knows where I am, he himself put me here, and if I said a word, he'd finish me off. And he can, it'd be no problem to him."

When Don reported back to McAllister, he counseled him to wait. Give it time, weeks, months, wait till it's all died down, then do whatever it is you need to do.

"I'm a star! I've hit the big time. Woo-hoo!"

Rob danced around the office waving that morning's Glasgow paper.

"Here, in features, my article."

Joanne and Don would have liked to see the paper but with Rob whooping and laughing, waving it above his head, dancing a demented war dance, they couldn't.

"Hey, Geronimo! Give us a look." Joanne grabbed the paper off him.

"Have it, I'm away to buy some more copies. I pinched this one from the guard on the train."

Rob went flying out the door, straight into McAllister.

"Sorry, boss. And thanks for everything."

"The lad did well," Don commented.

"He did that." McAllister agreed.

Joanne read quickly, then glanced at the editor.

"This is good. Did you help?"

"Not really. A bit of subbing. It's his work and his story."

"He makes it very alive."

McAllister nodded. "Let's hope we can turn out a newspaper with room for good, thoughtful stories."

"But we've still one more paper for this year, so off you go and shut yourself in your wee room and don't come out until you've produced a leader worthy of this new future you're on about."

"Yes, Mr. McLeod." And this time McAllister did as he was bidden.

As a wordsmith, McAllister prided himself on knowing an apposite word or phrase for every occasion, every landscape, every weather; but the past weeks were beyond description. He concluded that *dreich,* that good old Scottish standby, was far too mild for the scale of awfulness.

Christmas had come and gone. In the Highlands, indeed in most parts of Scotland, the Dickensian Christmas was for storybooks. Church on Sunday, small gifts for the children and a fancier dinner than usual was Christmas for Presbyterians and their ilk. New Year was altogether another matter. Hogmanay, the house clean and tidy, sideboards heaving with drink, table laden with black bun and ham sandwiches, radios were tuned to a New Year ceilidh and those with a television watched Andy Stewart and the White Heather Club, everyone waited for the chimes of Big Ben to strike twelve. Then the New Year toast, first footing, more drink, black bun, lumps of coal, and many kept the tradition of giving a peck of salt. Hopefully your first-foot was a dark and handsome stranger. The round of visits to every relative and friend and neighbor went on as much as a fortnight into the New Year and longer in the far-flung islands that had not yet adopted the Gregorian calendar.

The collective hangover of New Year meant nothing much was done until at least the third week in January. Too many drinks, too many visitors, cars that wouldn't start, buses that didn't come, freezing nights that turned daytime sleet into black ice, burst pipes, sodden gardens and a dank layer of coal and coke and wood and peat smoke, brought on a collective misery. And as often as not, the river was in spate and threatening to burst its banks.

Editorial finished for this week, McAllister reached once more for the list. He was convinced he knew who was responsible for the boy's death; the details of how he had died were a mystery; proving it was impossible. There was no evidence that would stand up to a good defense advocate.

At what point in his life the search for truth had become a quest, McAllister would never know. Coming to this small newspaper, having been given carte blanche to change it into what he knew it could be, that was a Herculean task that could not be completed by one man in one place, in one year. One decade might be more realistic. To change needed a change in the attitude of the community too. His time in Spain and his love of literature often conjured up memories that whisked him across the seas, across the Pyrenees, to mountains with no resemblance whatsoever to Ben Wyvis. It's a ridiculous thought; me — Don Quixote tilting at windmills, with Don McLeod as my Sancho Panza. He smiled a rare smile and the resultant twinge in his jaw brought him back to the here and now and the lost cause of justice.

The new version of the *Highland Gazette;* this could be a pioneering newspaper capable of tackling the great wall of silence surrounding the Church, the murky processes of the town council and the occasional rotten councilor like Mr. Findlay Grieg, who thought he was bomb-proof, the treatment of the unfortunates in children's homes and orphanages, the state of some old people's homes, which were only one step up from a poorhouse, our nineteenth-century prisons, our condemnation of unmarried mothers, our turning a blind eye to violence against women and children — the list could have gone on.

We continue to congratulate ourselves on what a nice wee town we have. Yes, there are many many good points about living here, McAllister acknowledged that, but until there is justice for Jamie, I'll not be able to appreciate them.

"Thank goodness I never say maudlin rubbish like this out loud," he muttered.

It wasn't until the end of January that McAllister had all he needed. DCI Westland had been gone nearly six weeks. Inspector Tompson was unbearably smug and completely safe. Father Morrison was dead and buried. The identity of the killer of wee Jamie would remain one of life's great mysteries was the common consensus.

The first piece of information came via the Reverend Macdonald. It was a completely innocuous conversation. Joanne and

Rob were typing away, chatting in between bouts of typewriter wrestling, discussing the use of Gaelic speakers instead of secret codes in the last war.

"They needn't have bothered with Gaelic speakers, anyone from Glasgow is completely unintelligible to friend and foe," she laughed.

"I heard that," McAllister said from across the room, where he was busy working on the layout of that week's edition.

"That was one of the problems my Annie had when she was a bridesmaid, she couldn't understand the accents of those wee Italian Scottish girls." She smiled at the memory. "And when the dreaded Inspector Tompson was questioning her, she missed a lot of what he was saying because of his accent and also because he was speaking at the poor child in his best Military Police sergeant shout."

McAllister and Rob simultaneously said, "What?"

"Didn't you know? My brother-in-law told me. Inspector Tompson was in the Military Police during the war. When he was demobbed, he became a policeman."

The second piece of information came from Jimmy via Don.

"I don't see how this will help any," he

said, "and my brother Keith willny swear to it, but he heard that sometime before I was there, Inspector Tompson was a part-time instructor at the boxing club in Glasgow. Early on in the war it was."

Another proof, or nonproof as McAllister termed it, he had kept to himself for some time. Comparing the photographs Don had singled out from the envelope still locked in the office safe with the group photograph of the boys from the boxing club, the one with Kenneth, his brother, and a very young Jimmy McPhee, the size was the same, the paper was the same, the printing looked similar, but so what? It proved nothing.

And finally the nontestimony of Davy Soutar. Don had checked, and yes, it was the man himself who had had Davy Soutar transferred from Barlinnie so he could keep an eye on him.

Then it was time. Two phone calls.

"I've got what you were looking for. I think we should meet," he said at the start of the first call.

"Tonight. Not too late. Seven, I said. Don't want to scare him off." The second phone call.

No turning back now.

■ ■ ■ ■

He parked the car between the streetlamps under skeletal sycamore trees, opposite the path to the Islands suspension bridge. He was early. He lit a cigarette and waited. The river with a low-pitched tinnitus roar filled the night. A car drew up behind him. The driver got out, checked in McAllister's window, then walked around, opened the passenger door and took a seat. The smell of Brylcreem mixed with that of new wool.

"Nice coat," McAllister said. "New?"

"What's this rigmarole all about then?" Tompson seemed nervous but still very much in control.

"As I told you on the phone, I've got what you were searching for."

"There was a proper police search. Anything you've found, if you *have* found anything, is police evidence."

"No, I don't think you'll want this handed over. You can probably wriggle out of a charge of destroying evidence but that's too big a risk, especially if the procurator sees the contents. Your military greatcoat was really of no consequence. But you were seen wearing it when you grabbed the boy.

"By a nine-year-old and a six-year-old, in

the half dark, and they told everyone it was a hoodie crow."

"Yes. But just in case anyone else saw a man in a greatcoat that night, you left Karl's coat on the canal banks. I presume you took his coat from the captain when you went to interview him on the ship. And I presume you were wearing your own coat when you put Jamie's body into the water, weren't you?"

"Pure speculation. You'll have to do better than that, McAllister."

"Davy Soutar. He was one of your earlier victims."

"I heard you wanted to speak to him. The prison governor asked my opinion, I told him you were out to make trouble, so you've no chance of getting near that thieving wee liar. And if by chance he does get to speak to you, his life will be no worth living. I'll see to that."

"You're wrong. I've heard his story. He passed it on to a friend — a friend who can give him protection."

"And who will take a criminal's word against mine? Wrong again, McAllister."

"Aye, that inquiry at the home you were all brought up in; you escaped that time, didn't you? Another of your victims? He couldn't take it anymore so he killed himself? And John Morrison Bain, he wasn't going to turn you in, was he? After all, he took the photos. But I suppose it's the way of it, first a victim, then a perpetrator."

"You know nothing, McAllister, nothing at all. I was an orphan, sent to that hellhole at five. John Bain was in the same dormitory. We grew up together, if you could call it that. We were survivors, friends, we looked out for each other."

Poor wee bugger, McAllister thought. He felt for the boy but not for the man; no wonder he is what he is.

"The boxing club?"

"Don't tell me there's something the grand know-it-all editor from down south doesn't know? But you'll not be here for much longer; I'm going to make sure you're out of a job."

"I heard you were an instructor there. A good place to find victims."

"My my, Mr. Big Shot, you really fancy yourself as the great detective."

McAllister clenched his fist deep in his pocket, the key biting into his palm. He had struggled with this moment over the past weeks, ever since Rob had discovered the photos. The key? The envelope of filth? The two incriminating pictures? Which would he show first?

Suddenly, he wanted this over with.

"I have the boy's door key. It didn't burn. The shoelace that it was tied to did. No wonder you couldn't find it, it was in there in the stove along with what was left of your old army coat. I tried it. It fits Jamie's front door. They're gone now, his mother and father, back to the Isles, couldn't stay here; what happened to wee Jamie, it broke their hearts."

"You haven't come up with anything that I can't explain away." Tompson laughed. "Is that it, McAllister? That's all you've got? You'll have to do better than that."

"So you did kill the boy?"

"No. And since you'll never prove anything, I might as well tell you. It was an accident. It was an accident I was even home at that time of the day. An accident I was there when the bell rang. I was about to go back on shift but when I opened the door, there he was; I picked him up to give him a shaking, put the fear of God into him. I closed my coat over him, took him over to John Bain's studio. John — Father Morrison to you — he had this harmless wee . . . idiosyncrasy . . . he liked taking pictures of boys. I got him over there but the lad had peed himself and wouldn't stop bawling so I shook him some more and he had some sort of fit, anyway he went blue, couldn't breathe, and he died. Weak, he was. Nothing we could do."

"And you didn't call an ambulance or take him to the infirmary."

"It was too late."

"And you couldn't tell the truth — that he'd died of fright, in case your past somehow came out." Tompson nodded. "So you took him up to the canal and put him in. Burned the coat in case there was any evidence, hairs and suchlike, and then played your part as investigator of the tragedy, finding a convenient scapegoat in the Polish man. That didn't stick. But so what? After all, who'd suspect you of all people?"

Tompson was nodding in agreement with McAllister's account, completely oblivious to the awfulness of it all. When the journalist stopped speaking, he, head down, gave a half glance toward McAllister to see if he had finished, to know if it was over.

McAllister finished his cigarette and sat still, staring into the overhead canopy of shaking skeleton branches outlined against the stars. He let the story settle. He was good at pauses. Then Tompson in his certainty, in his arrogance, once more misjudged the man beside him and allowed a small almost imperceptible sigh to escape. In unison, the leather of the car seat gave out a soft breath as the man let his bones relax.

That did it. When he was certain nothing more would be said, nothing added, no excuses, no sympathy expressed, no regrets, nothing, McAllister decided. Neither raising his voice, nor allowing emotion to color his words, holding tightly to the steering wheel to keep his hands from grasping, hitting, strangling, he began, telling it as though he was discussing an abstract puzzle that had nothing to do with the actual, physical abuse and the death of a wee boy.

"No, Tompson. That is *not* what happened. You *couldn't* call for an ambulance, could you? You knew there was physical evidence of what you had done to the boy; you knew he might tell, no matter how much you scared him. You couldn't risk that, so you killed wee Jamie. Then you concocted a story for Father Morrison. But that only worked so far. When the priest realized that you were back to your old perverted ways, and that you had killed the boy, he refused to help. He had come to the Highlands to put the past behind him. He was trying to atone for his sins. Maybe he swallowed your tale that the death was an accident. More likely he knew the truth but chose to believe you in order to protect the Church. He wouldn't report you, but neither would he cover up for you. And he couldn't continue to live here knowing what he did about you, so he left."

"He was my confessor, he couldn't turn me in. But John Morrison Bain was no longer my friend. God would be my judge he said. And now he's gone, very conveniently for me, and you will never be able to prove any of this. I, on the other hand, could easily make a case for Father Morrison being the murderer."

McAllister flicked on his lighter. He held up one of the photographs, one of the pictures of Tompson — hard to identify without corroboration, but it was him and a naked sniveling terrified Davy Soutar.

"Where did you get that?" Tompson lunged toward McAllister.

The passenger door opened. Jimmy McPhee reached in — a flurry of jabs, face, solar plexus, jaw again. He dragged Tompson out with the help of a brother. They suspended him between them, an arm around each of their shoulders, and with his feet dragging, for all the world like a New Year drunk, they half-marched, half-dragged the inspector along the path and onto the suspension bridge.

McAllister hurried to the policeman's car, dropped the envelope of photographs onto the front seat, and ran to catch up with the trio making for the middle of the swaying bridge.

"No need for you here." Jimmy had to shout above the roar from the weir not far downstream.

"Yes, there is."

EPILOGUE

Press & Journal
Wednesday, December 17
Dogs Find Body
A man's body was found yesterday in a snowdrift near Carrbridge in Inverness-shire. A local shepherd said his dogs located the body about a mile from the railway line.

No identification has yet been made. Detective Inspector Tompson of Inverness-shire Police said that it was still too early to speculate.

"The post mortem has yet to be performed and the body to be formally identified," he said.

Highland Gazette
December 23
Police Identify Body in Snow
By Robert McLean
A body found in the snow near Carrbridge on December 17 has been identified as that

of Father John Morrison-Bain, a well-known figure in the community. Discovered by a local shepherd who had been involved in the initial search for Father Morrison, the body had been buried in a deep drift. Identification was confirmed by a crucifix found on the body and by personal identifying features provided by the Army Chaplains unit, with whom Father Morrison had served during the war.

The man who found the body, John Blair, 56, of Auchterarder Cottages, Nethy Bridge, told the *Gazette* of the gruesome discovery.

"It was the dogs that found him," said Mr Blair. "What was left of him, anyway. Unfortunately some wild creatures had got to him and his eyes had been pecked out, probably by hoodie crows."

Hoodie crows are common in the area and are a notorious hazard at lambing time.

Highland Gazette
December 23
Obituary
Father John Morrison-Bain, 1904–1956
The interment service for Father Morrison was sparsely attended, with many friends and family unable to attend. A number of former students from the boys' boxing clubs that Father Morrison ran for many years

followed the cortege to its final resting place; most noticeably, the former Scottish bantamweight champion, Jimmy McPhee.

The career of John Morrison-Bain, or Father Morrison or Father Bain as he was also known, failed to fulfill its early promise. A foundling, he was raised in a church orphanage and began training for the priesthood straight after leaving school at the age of fourteen. At one time he was a highly regarded young sportsman and won prizes for his boxing.

His first appointment was as administrator of a boys' club in the Gorbals, where he also acted as boxing coach for eight years. At the same time, he taught sports part-time at St. Joseph's, where he had himself been educated. The school provides places for boys from families suffering financial difficulties, and its pupils often go on to join the church.

Soon after the outbreak of war he volunteered to serve as an army chaplain. He settled in the Highlands a few years after the war. Unfortunately no information is available as to his whereabouts in the intervening years. A church spokesman explained that many records were lost in the destruction of much of wartime Glasgow, as well as in the confusion that followed it.

A representative of the Highlands and Islands Constabulary refused to comment on an enquiry in which Father Morrison had been involved as an important witness at the time of his death. The *Gazette* has learnt that the case is now officially closed. Jimmy McPhee and other former students held a wake for Father Morrison at a local hotel.

Highland Gazette
January 27
Drowning Tragedy
The crew of a local fishing boat found the body of Detective Inspector Michael James Tompson in the harbour in the early hours of Tuesday morning.

Inspector Tompson had been missing for two days. A fatal accident enquiry will be held, but a police spokesman said there were no suspicious circumstances.

ACKNOWLEDGMENTS

Thanks to my early readers for their generosity and support: Jock Watt, Kate de Ruty, Deborah Aronson, Don McIntyre, Taliesin Porter, Sal Nolan, Trish Waddington, Kate Dagher. Thanks to Barry Oakley for his wisdom and faith in a struggling writer. A special thanks to Trinh Huu Tuan for believing in me as an author from the very beginning; to Robert Alan Jamieson, poet, writer, teacher and dear friend.

Thanks to my agent Sheila Drummond, whose tenacity is legendary; to my U.S. agent Peter McGuigan (aka the Boy) at Foundry Media for his amazing matchmaking skills; to Anne Cherry for a superb job — copyediting Scottish is not easy. And to my editor Sarah Durand for her wisdom and insight.

And of course, Hugh.

■ ■ ■ ■

A Small Death in the Great Glen
A. D. Scott

A READERS CLUB GUIDE

■ ■ ■ ■

INTRODUCTION

A young boy has been found dead in the canal, and the members of a small community in the Highlands want answers. Suspicion quickly falls on a Polish sailor who has gone missing from a Russian ship. The year is 1956, and foreigners to this small Scottish town are guilty until proven innocent. Despite a lack of evidence, the police and townsmen are ready to convict.

The staff of the town's century-old local newspaper — including new editor in chief John McAllister — may be the only people intent on finding the real culprit. But as McAllister is about to find out, the ghosts of his past connect him with the murder more closely than he could have ever imagined. Obsessed with the case, he is determined to uncover the truth. But preserving the status quo reigns supreme in the community; corrupt town clerks quietly go about their business, battered wives tell no tales, and highly-respected figures hold dark secrets behind closed doors.

QUESTIONS AND TOPICS
FOR DISCUSSION

1. John McAllister joins the *Highland Gazette* staff looking to make a change, but veteran editor Don McLeod initially refuses to go against age-old tradition. By the end of the book, Don begins to come around to McAllister's ideas. How else does the theme of "change" triumphing over "tradition" play out in the novel?

2. Though the battles are over, the war continues to touch the lives of A.D. Scott's characters. Select a few of the main characters and discuss the lasting effects of the war on each. Have any of the characters been impacted by the war in similar ways?

3. *"I'm not his possession. I think what I like."* While Chiara clearly rejects the notion of a woman belonging to a man, Joanne finds herself hard-pressed to escape Bill's grasp — and fist. What steps does Joanne take, physically and emotionally, toward re-

claiming herself from her possessive husband?

4. Joanne repeatedly claims that she will not leave Bill for the sake of her daughters. *"I must stay. For their sakes."* Discuss Joanne's thought process in this regard. How does her staying with Bill affect the children positively? Negatively?

5. Peter Kowalski, a Polish escapee himself, never hesitates to help a fellow countryman — even if it means putting himself and the Corelli family at risk. Is he right in doing so? Why do you think he keeps these encounters a secret from Chiara, his future wife?

6. When Karel "Karl" Cieszynski nearly fails in his self-proclaimed "mission" to bring the crucifix to Scotland, he is saddened beyond words. Why is it so important that the crucifix reaches Peter? What does this piece of jewelry represent?

7. The people of the town appear relieved when Karl is arrested for Jamie's murder. However, few seem to question whether or not he actually committed the crime — including Joanne. Discuss why the townspeople are so eager to sweep the whole thing under the carpet. What are they trying to achieve?

8. Discuss Wee Jean's relationship with

Grandad Ross. Why does Grandad Ross have such a soft spot in his heart for his youngest granddaughter?

9. Joanne and WPC Ann McPherson are examples of women who attempt to succeed in the workplace despite the many obstacles they encounter. If the two of them sat down in Gino's café for a cappuccino and a chat, what might their conversation sound like?

10. While blackmailing Councilor Grieg in his office, Joanne suddenly pushes for Grieg to acknowledge his daughter with Mhairi, even if only in private. Why do you think she does this?

11. Why does Annie ultimately decide to tell the truth? Do you think she fully realizes the implications of what she saw?

12. Is it a reporter's duty to print the truth, the whole truth, and nothing but the truth? Consider the information the staff members withhold from the paper; are their reasons for doing so valid?

13. Does McAllister's personal agenda against Father Morrison hinder or help his ability to perform his duty as a reporter? In the end, which is more important to him: avenging his brother's death or getting the story straight?

14. Do Inspector Tompson or Father Mor-

rison show any signs of remorse for their actions in the novel, or in their pasts?

15. *"We know evil exists. I try not to see it, but it is there, in big and small ways. And always balanced by good."* Mrs. McLean's words demonstrate her eternal optimism, even after having lived through two wars and their aftermath. How do other characters in the book demonstrate optimism for the future? Have any characters completely lost all sense of hope?

TIPS TO ENHANCE
YOUR BOOK CLUB

- Chiara and Joanne enjoy some of their happiest moments while in Gino's café. Meet with your reading group at a local café to discuss the book over a hot cup of cappuccino or some sweet ice cream.
- *"A newspaper was no place for a woman."* Joanne suffered for her decision to be a working woman — whether it be due to Bill's shaken ego, the community's glaring disapproval, or her own insecurities. Using the Internet or resources at your library, find out more about how women entering the workplace were viewed during the 1950s, both in Scotland and around the world.
- Rob and Peter's band, The Meltdown Boys, shock the glen with a style of music no one has heard before — 1950s American rock 'n' roll. Make a playlist of music from this genre, including "Rock Around the Clock" (Bill Haley and Comets) and

"Tutti Frutti" (Little Richard), the only two songs The Meltdown Boys know how to play. How has American rock 'n' roll changed since the 1950s? Why was it so shocking to the people of the Highlands?

- A. D. Scott uses her words to describe the visual beauty of the Scottish Highlands; why not try using a paintbrush? Have each group member select a descriptive passage as inspiration for a piece of art. After the creation session, group members can share their passages and paintings.

A CONVERSATION WITH A. D. SCOTT

What first drew you to the mystery/ suspense genre?
I love reading mysteries; I especially love novels that give a sense of time and place. My favorites are too many to mention but Donna Leon, Mala Nunn, Peter Robinson, Ian Rankin, Kate Atkinson, and Laura Lipman are wonderful. I love mysteries that immerse the reader in another culture so I am a fan of Scandinavian and Icelandic crime writers and the Aurelio Zen stories set in Sicily.

Is there a different process to writing a suspense novel than writing other types of fiction?
Writing a suspense novel makes the reader (and the writer) try to puzzle out what is going on, so a writer can use this curiosity to explore themes that interest them. For example, small town newspapers are a true

reflection of a community, every town has at least one and they haven't changed much in sixty years. What *have* changed are national newspapers and magazines — for better or worse is a matter of conjecture. So the writing process doesn't change, but the opportunity to reflect while plotting or solving the mystery are more.

A Small Death in the Great Glen has a large cast of characters, each of whom has his or her own thoughts and feelings. Was it difficult to develop so many characters in one book?
Sitting in cafés, traveling by train or bus, watching people as they go about everyday life, I find myself constantly imaging their inner lives. I give them family and friends, but more than that, I imagine their dreams. Sometimes this habit gets me into trouble; when I am telling a story, I have to stop and think, did this really happen or was it something I made up? People, characters, everyday life is fascinating and complex, much more so than big events.

Which character in your book do you admire most, and why?
What a tough question! I think Jenny

McPhee would be my choice; she is who she is, with no doubts, no questions. She is sure of her history, her family, and she can move around the country whenever the fancy takes her. I love strong women. Most of all I envy her singing voice.

Malla Nunn, author of *A Beautiful Place to Die*, commended you for your "intimate knowledge of the Scottish Highlands." Besides having grown up there, did you conduct any special research to add to the authenticity of your story's setting?

I have a detailed, large scale, contour map of the area printed in 1954. The colors are beautiful and the shades of green and brown and blue are a wonderful "aide memoire" to my childhood. Also, when I was at school we went everywhere by bicycle, often long distances, this is the best way to know and remember a place. In those days, even a nine-year-old could wander off on her own. A sense of smell is also important. Close your eyes, think of the time of year and remember what it smells like. This always works for me.

When did you first learn of "hoodie

crow," and why did you choose to reference it in your novel?

Hoodie cows were (are) scary creatures. The first time I remember encountering them was innocently watching newborn lambs cavorting in a field of snow. Then, seeing blood and a dead lamb, the farmer told us it had been attacked by hoodies. Horrible! The hooded crow, to give it its proper name, is associated with the faeries and there are numerous references to them in myths, legend, and folktales. "Twa Corbies" (Two Crows) is a famous Scottish poem or song where the crows sit on a dyke discussing dining on a slain knight lying beneath them. These are the tales and songs we grew up on.

Many characters in your novel are considered outcasts by the community, whether it be for their gender, occupation, or nationality. Can you discuss this theme and why it is so important to the book?

Another hard question — and a rather revealing one. Perhaps it is because I was one of those children who drove adults crazy, always asking questions, never content with the answer, always attracted to anything unusual, never to the safe and normal and, to me, boring town.

Which writers have had the most significant effect on your own writing? How did their work affect your own?
Robert Louis Stevenson (RSL), to us Scots, he is the novelist above all others. One of my ambitions is to visit his grave in Samoa and say "Thank You." Coorying under the quilt on a stormy, rainy, or snowy night and reading *Kidnapped* or *Treasure Island,* scaring myself, losing myself, in warm Caribbean waters or the windswept stormy Minch, every sentence was magic to me. He also showed me a life beyond a small town in Scotland and opened up the idea of living a life of possibilities.

What's next for the staff of the *Highland Gazette*?
In the next book the *Highland Gazette* starts to change and all I can say is that it is more of the same, but very different. As the *Gazette* expands, McAllister hires some outlandish new contributors, and the scene is set more on the east coast than out west. The theme came to me from the hymn "All Things Bright and Beautiful." There is one character in the new book that absolutely fascinates me and the more I explore this

person the more intrigued I become. There are also new characters that touch on Scotland's part in strange and exotic events in the Far East in the nineteenth century.

A Small Death in the Great Glen is your first published novel. Do you have any words of advice or encouragement for aspiring novelists?
Just give it a go, with no expectations other than the joy of writing, of creating. If you really want to write, write every day, a few words, a few lines, but commit to it whole-heartedly. Above all, read; read everything, anything, read voraciously, give up every-thing else to read, read, read.

ABOUT THE AUTHOR

A. D. Scott was born and brought up in the Scottish Highlands. She was educated at Inverness Royal Academy and attended the Royal Scottish Academy of Speech and Drama, followed by a period working in theatre, magazines, and newspapers. She has also lived and worked in Vietnam and China and presently lives north of Sydney, Australia.